To JULIE —
WITH THANKS —

Willie Cooper
JUL 04

SHERIFF SKINNER AND THE

PUZZLE RIVER
WATER WAR

Sheriff Skinner and the Puzzle River Water War
Published by: Primer Cap Pistol Publishing
October 2003

Cover Design: Joey Wu

ISBN: 0-9715542-2-6

To Eileen

Thanks to:

Glenna Goulet – *Transcriber*
Maurie Klimcheck – *Editor*
Archetype Book Composition – *Typographer*

CHAPTER 1

"We got trouble," expelled Sheriff Skinner dejectedly, as he plopped his long body into his desk chair.

"Looks like it's sitting down trouble, at least," said Sam, the chief deputy, not looking up from fixing a broken strap on his spur.

"Stopped by the new jail on the way back from dinner and Ortiz tells me the outside walls of the stable are to be board and batten," continued Skinner, pulling an oilskin pouch of tobacco from his middle desk drawer.

"Thought you was promised a brick jail?" Sam answered, working a rivet through a newly-augered hole in the strap.

"You're not going to hammer that rivet on that desk, are you?" asked Skinner, packing his pipe.

"Who, me? You know me better than that."

"I don't trust you around good furniture. You got that top all scraped up with your spurs, and it's not a year old yet," rebuked the sheriff.

"Mosely told him to make it of wood, only the inside wall is going to be brick. Ortiz says it will save almost three hundred dollars."

"Well, technically, the stable, even if it's adjoining, isn't the jail," pointed out Sam. "I think the good captain out-foxed you."

"I'm about to go fox hunting right now, soon as my dinner digests."

"Saw something in the Tucson paper that should make you rest easier." Sam tossed the paper to the sheriff. "There in the obituaries."

The sheriff sat up straight to read the column. "Well, what do you know? Our old prisoner, Jesse T. Wilbur, passed away in Yuma prison. Sixty-six years old."

"Now, aren't you ashamed you punched him in the stomach so hard he liked to gag?" said Sam, hammering the rivet on a worn horseshoe.

"Hell no, he was trying to hang us to that blue adobe's roof rafters. If the cavalry hadn't come, we'd be wearing wings right now."

"I'm not sure sheriffs go to heaven. Anyway, Cletus said he would have shot us first, rather than to let us choke. Said that big rifle of his would have busted our skulls up like a dropped watermelon."

"I don't enjoy you recounting that, as I've told you before," the sheriff replied, grimacing at the thought. "I wonder who will take over his ranches. How many does he have? . . . Three?"

"Did have," reminded Sam. "And he had four, but they was spread out. Those farmers along Puzzle River cut his holdings in two. Think he said something about a niece back East, when he wasn't cussing us out."

"They won't miss him, I'm sure of that," said Skinner, puffing a huge cloud of blue smoke from his pipe. "And if the niece has any smarts, she'll sell out quick, before those ranches start going downhill. It took a mean S.O.B. like Wilbur to keep them going."

~~~~~~~~~~~~

Captain Mosely was the Chairman of the County Supervisors. He got his captain's title from his former occupation as a riverboat captain on the Upper Yazoo. When the Union ironclads sank his boat, he converted Confederate currency to embargoed cotton, selling it at war's end for enough to make a new start in the West. He now was president and principle stockholder of the Green Falls Bank, which was the only financial institution in the county, through his adroit manipulation as chairman of the supervisorial board.

He was hurrying out of his bank as the sheriff tied off his big mare. "Hey, Captain," called Skinner, "hold up a minute. Gotta talk with you."

Mosely swiveled his silk-hatted head toward the sheriff, saying, "I'm late for dinner, and too hungry to talk here. Come on—you can watch me eat."

"I'll have some pie. Mrs. Purity makes good pies," said the sheriff, stretching his long legs to catch up with the elegantly dressed banker.

"Now, what's your problem?" said Mosely, between spoonfuls of pea soup.

"I've got a weasel for a chairman of supervisors," related Skinner. "A no-good, lying weasel who promised me a brick building and is trying to switch it to a house of straw."

"Not straw, my dear Sheriff," Mosely slurped, "but a rugged thing of beauty, reflecting the true architecture of the West."

"Bullshit!" retorted Skinner, trying not to let the pleasure of the pecan pie show on his face. "You promised me a brick jail. Not a board and batten shack."

"I see. You must have been talking to the builder."

"I have, and you are trying to pull a fast one on me."

"Not a fast one. Not a sneaky maneuver, but a sound fiscal necessity," said Mosely, pushing the soup plate away to concentrate on his sausages and sauerkraut. "Anyway, I never promised you a brick stable. A jail—yes. A brick stable—no."

"But the stable is attached to the jail. And it's a small stable, only big enough for three horses and some feed."

"You just don't understand economies, Skinner," continued Mosely. "Would you pass me that mustard pot? Using wood saves more than 500 dollars. And if . . ."

"Ortiz tells me 300 dollars."

"Never believe a builder, Skinner. They always estimate low. Do it to keep the job going."

"Your problem, Captain," said the sheriff, trying another tack, "is the expense. And you're right in saying the brick stable adds three hundred extra dollars . . ."

"Five hundred," interrupted Captain Mosely.

"If you insist," conceded Skinner.

"I insist."

"See, you're good on the financial shenanigans, but I'm worried about what would happen if some rioters set the stable on fire. The jail would go too, and everybody in it. That's my problem, not the money."

"It's not shenanigans, Sheriff," said Mosely, talking with his mouth full. "It's fiscal responsibility. I have to balance what comes in with what goes out. And on a big project like your jail, I have to . . ."

Mr. Ames, the livery stable operator, came up to break into Mosely's soft-soap to say, "I think I just saw the Purdy boys going into your bank, Captain, and it looked like George had a shotgun under his duster. Might be—you is getting robbed."

"Oh my Lord!" said Mosely, turning pale. "Do something, Skinner. We can't afford a robbery."

The sheriff jammed the last of the pie into his mouth to mumble at Ames. "Do they have anybody outside, holding their horses?"

"Not sure. Think so," said the liveryman, tilting his head to improve his thinking.

"Go out the back, Mr. Ames, and get Sam and Cletus here quick," said Skinner.

There was a man outside the bank, pretending to be tightening a cinch on one of the trio of horses he was holding, a Winchester nestled loosely in a scabbard close to his hands.

Skinner ran back into the restaurant's kitchen. "I need a box or a crate. Got one here?" he asked the sweating cook. "Fast," he added. The cook, lost for quick words, could only point outside to a vegetable crate half full of trash. Skinner grabbed the crate, garbage and all, and dashed back through the restaurant to the front door.

He stepped out, putting the messy-looking crate on his shoulder, hiding his head. The unshaven, youngish man by the horses paid Skinner no attention as the sheriff dodged around a pair of ladies to come close to the hitchrack.

Suddenly the sheriff pivoted to dump the dripping crate on the horse holder's head, jamming the damp garbage down over the man's hat until the bottom slats on the crate broke with a snap.

Skinner ducked under the hitchrack as the man struggled to pull the sloppy mess free. He had been better off with the slops, for as soon as the man's head was visible, the sheriff laid the barrel of his pistol across the man's dripping brow. The man crumpled, to lie still by the horses' hoofs.

The sheriff circled behind the horses, walking nonchalantly into the bank, his pistol held ready behind his coattails.

George Purdy turned towards the door as Skinner opened it, his shotgun swinging towards the threat. Skinner shot first, his ball catching the big man in the chest, staggering him backwards as his finger loosed a barrel of the shotgun's buckshot, ripping the door lintel just inches above Skinner's head.

The sheriff fired again, catching George in the throat, to pump out a scarlet spew of blood.

"Drop that gun, Sheriff." It was Bob Purdy, with a pistol at a man's temple. "Or the cashier gets it."

Irwin Smith, the bank's cashier, was shaking with fright. "Oh, God! Sheriff, don't let him kill me. I'm the sole support of my mother."

"He won't shoot you, because when he does, I'll plug him good," said Skinner. "Now what, Bob? I've got a deputy out back, and one out front with your unconscious friend. Give up and live through this; continue and you're dead."

"Go to hell, Skinner," said the hawk-faced brother. "I'm taking the cashier with me. If I'm hit, I'll kill him. I'll take him with me—either across the river or to hell. Go on—name it, Skinner!"

"Go ahead and leave, Bob. But you're not taking a dime with you. And if you don't like it, shoot Mr. Smith here, right now."

"I'll leave. He who runs away lives to shoot a son-of-a-bitch of a sheriff another day."

"Move it, Bob," growled Skinner. "But remember one thing; if you hurt Mr. Smith, that young fellow out there will never live to make it to jail. I'll personally blow him to hell, and swear he was running away. Hear that?"

"I hear. Now let me out of here," said Purdy, dragging the terrified cashier out of the bank. Outside, he forced his hostage into the saddle of one of the three waiting horses and vaulted up behind him, the pistol still menacing the man. With a snarled warning not to follow him, Purdy kicked the horse into flight down the crowded main street.

The sheriff was just swinging up into his own saddle when Cletus galloped up, to rein in his big dun to a sliding stop.

"Sam will be along directly," the mountain man yelled. "The call caught him in the backhouse."

"Hey, Ames!" called Skinner, whirling his eager mare, "send Sam after us when he comes. And take charge of that young fellow down there wearing that garbage." Then to Cletus, "Come on, we'll follow Purdy at a distance." The pair clapped spurs to their mounts, scattering the growing crowd.

When the sheriff and Cletus came to the river, they could see the outlaw's horse splashing through the shallows, close to the far bank. They could also see the hostage trying to regain his feet, after being jettisoned into the river.

Skinner pulled his horse to a cruel stop, calling to Cletus to get down and try a shot with his Winchester.

"Too far for my old eyes. Must be close to five hundred yards," said the old scout, handing the saddle gun to the sheriff.

"How much drop?" cried Skinner, jacking a shell in the chamber.

"At least five or six feet, little breeze down river," said Cletus, dismounting to hold the horses.

"Blam!" went the rifle in the sheriff's hands. And again he fired, reloading fast. Again and again he sent the heavy slugs arcing towards the far horseman now climbing the bank.

Purdy turned in the saddle at the bank's crest for a quick look at the shooter. He began to wave an arm in a disdainful farewell when he was toppled from the saddle, falling slowly as if he were suddenly too top-heavy to stay astride his laboring mount.

"By God," shouted Cletus loudly, trying to make himself heard above his buzzing ears. "I wouldn't have believed it if I didn't see it. Hell of a shot."

"Not that great," said Skinner, handing back the Winchester. "Took me eight shots. I had the law of averages on my side. Come on, let's go collect him."

Purdy was not dead, at least not immediately. The big .44 slug probably had tumbled at the end of its long flight to hit sideways under the outlaw's left arm, ripping a huge gash in his side.

The hatchet-faced outlaw tried to focus his dying eyes on the pair of lawmen as they rode up, but could only blink myopically. He could, though, raise a weak right hand. He pointed a dirty, gnarled, cowman's finger skywards, as if tracing a word that his voice could not make. For half a minute, the finger tried to talk. Then it fell back to earth.

"I guess they're right, after all," said Cletus, looking down at the bloody outlaw.

"What do you mean?" asked Skinner, watching a green fly land on Purdy's wound.

"He was trying to tell us something."

"We'll never know, will we?"

"That's what I mean," went on Cletus. "They're right. Dead men tell no tales. Maybe he was trying to tell you that was a great shot?"

"I'll accept that. Let's get him on his horse before these damn flies carry him off somewhere."

~~~~~~~~~~~~

The man riding in the middle leaned across her to spit a brown stream of tobacco juice out of the stage's door window. Again he managed to press her breast with his forearm—accidentally on purpose.

"You scummy sonabitch," she told herself, "that's the last time you'll pull that on me." Her suede-gloved hand fluttered, femininely, to adjust her tiny pill box hat. Then she awaited her quarry's next move.

The man was patient, playing his little game to while away the long, boring stagecoach journey. Finally he cleared his throat noisily as a prelude to another spitting and another stolen feel. He twisted his thin shoulders, starting his lunge towards the window.

His arm moved toward her bosom again as he sucked air noisily, preparing to spit, moving closer to her.

Suddenly she struck, the long needle-pointed hatpin sliding easily into the man's arm. He gave a shout of pain, swallowing part of his chew. Now he really had to spit, hanging onto the sill of the window. The pin with its tear-shaped, pearled head, stuck out of his arm, impervious to the man's hacking.

Finally, the coughing fit finished, the man looked at his arm and the pin in disbelief.

"Oh, there it is," said the young woman, pulling the offending hatpin from the man's arm. "I thought I'd lost it. They are sharp, aren't they?" She smiled sweetly, giving a slight wink to the big Negro woman riding across from her.

"You should be more careful, Missy Wilbur," said the silk-clad Negress. "You could have hurt the poor man. 'Specially if it got in his lower parts." The big woman started a rumbling chuckle, much as a volcano announces a coming eruption.

"Thank you, Aunt Polly, I'll remember that," said the young lady. She turned to the red-faced man. "Won't we?"

~~~~~~~~~~~~

The big man wiped the blood from his mouth with the back of his hand, set large tree-like legs under him to rush at the smaller man before him, head down, aiming for the slighter man's breastbone. He was fast, this big man—and tough—tough as twenty years of bulldogging longhorn cattle makes a man.

But if the big man was fast, his opponent was greased lightning—dodging the rush to hook hard fists into the big man. Then, the big man was whipped. But, though groggy and bleeding, he had too much pride to quit. He shook his big head, tottering on rubber legs. His big fists were down by his hips. He looked like a bull waiting for the matador's thrust.

The smaller man obliged him, clasping his fists together to batter the big man to his knees, then kicking his head to sprawl him between the aisle and feed bags.

The victor leaned against a post in the stable to catch his breath. He was of medium height and weight, looking to be about thirty. He carried himself with an inner authority that not only rested on his heavy shoulders and hard fists, but on his natural intelligence and ranching knowledge.

He went over to the silent big man to grab a big hand and drag the man out of the stable to the water trough. In a show of strength he lifted the big man and threw him into the water.

For a moment he feared the big man was dead, as the large man sank down beneath the water, the eyes in the oversize head still rolled back into his skull.

Then the water exploded as the big man surfaced, sputtering and spewing out green water in a spray that would make a whale proud.

"God damn, Hughie," puffed the big man, "you whipped my ass good."

"That I did, Bert. You hollering uncle?"

"Hell, yeah, you'd probably drown me in this damn trough if I didn't. I guess I knew all along you'd be a better foreman than me. You think on your feet better than me. But I just had to give it a try. Does this mean I gotta leave?"

"Not if you can take orders from me," said Hugh. "You're a damn good hand."

"I'm a top hand, Hughie. But you're the foreman of the Double Bit, at least 'til the new owners show up."

"I just hope I've got time to shape this spread up before then, or we'll all get kicked out on our ear."

"Wouldn't be your fault, Hughie. What with the old foreman getting killed and old man Wilbur pitting you and me against each other for the job. Why'd he do that, anyway?"

"Just pure meanness, Bert. Like people watch two dogs fight. But he screwed himself when he ended up in jail, without a foreman to run this place."

"Well, he's dead now and I'm beat up. What are you gonna do now?"

"Bring our cows in where them damn nesters can't get at them, and get a good count. Yeah, and put the fear of God in them farmers."

~~~~~~~~~~~~~~~

His younger sister slipped and fell in the mud as she tried to climb the slippery river bank.

"Augie!" she cried, "Help me. I'm all schmutzig."

"Wait until I get the horse up first," the fourteen-year-old boy said, pulling the stubborn horse up the slick bank. Once on top, he dropped the lead to plod back down to his little sister, still mired in the mud. "Mutte will be angry if she sees that mud. You go back and wash off in the river, while I do the watering," he said, pulling her upright.

"I hate watering cabbages," pouted the little blonde girl, with the seriousness of a frustrated eight-year-old.

"We all must work, Trudy," replied her brother, "at what we can do. That's the Lord's way, Vater says."

"If God can see everything, He must have seen me fall down in the mud, and felt bad."

"But He saw you get up, too. And now you're cleaning yourself and will soon be helping me water the cabbages. He would be proud of you. And I know the elder would be, too."

"I don't care, I don't like mud. I don't like the elder, either. He looks at all the girls funny. I like feeding the chickens. Why did Mutte make me help with the watering?"

"You're getting too big for the chickens; it's Katrina's turn now. Clean up and I'll be back for more water soon." The boy left to go back to the horse, now grazing on some tender grasses at the bank's edge.

The horse carried two fifteen gallon bladders, strapped to the sides of a pack saddle. The bladders were each made from a whole pigskin, of which only one front leg on each remained. These were connected to leather hoses, now looped over the top of the pack saddle.

Young Augie led the horse to the cabbage row, where he had previously run out of water. Then, with the horse's lead between his teeth, he took the two slim hoses down from the pack saddle and walking slowly, bent almost double, he moved down the furrow directing the life-giving stream of water at the rows of cabbages on each side, pulling the patient horse behind him with jerks of his head.

Augie's family were German immigrants, seduced to America with stories of untold wealth lying just under the rich soil of the virgin prairie. "A cornucopia of abundance," the railroad's European agents said, as they robbed the trusting settlers of advance fares and commissions.

Now, after an odyssey of several years, in which they were chased from what they had thought they had paid for in good faith, their little sect had settled on federal land, intending to prove up their ownership on the riverbank sections and make them legally theirs.

This was the Puzzle River Valley. The early Spanish called it Rio de Confusion, because of the river's course, some places above ground and, in other stretches, below the ground. About three miles below the settlement the Puzzle River dived underground not to come up again until it pooled sluggishly into the Little Fish, the river that partly circled the town of Green Falls.

Although the good, God-fearing Saxon settlers understood European war, with its many small kingdoms' unrest and suffering, they had no understanding of the importance of water in the West. Everyday, under the blazing Arizona sun, they gave their crops water.

For every ten cabbages young Augie watered, a rancher's calf could be nourished—and the ranchers had no affection for cabbages. Perhaps for barley and oats, but not for cabbages. And that was the essence of the problem brewing on the Puzzle River.

But it was to get worse. Firm in their beliefs, the Germans, displaying all their traits of thoroughness and persistence, were building a dam upriver to be connected to their farms by a network of canals. Not just an earthen dam, haphazard in design and durability, but a stone dam with twin paved flumes to economically use almost every drop of Puzzle River water. Yes—the Germans built well.

And the cattlemen saw the Saxons' work and were not pleased. They saw the immigrants dig their deep, massive footing across a narrow cleft in the river's walls the Germans called Steinigportal; diverting the river across their foundation in two big, temporary, wooden flumes, each big enough to hold a freight wagon. The diversion, alone, took three months of labor for forty men and boys.

Now they had split their labor with half their force at work in a quarry and the remainder either transporting the stone blocks on a wooden-railed gravity railway or placing the one-ton stones on the dam's faces. Smaller rock and rubble were placed between the faces, in the thirty foot space left for that purpose. Wagonload after wagonload of clay was tamped between and over the rubble, securing the massive ballast to the cleft of Steinigportal.

All this the cowmen saw—and they feared for their own proper share of the waters of Puzzle River. They looked among themselves for guidance and leadership, and found only hot-heads who thought that bullets and black powder were the only answer. Perhaps it would come down to that in the end. But their leader was coming, unbeknownst to them all, and certainly to herself, as well.

CHAPTER 2

The striking part of their appearance was the three large wagons they drove—big, high-axled wagons with broad extra-stout wheels that could devour rocky trails or cross country badlands. There were nine of them in the party. They were a band of cowhide thieves.

Judd Payton was bossman and hunter—along with Smokey Watson, his cousin, who was scout and hunter. This was almost a family affair, with three of the six skinners being relatives, as was old Uncle Walter Watson, the cook and driver of the smaller utility wagon that carried their stores.

Every wagon was overdrawn—with an extra set of big mules, for this was the fundamental of their business— speed. They had to locate a poorly guarded herd and silence the herders—to slaughter and skin the herd speedily and efficiently. Then with the heavy, wet hides tied on the big wagons, they would race off to sell them to the ever present hide merchants, notorious for never checking a brand.

In early Arizona the cowhide was more negotiable than the cow itself, because the demand for beef was satiated, swamped by the oversupply of range cows due to the war and the difficulty of getting a herd to market.

Eventually, railroads and trailherds to the railheads would solve the problem. But right now, most ranchers were desperately cow-poor, having few dollars to pay for herders, thus setting themselves up as prey for the hide snatchers.

Now, the hiders were leaving Tucson by the light of a weak moon, their strong teams pulling the empty wagons easily. Their mules had no bells to jingle a happy tune, which was appropriate, as this was a dark convoy, sneaking out of town to do dark deeds.

As Judd Payton, an easy-to-smile man, would freely admit. "It's a nasty, thieving business, but a good living, all the same." And this night, he lead his party off to tap Green Falls County's livestock.

~~~~~~~~~~~~~

Doctor Seevers was at the old jail in the stage company compound treating the new prisoner when the sheriff and Cletus came back with Bob Purdy's body tied to his horse. The cranky old ex-Army surgeon verbally abused the sheriff as soon as he saw the lanky sheriff duck through the door.

"Damn it, Skinner. What did you hit this poor boy with—a crowbar?"

"Just my Colts barrel, Doc," confessed the sheriff. "But I must admit, I was too busy to pull my punch. Is he bad off?" He went over to the doctor's patient, lying unconscious on the table.

"You busted his skull, that's all. I've been picking pieces of bone out of his frontal lobes. I sent Sam off to that jeweler of Gomper's to get a thin plate of silver to patch the hole with. If this works, I'm going to quit Green Falls and go to New York to practice cranial surgery. I'll make my fortune. I'll buy a silk hat and go to those operas every night."

"Wouldn't that cut into your drinking time?" asked Cletus, racking up the Winchester.

"Naw," said the white-haired doctor, sloshing whiskey over the oblong hole. "They have intermissions, where you can buy champagne. I'd take three or four glasses back to my box. Drink them there. Now, if that rebel deputy of yours ever gets back, I'll slap the patch on and sew him up. Maybe I'll write an article about this in the medical journal. New York—here I come."

"Don't look now, Doc," said Cletus, "but your patient seems to be holding his breath."

"What?" shouted the old doctor. "Can't be." He put his ear to the youth's shiny chest. Then turned his head, to use the other ear. Raising his head, he put two tobacco-stained fingers on his patient's throat. After a few long seconds of fumbling for a pulse, he gave up.

"Damn you, Skinner!" He interrupted himself to take a gulp of whiskey from the bottle next to the youth's head. Finished, he looked at the bottle and took another drink.

"Damn you, Skinner, there goes my New York career. Now I'm stuck in this dust bin of a town."

"No opera, Doc?" said Cletus, trying to keep a straight face.

"And no champagne, or silk hats either," added Skinner. "Only the Drovers Rest and red-eye whiskey."

"Bullshit!" said the doctor, seeing no humor in the loss of his new career. "You just kill this poor young man, and here you are, joking about his death."

"Not joking about your poor young bank robber, Doc," said Skinner. "Just commenting on how you were hoping the hole in his head would get you a big practice back East. Everything's crude here, Doc; justice, medicine, working and living conditions. And I'm afraid . . . our humor, too. That's an apology to the fine doctor that fixed my hernia last year, before it killed me."

"Why don't you button that gob of yours? Don't you think I feel bad when I lose a patient? This was just a kid, practically."

"A kid that got mixed up with a badman's business, Doc," Cletus said. "He took his chances and lost, that's all. Happens all the time; to miners, cowboys and everybody out here."

Just then the door opened to Sam. "I've got that silver plate, Doc. It's hammered real thin, sort of concave-shaped, too."

"Is it smooth?" snapped the old doc.

"Sure is, Doc—polished-like."

"Then, Mr. Deputy," said the doctor, loading up his satchel, "shove it up your butt and call yourself silver-ass." He strode out the door, slamming it hard against the doorjamb.

"Holy Pete," said Sam. "Did I say the wrong thing?"

"Don't worry about it, Sam," said the sheriff. "He just feels bad about losing this kid. He might seem cranky and mean on the outside, but he's sweet butter inside."

"He could have fooled me," said Sam, looking at the shiny piece of silver in his hand.

~~~~~~~~~~~

She came in on Tuesday's stage from Tucson, to take a room for herself and another room for her maid.

"And," she told the hotel clerk, "I need a message sent to the D B Ranch. It's supposed to be somewhere near a river called Puzzle."

"I can find a man who can find it, Miss Wilbur. What would the message be? Would you like a pen and paper?"

"No, just tell whoever is in charge out there to send a comfortable conveyance for my maid and myself and our luggage. Tell them I'm the new owner, and I don't please easily."

"I'll have the message sent off immediately," said the clerk, ducking his head ingratiatingly. "Would madam care for a bath? We have a bathing room on the second floor, but I'm afraid there's a 75 cent charge—the water you know— and the maid's time."

"Sounds heavenly. By all means. Call me when it's ready, and not too hot, please."

"Certainly, Miss Wilbur." The clerk banged his bell for the uniformed old man who was the bellman.

~~~~~~~~~~~~~~

"Got good news for you, Skinner," said Mr. Hansen, as he washed up at the new soapstone sink.

"Good—I can use it today. Did you hear about the fracas at the bank?"

"That's what the good news is about," said the old man who, it seemed, would be the Skinner's boarder for all time.

"Manny Ortiz told me that Mosely told him to forget about the wood and make the stable out of brick. That's why I'm a little late for supper, had to stop by the lumber yard and cancel the siding. Wow, stuffed pork chops. Missus, you outdid yourself."

"You're always so appreciative, Mr. Hansen," said Gen. "Not like Sylvester, who takes his food for granted. Here, try this applesauce. The dried apples came from a fresh batch. Quite sweet."

"Very tasty," complimented Hansen.

"Did Manny say why the Captain changed his mind?" asked Skinner, pouring the brown gravy over his rice and mixing it up with his fork.

"Said he's afraid that if there's a riot or something, the stable could be set on fire if it was wood. Told Manny how he's got to think of everything, even when it comes to the sheriff's building."

"The perfect politician at work," commented Skinner, buttering a thick slice of freshly-baked bread.

"That bread might be too fresh for your stomach, Sylvester," said Gen. "I've got some of the old heel left. It will lay easier on your stomach."

"Not necessary. My stomach is just fine today. I could eat a box of worms and not notice a thing."

"Worms? Who would want to eat worms?"

Later that evening, when the cramps hit him, the sheriff wished he'd had the worms rather than the fresh bread. But he did not tell his wife.

~~~~~~~~~~~~~

There were a dozen cowmen waiting in the hotel's plush lobby, standing about self-consciously in their best clothes, darting glances at the costly furnishings thereof. Then they saw her come down the wide stairway, followed by her big maid, and they knew that this was their new owner. They stopped their quiet banter to pull off their hats and to stare at her.

She was certainly worth a stare, with her tall, slim figure encased in a form-fitting green frock that not only emphasized her body, but also matched her green eyes and complimented her coppery hair, today done up in a silver-threaded snood.

Perhaps, a purist might say her mouth was overly wide, and her chin a bit large and determined, or her green eyes were on the hard side. But the cowmen below her were not purists, but lonely men, forged by their profession into a society of men. Not as pious and chaste as monks, but similar in their insecurity towards women.

Opal Wilbur stopped her descent, to let the men get an eyeful of her charms. She knew she was beautiful and had used her attractiveness as a tool since she was a child. At boarding school and finishing school, her beauty was a two-edged sword, cutting her classmates into those who jealously hated her and those who adored and followed her.

Now, with her parents gone and her only brother missing at Vicksburg, with her annuities becoming more slender each month, she stood before her men trying to impart upon them her resolution to succeed at this opportunity.

At last, one man stepped forward, if not in homage, at least in greeting.

"Miss Wilbur, my name's Hugh Foote, with an e on the end of my Foot. I think I'm the new foreman of the D B. We'd all like to welcome you to Arizona. And we were sorry to hear of your uncle's passing away like he did."

Opal Wilbur looked down from her stair step at the handsome cowman, seeing an intelligence and presence of mind behind his lifted gray eyes. She also noted how he ran those eyes impudently over her body.

"Uncle Jesse was a mean old son-of-a-bitch," she said. "But he knew how to run a ranching business. My father always said I took more after Uncle Jesse than I did to him. I hope to prove him right. Mr. Foote, why do you only think you are the foreman of the D B? By the way, what do the initials D B stand for?"

"Stands for Double Bit, like in a horse's mouth. And I'm not really sure I'm foreman, for sure. When the old man . . . I mean your uncle . . . died, he hadn't replaced the old foreman, who got busted up by a cow and killed. Mr. Wilbur sort of enjoyed seeing me and Bert Massey fight over the job."

"That's me, ma'am," said Big Bert, wiggling his hat slightly to catch her attention.

"And now it's decided?" Opal questioned.

"Yes'm, Hughie tromped my butt, day before yesterday." The other cowmen grinned at this—chuckling, to crack their weathered faces.

"I'll put you on probation for a while, Mr. Foote, to see if you can follow orders. Now introduce me to these other men," she said, stepping down from her perch.

The other men turned out to be managers, foremen and a few top-hands along as an honor to their service or longevity. Represented at this meeting were the D B, the headquarters ranch of Wilbur's holdings; the Running W, the largest in acreage, and the hilliest; the Lazy J, across the ridge in Palisade Valley; and the B R, Wilbur's small breeding ranch which specialized in raising horses, both for the Wilbur ranches and for outside sales.

This ranch, according to Hugh Foote, making the introductions, was also involved with a new program to upgrade the Wilbur cattle by breeding bulls. The manager of this ranch was an aristocratic-looking, youngish Mexican, a scion of a famous south-of-the-border breeder of fighting bulls.

All the many names, faces, and their positions, failed to fluster Opal Wilbur. She seemed to automatically file the information in her mind.

As the last employee was introduced, and his name and face noted, Miss Wilbur pointedly asked Hugh Foote the thought uppermost in her mind.

"Now Mr. Foote, you have introduced managers of the four different ranches. Who, may I ask, manages and coordinates the activities of all these ranches? In other words, who's the general manager?"

Hugh Foote looked her in the eye, a trace of a smirk on his tanned jaw. "Well ma'am, now that your uncle is gone . . . I reckon it's you. Just you."

"Thank you Mister Foote," said Opal Wilbur, eyes suddenly turning to green ice. "And from now on, refer to me as Miss Wilbur, not ma'am." She turned that freezing look on the rest of her employees. "Do you all understand that, all of you?" All present nodded assent, silenced by the intensity of her character.

"Now gentlemen," she said, a hint of a smile cracking her stony, beautiful features, "I'd like to buy you all a drink in the lounge. Please follow me." She marched into the gentlemen's lounge trailed by her troops, to the shocked stares of the morning drinkers.

"Barman," she ordered the gap-jawed bartender, "give us three bottles of your best whiskey and glasses all around." Soon every employee held a large jigger of Kentucky's best.

"Just half a glass for me, Mr. Foote. I get mean with drink."

"Don't want that then, Miss Wilbur," said Hugh, pouring exactly half a glass. "You seem pretty mean already."

"Mr. Foote, you haven't seen anything, yet." Then she faced about, raising her glass. "Gentlemen! To the prosperity of Wilbur Ranches." She drained her glass in one quick gulp.

"To prosperity," echoed her employees, tossing down the dram.

"Finish the bottles, gentlemen, while I enlighten you about how I feel.

"Number one is that business is like war. If you fail you die, in war. In business, if you fail you die . . . broke—and nobody cares.

"Number two, you're either with me, helping me in every possible way or you're against me; and I'll get rid of you. Try any tricks on me, such as kickbacks, under-the-table payoffs or whatever, and I'll prosecute you. Or," at this she cracked a venomous smile at the wide-eyed assemblage, "much, much worse. This is not only a threat, it's an absolute, goddam promise.

"But, don't, I repeat, don't be afraid to run your jobs, honestly and rightly. Don't be afraid to make changes that will help Wilbur Ranches. That's your jobs as managers. Consult me, though, on anything that's major or expensive. I might look rich, but I'm not. I think they call it being cow poor." This brought a little titter from the listeners.

"Now climb back on your horses, and go back to work. Tell your crews that you've got a crazy bitch of a woman boss who's going to make Wilbur Ranches the best in the West. Best in cattle, salaries and places to work. I thank you for your time. Goodbye, I'll be seeing you soon."

The men—dismissed—left quickly and quietly, as if afraid to trade their thoughts. Only Hugh Foote remained to tell her that he had a man outside with her uncle's old buggy to carry her to the D B.

"Good. When you leave, have him put our baggage aboard. And one more thing, Mr. Foote."

"Ask away. Be glad to help."

"I don't need you as a confidant, Mr. Foote. I just want to know who Uncle Jesse had for his ranch regulator. I have been given to understand every large ranch hires an enforcer to police its borders and such. Why wasn't he here today?"

"That's an easy one, Miss Wilbur. He was shot dead by the sheriff of this town a while back when your uncle had a run-in with him about some Indians that your uncle wanted killed."

"Is that when my uncle was arrested?"

"The same time," said Foote, smiling wryly, remembering the scene. "Your uncle told this man, Art Auldt, to shoot the sheriff. Art started to oblige, but the sheriff got him first. That was the end of Art. And incidentally, your uncle."

"Thank you, Mr. Foote. I'll see you later on at the D B. Is a room prepared for me, and also my maid?"

"I had the cook sweep out your uncle's room. He had a lot of stuff we didn't know what to do with, so we just left it for you to sort out. Frankly, we're cowmen, not chambermaids." He nodded a quick goodbye and left her alone to the stares of the bar's regulars.

CHAPTER 3

"Right this way, Miss Wilbur," said Mr. Smith, ushering Opal Wilbur before Captain Mosely's big desk. He then introduced her to the banker and moved away—to hover within hearing.

"Well, Miss Wilbur, what can we do for you?" Opal was dressed in dark traveling clothes, her flaming hair again sheathed against the dust.

"I understand my uncle had an account here?"

"A drafting account. Mr. Smith, the Wilbur account please." Smith went to a shelf to bring back a slim ledger. Mosely familiarized himself with the final page.

"Down to $367.54. It's in probate, you know. Court disbursed over $2,300.00 last month for salaries and supplies to keep the wheels rolling. The account has a $5,000.00 draw, though, at 3/4 of 1% a month, when that $367.54 is exhausted."

"That's my line of credit?" asked Opal Wilbur. "$5,000.00?"

"Jesse never needed more. A note could be arranged. Of course, collateral would be necessary."

"It looks like I need to sell some cows off, to meet obligations," said Opal, eyes focused on Mosely.

"Well, that's what your business is about, isn't it, Miss Wilbur? I hear the government contract at Ft. Lowell comes up next month. Course, the Tucson spreads seem to think that's in their bailiwick. Your uncle used to have an agent in Tucson.

"Seems to me, Miss Wilbur," went on the banker, "that you need to get this probate business cleared up and find someone to manage your ranches."

"I intend to manage them myself," she said in a voice that defied argument.

"Oh my," said Mosely, "well, well."

"Do you know who my uncle's attorney was?"

"For his trial he had a Tucson lawyer. The trial was in Tucson, you know. Too volatile to have it here. 'Specially with the local judge charged also."

"What about for his business here?"

"He used Aaron Sawyer," said Mosely. "But he died in a courtroom shooting a while back. Your best bet is to see David Rose. He's new, but good. Office is across from Gomper's, upstairs."

"One more thing, Mr. Mosely."

"It's Captain, Miss Wilbur. I was a steamboat man before being a banker. Yankees sank my boat."

"Oh, I'm sorry," Opal said, eyes softening.

"Aw—it was the War. But she was the prettiest thing on the Upper Yazoo . . . least for awhile." He sniffed hard.

"But what is it you need?"

"I need a secretary, an educated woman who can write letters and do accounts, who would live at the ranch and help me run the account side of the Wilbur Ranches."

"Would this lady have to be real active? Riding, walking a lot?" Mosely asked.

"Not really. Once a month around to the ranches, to check accounts. Could use the buggy and a driver, though."

"I know of a woman, Beatrice Cole, who practically ran a mining supply company for a worthless husband. One day she and her little boy were crossing Main Street, when a runaway hit them. The boy was killed and Beatrice lost a leg above the knee.

"To make a long story short, her husband left her, selling his business. Now she supports herself keeping accounts for a stinking saloon down towards Spanishtown, named The Dead Dog. She walks with a crutch, slowly. And the amazing thing is that she's not bitter. Turned real Christian, though. Does a lot of New Testament reading."

"Beatrice Cole, Dead Dog Saloon. Thank you, Captain, and I'll probably need that $5,000.00 in the drawing account. At least, until I get things straightened out."

"Get that probate cleared and it's yours," said the banker, helping her out of his bank.

~~~~~~~~~~~~

It was daylight. The hide thieves had stopped to take their rest in a lonely, blind canyon. There were guards posted, though. Always, they had guards posted or mounted videttes to protect themselves from those from whom they stole or would soon steal.

The camp was starting to stir. The smell of fresh coffee and bacon floated from Uncle Walter's flameless, smokeless, coal oil stove. One of the skinning men went out to the mule line to treat a mule's bad eye.

"Rider coming in," called down a sentinel on a commanding high point. "It's Smokey," came the reassuring shout.

The short scout threaded his horse through the boulders of the steep path to come out on the little valley's floor. He got down tiredly from his lathered horse to start stripping it of its equipment.

Judd Payton, the thieves' leader, quit talking to Uncle Walter to walk over to the scout, who was wiping the sweat from the patient roan.

"So, what's the word?" Judd asked the stubby scout.

"Two words. Easy pickings," said the smaller man. "But it means a long night getting into position. It's about a twenty-five mile ride, sticking to the trail."

"Any chance going cross-country?"

"Too damn many barrancas to get around. Gonna have to take the Green Falls trail, at least part way."

"Where is this place? It ain't the Charleton spread, is it?"

"Hell no, not getting mixed up with that bunch of vaqueros. This is across the river. The Running W. They got a herd tended only by an old man and a young boy. Should be a snap. Two hundred hides, at least—maybe more."

"Sounds good, you gonna turn in?" asked the boss.

"Soon as I take care of this nag and get some food. Wake me up about four miles past Mesa Grande, and I'll guide us through them nesters to get to where we're going."

⌁⌁⌁⌁⌁⌁⌁⌁⌁⌁

"You got a minute to spare me?" asked old Hansen, the carpenter who built Skinner's house. After completing the job, he still stayed with them, bunking in the none-too-big woodshed and taking meals at the kitchen table. He was addressing the sheriff, looking up through the front porch balustrade. Skinner folded up his newspaper.

"Always have time for you, my friend."

"You'll probably just say I'm a crazy old man," said the quarrelsome carpenter.

"I probably will," said Skinner, "but test me—anyway."

"It's about Henderson's saw. Bob Murdock bought it. I wanted it, but Murdock ended up buying it. And for a song, too."

"You have succeeded in completely confusing me," said the sheriff, knocking out his pipe on the porch rail.

"I'll start at the beginning. Always knew you was slow."

"Please do," replied Skinner, taking no umbrage.

"Charlie Henderson was a hell of a good cabinetmaker. He had to retire about six months ago, 'count of his arthritis. Hurt to grasp anything—had been getting worse over the years. Mind if I sit down?"

"Be my guest. Care for some pipe tobacco?"

"You ain't got a cigar, do you?"

"'Fraid not," answered Skinner, packing his pipe.

"That's all right, then. Let me go on."

"Do, indeed."

"Charlie's hands," said Hansen, remembering where he had left off. "All swollen up and sore. Had to quit. I tried to buy that handsaw from him. You know, that beautiful little Swedish one. Twelve point, blade almost as thin as paper, but such good steel, you could almost bend it double."

"A fine saw," said Skinner, helping the story along.

"Sure was. 'No,' Charlie said. 'I'm keeping my toolbox with me 'til I die. Had 'em all my life. Won't give 'em up.' That's what he said. I think he was hoping for a miracle. To heal his hands, I mean. Probably listened to that landlady of his, that Mrs. Robinson. She's real devout, you know."

"What about the saw?" said Skinner, putting a match to the pipe bowl to puff out clouds of blue smoke.

"That comes later—just wait. Where was I? On yeah. Well, Charlie died a while back, when you was back East, hob-nobbing with President Johnson. So I goes to his funeral and, afterwards, asks his landlady, Mrs. Robinson, if Charlie's tools was spoken for."

"Yes," said the sheriff, almost plaintively, anxious to resume his paper before it got too dark to read.

"Now, listen to this. She says that Charlie sold them to some fellow leaving for a job in Denver. Took the whole she-bang, including, get this, the pretty little Swedish saw."

"'Bye, 'bye Swedish saw," said Skinner, seeing light at the end of the tunnel.

"Not at all. Just hear me out. Now . . . today I goes over to Gomper's to buy hinges for the jail's front door—need big bronze ones for the door, 'cause it's real heavy. Actually, these hinges were red brass, not bronze, but Gomper don't know hardware that good."

"The saw, Mr. Hansen, please," sighed Skinner.

"Just giving you the background. Don't have to get huffy, you know . . . Well, there I was in Gomper's Department Store, when who do I see but Bob Murdock there, building shelves for Gomper. And guess what he had in his hands, cutting the trim for them shelves?"

"The Swedish saw, no doubt."

"Yep, must have given away my story," said Hansen.

"You told me at the beginning that Murdock had it."

"Well, it was Charlie's old saw. Even had his initials on the handle, C.H., plain as day. Burnt right into the wood."

"So, where did Mr. Murdock get the saw?" asked the sheriff, hoping his voice showed enthusiasm.

"That's the mystery. That's why I'm telling you all this. Listen up. Bob Murdock bought it at that pawn shop down near Spanishtown. You know, by the live chicken place. Was right out front in the window. Bob recognized it right away; didn't even need to see the initials on the handle."

"My word," said the sheriff, feigning complete interest in Hansen's tale.

"And get this, Bob paid only $1.50 for the saw. God, what a bargain!"

"Only $1.50?"

"What do you think?" said the old man, expectantly.

"Think of what?" replied Skinner, caught off guard.

"Why did Mrs. Robinson lie to me about the saw? I got a hunch she killed Charlie and sold his belongings. He had a lot of other stuff. Had a big stamp collection, five or six big books of them."

"How did your friend Charlie die?"

"I heard it was old age. He was strong as an ox, except for his hands."

"Now that you've told me," asked Skinner, "What do you want me to do?"

"Investigate it, you dummy. Ain't you a trained investigator and lawman? Foul play's been done, and it's your job to clear it up."

"I'll check into it. Will that make you feel better? Where is this landlady's house located?"

"Just past Dora's. About the second house across the street. Its got a wrap-around front porch, can't miss it. Will I get a reward if she murdered him?"

"Don't count on it for your old age."

"That's all right. I'd rather stay here anyway," said the old man.

~~~~~~~~~~~~~

"I want to go with Augie," said Trudi Damm, trying to pull away from her mother.

"No, Liebling, only the older boys and men can go to the drill. That is Major Riemann's order. But you can watch them, if you don't bother them."

The farmers had gathered after church to drill on the flat field next to the church. The field was large and would someday be filled with graves, although at the present, only a few graves were seen, close to the new wooden church.

The company's sergeant-major drilled the seventy-odd men and older boys, marching and counter-marching them back and forth across the dusty graveyard under the scrutiny of their company leader, Major Riemann.

Riemann was a veteran of Rosecrans' German Union Troops, having worked his way up through the ranks of a Wisconsin regiment. At Murfreesboro he was wounded, his elbow being shattered. Luckily the wound didn't lead to the normal amputation, but the bones had fused to give him a stiff arm, in the bent position.

While he was recuperating at home, his wife and young daughter were struck down by typhoid. A lonely, driven man now, saddled with the responsibility for this small community, he was a dedicated, but mirthless, leader.

Hans Klaus, the sergeant-major, halted his panting troop, allowing them a short rest while he conferred with the major.

"Except for the few veterans, it seems almost hopeless, Major," said the rotund sergeant, fanning himself with his straw hat. "Especially with only a few hours every Sunday."

"We're fortunate the elder gives us that on the Sabbath, Hans," said the tall, greying major. "When the rifles come, I think we'll see a change. Let me talk to them now. Go out and bring them to attention."

The sergeant-major strutted back to the resting company to call them to attention.

"Men," the major told them, "I want to thank you for giving up a portion of your Sabbath to train for duty in our militia company. Some of you ask whether this is really necessary. This is America, you say. We did not come so far from our homeland to be conscripted by an army, even if it's a very tiny one. We did not leave one Bismarck to come to America to march on Sundays to the cadence of another Bismarck.

"Am I Count Bismarck? Is Sergeant-Major Klaus a Prussian martinet? No, I'm a crippled engineer, trying to make a dam, and Sergeant Klaus is our baker. We are just citizens helping other citizens to protect ourselves against the renegades that prey on settlers here in the West.

"You are training to protect your families. Soon the rifles that General Schurz found for us will be here, and then you will train with them, learning all the many skills of a soldier. But for now, you will learn to march, wheel, form ranks and to assume the posture and the smartness of a soldier.

Remember, you have an advantage over other men, for you are Saxons. The blood of warriors flows in your veins.

"Remember that when the Roman emperors, chiefs of millions of soldiers in the powerful legions of the Roman armies, would organize their own personal companies of bodyguards, they would recruit the warriors of Saxony, as the fiercest of all the world's fighting men. That is your heritage. Here in this new land, this Arizona, is your destiny. Be proud. Be strong and be loyal to your families and your community. May God bless you all, and may He bless our enterprise . . . Take charge, Sergeant-Major, and drill them hard and well."

~~~~~~~~~~~~~

The dark shadow of a form came out of the murk, to lead the big mule up to the wagon, and then, with an awkwardly held hand on the mule's muzzle, pushed it gently into its position against the wagon pole. The old man came with the lantern and leaned behind the animal to fasten the chains.

It was just a few minutes after four, but neither the old man nor the misshapen youth had a clock to wake them, for habit sufficed—the routine of a seven day work week that dictated a round trip to Green Falls every day of the year to pick up manure for the growing fields of the Puzzle River farmers.

Paulie Vogelnester was born in agony, to live with affliction. He was ripped cruelly from an expiring mother; his infant body jammed by a breech birth. The tardy doctor was trying only to save the mother, the mistress of a prominent nobleman. But the little broken body fooled all, to live, though grotesquely deformed from head to hips. Only the baby's extremities were near normality.

The young monster was to have been smothered and quietly buried. The nobleman's confessor, though, alerted to the problem through court intrigue, persuaded the count to raise the monstrosity in anonymity as a penance for his lust. A poor, childless widow was recruited to care for the deformed boy. This good woman, suddenly well-off, married the old man who now held the lantern. The woman, sadly, died of acute sea-sickness on the long trip to America.

So it was that Groszvater Vogelnester and his foster son Paulie, exiled by the lad's deformity, became the haulers of dung.

Actually it was a good job, as employment went in the West, once the smell and stigma of animal waste was accepted and forgotten. The trip, unloaded, to Green Falls took four hours, during which Paulie or Groszvater could doze. Then it took several hours to load the big wagon. Lunch was a quick affair, and then they would start back to the Puzzle River. The return with the heavy load took longer, but they would be back by six to pull the pins on the wagon's big bottom dump doors, in the field selected. Then it was time to groom and feed the mules, eat their supper and seek their pallets in the mule stable.

Paulie Vogelnester, although misshapen in body, was not an idiot. In fact, he had a nimble mind, though he was somewhat pressed on occasion to perform physically to his mental commands. Not from lack of strength, for he was very strong of limb, but from the acute curvature of his spine and derangement of his hips.

The ugly child, rejected by playmates, found solace in the written word. His adoptive mother taught him to read, but with her limited education, was soon left behind by her bright student.

Paulie was seventeen, his twisted torso banded by thick muscles developed by his body to spite his malfunctions. His arms, swinging from twisted shoulders, were long and corded muscularly, almost ape-like. His right hip, uneven with his left, caused him to assume a strange gait, in which the left foot would step off smartly, hoping to be backed up by the shuffling right.

While on the ship to America, some uncaring stranger remarked that Paulie looked similar to Victor Hugo's character in his new book, "The Hunchback of Notre Dame." From that time on the children of the group called Paulie 'Quasimodo', even though they had never read Hugo's story. Such is the cruelty of children.

~~~~~~~~~~~

Beatrice Cole was retrieved from Green Falls the next day. Although her arrival was welcome, it made a bad situation worse. There was only one bedroom in Uncle Jesse's not commodious house, and Aunt Polly was already complaining about sleeping in the kitchen.

Opal turned the parlor into bedrooms for her new secretary and her maid, temporarily tying wagonsheets in place as partitions.

Beatrice Cole went immediately to work, attempting to make sense out of Uncle Jesse's jumble of accounts.

Opal asked Hugh Foote to find her a sure-footed mare, and he told her he would send to the B R for a suitable horse; a small, pretty mount being unavailable at the D B.

That evening, over supper, Beatrice Cole came up with the name of a possible regulator for the Wilbur Ranches. Her saloon experience gave her an encyclopedic, if unsavory, knowledge of men who carried a gun for more than social decoration. A letter to the man would be sent off tomorrow with the wagon going to Green Falls for the partitioning materials.

Opal, between sessions with the lawyer, David Rose, secured the services of a cattle agent in Tucson. She had him bid on the coming Army contract, making sure the bid would be at least 10 percent below what would, hopefully, be the lowest bid. Opal desperately needed to have operating cash, even if they lost money on this particular contract.

The next day Señor Pedro Aviles, the grandee-like manager of the breeding ranch, personally brought over a sleek, small mare for Opal's approval. The man was very handsome and courteous, practically falling all over himself in his attempt to please Opal.

Beatrice Cole took the smile from his face and the twinkle from his eye when she told him to send his account books to headquarters for audit. Suddenly the big, strong, self-assured manager melted into a stammering weakling, full of alibis and excuses.

"Just send what you have, Mr. Aviles, and from now on don't skip the paperwork," said Beatrice.

"At your peril," added Opal, disappointed in the man. Perhaps he knew breeding, but a manager wore many hats, and she thought, wryly, a female manager of managers needed a halo, or at least a pair of wings.

CHAPTER 4

After checking on the progress of the new jail, Skinner turned Gertie towards the boarding house of Mrs. Robinson, kitty-corner from Dora's house, that was not a home. The Robinson house, as its sign proclaimed, was "Where Gentry Lodge." It did have a wrap-around front porch, although narrow, more like a balcony, thought Skinner.

It also had a handsome, cast-iron carriage boy out front, in the image of a Negro boy jockey, his shiny black hand holding a brass ring to which the visitor could tie his animal.

The front door contained one of those fancy new pull-bells, which Skinner pulled, setting off a double-ring of the inside bell. Hearing no footsteps approaching, the sheriff pulled the rod again, the door being opened in mid-ring by a stern-faced, older woman.

"If you're seeking accommodations, we fill our rooms from a waiting list," stated the greying woman brusquely.

"Thank you, but I'm seeking a Mrs. Robinson. I'm Sheriff Skinner."

"Oh, aren't you the one that killed those men a few days ago?" she asked, eyes widening.

"This is on an entirely different matter, ma'am. Are you Mrs. Robinson?"

"Why, yes. I'm Mrs. Robinson. Robinson was my maiden name. My late husband's name was Stugpool. When he died, I reverted to Robinson. Never liked the name Stugpool. Is that what this is about? Should I have gone through the court to change my name back?"

"I really can't say, Mrs. Robinson, but a lot of women seem to use their maiden names. I would think it would be legal if you weren't trying to illegally deceive people. But you'd really have to ask an attorney about that—to be sure."

"Then, what are you here for?" she said, her large figure still blocking the doorway.

"I'm checking on the death and estate of a man named Charlie Henderson," said Skinner, watching her eyes.

"Yes, old Charlie was a lodger of mine," she answered, eyes never wavering from Skinner's face. "What are you concerned about? He died in bed, you know—weak heart, the doctor said." A vein in her temple suddenly started pulsing bluish blood.

"There was a question about Mr. Henderson's effects," said Skinner severely, determined to keep the pressure on the woman. "Whether they were distributed properly."

"Didn't have much—them Shakespeare books, and some clothes. Undertaker came for his Sunday outfit, to bury him in."

"I was led to believe he had a valuable stamp collection and a chest of tools."

"You've been talking to that Hansen, haven't you? That old drunk put ideas in your head, didn't he?" she spat out, scathingly.

"What did happen to his tools, Mrs. Robinson?" Skinner asked harshly.

She looked away from his face to say, "I don't know anything about his tools. Weren't in his room when he died. Had four dollars in his pants. The undertaker made me sign a receipt for it."

"And the stamp collection?"

"Just one book. It's in a box in the shed. I was keeping it for his relatives, if they come."

"Only one book?"

"That's all I found. That and some old clothes. It's all in the box."

"I'd like to see that box, if you don't mind, Mrs. Robinson," the sheriff said impassively.

"I guess you public people got all day for foolishness. Well . . . come on, I'll take you to the shed," she said, coming out on the porch and shutting the front door behind her. She led the sheriff around the porch to a set of steps going down to the side yard. The shed stood in the corner of the lot behind the privy.

She unlocked the brass padlock with a key from a keychain recovered from her bosom. "Just stay there," she ordered. "It's dark, but I know where I put it."

"Wouldn't think of you lifting a heavy box," said Skinner, following her into the gloom of the shed.

"That's it, there on top." She started to pull a lug-sized vegetable crate from a pile of boxes.

The crate was labelled "Henderson," in black crayon. "Here, I'll get that," said Skinner, grabbing the box from her. Not so fast, though, not to see several other boxes so labelled, with "McFee," "Smith," "Borge" and "Peoples."

"Thank you, Mrs. Robinson. If any heirs come looking for this, send them to me. It's in my hands now."

"It certainly is," she said bitterly. "Here I try to do a good turn and get no thanks for it. That's what I get for taking in these old men—serves me right."

"Now, now, Mrs. Robinson," chided the sheriff, "a lot of our good works are often misconstrued by people who don't know all the circumstances. I'm in that category quite often, myself. Remember how you asked about myself and those bank robbers just a while ago. I live with that all the time."

"Yes, but I don't go around shooting people," the woman said, looking hard at the box in Skinner's hands.

~~~~~~~~~~~~

Smokey Watson, the scout for the hide thieves, took the wagons off the road to Green Falls, putting them on the old Eagle Pass Trail, seldom used now with the demise of Comanchero traders. Then it was down that poor trail to cross the Little Fish at Rocky Ford, where the water barrels were filled.

Then it was on, leaving the Eagle Pass Trail to pick a winding cattle trail through the badlands bordering the Puzzle River, crossing the underground portion of the river. Now the going was easy and the big mules were whipped into a mile-devouring trot to arrive at a concealing copse of pine. They came at the beginnings of the false dawn, when the glow of the rising sun hints at tomorrow, then seems to vacillate on its delivery of the new day.

There, below their clandestine camp, was the prey, a medium-sized herd of longhorns, still dormant in the murky darkness of the lower valley. Today the thieves would rest, waiting until later in the afternoon to do their work. Tomorrow at this time they would be pushing back through the badlands, loaded with stolen hides, leaving the carcasses of almost two hundred cattle for the feathered and the four-footed scavengers that were always near.

But as carefully and secretively as the thieves marched, they were seen. Not recognized, though, for what they were—for Paulie and Groszvater had no experience with hide thieves. But they were surprised to see the dark convoy pass before them in the night, and were worldly enough to realize that the shadowy wagons were somehow sinister.

~~~~~~~~~~~~

"It somehow don't seem right, Miss Wilbur, you riding like a man, rather than using a sidesaddle like a . . . like a . . ."

"Lady," said Opal Wilbur, cutting off Hugh Foote's fault-finding of her decision to use a small saddle found in the tack room. "Pray, Mr. Foote, what physical facts do you use to support your argument?"

"Well, er," he stammered, "ladies are built different than gents, where they fit the saddle, I mean."

"Are you saying that the male genitals make it easier to sit a saddle, help cushion the pelvis, is that it?" she said, enjoying Foote's embarrassment.

"Well, ah, not really," he said, red-faced.

"For your evidently limited knowledge of the female body, Mr. Foote, a female has a wider pelvis than a male, making riding astride easier than for a male. Also, the female anatomy places the woman's principal muscles in the lower torso and thighs. Not limbs, my red-face Mr. Foote, but thighs. A woman's strength is designed to deliver babies. Of course there's a few days that a woman may not be comfortable riding astride, but I let you guess about them, Mr. Foote."

"Not me, Miss Wilbur, I'm not good at guessing," said Foote, trying to regain his aplomb.

"It's nice to hear there's some area you're not superior in, Mr. Foote. Makes you a little more human."

"Oh, I'm human all right, Miss Wilbur. If you prick me, do I not bleed? If you tickle me, do I not laugh? If you poison me, do I not die?"

"Very good, Mr. Foote, only it should be in the plural," said Opal, surprised at the Shakespeare.

"Thought the singular would be more apropos of my situation," said the foreman. "Now let's see if we can find a bit for your mare."

"Good, then when my horse is ready I want you to point me in the direction of the Running W. I want to look them over."

"You better take your nightshirt with you, 'cause you can't make it back here before dark, not unless you're like one of those Pony Express riders."

"Then I'll take a blanket roll and saddlebags, and come back tomorrow."

"Miss Wilbur, I know you're a tough, determined lady, but would you do me a favor and take Bert Massey with you? He knows the way, and I can spare him for a couple of days. It would sure make me feel a lot better. 'Specially with you on a new horse you're not real familiar with yet."

"Why, Mr. Foote. I do believe you are worried about little old me," said Opal, mimicking a Southern accent. "I accept. But I had the feeling you would be glad to see me ride off, never to return."

"Not so, Miss Wilbur. What with that family of yours, I'd probably end up with an even meaner relative."

~~~~~~~~~~~

Major Riemann waved his good arm to signal that the mark was on the level, then raised his face from the dumpy level. He was surprised to find a small circle of men around the instrument, waiting to gain his attention.

"What's this?" he questioned. "Is something wrong?"

"You could say that, Major," said a man named Gruber, "We need to talk to you. Isn't that right, Damm?"

"Ja, we must talk. For better or worse. We must talk now."

Riemann looked around at the men. God family men; hard workers, all of them. And more, they were the leaders of the community, not given to flighty pronouncements or quick decisions.

"So, say your piece. What is bothering you?"

"Major, we—" started Gruber. "Oh, you tell him, Damm. I talk too rough sometimes."

"What we mean, Major," said Damm, suddenly finding his big, cracked hands to be interesting, "is that we all believe in this dam. We know our future depends on having water."

"Then, what's the problem?" said Riemann, trying to drag out Damm's story.

"We need to get more crops in. We have no reserve," blurted out Fenstermacher.

"What we mean, Major," put in Damm, "is that we need more balance between working on the dam and putting in crops. You know back in the old country the counts and the barons always had projects going on that took many men. Churches, castles, canals—always big jobs that took many years, sometimes a generation or more to finish. But always the Edelmann would understand that without bread, or feed for the animals, we could not finish his big work. Now we have the same problem here."

"Without bread, we cannot live, Major," said Gruber.

"What do you ask of me?" asked Riemann flatly.

"We would like a meeting of the whole community," said Fenstermacher, "to discuss this with all, and make the correct decision. The future of our colony depends on this."

"Schedule your meeting. Then we will decide," said Riemann. "Now—can we get back to work?"

As the men went back to their jobs, Kurt, the survey assistant, came clumsily up to the major. "You hear that, Kurt?" asked the major, shouldering the level and tripod.

"Ja, Major, it's the grasshoppers," said the dwarf. "The farmers fear for the grasshopper. Me, too—I'm closer to the ground."

~~~~~~~~~~~~

Vern Miller was the Postmaster of Green Falls. Skinner caught him sewing up a canvas mail sack.

"Hello, Vern," said Skinner. "Need to pick your brain."

"Too late, Skinner, it's picked and shipped out to parts unknown."

"I hear you know something about stamps," continued Skinner. "Not real postage stamps, but the kind people collect and put up in albums."

"What brings about your thirst for knowledge, Sheriff—thinking of collecting stamps? My advice is, don't. Turns a man into a social hermit, depriving him of the many pleasant hours he would get listening to shrewish wives and quarreling offspring."

"That why you collect stamps, Vern?"

"You found me out. It must be that detection streak in you lawmen. Now, what can I do for you?" He knotted the heavy thread, cut it with his teeth, then threw the repaired bag on a stack, to grab a rent sack from another pile.

"I have here, a stamp album, from a person recently deceased," said the sheriff. "He was supposed to have other books, but they seem to be missing."

"Let me see it," said the postmaster, putting aside his work to take the album to the window.

"This is Charlie Henderson's first album. I recognize his hinges," said Miller. "This was before he started to specialize. Charlie was in our Philatelic Society; in fact, he was past-president. He had trouble lately on account of his fingers, but he persevered. What did you say happened to his bisects and overprints? That was the valuable part of his collection."

"His what?" asked Skinner, confused.

"Charlie had an album of bisects, such as when they take a stamp and cut it in two or even three pieces to use for less expensive postage. And he had two albums of overprints or surcharges. These are stamps that have their value changed, mostly to fill a shortage of a particular denomination."

"You say those albums would be valuable. How much would you say they would be worth?"

"I could only guess. If I had the albums, I could try to match them up with my Brown's Catalogue and get some kind of an estimate," said the postmaster.

"How about taking a guess, Vern? I need to have some kind of an idea of their worth."

"I don't know," said Miller, thinking. "Over a thousand dollars, probably. Some of his collection was damned valuable. And this was the only album that showed up?"

"That's all his landlady said she found. What's that worth?"

"Not too much. He was just getting into the hobby. Was pasting up all kinds of stuff, based mostly on looks. And some of the issues were just junk that the hobby houses sell to school kids. Maybe thirty-five bucks, not much more."

"Well, thanks, Vern," said Skinner. "Looks like Mr. Henderson's estate was robbed, unless he sold the albums before his death."

"Charlie wouldn't have done that. Those stamps were like his children to him. In fact, in my case, I am only too willing to sell a child or two. Know any friendly Apaches?"

"'Fraid not, Vern," said the sheriff, chuckling. "They've all gone south for awhile."

~~~~~~~~~~~~

It all went as planned, except the younger herder proved tough to kill, making Judd Payton, the hide thieves leader, ride out to his fallen body to provide the coup de grace with his pistol. All the shooting had spooked the herd somewhat, and Big Judd and Little Smokey had to do some riding to push the herd back to the big wagons, where the slaughter commenced in earnest.

The skinners were good, and fast, using mule power to help peel the wet hides from the heavy carcasses. Uncle Walter cut several choice lumps from a younger cow, burying them in a small pit with wood coals for their traveling food, for it would be breakfast on the run, once their night's work was done.

They worked steadily, only pausing to sharpen their now slippery skinning knives, or to lead another wild-eyed beast to their bloody butcher ground. Soon the moon came up and with it a sharp breeze to push away the stink of fresh blood. The coolness felt good to the sweating men, invigorating their bodies.

Around ten Uncle Walter lugged around the big coffee pot, to give each man a syrupy-thick cup of his celebrated hide-runners' coffee, sweet with chicory and rum.

Then, by an hour past midnight, it was over, and all hands were necessary to fight the heavy hides up on the wagons and lash them down for the rough ride to market.

As the men stood around a large bucket of hot soapy water, trying to scrape the tallow from their arms, Uncle Walter dug up the roasted beef, slicing it in wide, tender slices to layer them on not-so-fresh bread. Quickly, the wooden platter was emptied as the men took their sandwiches with them to their wagons.

Then, at a soft call from Judd, the brake levers were released and the reins shook out at the patient mules as the loaded wagons wheeled into line, forming up their ghostly column. By four o'clock the wagons had crossed the trail to Green Falls and were filing towards the badlands.

That morning Paulie Vogelnester and Groszvater did not see the phantom convoy, but they noted its deep wheel marks where they crossed the trail, and they again wondered.

~~~~~~~~~~~~

Opal Wilbur and Bert Massey left the Running W soon after dinner, which turned out to be a rather grand affair because their cook, Sparky Anderson, needed to show off his culinary talents to the new boss lady.

This display of cookery bothered the manager, Bob Bennington. He was afraid if Sparky showed off too much, the new owner might steal his talents for the headquarters ranch, a catastrophe for the men and morale of the Running W. He was also bothered by the fact that the rider he had sent out to bring in old Stanley Hopkins from the west range had failed to return.

Bert and Opal were gone from the big ranch only about twenty minutes when they saw a swift-moving rider giving chase. The rider was waving his hat as he galloped, trying to attract the attention of the new owner and her companion.

"Something's wrong, somewheres," said Bert, pulling up his big roan. "We best wait and find out."

It was the rider sent to bring in old Stanley Hopkins, his horse lathered from the exertion. "Ma'am, we've got trouble!" the young rider said excitedly. "Old Stan's dead and so's Jimmy Rodgers, and the herd's all killed for their hides. It's horrible!"

"You better take that nag back, he's finished for today," Bert told the young rider. "Where did this happen?"

"Up at the salt spring, this side of the canyon. 'Bout two miles from the line shack. God! Jimmy's head is all splattered about. He's my age, you know. Got folks in St. Louis."

It took Bert and Opal almost an hour of fast going to get to the scene. Bob Bennington and half a dozen hands were there, wrapping the dead men in their slickers.

Opal was shocked at the carnage. She had never seen a skinned cow before, and now she looked at two hundred yellow carcasses, scattered over the killing ground. These lumps were her cattle, some of their legs drawn up stiffly in death, as if beseeching some bovine deity for help.

Bennington had to call to her twice to interrupt her dismay.

"What was that, Mr. Bennington?" she asked, breathing deeply to shake off her revulsion.

"I said—we'll have to send for the sheriff," said the fatherly-looking manager. "Not that it will help much, but it needs to get on the record."

"Can you send someone?" said Opal.

Bennington went out to a young cowboy to tell him to ride to Green Falls for the Law.

"Who did this, Bert?" asked Opal.

"Wouldn't put it past them damn Krauts," answered the big man. "They hate our guts, and the feeling is likewise."

"Wasn't the sod-busters, Bert," said Bennington, coming back to hear Bert's outburst. "Was hide thieves. Had three big wagons and one small one. Tracks heads south. I sent Shorty Ames and Blackie Thompkins to follow them."

"Just two men?" questioned Opal. "Will that be enough if they catch up with the outlaws?"

"Not if it's an all-out fight. The problem is, Miss Wilbur, I don't have enough men to mount a posse to follow them. What with these two," he pointed his head at the slicker-wrapped bodies, "already down. Two men was all I could send without stripping the ranch. You know we got a pretty slim payroll nowadays."

"I know," said Opal tersely, "and no regulator since the last one was killed."

"That's right," said the manager. "Need a regulator—bad. What Bert here says about the nesters is pretty close to the truth. I'm almost sure they're eating our beef. Never find any strays down that way anymore—towards the river, I mean."

"I've sent for a regulator, Mr. Bennington. My new book-keeper recommended someone. Hopefully, he'll be on the job soon. Maybe we can prevent future outrages like this from occurring."

"You couldn't tell me this new man's name, could you?" asked the manager.

"His name is Captain Cabot. He is supposed to be quite experienced in these matters."

"If it's the Captain Cabot I'm thinking of, Miss Wilbur, he sure is."

"That's nice to know. One thing more, Mr. Bennington—I've put an offer in to the Army for the September contract; 250 prime beeves. How will today's massacre effect our ability to meet that contract?"

"The Army contract? The ranchers in Tucson won't be happy about that. No sir-ee."

"That is just too bad. We need cash, badly. Now, answer my question."

"Miss Wilbur, there's cows and then there's prime cows. This herd here was mostly prime, good sized. They would have made a giant step toward filling a 250 cow herd. Probably weren't fifty culls out there. Now I'd be pressed to come up with 150 head—prime stuff, that is."

"All right, Mr. Bennington, gather up that many and work them toward the D B. I'll get the Lazy J and the D B to scare up the rest."

"Miss Wilbur, I gotta tell you this, them ranchers in Tucson ain't gonna be happy about you busting into their Army contracts. They're awful friendly with the government inspectors. Them inspectors are going to go over any herd you take them with a fine tooth comb; let me tell you."

"You just give me 150 prime beeves, Mr. Bennington," said Opal, "and I'll worry about the inspectors."

※※※※※※※※※※

"No jelly buns?" said Sam. "You didn't bring any buns?"

"Too close to dinner," said Skinner, putting down the box of Charlie Henderson's clothes and the album. "Didn't want to spoil your appetite. And I bought yesterday, anyway. It was your turn today."

"But you had to pass the bakery to check on the new jail."

"They got a man digging for the outhouse," said Skinner. "I told Manny what I wanted, a good stout partition between the prisoner side and the officers' side."

"Did you tell him about that article in the paper about that jailbreak in Kansas where someone hid a pistol under the sitting-down box?"

"Sure did. He's going to put a hasp on both doors so we can padlock them up," answered the sheriff. "'Course, it's going to be wooden wall . . . conceded that to Mosely."

"Make it easier to move, if it's wooden. When I was young my daddy moved our backhouse at least . . ."

Sam's outhouse oration was suddenly interrupted by the dishwasher from the Congress Hotel.

"You gotta comes muy pronto, Señor Sheriff. A man has a bomb tied around his stomach. He say he's going to blows everybody ups in the air."

"I think it's time for my dinner," Sam joked, getting up to unlock the Winchesters.

"Think we'll try the cuisine at the Congress," Skinner said. "Where is this man?"

"In the upstairs—the manager he sends me—maybe I stay here for awhile?"

"'Fraid not. Go back to the hotel. We'll be right along," Skinner told him. Then to Sam, "Give me that shotgun." He opened his bottom desk drawer to grab a handful of shotgun shells.

The man was on the second floor, in a room that opened onto the big canvas-floored porch.

"Why are you doing this?" shouted Skinner at the man, partially seen through his half-opened room door.

"God talked to me this morning as I ate my oatmeal," said the man, almost inaudible from behind the door.

"What did God tell you to do?"

"He said I should lead His people and tie dynamite around my body and hold the bottom half of an oil lamp to light the dynamite."

"Where did God want you to lead His people . . . er Mister ah . . . what's your name?" Skinner shouted.

"Phipps—George Phipps. That's spelled P-H-I-P-P-S. And God wants me to lead everybody to Natchez, Mississippi."

"Why Natchez, George?"

"On account of John the Baptist will be there, and he will baptize everybody, to the least swaddling infant, He said."

"Baptize everyone in Green Falls?"

"No, the whole world. The Mississippi is very wide there, I'm told."

"The whole world, George?"

"'The host of nations, shall ye gather.' That's what He said."

"Over your oatmeal this morning?" Skinner yelled.

"My mother gives me oatmeal every morning, when I come back from working in the mine. It's good for you, she says."

CHAPTER 5

S mokey Watson, the hide thieves' scout, was hunkered down behind a respectable boulder, watching the back trail. The big wagons had splashed through the Little Fish almost two hours before, and soon Smokey would leave his concealment on the south bank to catch up with them before the night passage through Mesa Grande.

Then he saw them, two men cautiously working their way down the north bank. They were spaced apart, with the taller man doing the leading by following the deep wheel ruts of the heavy hide wagons.

"Damn," Smokey said quietly to himself. "Why can't they let a body be?" He jacked a shell into the Henry and raised its folding peep sight to 150 yards.

The first man raised a hand, signaling to the man following. The second man stopped his horse, still on the bank, to watch the first man slowly move his mount down toward the water.

Smokey waited, holding his breath, until the tall man's horse was hock deep. The man stopped his horse, giving it a quick drink. With the horse's head down, the man made an inviting target.

The stocky scout fired, to watch the man slowly tip off his mount and fall into the shallow water. The second rider jerked his horse around, racing behind some large rocks.

Smokey fired two quick shots at the second man's shelter and then ran to his horse and galloped up the trail.

Shorty Ames, the second rider, waited for a long time behind the safety of his rock. Finally he burst out from behind the rock in a gallop, spurs savaging his mount, fleeing toward safety.

~~~~~~~~~~~~~

The rifles came that evening; eight long, heavy boxes, each holding ten of the long-barreled Spencers. Accompanying the repeating rifles, were ten squat boxes of .52 caliber rimfire cartridges, 1,000 rounds to each box. General Schurz had also sent cartridge pouches and— surprisingly—bayonets.

The German settlers had laid out their community in the style with which they were long familiar, the European village plan that placed their houses and barns together around a town square fronting their church.

Now, as the men of the community came from their labors, they saw the boxes of weapons heaped solidly before their church, and they felt comforted by the very presence of the arms. Major Riemann called the men and the older boys of the community to form ranks to receive their rifles. Quickly the boxes were pried open, and each member of the defense company was given one of the heavy rifles and its accessories, except for the ammunition.

The sergeant-major, flanked by the pastor and the major, handed each man a rifle and equipment, as the pastor warranted a short ceremony over each man's investment.

"Use this weapon to defend yourself, your family, your community and workplace. Be faithful to your orders and your comrades with the knowledge that God is always with us. Do you so swear now, as you take this rifle from your officer?"

Each recipient, lantern's light casting an amber sheen on his solemn face, knelt before his leaders, vowing his honor in acceptance of the rifle.

The rifle investment ceremony took over an hour, a time of somber ritual, a soldier's sacrament. But the custom reinforced the stolid German character by appealing to his sense of community and heritage.

When the last man had returned to ranks, Riemann called the men to attention to explain the great cost and the difficulty of the procurement of the weapons and their importance to the colony's welfare. He told the men to take their rifles home and clean them thoroughly and to learn the weapons' parts and operation. On the next Sunday afternoon they would march to the quarry to fire the weapons.

~~~~~~~~~~~~

"How did you get the dynamite, George?" shouted the sheriff. "I hear it's hard to get."

"Not for me," said the man behind the door. "I'm a mechanic working on that new steam pump. I'm good at locks. I took twelve sticks of forty percent. Got it all tied around my stomach. Have you notified all the many tribes of the Lord? We have to leave for Natchez soon."

"Takes time to write all those letters, George. Can you help us with the names of all the tribes? Let me go get a paper to write on."

Then, Skinner backed down the hotel corridor to talk to Sam.

"Can you get on that porch and get a shot at him?"

"It'll mean a head shot," said Sam. "Don't want to hit that dynamite. That would be the end of this hotel."

"Not to mention you and me."

"I'll give it a try," said Sam. "Keep him talking."

"At least he seems talkative," said Skinner, mostly to himself, as Sam had rushed off down the hall.

"George, you still there? I'm ready," hollered Skinner.

"Ready for what?" came the voice behind the door.

"The tribes, so we can send them your message."

"What tribes? I'm afraid of Indians. So is mother."

"The tribes you're taking to get baptized."

"Baptized?" came the voice, questioningly.

"That's what you said," shouted the sheriff.

"No, I didn't. Don't put words in my mouth. I'll blow up the dynamite right now."

"George, how would it be if I brought your mother up here to talk to you?"

"Don't want her here. It's always, 'Georgie do this' and, 'Georgie do that. And don't forget to bring in the wood and don't dump the ashes too close to the house. They blow all over and get the wash all dirty.' No—I don't want her here. Maybe I'll blow myself up, right now."

"No, George!" shouted Skinner. "You can't do that right now."

"Why not? How far is it to Natchez?"

"A long way. And you can't blow yourself up now, because it's too close to dinner."

"What time is it? Mother gets angry if I'm late for dinner."

"Almost noon. Why don't you let me watch your dynamite while you go eat? I'll keep it safe."

"No. God told me I need the dynamite. I was supposed to do something with it. I'll remember in a little while. I forget real easy since the accident."

"What accident was that, George?" yelled Skinner.

"When that thing hit me in the mine. Mother said I was asleep for five days."

"What was the thing that hit you, George?"

"I don't remember, but the doctor shaved my head—at least that's what mother told me."

"When did that happen, George?"

"I don't want to talk about it. I'm gonna stop talking with you, you're trying to . . ."

Suddenly the door slammed closed before George's sagging body, as the sound of a shot exploded from the porch.

Skinner ran to the door, pushing it open against George's bloody body. Sam forced the French door, to step in from the porch, Winchester in hand. George Phipps was now sprawled beside the door, his skull shattered by the Winchester's big slug.

The oil lamp luckily was smothered in its fall against the carpeted floor, just a dark smudge marking its landing.

"That was one tough shot," said Sam. "That glass door was reflecting the sun. Hard to figure where to shoot."

"Well, it's over now," said the sheriff. "Mr. Phipps won't have to worry about the ashes anymore."

"What ashes?" said Sam. "I thought he was a mechanic gone loco."

"He was," said Skinner. "He didn't like to take out the ashes."

"Neither did I, when I was a kid. Mother always made me carry them way off, so they wouldn't blow on her wash line."

"That was his trouble, I guess, Sam. That, and a hurt head."

"I don't know about then," said Sam. "But he's sure got a bad head now."

~~~~~~~~~~~~~

"Well, finally the Lord and master arrives for his dinner," said Gen. "I had to feed Mr. Hansen forty-five minutes ago. He had to get back to work."

"I hope he left something for me," said the sheriff. "I was delayed by a call to the Congress Hotel."

"It was bacon and liver, but the bacon's all gone. I had to make a little brown sauce to keep the liver from drying out. Now the mashed potatoes are all cold. I'll make them in potato cakes for you. Just go wash up—it won't take too long," said Gen, throwing kindling on the still hot coals of the new range's firebox.

"Take your time, my sweet, I could use a little relaxing time," said Skinner, going out to the back stoop to wash.

"And oh, Sylvester," said Gen, putting a scoop of butter in a cast-iron frying pan. "While you're out there, will you dump out those wood ashes in that lard bucket, please?"

"Yes, ma'am," said the sheriff, "and not too close to the wash, I imagine."

"What foolishness, Sylvester," reproved Gen, above the splatter of the butter. "This isn't Monday. Put them around the rose bushes out front."

~~~~~~~~~~~~~

Skinner had just returned to the office to sit down to a pleasant pipe-smoking session after the dinner, when the young galloper from the Running W came rushing into the office to spill his story of murder and hide stealing.

The sheriff and his evening deputy, Cletus McCoyne, listened to the excited cowboy with the unpleasant feeling that this particular crime would net no offenders, at least for today.

"Will that horse make it back?" asked Skinner. "We could use a guide."

"If we don't go too fast. She's got a lot of bottom," the youth answered proudly.

"We won't go too fast, don't worry about that," said Cletus. "We're too old to tear up trails anymore."

Sam came back from his late dinner as the sheriff and the big mountain man were loading gear on their horses. The sheriff told Sam about the trouble and that he was taking Cletus with him to check out the murder location. "And stop on your way home to tell our wives we won't be back for awhile," said Skinner, tying on a blanket behind his saddle.

It took two hours at a good trot to get to the sad spot. An older, worn-out-looking cowman had been left at the scene. He was sitting and smoking in the shade of his patient mare. "They all went back to the W," he said, crawling out from under his dun. "I was supposed to show you them wheel ruts, case you couldn't find 'em. They runs down from their camp up there."

"Then, show us," said the sheriff, keeping a tight rein on Gertie, who was nervous with the huge swarms of flies feeding on the carcasses. "This isn't such a great place to spend the day."

"Just flies," said the old man. "You get used to 'em."

Once the elderly cowman showed the lawmen the wheel tracks, Skinner told him to ride back and tell the manager that he and his deputy would follow the tracks for awhile. The old man nodded and turned his horse toward the ranch.

"You go along, too, sonny," Skinner told the young galloper. "That horse of yours is worn out." Then, turning to Cletus, "But first I want to check on this camp that the old man said the hide thieves laid up in."

They backtracked, following the lighter wheel tracks of the empty wagons, riding up the hill to the grove of stunted pine.

"They're clean campers," said Cletus, swinging down to load his horse. "I'll say that for them. And that's mule dung, most of it, anyway. So they're pulling the wagons with mules."

"How can you tell?" said Skinner. "All manure looks alike to me."

"I know my shit," laughed the old scout. "A good tracker can tell you all about the animal he's chasing, just from checking the droppings. See that?—corn kernels. Those hide thieves fed good."

"Hold on, Cletus—found something," said Skinner, noticing some paper scraps in the brush.

"Talk about shit," laughed Cletus, "You found the hiders' privy."

"Now let me examine this fecal find," said Skinner, "and see if I can come up with something." He broke off a stick to stir up a disgusting scrap of newspaper. "It's the Tucson paper. They're from Tucson. How's that for detective work?"

"Not so great, everybody within a hundred miles wipes himself with the Tucson paper. What you need is a love letter written to some lovesick hide thief, complete with his name."

"How many wagons do you figure, Cletus?" asked Skinner.

"Three big ones with six-inch wheel rims and one smaller one with about a three-and-a-half-inch rim. And big teams, almost double-teamed. They're going to be hard to catch," said the scout, shaking his head negatively.

"We're not catching them here," said Skinner. "Better get going." They were crossing the trail from the settlement at Puzzle River to Green Falls when they came across Shorty Ames coming back from the ambush at the Little Fish.

Shorty Ames was a member of old Jesse Wilbur's armed mob that almost hanged the sheriff and Sam six months previously, so he was easily remembered by Skinner, who prided himself on never forgetting a man that tried to hang him.

"Hold on, Ames," yelled Skinner. "What's the hurry?"

"We was following the hide thieves, me and Pete—Pete Turner. We got ambushed when we tried to follow them across the Little Fish. They opened up and got Pete. Must have been six or seven of them. I charged at them, shooting like crazy. Sure that I got a couple of them. But I seed that Pete was dead, so I hightailed it out of there. Come right back—I was gonna tell Bob Bennington, our manager."

"So Pete is back at the river?" asked the sheriff.

"Yeah—dead. In the water. But I'm sure I got a couple of them," said Ames, not meeting Skinner's eyes.

"Go on back. Tell them we're following the outlaws."

"What about Pete?"

"What about him? He's dead, isn't he?" said Cletus.

"I mean what about his body?" said Ames.

"Tell Bennington to send some men to collect it. We're busy chasing outlaws," Skinner said roughly. "Come on, Cletus, there's not much light left."

~~~~~~~~~~

The sheriff's visit bothered Mrs. Robinson. Later that night, when her elderly boarders had turned in, she took the lantern and went out to the woodshed to break up the boxes which were labeled with the names of former lodgers. The few almost worthless possessions, such as shaving items and trinkets, she threw into the privy and shoveled lime over the ooze that was their resting place. The boxes she chopped into small pieces and placed on her stove wood pile for immediate use. The clothing articles she tore into strips and would make them into a rag rug, for she took pleasure in having a memento of her adventure. For it was not every day a widow-woman could make a killing in her business.

~~~~~~~~~~~~~

The next evening, the night after the rifle investment, the colony gathered to have their meeting concerning the farmers' complaints. The monthly Saturday night social was canceled, to the dismay of the women, especially the husband-hunting young girls.

All the men of the community were present, as were many of their wives. The pastor opened the meeting with a short invocation, asking the Lord to guide their thoughts and actions in this meeting, and in their daily lives.

Then the elder, the venerable dean of their colony, Hienrich Kolb, took charge of the meeting, placing himself between the two factions as a moderator.

The elder asked the farmers to state their argument first, requesting Franz Damm to take the floor. Damm rose to his feet and looked almost apologetically at his fellow community members. Then, raising his lion-like head, he looked at Major Riemann and pointed a work-ruined hand at him.

"Major Riemann is a fine man," he said, slowly enunciating every syllable. "A fine engineer, a respected and experienced soldier. A good leader in all but one element. He is not a farmer.

"I am a farmer, as are most of us here. Our fathers tilled the soil, as did our grandfathers and their grandfathers, and on back into the history of our families.

"We have seen good harvests, when the grain spilled from our granaries. And we have seen bad years, when we had to eat our brood sows and make our seed grain into bread. But always we survived—somehow. We continued to grow our crops, even though we had to give our masters their giant shares, even when we had to give them our sons for their armies, spilling their young lives in stupid shows of power.

"Now we are in America, where we are the masters of what we do, or what is asked of us to do.

"This dam we are making is most important. This Arizona is a dry country where every drop of water is like gold." He used the word 'Goldstück,' a gold piece.

"We farmers understand water, but we also know when we must plant, so we do not have to go hungry and have to eat our brood sow and our milk cow. We must put more grain in the earth or we will not have bread. Always there will come a bad year. A year when the rust comes, or the tiny insects or the big grasshoppers. We must have enough surplus grain to feed us . . . when the bad year comes.

"Please, my men and women, allow every farmer enough time to plant more grain. You, my friends, can set the amount of land each man can additionally set to plow. But plant we must, or we will starve, if not this year, then the next."

He looked around at his audience, the tears from his eloquent entreaty running down his weathered checks, giving mute testimony to his earnestness. Then, nodding his leonine head, as if to himself, he took his seat.

A murmur of voices rose at his sitting, which was quickly stilled by the elder's upraised hand. "Major Riemann, will you now present your contention?" he asked.

"Thank you, Elder Kolb," said Riemann, rising to face the assembly. "To tell you the truth, I came here to argue against this planting. I was going to say that we must endure; we must continue construction, as every day we work puts us closer to the day the dam will be finished and we have the water we need.

"But, Brother Damm, with his heartfelt plea, has convinced me that I have been shortsighted. Perhaps it was my ego. If it was, I apologize to all. I here and now indorse Brother Damm's plan. But I would like, with your permission, to modify the planting. I want to make a giant gang plow, with four large plowshares, pulled by sixteen animals, and a harrow of the same size. These would be driven by only half as many men. A three man crew would plow all the new fields and plant the corn for all the families."

"Corn?" The assembly gasped, almost as one voice.

"Yes. Although, as Brother Damm says, I'm not a farmer, I am convinced that we can additionally irrigate only corn, until the dam's flumes are built. Now—shall we discuss this new idea?"

CHAPTER 6

I t was dark when the sheriff and Cletus came to Mesa Grande. A solitary tallow-dip lantern, hung on the store's porch, barely managed to give them a weak welcome.

The hamlet of Mesa Grande contained only three buildings, the largest of which was the Swanson combination general store, post office and saloon. Bracketing the store was the quarry office on one side and a corral and covered shed used by freighters as an overnight stopping place on the other side.

Mesa Grande, named after the table-top feature of the mountain plateau, was the half-way point between Tucson and Green Falls. It was the natural resting place for travelers moving between those towns.

The saloon's interior was blue with tobacco smoke, and had the sharp smell of stale beer and the unwashed bodies of its hard-drinking customers. Skinner had met the proprietors, Mr. and Mrs. Swanson, previously, when the stage had stopped there during his course of employment.

"What brings the law to Mesa Grande?" asked Mr. Swanson, squeezing out his bar rag on the floor at his feet. "Not another stage robbery, I hope."

"Hide thieves this time, Mr. Swanson," said Skinner. "But give us some beer, we've got thirty miles of thirst."

"And food," put in Cletus. "I'm starving."

"Got some pretty fresh crackers and a hunk of passable cheese. Got some pickled eggs, too."

"Bring them all," Cletus ordered, "and some mustard, if you got any. I'm a mustard man."

"And all the time I thought you were a mountain man," said Skinner.

"I'm a mountain mustard man," affirmed Cletus. "Some like tomato sauce. I like mustard. Lots of it. That was the trouble with the tribes—no mustard. Sometimes salt, but no pepper or mustard."

After they had stuffed themselves on crackers, cheese and pickled eggs, Skinner waved Mr. Swanson back to their section of the rough bar, in search of information.

"Now, Mr. Swanson, we need help. I think the hide thieves came this way last night. Did you see any big wagons go by last night?"

"Last night?" echoed Swanson. "Not me. Closed up the bar around midnight, not much business, anyway." He turned to a heavy man who was playing cards with Mrs. Swanson. "Hey, Jessup, come here a minute, will ya?"

The fat man at the table sighed and threw his cards down and struggled to his feet. "Now what?" he asked querulously, wiping his shiny face with a soiled white handkerchief.

"Did you hear or see any big wagons going past here last night?" asked the sheriff.

"Yep," said Jessup, stuffing the handkerchief back in his pocket.

"You did? When was this?"

"Which batch? There was two parties."

"Two parties?" questioned Skinner.

"Certainly," said Jessup knowingly. "First bunch was the wagon with that steam boiler and the machinery. Pumps, I think they was. Round about ten o'clock. Spent the night next door after Mr. Stick-in-the-mud kicked them out and locked up the bar. Chased me out, too. And I'm his best customer."

"And there was another group?" the sheriff persisted.

"Late, must have been around two or three, dark as hell. I had to make a trip to the backhouse. I think it was that rotten cheese of yours, Swanson. I generally have a cast-iron stomach, you know."

"Get back to the second bunch," steered Skinner.

"Four wagons; three big ones, one little one. Well, not real little; more medium-sized, like a farm wagon. And quiet, no jingles, no squeaks. Sort of ghostly, if you know what I mean. No lights, neither. Not before or to the rear."

"Which way were they going?" asked Cletus.

"Oh, to Tucson, I guess. Headed that way, anyway," answered the fat man.

"What's going on here?" said Mrs. Swanson, butting in on the questioning.

"The sheriff thinks a bunch of hide thieves came past last night," her husband told her.

"They killed three cowboys over past Puzzle River," said the sheriff, "and got away with two hundred hides. They have a fertile field over there for hide thieves, and I imagine the robbers will come back for a second helping. That's where I need your assistance."

"Me?" said Mr. Swanson. "I'm too busy tending bar, and taking care of the post office."

"There would be some recompense involved," continued Skinner.

"How much?" said Swanson quickly.

"You haven't heard what I need done."

"Go on tell us. We can use the money."

"I want you to sweep a two foot wide path across that road every night, just before dark. Then first thing every morning, check that path to see if the hide thieves came through during the night. If they did, ride like hell to Green

Falls and let me know the robbers are out, and on the prowl. I'll give you a 25 dollar reward for this information."

"I can't leave the post office. Besides, I'm not much of a rider," said Swanson, lamely.

"I'll do it," said Mrs. Swanson. "Hell, I can ride a horse. Can shoot, too, just ask that other deputy of yours, Sam Buller. I killed that mail robber last year, back in the quarry. Shot the hell out of him. But I want something myself."

"What's that?" said the sheriff. "Better not cost any money."

"Just a badge. Want you to make me a deputy," said the feisty woman. "Then when we get trouble here, I'll be the law and I can lock them up in the cool cellar, legal-like."

"It's a deal," Skinner told her. "Just don't shoot anybody who's not shooting at you. Hold up your right hand. I do hereby deputize you a special deputy sheriff, Green Falls County, Mesa Grande Station. I'll send you a badge in the mail. Now, how about buying your boss a drink, to celebrate your new official position, Deputy Swanson?"

~~~~~~~~~~~

"I'm going to need my rifle, Sterns. Got a call for my talents," said the greying, thin man.

"Do you mean you want to redeem it? It's $27.00 now. It went up another dollar last Monday. That's the agreement you know; a dollar more every Monday."

"Get me the rifle, Sterns," ordered the man, laying two twenty dollar gold pieces on the counter. "I got a good advance."

"Sure thing, Captain Cabot," said the pawnbroker, unlocking a cabinet and taking out a heavy .56 caliber Colt revolving rifle. "I'm glad you're redeeming it, as I'd have trouble selling it. Too many accidents with these Colt rifles. The side flash tends to set off the other chambers, and there goes the shooter's hand."

"So I've been told," said the wiry, well-dressed man. "I never have any trouble. The secret is beeswax. Close off the chambers of the cylinder with beeswax, and they don't flash over." He had brought a leather box-pouch with him and carefully placed the three extra cylinders for the rifle in their felt-lined recesses. Then he closed the pouch and hooked the fastener.

The shopkeeper watched the captain stow away the deadly cylinders, fascinated both by the man's deft actions and his fearsome reputation as a man-killer.

"Can I sell you anything else you could use, Captain?" asked the pawnbroker. "Got a practically new .36 Derringer. You can almost hide it in your hand."

"I do my work at long range, Sterns, with this," said the captain, giving a little love pat to the heavy rifle. "'Never let an enemy get too close,' is my motto. Right, Sterns?" This last in an icy voice.

"We are friends, Captain," said the pawnbroker, taking a step backward from the counter.

"But it's those Mondays that worry me, Mr. Sterns. Sometimes I feel those dollars get in the way of our friendship. All of a sudden you're squeezing a dollar out of me, every Monday."

"You know, Captain, you're right," said the storekeeper, suddenly dry in the mouth. "I'm glad you brought that up. Friends got a duty to each other, you know."

"Oh, I know," said the captain, a hint of a smile on his tanned face.

"And I'm going to waive the interest charges—how's that? Just the twenty I loaned you. Here—take back this other twenty." He pushed the coin at the captain with a pudgy finger.

"That's what I call real friendship, Mr. Sterns. It's a pleasure to do business with you. And may I come back again, if I need our friendship in the future?"

"Any time, Captain," said the perspiring pawnbroker, escorting the captain to the door. "I'm always open to my friends."

The captain smiled and left, with the shop owner quickly shutting the door. "Whew," Sterns whispered to himself, "with friends like you, who needs enemies?"

The old Negro, who had waited with the two animals outside the pawnshop, smiled to himself as he saw the relieved shopkeeper usher his employer out. He took the heavy rifle from the captain and slid it into the chamois rifle cover that he had held. Then, pushing the captain's grey away from his mule, he held out the stirrup for the captain to mount.

"Thank you, Nappy," said the captain. "Hand me that duster, will you? It's a long ride to Puzzle River."

The Negro dug out a tan duster from a valise tied to the mule's saddle and handed it to his master. "Looks like Mr. Sterns was glad to see you go, Cap'n," chuckled the old man. "Did you arrange a discount again?"

"Friendship, Nappy. The blessings of good fellowship."

"Might be, Cap'n, but I believe Col. Colt had a lot to do with it."

"You could be right, Mr. Napoleon," said Captain Cabot, heading his horse down the dusty street toward the Green Falls trail.

"And here we goes again," said the Negro, kicking his mule into a trot to follow his master. "A body here, a body there, it's how we gets our daily fare . . . get along, Mr. Mule."

~~~~~~~~~~

"You're home quick this time," said the motherly-looking woman, helping her husband down from the empty hide wagon's high seat.

"Tell that to my rump, and you'll get an argument," replied Judd Payton, attempting to flex a sore back. "Think I sprung something. Them hides get heavier every year."

"Everything go all right?" questioned the woman. "Where is Uncle Walter?"

"No problems, and Walter's taking on supplies for the next trip."

"How did Joey work out? I still think he's too young to go along on big raids."

"A true Payton. He was ripping off hides like he'd been doing it all his life. Did his share of driving, too."

"He should still be in school. I always hoped for a doctor or a lawyer in the family," said the wife. "Now he'll never quit hiding—seems to get in your blood."

"I was hiding when I was thirteen. Your grandson is almost fifteen, and big for his age. And then a hide only brought six dollars, when we could find them to snatch. This batch brought fourteen. Figured 203 at fourteen, came out to over $2800. Boys' shares came to $750; another $400 for Smokey and Walter; $560 for the mules' rent; $120 for the hide wagons; $200 for grain and harness; $50 or $60 for our grub—leaves us over $750 profit."

"That's wonderful, dear," answered his wife. "At that rate, this ranch will be paid off sooner than we thought."

The couple had to move out of the way to allow the animal broker's men to unchain the mules from the big wagon and move them to their own corral and facilities, away from the Payton's big ranch house.

The woman watched the men moving the teams off to the broker's corrals. "$560 seems like a lot to pay for animals you only use three days."

"It's top dollar all right, but you get what you pay for. This trip we used fifty-six animals, which is a hell of a herd of mules. These fellows take away all the problems of making up the teams. All the feeding, shoeing, training, doctoring and replacement is all done by someone else, letting me concentrate on my one big concern."

"What's that?" asked his wife, taking his arm for the walk to their home.

"Finding new herds to tap, where we won't have trouble."

"Any ideas on next week's job, dear?"

"Thinking about going out past the tanks. The old haciendo out there died, awhile back. They might just be ripe for a raid. Smokey's going to scout them out tomorrow or the next day. Now, what's for dinner?"

~~~~~~~~~~~~~

It most surely was the flies that sickened her. Opal had felt nauseated looking at the field of yellowish lumps that represented four thousand dollars of her fast evaporating fortune. The sight of the rain slicker-wrapped murdered employees also had shocked her senses, as she watched Bennington's men struggle to get the uncooperative corpses tied down onto equally obdurate horses.

But it was the flies that sickened her. The millions of voracious flies. A buzzing, green-glinting blanket, a living verdigris of droning insects, frenzied in their ravenous rapture of feeding. A disgusting sight, coupled with the ever-increasing clouds of coursing flies, attacking both man and horse. An awful sight; a repulsive situation.

She had to leave, or she would embarrass herself by vomiting in front of her employees. She urged her little mare out of the swirling flies, very content to let her workers perform the necessary duties.

When they were finished, the corpse-carrying horses were led out of the awful mess. An older hand was detailed to wait for the Law, and to point out the wagon tracks of the outlaws and where the murderers had camped before their onslaught.

The group left the scene of slaughter. Silent in speech; somber in attitude; all wanting to leave this dreadful place and return to the rustic normality of the ranch, where a fly was a nuisance, not a menace to breathing.

Supper was a sad affair, even though the Running W's talented cook dished up a fine meal. They all had left both appetite and agreeability back at the massacre site.

This mood was not helped with the arrival of Shorty Ames, with the news of yet another man lost. The news that the sheriff and a deputy were at work trailing the outlaws was accepted with a lack of optimism. Nothing would bring back the three dead friends, or salve their pride and conscience about the lost herd. Supper was, even with the good food, not a good mealtime.

Bennington had turned over his bedroom to the owner. A man's uninviting room, smelling of tobacco and sweaty clothing. On a lumpy, thin mattress and coarse blankets that never knew sheets, Opal put in a bad night. A long time of bad dreams and tossing recollections.

Morning brought only light, not solace or solution. But the wash-up water was chilly and invigorating, the coffee hot and thick, and the pancakes dollar-sized and crispy-light. The heated sorghum syrup melted the still-sweet crock butter on the plateaus of stacked pancakes, to marry with them, flowing across the lowlands of the bacon and eggs, to puddle in sweet circular lakes at the plate's rim.

With an admonition to the manager to remember the gathering of a new market herd and a too-formal goodbye to the bereaved cowhands, Opal and Bert left the Running W and made the long trip back to the headquarters' ranch.

Once at the headquarters' ranch, Opal found Hugh Foote to be all soothing consolation and sympathy about her loss.

"How did you find out?" she asked, knowledge of the tragedy becoming suddenly personal, a private sorrow, to be locked in her breast, and brooded over.

"News travels fast," Foote answered, with his little boy's wry smile. "And bad news travels even faster. You've got to expect things like this to happen. Lightning can chase a herd over a cliff, or they can get into jimson weed and die of poison. Them big white flowers sure look tasty to a hungry cow. And then there's the ticks that sicken a critter to death and that new anthrax that will even kill a man. Then there's . . ."

"That's quite enough, Mr. Foote," Opal said sharply. "I don't need any dirges from you today. I'm going to turn this page and go forward with resolution and good sense. As you so kindly reminded, these things are part of the cattle business and must be expected and dealt with.

"I suggest, Mr. Foote, that you pick up your crying towel, and get back to your duties, one of which will be to round up at least 50 prime beeves for the Army contract. We have to make up another herd to replace the slaughtered animals."

"Fifty," said Foote, the smile gone. "Just like that."

"Just like that, Mr. Foote," Opal said acidly. "Hopefully, you can find them—that is, if you want to continue as foreman."

~~~~~~~~~~~~~

Perhaps Hugh Foote thought that his boss had thrown off her black mood, but Aunt Polly knew better. She had known Opal since young childhood, when Mr. Wilbur had hired her, a twenty year-old house girl who had suddenly become too big and too smart for the scullery. She was sold away from her mother and smaller brothers to a Maryland house that needed a colored girl to dress and pick up after a spoiled four-year-old rich girl with flaming hair.

Polly knew Opal's every mood, and she half believed that she could read the girl's mind. She knew, though, that she could read Opal's eyes. From the icy green spark of anger to the green slate of contempt, the girl's eyes had always betrayed her disposition. Now Aunt Polly was looking at eyes that told of defeat and the hurt of failure. Aunt Polly tried to cajole her into eating.

"I gots some nice chicken soup, honey. With those big flat noodles you likes me to make. How about I cuts some nice slices of breast meats and makes you a nice sandwich to have with the soup? I can cuts the crusts off, just the way you likes."

"Just the sandwich . . . And some tea, Polly, in my room," said Opal flatly. "I want to think."

"Honey, you be better off coming out of that room and talking to folks. Get your troubles out in the open and off you minds. It's no good for you staying cooped up in deres."

"Do what I tell you; you're not my keeper," spat out the young woman. "Or you can get on that stage coach and go back to mother. You'd make a good washerwoman; you talk enough." The bedroom door slammed behind Opal as she retreated into her privacy.

Polly stared at the door, shaking her round head. Then she laughed, the eruptions coming from the vast vault below. "Well, leastways I got you mad—that's a start, anyways." She went to slicing the chicken.

~~~~~~~~~~~~

The major consulted his watch again. It was a half-to-two. Smiling slightly, he nodded to young Rudy Goldfarb, the company's drummer boy. The boy came to attention and brought the drumsticks up to his eyes in salute, then brought them crashing down down on his field drum, banging out the call to assembly.

Slowly Der Platz started filling up with the rifle-carrying soldiery of the defense company. Each man's hat or cap was adorned with a green cockade pinned to the front. The cockade was a broad green ribbon pleated horizontally several times to denote the green falls of the county's name. The citizen-soldiers were very proud of their emblem and their newly-issued arms.

Major Riemann had the rotund sergeant-major march the company to the quarry, two miles off. He then rode out on his horse, accompanying the wagon that carried the exercise's allotted ammunition. Onkel Pfaff, a septuagenarian who once served as a surgeon's assistant in a Hanoverian regiment, rode beside the wagon's elderly driver, to handle medical emergencies.

Once at the quarry, the company was divided into veterans and recruits; with training and firing practice to accommodate each group. The forty older men each fired twenty rounds, becoming familiar with their weapons and adjusting their rifle sights as necessary.

The younger men were a different story, trying their instructors' patience. The big .52 cal. rifles were heavy and had a hurtful recoil, causing the young recruits to flinch or otherwise throw their point of aim from the target. But, by session's end, most of the young soldiers were managing to strike somewhere near where they aimed.

This afternoon had provided valuable training for the company, Major Riemann later told the settlement leaders, but more firing practice was indicated for the near future. Also, since more than 1500 cartridges were expended, an order for additional ammunition was prepared for mailing to General Schurz.

Major Riemann was also making plans that would, with the construction of strategically placed walls, link the perimeter houses of the settlement into a rough fortress; enough to protect against Indian raids.

He was also talking with the elder about the possibility of giving arms training to some of the older unmarried women, as they now had an assortment of older rifles and shotguns available, due to the issuance of the Civil War weapons sent by General Schurz. The elder was against this idea, because he believed that a woman's place is at her home and hearth.

But the major was a man not easily dissuaded, whether it came to water or to war. He would persist.

CHAPTER 7

I t was about an hour after midday, with a hot desert wind that burned any exposed skin. Skinner and Cletus rode with gloves on their hands and bandannas on their faces. Though it was a downhill ride from Mesa Grande, the horses were tired and heavily lathered.

With obvious relief, the sheriff and his deputy splashed their mounts across the river's cooling wetness and rode up Main Street to their office.

"Go on home, Cletus," Skinner told the big deputy. "Get some rest and get back around seven for the saloon patrol."

"Sounds good to me. If you're going in, will you take this in for me?" The mountain man handed Skinner his Winchester. "I'll clean them up tonight," he said, pulling his horse around to head for home.

Skinner pushed open the door, both Winchesters in his arms, to find his chair occupied by Doc Seevers, the old Army surgeon, one of two doctors in Green Falls. The doctor was drinking coffee out of the sheriff's cup and clutched a half-eaten jelly bun in his clawed, arthritic fingers.

"Oh, excuse me, mister," joked Skinner, laying the Winchesters on the table with a clatter. "I thought you were the sheriff."

"Could be," snapped the cantankerous doctor, "if there was more money in it. Lawmen get the glory, but it don't buy much. You should sit down. You look like you're all in."

"I would—if a certain small town quack would get his skinny butt out of my chair."

The doctor popped the remainder of his jelly bun into his mouth, saying, "If that's the way you treat highly esteemed medical professionals in this office, I want out. Take your cup. Take your chair—and I shall leave. I can tell when I'm not welcome. Besides, whoever made the coffee put too many eggshells in it. Got a lime taste to it."

"Well—thank you, Doctor Seevers," said Sam. "See if I give you any more of my grandmother's secret recipe coffee."

"Probably had to keep it secret or she'd be indicted for poisoning," said the doc, heading for the door.

"Hey, Doc," said the sheriff, giving his cup a wipe with his dusty bandanna, "Talking about poisoning, I need some information about a case I'm working on."

"Oh, no," answered Seevers. "Not another game of twenty questions. Will I get a fee out of this?"

"Not if I can help it. You doctors make too much already. But I got a lot of glory to spread around."

"Touché, Skinner. Give me a question. You've got my curiosity up."

"Got some names to throw at you. See if you can illuminate a hick sheriff with a sore backside."

"Go on . . . shoot."

"McFee, Smith, Borge and Peoples," spat out Skinner rapidly.

"Four old men who died of old age," answered the doctor, just as quickly.

"Are you certain—that they weren't poisoned?"

"Not enough to put money on it. Why?"

"I'm checking into an old fellow named Charlie Henderson, who died a few months back, and have found a few irregularities concerning his estate. When I questioned his former landlady, I found boxes with those four names on them—in her woodshed."

"And that's why you're asking me about their deaths?"

"That's it. What can you tell me?"

"As you're aware of, in this county a certificate of birth or of death is not required," said the doctor, trying to find a clean cup in the jumble of cups on the shelf.

"Someday, like in New York or Chicago, it might be—but not now. So, in consequence, babies are born unknown to the Territory of Arizona. Maybe their names are put down in the family Bible—maybe. The same is true of most deaths.

"Generally, only the violent deaths are recorded, mostly in the local newspaper, as events of local interest. Sometimes a report of these deaths is sent to some bureau in Washington, if it's a wagon train massacre or something. Mostly, the deaths fall through the cracks in the floor."

"So, how did you know about McFee, Smith, Borge and Peoples, then?" asked Skinner, getting up to pour himself a cup of coffee only to find the pot empty. He shot Sam a reproachful look. Sam shrugged, pointing to the doctor, who was drinking the last cup from the pot.

"Luther Borge was one of my patients," went on the doctor, "as was Charlie Henderson. Borge was an old soldier—knew him at Ft. Dodge, a long time back. He was suffering from heart trouble. Sounded all mushy, which generally means the heart valve's defective. Like in a water pump that has a leather flapper that's partly worn away."

"What was Henderson's condition?" said Skinner.

"Pretty fair, for an old geezer, except for severe arthritis in his hands, wrists and one elbow."

"So, what killed him?"

"Beats me. I heard about Charlie from Vern Miller, the postmaster. Charlie had told him that he was a patient of mine. They were in some kind of a club together."

"And what about McFee and Peoples? How did you know them?" continued the sheriff.

"McFee used to be head bartender at the Drovers. That was before your time, when it was new. Diamond Dick McFee, hell of a nice fellow. Knew everybody in Green Falls by his first name. Hell of a shame."

"What do you mean, shame?"

"He got shot in the throat one day by a girl who tried to shoot an ex-boyfriend. I had a hell of a time saving him. He ended up with a lot of scar tissue. Had to end up eating mush all the time. Like a gruel. That's why he got mad at me and started going to that Frenchman over at the Association. He just ended up starving to death. Read his obituary in the paper. Guess that French doctor couldn't help him, either."

"Why did they call him Diamond Dick?" asked Skinner.

"Big diamond stickpin in his cravat, and diamond cuff links. He was flashy—was Diamond Dick."

"And Peoples—how did you know him?"

"Didn't."

"Didn't?" exclaimed Skinner. "How did you recognize the name?"

"From Charlie. Old Charlie told me about Pop-Eye Peoples. Wanted to know what made his eyes extrude. And how he was a miser. Was always telling jokes about how cheap old Pop-Eye was."

"Very credible, Doc," complimented Skinner. "You're positively an encyclopedia of Green Falls citizenry."

"Should be. Been owed money from most of them. That reminds me, did you ever pay me for that hernia of yours?"

~~~~~~~~~~

Opal Wilbur's fit of depression, thankfully, lasted less than a day. Those gladdened by the raising of the funk siege were secretary/bookkeeper Beatrice Cole and ladies' maid/

cook/confidante Aunt Polly, who had quickly found out that the headquarters ranch house was too small to house non-speaking factions. Even though the parlor had been trans-formed into two cell-like bedrooms by one of the older hands who was reasonably skilled in hammer and saw, the bun-galow—a new word for any shack with a porch—was cramped.

On the second day of her return from her herd's death scene, Opal awoke refreshed from her catharsis. Fresh and free from doubt or dilemma.

She stripped the damp and acrid nightwear from her body and the rumpled bedding from her bedstead, calling out to Aunt Polly to drag in the wash boiler and buckets of warm water. "I'm going to cleanse myself of bad feelings, Polly. And bring me strong soap—the brown kind. Maybe I can burn off a layer of sweetness and charm."

"Angel darlings," laughed Aunt Polly, "Doan' you scrubs too hard, 'count of you ain' got too much of that, nohows." Thirty minutes later, Opal emerged from her room, shining and vibrant—ready to fight for her small domain. A Boadicea, the warrior queen, ready for battle.

The day brought an ally, not an adversary. It was Captain Cabot, still cool-looking and dapper despite the searing heat. He was trailed by his faithful mule-riding servant, Napoleon.

But Captain Cabot was not a comic character. He was flesh and blood, though lean of flesh, and perhaps—thin of blood.

She met him in the kitchen, apologizing for the lack of a parlor due to the need for more bedrooms. He smiled at this, almost regally, certainly patronizingly, and checked the prof-fered kitchen chair for dust before he sat down.

Opal seated herself to thank him for coming, then paused—expecting the man to respond gratefully for the employment.

Captain Cabot nodded acknowledgement and almost smiled, his tight, bronze face cracking slightly. He sat for a long, awkward moment, then crossed his legs, making a face at the dust on his shined boots.

"I imagine it's proper," he said finally, breaking the strained silence, "for me to also show some appreciation to you. Perhaps as a measure of fealty. But I won't. Our relationship is mutually beneficial. You have a measure of peace, and I receive a measure of your wealth. Notice I say measure, for you will never be completely peaceful here. And although I get a measure of your wealth, like any hired hand, always feel my talent has been sold too cheaply in the marketplace."

Opal broke in, not wanting the man to monopolize the meeting, to ask the derivation of the man's title of Captain. Was it earned somehow, or awarded honorably?

"A captain—to be sure," said the thin figure in black, "of the briny seas and the muddy trenches. On the silver deck of a blockade runner," he continued, almost dreamily. "Then, when the proud cause was near gone, I took my crew to fight on land—Southern land. We were to go down, swords in bloody hands, on the broken battlements of our noble intention.

"But then reality arose before us. The miles—long lines of shattered men stumbling away from the enemy—to anywhere that seemed safe. And half my brave crew fled with this pitiful remnant. Whether in good sense or cowardice, I do not know. Both were true. The rest of us went on, mostly to oblivion. I was felled, not by shot, but by sickness. A disease that fouled me from boots to breeches, wasting my body down to that of a child. I would have succumbed had not my servant, Napoleon, out there, carried me away and nursed me, finally, to health." He shook his head at this, as at something distasteful, before going on.

"And now I am what is sweetly called a regulator, or an enforcer, as if to put a sweet name to dreadful work. I am a killer of men.

"Look at me as a smoother of society. An artisan who rasps the rough projections even. It pleases me to look at myself as a traveling sword. A knight-errant—if you will. Certainly without the purity of a Galahad, but not a Modred, either."

"But aren't you afraid," asked Opal, "to always be the hunter of men? Afraid of losing objectivity; becoming just a lion; always on the stalk, killing only for your supper?"

"My dear girl," and this time he laughed, "I say girl because you see the world now only in the basic colors, whereas someday you'll see things in the softer half-shades, where good is qualified by a dab of doubt, and evil is graced by the worth of noble intention.

"If I allow myself the indulgence of a philosophical veneer, or a holier-than-thou suit of armor, it would cloud my vital sense. It would lower a gauze veil of ethics and religion over my shooting eye, placing me at peril to the very people I must remove.

"No, I look at myself as God, if there is one, looks at me. I am what I am. A killer of bad men. You—who hire me—judge them. I only destroy them, as you would remove a stinging insect that threatens you.

"Now from the ethical to the pragmatic. I would discuss my compensation and my living arrangements. In defense of the former may I say that I am a poor man, without funds. In truth, I had to recover my rifle, the tool of my trade, from the pawnbroker before I could leave for this welcome assignment."

"According to my uncle's records," said Opal, "our last regulator was paid 75 dollars a month and found. That's almost twice what our top hands receive. So it seems rather princely to me."

"Not to me, madam. If it is princely, this must be an extremely tiny principality," belittled the man.

"What salary do you think proper, Captain Cabot?"

"$150 a month and found, plus bonuses."

"You're not serious! My managers only make $90," Opal burst out.

"I'm a serious man, madam," replied the captain. "Do I seem to joke?"

"Call me Miss Wilbur," Opal said, tight-lipped in anger. "I'm not old enough to be thought of as madam."

"Perhaps that is why you feel that figure excessive. A lack of experience, no doubt, with a regulator's duties. What did you say happened to this economical man you previously had?"

"My uncle hired him. He was killed trying to protect my uncle."

"I see," said Cabot succinctly. "Do you?"

"What do you imply, Captain?"

"The obvious. You get what you pay for, Miss Wilbur."

"What's this bonus business?" said Opal, green eyes flashing sparks at the thin man across from her.

"I get a fifty dollar bonus for each man I have to do away with."

"Fifty for a man," snarled Opal. "How much for a woman—twenty-five?"

"You are being facetious, Miss Wilbur. Is $50 too much for a man's life? Seems a small price to me." He paused briefly, then continued. "I have the feeling our talk is going sour. I wonder if you really want an experienced regulator."

"I do need a regulator, Captain. But I just can't pay you $150 monthly. I'm cash poor and cow rich. What if I give you your pay in cattle?"

"Sorry, Miss Wilbur," said the captain, smiling, "I'd never make a cowboy. I'm no good with a rope. But I will modify my salary proposal. $100 a month and found for me and my servant, but the bounty would go up to $150 per man."

"That sounds much better, Captain Cabot," said Opal. "It's a deal."

"Very well, Miss Wilbur. Now I'd like to bring up the matter of my accommodations. As you know, I am a gentleman and will need a gentleman's lodgings."

~~~~~~~~~~

"I don't know, Sheriff," said the new prosecutor, Aaron Rose, getting to his feet to look out his office window at Main Street below. "If this was back East, I could go before the Grand Jury, maybe not to get an indictment on this Mrs. Robinson, but at least to secure a recommendation to seek a warrant to search her house for evidence."

"This isn't Boston, Rose," said Skinner. "You got to break new ground out here."

"I wish it was that easy," said the young attorney, turning back to Skinner. "We don't even have a judge available to issue a warrant. I will, though, write to Tucson for one, but first you'll have to give me all the facts for my request. Don't leave anything out. Every little thing is pertinent to . . ."

Suddenly Deputy Sam burst into the office, hot and huffing from the exertion. "Gotcha! Knew I'd find you here or at the bakery."

"It's trouble come knocking on your door, Mr. Rose," said Skinner, uncoiling himself from Rose's side chair.

"No time to knock," corrected Sam. "It's a bloody mess. Come on, follow me." He whirled out of the room.

"Come on, Counselor," Skinner said, "do you some good to be in on the beginning for a change."

Out on Main Street the young prosecutor allowed himself to be hauled up behind the sheriff on his horse. Then, with Sam leading at a fast pace, they were off, Rose hanging tightly to Skinner's waist for fear of falling.

Their destination turned out to be halfway up a low hill west of town, called Chinaman's Ridge. The Chinese laborers had been run out of town by the resentful white miners two years previously, but the name still stuck to their left-behind nest of mud and wattle shacks.

Sam passed the only substantial building on the hilly enclave, a low adobe brick saloon called the Grandview, to strike off up a fecal-scented alley cut by an open sewer-ditch which zig-zagged down its length.

The house was marked by a collection of the curious. A crowd of several dozen, content to soak up the morbid moment. Anything to escape the hot boredom and drudgery of their shallow lives.

Sam let his horse push its way through the chattering crowd, to swing down, tying off his horse on a stout picket of a high-set window. Several of the bolder spectators stood in the open doorway, calling out to the crowd the horrors of the bloody rooms.

Sam chased them out, slapping at them with his hat and cursing them for their disrespect.

The sheriff could see why the scene had attracted the curious. It was an eyeful. Repulsive and shocking, with blood and body parts scattered fiendishly throughout the three room mud shack.

He took a deep breath and was immediately sorry, for the stink of blood and excrement brought back the memories of the stench of war. Here the smell of gunpowder was absent, the murders evidently done with a ruby-red smeared hatchet left embedded in the blood-drenched, headless torso of a young child.

"How many in here, Sam?" asked Skinner, holding his bandanna to his face.

"From what I can make of it—almost said, pieced together—it's two kids and a woman. I'll know more later when they're laid out."

Suddenly the young prosecutor bolted for the door, driving the bystanders to flight with an eruption of vomit.

That brought a smile from Sam, who said, "That's one way to scatter a crowd. Maybe should remember that the next time we have a riot."

Skinner went to the door to talk to the crowd, trying not to notice Mr. Rose, who was wallowing in nausea while clutching Sam's stirrup to support himself as he retched his breakfast under the stoic horse.

"Who found this mess?" said the sheriff, tucking away his tell-tale bandanna.

"It was my Billy," answered a red-faced, thin woman pushing a rickets-legged boy out of the crowd. "Tell him, Billy, don't be scared."

Billy stared at the tall, black-clad sheriff with the wide eyes of a frightened animal, mute with the memory of the slaughterhouse, still there, open-doored behind the big lawman.

"I think he's ascared," excused the woman, putting a grimy hand on the boy's dirty cap. "He went to the Schwarzsteins' to pick up Fritzi to go to school. Does it every day, you know.

"First thing I knows, he's running in, screaming about all the blood. So I goes and looks, and God help me, it's horrible. So I runs down to the saloon and tells Mr. Felton and he sends old Amos to fetch you all."

"Their name is . . . er . . . was Schwarzstein?" asked the sheriff.

"Yeah, they was German. Frieda, Fritzi, Helga, and the man's name is Hugo—Hugo Schwarzstein. Did he do it, mister?"

"Too early to tell. Where did he work?"

"In one of the mines; one of the small ones, I think. He got fired from all the big ones for drinking too much. He was always getting drunk and beating on Frieda and the kids. Broke the girl's arm last year. My husband and some of the men went over there to knock him around, but Frieda stopped them. Bet she's sorry now, huh?"

"I imagine so," said Skinner. "What's Mr. Schwarzstein look like?"

"I dunno, sort of short-like, but not too short, yellow hair, going gray. Thick-like in the neck. And oh—got funny ears. You know—all crumpled-up like. Frieda said his father used to box his ears a lot when he did something wrong. Back in the old country. I guess they was real strict back there."

"Thank you. I want my deputy to get your name and address for the record."

"Does that mean I have to go to court?" said the thin woman. "I don't think my husband would like me to go to court."

"That's a long way in the future. Don't worry about that now. Might not happen." He turned to the prosecutor, now standing wanly, holding on tightly to the horse's halter. "Isn't that right, Counselor?"

"Anything you say, Sheriff. Can we go now?"

"Soon as I get Sam lined out on this. Just hang on to your friend there; I won't be long. Then I'll drop you off on the way to Marks' place."

CHAPTER 8

"**O**w many?" said the wizened little man named Griff, in his whiny, cockney accent.

"You heard me; eighty-two feet," said the balding, heavy-set man across the table.

"How come eighty-two feet, Mike?" said the third man, shaking salt into his beer. "Where did you come up with that figure?"

"It's mathematics, Harvey. Simple mathematics," said the man called Mike, in a superior tone. "Look, that old level is 50 feet below the surface—right?"

"We know that," Harvey said. "Tell us what we don't know."

"Just shut up and listen and we'll be rich. Now the Association's strong room is approximately 65 feet from that lateral, if you measure on the surface. That makes it 82 feet at about a 35 or 40 degree angle, I'll get that part figured out when I graph it. Then I'll make an angle plate we can set to a plumb line."

"'n' 'ow much silver is there?" said Griff.

"Depends when we hit it. The idea is to break through just before they make a shipment. Let it accumulate, you know."

"We'll never do it without the foreman's with us," said Harvey. "Never in a hundred years. He'd know we was digging someplace else."

"'Fraid you're right," said Mike flatly. "And he's going to want a big cut, big as us, dammit."

"Me old man use to say its costs money to make money," put in Griff. "Looks like 'e was talking to us about this silver."

"What about the strongroom floor, Mike? What's it made of? How much trouble will it be to get through it?" asked Harvey.

"It'll be tough," admitted Mike. "Twelve inches of concrete with one-inch iron bars embedded halfway through. The bars are laid in an eight-inch grid. So it means probably having to cut a couple of bars to let Griff get up there."

"Me?" said Griff, "Why me?"

"For your sweet disposition, and your skinny ass. You're going to pass us down the bullion."

"Get back to that floor," said Harvey. "How are we getting through?"

"Don't worry about it. That's why I want Olly in on this. He can make nitro talk. He'll figure it out. You know what is going to be our biggest problem?"

"What's that, Mike, hiding the spoil?"

"Nope, believe it or not, getting a half-ton of silver out of the mine, without getting caught."

"'ow are we doing that, Mike?"

"Working on that, too. Harvey I want you to sound out the foreman; you're more friendly with him, than me. It will be a ten percent share for us three, the foreman, and Olly. That will leave half for all the others. I figure six men plus the lift operator, and one of that six will have to be a freighter to move the stuff from the elevator."

"I better drink me beer up quick," said Griff, rubbing horny hands together in happiness. "'Cause it's gonna be champagne later on."

~~~~~~~~~~~~~

The neighborhood had taken little note of the portent that threatened the Schwarzstein shack. The almost nightly ritual of rantings and abuse had paled to an ever-nightly fact of life. Drunken Hugo was on the rampage once again.

But that night was different. Any shred of sense or moderation had suddenly fled. Nothing curbed Hugo's fury; not exhaustion, drunken stupor, nor sexual frenzy, all of which previously had worked to limit the brutal beatings.

Then—it was too late. They were dead and dismembered; flung about the wretched rooms in the horror of havoc. Hugo walked out of the blood-strewn house in a daze and staggered down the dark streets.

"Served them right," he mumbled excuses to himself. "No damn respect. Lousy bitch, never appreciated anything. Rotten kids, always siding with their Ma. Well—I showed them who's boss. Too late now. They'll hang me if they catch me. Stinking bitch . . . why'd you have to die so easy? God—I got bad luck. Got to get away from here—they'll hang me for sure."

Finally—after straggling about for hours, Hugo found a hiding place. He burrowed deep in a haystack, near one of the big horse corrals that held mine animals. He slept the guiltless sleep of the psychopath, whose perversity knows no obligations except to itself.

He awoke, if not clear of mind, at least in comprehension of his danger. He would be hanged, if caught. He slowly parted the hay from the mouth of his hiding place. All he could see was an old man and a crippled youth loading a large wagon with manure from one of the many mounds piled about the large corral.

Quickly, without being seen, he crawled from hiding, brushing the hay from his clothes, running a grubby hand through his hair.

He approached the two, who were intent on their work. He caught some German words passing between them. "Are you German people?" he asked in his slurring German of Southern Germany.

"Yes," said the old man, stopping to look at him. "We are German. Why do you ask?"

"I would help you with the dung, if you would give me a ride with you. I need to get out of this town," smiled Hugo, trying to look friendly.

"Why?" asked Paulie, still shoveling manure. "Is that blood on you? Are you a criminal?"

"Who—me?" said Hugo, suddenly noticing his hands and the blood splatters on his clothing. "No. It was a fist-fight. Yes—with my foreman, a dirty Irishman. I beat him pretty bad—but it was a fair fight. Now he will get me in trouble. He hates Germans. Please help me. You must. I'm a fellow German."

"Let him help, Paulie," said Groszvater. "I'm tired and he can use my shovel. Then we'll take him to the river. It will be all right. He seems like a good fellow. What do you say, Paulie?"

"What is your name? What do you do?" asked Paulie, suspicious of the man.

"I was trained as a stonemason, but here I work as a miner—a terrible job."

"And your name?"

"Ah—Hugo. Hugo Dunkelmehl."

"Let him help, Paulie. We'll be done faster and it's so hot today, it makes me feel old."

"You *are* old, Groszvater," laughed Paulie, his odd shaped head not quite able to make a recognizable grin. "Go on—rest. He can take your shovel, but at the river we must leave him to himself."

"Thank you, thank you," said the new Hugo Dunkelmehl, "you'll not be sorry. I'm a hard worker."

~~~~~~~~~~~~~

Three days later Smokey Watson returned with his scouting report on the big Spanish rancho under consideration for the next hide theft.

"Lots of cows, Judd," he told the hide thieves boss. "Only, the close ones are pretty well scattered."

"It's a lost cause, then?" said Judd Payton.

"Not really—but it will be a hustle. They've got a good-sized herd over by the red bluffs."

"The red bluffs?" questioned the boss. "That's a day's march from Agua Mala—ain't it?"

"Well," said the old scout, attempting to put a good face on his news, "maybe eight hours in and ten to get out—hopefully in one piece."

"What about the rancho's people? They got any line riders that could spot us?"

"They had a half-ass calf-branding operation going on over west of the tanks. About half a dozen men and a grub wagon. They're set up by a spring there. That's all I saw, anyway. Shouldn't bother us—we'll be ten miles from them."

"I value your advice, Smokey," observed Payton. "Do you think that herd is too far for us? We've been lucky. Are we starting to crowd our luck? Are we getting too overconfident lately?"

"I don't know, Judd," replied the scout. "I figure we've been making our own luck lately—with good planning and follow through. And I think that'll be the case with this raid on the rancho. I've got an idea that will get us past Agua Mala with nobody ever thinking that we're after hides."

"An idea, Smokey? I thought you saved your ideas for your time off with them painted ladies of yours."

"Go on laugh, if you've a mind to. But I got an education, you know. Went through the sixth grade before my pa died and I had to support the family. That's where I got the idea."

"From supporting your family?" asked his boss, puzzled completely.

"Naw—from school," continued Smokey. "Miss Wright. She was the schoolteacher. Read to us about that wooden horse of Troy, and how the Trojans pulled this big wooden horse into the city. And how it was full of Greek soldiers that ended up opening them big gates and capturing the city."

"And you're gonna make a big wooden horse full of our boys and skin out a herd?"

"See—that's the trouble with you birds from Missouri—not one bit of imagination. Just plug in your ear trumpet and listen to old Smokey and I'll tell you about another kind of wooden horse."

~~~~~~~~~

"What's this about you wanting to leave us?" scolded Jesus Ocampo, trying hard to keep a straight face.

The young vaquero stammered out his answer to the steward of the big rancho. "It's just a quick trip home—to see my family, Señor Jesus. Only a week or so."

"Hah—you say a week?" scoffed the manager. "It is a three days walk to your home in Agua Mala. Are you to spend only a day in the bosom of your family?"

"I . . . ah . . . I hoped to take my horse. I mean the horse of the rancho—that I ride," confessed the young man. He was hardly more than a boy, a fact borne out by his straggling attempt to grow the drooping mustachio popular with the vaqueros.

"So you would take the horse of the rancho?" snapped Ocampo. "What else of the rancho's property would you take? Perhaps a new blanket for some pretty girl you would like to impress?"

"Oh no, Jefe!" cried the young vaquero. "I will take nothing with me that is not my own . . . except . . ."

"What's that?—A fat cow?"

"No, no, Jefe—but I would like to take some of my pay to my mother. She has need of money, with my father being sick."

"What sickness does he have?" the steward asked softly.

"The usual. But, along with the troubles of his mind, he has lately started a shaking of his head and his body—at least that is what was written in the letter I received from the alcalde."

The steward pulled out a ledger from a desk drawer and opened it to run a callused finger down a column of figures. "Seven weeks' pay due as a vaquerizo, a herdsman. How long have you been with us, my boy?"

"Almost six months, Señor Jesus."

"If I made you a full vaquero . . . Would you be worthy? You are still very young."

"I would not disappoint you, Señor Jesus. I make you this promise," said the boy, trying to force his voice into a lower register.

"Good," beamed the steward. "Give me your hand on that promise." He shook the youth's hand solemnly, making a little ceremony of the promotion. He noticed the boy's eyes suddenly water and thumped the new vaquero's shoulder affectionately to dispel any unnecessary sentimentality.

"I'll give you two months vaquero pay," said Ocampo, "and tell the storekeeper I said to give you a new blanket and a bag of grain for the horse. I don't want that animal coming back with its ribs sticking out."

"Si, Señor Jesus. Thank you. I won't let you down."

"You better not. I don't like people to see that I make bad judgments. Now go. Here is your money and don't get any of those pretty girls in Agua Mala in trouble. There is plenty of time for that later—when you get older. Look at me. I'm still too young, myself."

~~~~~~~~~~~~

Paulie Vogelnester had argued against it, but Groszvater insisted, stubbornly, that Hugo Dunkelmehl should be taken to the German settlement. Finally, Paulie relented; more for his grandfather than for this German-speaking stranger who suddenly popped up seeking asylum with them.

So, instead of dumping their manure load in the designated field, they took the odorous load into the village, to the elder's house.

The elder, called from his supper, was angry to see the manure wagon parked in the village square. He was instrumental in the paving and the well-digging that graced the "Platz" and began taking Paulie and Groszvater to task for bringing such a conveyance onto the patterned cobblestones of the square.

After a while, though, the elder allowed the dung carriers to state their case. Paulie found himself in the strange position of putting forward Groszvater's arguments for bringing Dunkelmehl to their settlement.

"Ach, die Irlander," spat out Herr Kolb. "They're all savages—with no sense of values or discipline. I can understand this man having trouble with such people. Remember that mate on the ship from Hamburg? A dull-witted ox. Always shouting and hitting with his fists. Even threatened me once—when I was sick on the wrong side of the boat."

"So . . . can I stay with you, Your Honor?" asked Hugo, hat in his hands, a pleasing smile on his bristly face.

"You say you were a stonemason?" asked Kolb.

"Yes, Your Honor. In Kaiserslautern, Your Honor. I worked nine years there, including my apprenticeship. Five years on the Katholik Cathedral there, Your Honor, and every stone a work of art."

"And why are you here in America? You—who are such a fine stonemason?"

"A woman's wrath, Your Honor," replied Hugo shaking his head at the faked memory. "I took my lodging and meals with a widowed woman on Pariserstrasze. Somehow, but not of my doing, she thought I would marry her. When I refused, she denounced me to the police as a revolutionary. I was arrested and tortured by the police. They wanted names of my confederates. I had no confederates—I was just a simple stonemason. I escaped from the police while being moved to the prison at Zweibrücken and fled to France. My brother sold a fine team he owned and sent me the money to get to America. Just in time, too, for the secret police were asking around Sedan for me."

"And you're unmarried?" probed the elder.

"Ach—ja, Your Honor. I may never marry, that woman gave me such a damn time."

"Are you a God-fearing man Herr . . . ?"

"Dunkelmehl, Your Honor. I was brought up in a strict Lutheran family, but then I was orphaned at thirteen and apprenticed to a blasphemous master. I was held back from the faith by this profane man. Perhaps now, Your Honor, with your help and the charity of your community, I can come again into a Christian life."

Paulie and Groszvater both stared at the suddenly eloquent stonemason. Hugo Dunkelmehl, though, was talking for his life. A denial to this settlement could very possibly be a death sentence for him, to be cast adrift on the harshness of the Arizona desert.

"Fear not, my good man," stated Herr Kolb piously. "You have brought your skills to the correct place. Have you eaten? Come into my house. Come sit at my table. I welcome you back into the fold of the Almighty." As he ushered Dunkelmehl into his house, he turned to Paulie and Groszvater.

"What are you two waiting for?" he asked harshly. "Get that stinking wagon out of my square and never bring it here again—understand?"

Groszvater grinned sheepishly at Paulie and made an old man's exaggerated shrug. "Come, Paulie, our stinking carriage is not welcome on the clean stones of Herr Kolb's Platz—only on the fields that grow our food."

They could see the great dust cloud coming, hovering in the hot still air of midmorning. It announced the advent of the herd from the Lazy J, Opal's farthest ranch, thirty miles away in the Palisade Valley.

Hugh Foote had ridden out yesterday to spend the night with them at Black Creek Flat. Now, he came back to the headquarters house, riding at an easy lope, his wiry body seemingly molded to his horse.

Opal met him at the porch, a small cramped affair, seemingly stuck on the house as an afterthought by her frugal uncle.

"How many?" questioned Opal worriedly.

"My goodness," teased the foreman. "Not even a 'Good morning, Mr. Foote.' You just got to jump right down to business."

"Let's hope, Mr. Foote, that someday in the future I'll have time for pleasantries—and simple-minded remarks from the help. But right now it's business—pure and simple—night and day. Your report, please."

"One hundred fifty-three all told," Foote said quickly.

"And in what condition?" Opal had caught something covert in Foote's declaration.

"That, boss," admitted the foreman, "to change around an old saying . . . is a cow of a different dimension."

"How bad, Mr. Foote? No—just tell me how many you think will be acceptable to the Army."

"Well, of course I'm no government inspector, but if I was buying 'em, myself, I'd whittle down this herd to around one hundred fifteen or twenty. And that's not taking in account driving 'em to Tucson. That'll make 'em skinnier yet."

"Why did Thompson send along those culls? Did he expect I can sell them?" Opal asked angrily.

"I think you got old Blackjack spooked. He's a good man. Knows a lot about cattle and how to keep 'em alive in those hills that got more rocks than grass. Just not used to putting up with a new step-mother, I guess."

"And you are, Mr. Foote?" said Opal, sarcastically.

"Guess it's 'cause I'm not afraid of women. Like 'em, in fact. I even got along with my sisters, believe it or not."

"Oh, I believe you, Mr. Foote. You seem to be very accommodating, when you want to be."

"Why, thank you, Miss Wilbur. That's your first compliment to me. I'll sure enough treasure it."

"That wasn't a compliment, Mr. Foote. Just a comment. Now, where are we going to graze this bunch—for the time being?"

〰〰〰〰〰〰〰

"Who says the legal machinery grinds slowly?" exclaimed Prosecutor Aaron Rose. "Here's your search warrant, all signed, sealed and delivered in what?—four days?" The young attorney was all smiles.

"Not quite delivered," Skinner said, reading the document. "But it soon will be. Sam—go pry Cletus out of the stable. We're going to serve this right away."

"Isn't it pretty late in the day to be bothering the lady?" questioned the prosecutor.

"Now who's talking about the law's slowness?" answered the sheriff. "No, she'll be busy feeding her boarders. Keep her flustered and upset. Maybe she won't be so smooth."

The three lawmen tied their mounts to Mrs. Robinson's cast-iron horse holder. As hoped, they caught her making supper. "My God!" she fumed, rushing back to her kitchen to stir a cornstarch pudding frantically. "I can't leave this pudding or it will burn. Come back tomorrow."

"Nothing doing, Mrs. Robinson," stated Skinner. "You just keep on stirring. We'll get along fine without you."

"What did that paper say you're looking for?" she fumed.

"Property belonging to the estates of Misters Henderson, McFee, Smith, Borge and Peoples."

"You'll not find any. They didn't have nothing."

"Then you shouldn't mind us looking, should you?" reasoned Skinner.

"I just don't want you making a mess of my lovely house, pulling things out and all," she argued.

"I assure you, Mrs. Robinson, everything will be returned as it was," promised Skinner. "Now—which is your room?"

"It's here on the first floor. That door that says 'Private.' Actually, it's a little sitting room with a bedroom to the rear. The sitting room is my office, what with the desk there."

"Is the desk locked?"

"I was afraid you'd ask that," she said, suddenly stirring the pudding with great industry. "I misplaced the key last week, somewhere, and was going to call the locksmith."

"Don't worry yourself, Mrs. Robinson. Deputy Buller, here, is quite talented at forcing locks—aren't you, Sam? You'll hardly notice where the wood cracks."

"The secret is in twisting my boot knife in the right spot; otherwise the whole board splits," confirmed Sam, an evil grin on his face.

"Wait a minute! Hold on! It just come back to me!" cried the woman, taking the thickened pudding off the range and setting it on a red floor tile lying on the kitchen table. "I suddenly remembered . . . Look in that blue bud vase on top of the desk. I bet that's where I left it."

Skinner nodded to Sam, who disappeared into the woman's room. Seconds later he was back, displaying the key. "Talk about jogging a memory," said Sam with a straight face. "Ain't that amazing. One minute her mind's blank and the next she's suddenly remembering where she put it."

"Let's hope that's an omen, Sam. Could be we're going to find a lot of hidden things. You and Cletus get started in her room. I'm going to check the woodshed."

CHAPTER 9

T he two led their mounts down the side of the ravine, stumbling over unseen obstacles in the dark. Suddenly they were before the dark loom of one of the water diversion trestles.

"This should be adequate," said Captain Cabot, thumping the heavy timber.

"Sure is wet under here. Likes standings in a rainstorm," commented Napoleon.

"We'll be out of here quick enough. Dig out that bomb of yours."

"Not mine, Cap'n. This is your idea. I'm jes totin' it in my saddlebag." The old Negro fumbled in the bag to pull out a thick pottery crock and pass it to his master.

"Next time, Napoleon," chided the captain, "please try to find a more appropriate container. A marmalade crock seems rather frivolous for a bomb."

"Ha," cackled his servant. "Not much of a bomb no ways—lessen a pound of powder."

"It's not the blast . . . it's the thought behind it. It's the starting gun in the great Puzzle River range war. Where's those burlap strips? I'll hold the bomb against the timber and you wrap the strips around it."

It took longer than they had thought but finally the crock was secure. Cabot sent Napoleon with the mounts back up the bank to safety. Then, holding his hat over the bomb to protect the fuse from the leaking flume, he lit the fuse with a sulphur match.

They were over half a mile away when they heard the bang of the explosion.

"That's it, Napoleon. Let's see how those Sauerkrauts like that. Hopefully, they'll come out mad and buzzing."

"Yessir, Cap'n. But jes maybe they be like yaller-jackets—that can sting real good."

~~~~~~~~~~~~~~~

Hans Klaus told everyone that he heard the explosion first. Actually, it was his young apprentice who had gone outside for an armful of firewood for the oven and had rushed back to tell the stout baker. The two bakers were the only German colonists awake in the village. They had started their day at midnight, preparing the bread dough. Old Forstmann, the seventy-year-old fire guard, was supposed to be awake, and he adamantly backed up the baker's report, even though the old man had been dozing as usual.

The baker, though, was also the militia company's sergeant-major and knew his duty. He went directly to the major's house to pound on the door. After a wait, it was opened by Riemann, his riding breeches pulled over his nightshirt, giving his waist a lumpy look.

"An explosion, Herr Major," reported Klaus, a floured hand to his baker's cap.

"Where? . . . What direction?" questioned Riemann, voice still hoarse from sleep.

"The boy—I mean—it was from upriver."

"The dam? . . . Wake Sgt. Kiefer. Kiefer and six other riders. Sixty rounds each for rifle. Thirty for pistol. And tell him to bring material for torches. I'll meet them in fifteen minutes by the well."

"You don't want me, Major?" said the sgt. major, stiff at attention, the white apron cascading off his big stomach.

"Not tonight, Hans. Go back to your bread. I'm saving you for the big one. Can't rob all the soldiers from the village just for a patrol action."

The major's group of mounted infantry stopped half a mile from the dam to dismount and turn over their horses to two horses holders. Then, the six unencumbered men formed a loose skirmish line to approach the dam through the darkness.

"I smell gunpowder, Major. Up ahead," reported Sgt. Kiefer, coming back to the major's position.

"Take two of the men from the left to cover you and follow your nose. I'll take the others across the top of the dam. Give an owl hoot if it's safe for us to close in." The sergeant grunted his obedience and disappeared into the gloom.

The major found the right wing of his party and they began feeling their way out on the rubble-filled core of the dam. At the first diversion flume they stopped, expecting trouble. The rushing water of the flume masked their pounding hearts.

Suddenly they caught the owl's cry and the major led his men forward.

"I need to make a light," called the sergeant from below.

"Make a light and stand clear from it for a time," ordered the major.

The torch revealed the wreckage of the broken flume support. It was a wonder that the diversion flume had not collapsed. If it had been winter, with the increased winter runoff, it would have fallen.

They waited a while to see if the torch would invite shooting. Then, the major called for more light and a search for tracks or other things not in order. He posted one sentinel on the dam's top and crawled down the flume trestle to the apron before the dam.

"Hoof marks, Major," said Sgt. Kiefer. "All around under the flume."

"See how far up the bank they go, Sergeant. Take a torch and a man with you. I'll send for the horses to be brought up."

It took Sgt. Kiefer over twenty minutes to return. By that time the horses had been brought up.

"The hoofmarks show two animals, Herr Major," reported the sergeant. "The two men mounted up there, on the top of the bank."

"Why do you say animals—rather than horses?"

"Walter thinks one of the animals was a mule, Major."

"A mule? How can he tell? Especially in the dark?" questioned the major.

"You know Walter, Major. He thinks he's an expert on draft animals."

"Walter—come here," snapped Major Riemann. "What's this about a mule?"

The greying man tried unsuccessfully to click his heels, his shapeless boots only making a soggy sound on the water-soaked apron of the dam. But he did make a passable salute to his officer.

"It was a mule, Major, and a horse. The both of them."

"How did you tell it was a mule, Walter?"

"If you'll pardon me for the statement, Major, you're not a plowman. When it comes to plowing, a horse is good, as is a mule, Herr Major. But when it comes to gentle cultivation, weeding between the rows of cabbages, nothing is as good as a mule."

"Why is that, Walter? Come on," urged the major, not expecting a lesson in plowing.

"Because, Herr Major, the horse scuffs up the furrows with its hoofs. Digging in at the toe, you see. Very unsightly and hurtful to the drainage. The mule, on the other side,

Major, places every foot down flatly, disturbing not the soil. The second animal was undoubtably a mule, Herr Major."

"Thank you, Walter," commended the major. "We are indebted to your knowledge."

"My pleasure, Herr Major," said the man, beaming under the praise.

Riemann turned back to Sgt. Kiefer. "Sergeant, I'd like to send Senior Private Lander back to the colony with a message of what has happened here, along with repair instructions. Then the rest of us will push on after the men that caused this damage. Perhaps you can strike out now with Walter and pick up the trail. We'll follow shortly—as soon as I compose the message."

The sergeant grunted and nodded to Walter, and the pair left, leading their mounts up the indistinct trail to the bank.

~~~~~~~~~~~~~

The hide wagons left Tucson at midnight. The wagons were quiet as they traveled down the rutted, bumpy road. An effort had been made to still the many jingles and clinkings of harness and running gear, but the most important effect was that the appearance of the hide wagons had been changed.

No longer did the three big wagons look like flatbed hide wagons. Now they seemed to be freight wagons, with false sides restraining cargos of make-believe boxes and machinery crates. The drivers and skinners no longer were dressed in their customary soiled and greasy leather garments. They wore the canvas pants and check shirts of freighters or the blue canvas coats of mechanics and millwrights.

Judd Payton wore a starched collar and a tie along with a business suit and Wellington boots, trying to look like a mining engineer. Perhaps he wasn't a Greek bearing gifts, but he was doing his part to perpetuate the hoax. They all were—for their necks were in the noose now that they were off on a raid.

~~~~~~~~~~~~~

The digging to the treasure room went swiftly, partly because this tunnel was much smaller than that of the normal mining bores. With less soil to move, the underside of the treasure chamber was reached on the fourth night.

Olly, the powder man, was brought up the steep bore to solemnly gaze at the rough concrete of the floor.

"Looks awful solid, Mike," Olly observed. "Can we drill holes for the nitro in it?"

"I'm afraid of the noise," said Mike. "There's just too damn many fellows around here that know exactly what a drill sounds like. We just can't chance banging on that concrete."

"We're going to need a compass. A good one, to try to find the steel bars inside the concrete," said Olly.

"I'll see if I can borrow one from the survey office," agreed Mike.

"I got it—acid!" exclaimed Olly suddenly.

"Acid?"

"Sure—we'll dissolve the concrete with muriatic acid," grinned Olly. "A rubber hose hooked to some kind of squeeze bulb. Just squirt holes in the concrete."

"Sounds scary to me, all that acid dripping on you. How many holes do you have to have?"

Olly thought, using his fingers, including his two half-fingers, to help in his computations. "Twelve," stated Olly. "Six inches deep, at least an inch in diameter. I'll give you a brass dummy bottle to check the holes. We can't force the bottle, you know. Nitro is very unforgiving."

"How will you seal them in the holes?" asked Mike.

"I'll stuff clay around the cap and the fuse and then put a timber collar under that with a beam to the tunnel floor."

"Any problem with the nitro—got enough?"

"Just—I've been stockpiling it ever since you told me about this job. You find that compass and hopefully mark the position of the bar grid you want to enter at. Then make your holes on a one foot square. Then let me know, and we'll figure what's next. How's that?"

"You're leaving me to work out that acid business?"

"Why not? You're a smart man. You'll think of something. I'm the powder man. I've got enough worries about the nitro."

~~~~~~~~~~~~~

Sam came into Mrs. Robinson's woodshed to report on the search of the landlady's office. The sheriff was frustrated and angry with himself for not finding any incriminating evidence in the shed. The labeled boxes were gone—and the suspect's woodshed looked like any other woodshed—stacked with stove wood and junk, but devoid of clues.

"She's got a healthy bank balance," Sam reported. "Over eight hundred, according to her bank book. But nothing really suspicious. Cletus is checking out her bedroom. Hasn't found anything interesting."

"A wasted effort?" asked Skinner petulantly.

"So far, anyway," answered Sam, looking over the stacked wood. "Are you going to need help uncovering what's under here? She sure left a telltale sign, taking wood from the back of the pile."

"I was wondering if the back end was drier," said Skinner lamely.

"Sure looks the same. Let me tell Cletus that I'll be helping you out here for awhile and I'll be right back and we'll get at the front of that pile." Sam vanished out the door, leaving the sheriff to mentally kick himself.

"What a fool you are, Skinner," he muttered to himself as he took off his coat and rolled up his sleeves. "Talk about not seeing the trees for the forest. You can't see firewood for the firewood."

Sam came back and they started stacking the pile outside the shed. Skinner found himself almost hoping they would find no irregularities to bruise his ego.

The box was at the bottom, nestled against the shed's wall and the second row of stove wood. It was a tea box full of men's shoes and boots, mostly in good condition.

"How many pairs do you think, Sam?" asked the sheriff, as Sam browsed through the box.

"Ten or twelve. Different sizes, too. Here's a pair of patent leather pumps. Help me lift it out—it's jammed against the wall." They tugged the box free and brought it outside where the light was better. Sam started arranging the shoes, lining them up beside the tea box by pairs.

"Eleven pairs," counted the sheriff.

"Four different sizes," added Sam. "Not too moldy, either. Spider in that half-boot, though. It's gotta find another home now."

"Talk about spiders," said Skinner sotto voce. "Here she comes, hot-footing it out here."

Mrs. Robinson fired the first salvo at a range of twenty feet. "My God, Sheriff, you're tearing my woodshed apart. I'll have to hire a man to re-stack all that firewood. Have you no respect?"

"Is that 'respect,' Mrs. Robinson, or is it 'suspect'? I've got a lot of suspicions about you," shot back Skinner. "We just came across your cache of men's footwear. Why were you hiding a box of shoes and boots under your stove wood?"

"Why not?" she replied, looking the sheriff in the eye. "I had to store them somewhere. But if you really want to know—it was that lazy Tittle. I had the box in the shed and he was too lazy to move it when he stacked the wood there."

"Tittle? Who's Tittle?" questioned Skinner.

"He's a handyman," put in Sam. "Does minor repairs and clean-up jobs. My landlady has him beat her rugs."

"And that's how the box got buried?" Skinner asked the landlady.

"Your own deputy just said so. Take the wax out of your ears."

"No—my ears are fine. Sam only said that this Tittle is a handyman."

"He's as dumb as you, probably."

"You haven't told us whose boots these are."

"Go to hell. That's for me to know and you to guess about."

"I'll tell you what, Mrs. Robinson," replied Skinner angrily. "I'm going to find out for sure and I got a hunch that these shoes will come back to haunt you."

"Haunt me?" she scoffed. "My conscience is clear. I sleep the sleep of the innocent. Now, you assholes, put that stove wood back in my shed like this damn warrant promised or I'll find a lawyer that'll burn your butt."

"The box of shoes is evidence, Mrs. Robinson," Sam broke in to confront the women. "We'll keep that for a while. Now you go back into your house before you get the sheriff so upset that he will blow you to pieces."

"He wouldn't dare," said the woman, more softly and with less confidence.

"Don't bait me, madam," rasped Skinner. "I'm not used to it."

"Well—stack it neatly, just the way I had it," she said, leaving quickly.

"Just the way I had it," echoed the sheriff, giving Sam a big wink. "Not the way Mr. Tittle did it. Come on, Mr. Chief Deputy—I'll toss and you stack. Maybe I can work off my killing urge."

~~~~~~~~~~~~

"They's here, Cap'n, an' theys looks angry—like them bees."

"Thank you, Napoleon," said Capt. Cabot, rolling away from the dead tree he had used for a backrest during his nap. He went over to his horse, gave it a love pat on the withers, and slid the Colt rifle out of its scabbard. He unwrapped the protective chamois covering and threw it over his saddle. Rifle ready, he walked over to the rim of the dry wash in which they were hidden to look down at the coming horsemen.

There were seven of them. Two were out front reading trail, but not bunched up. The other five were back further in an arrow formation that spread out over several acres.

"Very creditable," Cabot muttered half-aloud. "Shows training. Not going to get a bonus today, looks like." I could get a couple, he thought—but they got a chance of getting me. Today I'll just show them a bit of bravado—to fan the fire.

He raised the rifle's peepsight, adjusted it to 200 yards and waited for the leading pair to ride into range. Then, the tracker was close enough and he fired at a point two feet to the side of the rider's head.

The two scouts immediately wheeled to gallop back to the main party, who had dismounted at the shot. The two trailing men rushed up to grab the group's horses and retire further down the slope.

"That's far enough!" shouted Cabot. "You're on D B land now! Move off—if you know what's good for you!"

"We are from the farm settlement," called back the major. "Someone tried to damage our project. Now we are on his trail."

"No bombers here, go back—you're trespassing. The next shot will be closer."

～～～～～～～～～

"That was a shot—wasn't it?" asked Opal, reining in her mare.

"'Fraid so," answered Hugh Foote laconically. "Want me to check it out? Sounds like it came from over that rise. You could stay here out of sight."

"I'm the owner, Mr. Foote, if you haven't forgotten. That means taking any risk I ask of my help." She kicked her horse into a gallop, heading for the crest of the rise. Foote put spurs to his mount, getting out in front of her.

He reined in at the top when he saw the dismounted men with rifles below him on the slope. Opal came up just as someone below shouted a warning about trespassing.

"That's your newly-hired enforcer—greeting them Sauerkrauts," he told Opal. "Should I butt in?"

"I want to find out what the trouble is. Give them a hail and say we're friendly."

Foote stood up in his stirrups and yelled down the slope that they were coming down and not to shoot. Then he walked his horse down the stubbly slope. Opal followed her foreman, trying to show determination on her face.

As Foote and Opal came up to the shallow gully, Cabot emerged, ducking through the brush that lined the ditch. He carried the heavy revolving rifle at high port as if reinforcing his intention to fire at any time.

"Good morning, Miss Wilbur," he grunted, not taking his eyes off the farmers. "Got some trespassers this morning. I'm warning them off."

"Yes—I heard you fire your warning. That's why we're here. I'm going down to talk with them."

"That is a bad idea, Miss Wilbur. These men outnumber us. They could shoot us down easily."

"Why, Captain Cabot—are you showing fear?"

"No, Miss Wilbur. I am cautious—when it comes to your safety," purred the captain.

"Thank you for your concern, Captain. I am going down to talk with those men. I think it would be a good idea to put your rifle out of sight, so as not to antagonize them. As you say—there are more of them." She kicked her horse into a walk. Hugh Foote followed her.

She pulled up at the line of armed men. "Who speaks for you?" she commanded. "I am the owner of this ranch. Please state your business here."

Riemann arose from behind a thin bush. "I am Major Riemann. I am the military and construction leader of our settlement."

"Why are you trespassing on my land?" demanded Opal coldly, her green eyes glinting anger.

"I ask your pardon, madam, for our intrusion. We are following the tracks of two riders that damaged our construction project last night. Now we were fired upon here. What are we to think?"

"Captain Cabot fired that shot as a warning—not to injure," replied Opal. "Mr. Foote, please call Capt. Cabot down here."

Foote hollered up the slope and Cabot came down on his horse, trailed by Napoleon. Cabot had his rifle conspicuously across his pommel.

"Captain Cabot," asked Opal when the enforcer was down with the group. "This man says they are following a party that did damage to their project last night. Have you seen such men?"

"No, Miss Wilbur," answered Cabot, with a thin smile. "Napoleon and I were out for a fat hare. Haven't seen hide nor hair of anything, including the hare."

"Does that satisfy you, Major . . . Riemann, was it?" asked Opal, glowering at the major.

"Not really. But for today—we shall withdraw. Madam, I'm looking for peace, not confrontation or a fight. But please remember that I have to do what's best for my community. If we are attacked, as we were last night, prudence dictates that we must reply—with force. Is that clear, madam?"

"Is this a declaration of war, Major?" spat Opal.

"Only a line drawn in the sand, madam," said the major.

"What about the water?" burst in Hugh Foote. "Are you drawing a line down the river—saying what's yours and what's ours? We got cattle that depend on that water. I'm not even sure we should share it with you damn Sauerkrauts."

"We will share it—fairly," stated Riemann.

"And we should believe you?" scoffed Foote.

"Not me, the Department of the Interior, as Arizona is a territory, not a state. A commission is being formed to rule on the water rights. You ranchers will give testimony to the commission about your needs."

"Who says so?"

"Senator Schurz has petitioned the Department of the Interior for the water allocation. We want to be certain, legally, of our water rights. We must, before we can plan on new cultivation. It would be foolish to plant crops if proper water was not available."

"You know, every year is different," said Foote, unconvinced.

"We know. We're working with what records are available and a study of tree rings. Also, the river bank etches its flow on certain areas of the river bank. We are trying to take a scientific approach. We have to. Water is life here."

"It's life and death, Major. Especially if you're a thirsty cow. If our cows die, I wouldn't give a dime for your settlement's chance of survival."

"That's enough, Mr. Foote," said Opal, putting her horse between him and Riemann. "If there is to be threats, I will make them, not you."

"No, madam," said Riemann. "This is good. This talking. It helps to establish our positions."

"I think it would be good if you left now, Major. If we see any strangers around, we will question them about your damage."

"Thank you, madam," replied Reimann, touching his hat with his good hand. "You are an extremely attractive woman and it has been my pleasure to meet you. Perhaps I could see you again under more pleasant circumstances."

"Perhaps, Major—just perhaps," she said with a grim smile. "Come, Mr. Foote, let us return to the D B. I've got some letters to write." She took her group back up the hill—Napoleon bringing up the rear.

"Call up the horse holders, Sergeant. We will return, also. We've learned what we came for," said Riemann coldly.

The sergeant waved his hat to call up the horses. Then he turned back to the major, saying softly, "And the Schwarzer rides a mule, Major."

Riemann slowly nodded the affirmative. "And the Negro rides a mule, Sergeant." They headed back to the settlement at a walk.

CHAPTER 10

Agua Mala was a bad place to live, but there was work there. Good money to be made in the quicksilver mine. The mercury they mined was most necessary in precious metal extraction, and there was work for all who could work.

That, however, was the problem at Agua Mala. Many of the workers had become ill. Insanity and nervous disorders struck the hapless citizens. Many babies were born either stillborn or deformed. The people blamed the water and many would not drink the evil-tasting water, electing to pay steep prices for transported water. These people, though, also succumbed to the maladies.

The young vaquero had come back to his family late in the evening. He had given most of his money to his mother and she had rushed out to purchase food and drink, for a small fiesta for the newly-made vaquero. And so the family had a fine, filling meal, with a roasted chicken and pieces of thinly-cut beef and cheese to put inside their tortillas.

The father, though, had worsened. He could not recognize his returned son. He could only lie near-naked on a straw-filled pallet, twitching his head frantically he struggled forever at his bonds, soiling himself as like an infant.

The next day the young man walked to the mine with his friends from boyhood. They joked as they went to the great sore in the hill that was their work. His friends called the young vaquero a nursemaid to the cows. But he could see their envy, or perhaps it was the pride, in their faces, that this friend of theirs had work with the cattle—out in the open, not in the acrid warrens of the underworld.

The next evening he was invited to visit one of his sister's friends, who had also included several young women. One girl, a doe-eyed fifteen-year-old with an eager laugh and a ripe body, impressed him to the extent that he gave her his new blanket. A shy offering from one child to another that bespoke the hopes of youth—regardless of the present, oblivious to the future.

Now, it was the early hours. The time when the owl hunted, while the rooster clung sluggishly to its perch. The young vaquero could not sleep. He could imagine the melons of the girl's breasts, the strong lines of her thighs and the whiteness of her open smile.

He crept from his bed, stepping out into cold, starry night to clutch a roof support. He enjoyed the night. When he herded the cattle—back on the rancho—he would sing little songs to them, reminding the cattle that they were safe. He rode between them and the wolf or the lion . . . for his song said it was so.

Then, he heard the hoofs and the muffled creakings of the wagons. He ran, barefoot in the alley's dirt, to the main road from Tucson, at the alley's end.

The big wagons passed him at a mile-devouring trot, the huge mules pulling the large wagons easily. Even the village curs were leary of this dark convoy—not barking, content to sniff and skulk at the wagons' moving perimeters.

Suddenly they were gone—disappeared up a narrow trail to the back country. North, in the direction of the hacienda whereon the young vaquero worked. Only the airborne dust, invisible in the dark, and the wheelruts of the wagons, pressed into the thick powder of the dirt road, were testimony to their passing.

The dogs returned to smell at the legs of the young vaquero and to make their marks on the alley's adobe homes. Then they left for more interesting places, leaving him alone. He walked onto the main road and ran his fingers across the wide ruts left by the wagons.

And then, squatting in the dusty road, breathing the dust of their passage, smelling the animal odor of the mules' dung, he found the plain fact that would forever change his life. He rose to his feet, certain of his course, confident in his competence.

Twenty minutes later he was on his horse and headed back to his steward, Señor Ocampo.

~~~~~~~~~~~~~

"I know, I know, Van," pleaded the sheriff. "I know you've a newspaper here—not a shoe store. Just think of the story you might get. Could sell a thousand copies."

Charles Van Doormann, newspaper publisher, looked skeptically at Skinner's display of shoes. Sam had nailed all of Mrs. Robinson's shoe cache on a ten foot board. "And you want me to fasten this pediformatic perversion over my sidewalk newspaper?"

"That's it, Van," soothed Skinner. "Hopefully, somebody will recognize some of the shoes and we can link them to people, hopefully, victims."

"And you'll give me the whole story if I put up this board and make a sign explaining same?"

"Don't put Mrs. Robinson's name on the sign. I might get sued," cautioned the sheriff. "Now—how about it? Do we have a deal?"

"I'll have to borrow a ladder, I guess. All right. But don't forget to let me have the story. Do you think she killed these fellows with an axe? Axe murders always sell good. A lot better than poison, you know."

"You just had a bloody murder last week, when that Schwarzstein fellow slaughtered his family. Aren't you ever satisfied?"

"Hey, Skinner—that was last week's paper. That's on the bottom of birdcages already, or wrapping up your liver and pork chops. I always gotta think of my next edition."

"Goodbye, Van. Thanks," said Skinner. "Gotta buy Sam some buns, or my name is mud."

He saw the crowd on his way back from the bakery. The press parted when they saw the sheriff. "What's happened?" he demanded, swinging down from his horse, Gertie.

"He never seed it," cried an ashen-faced matron. "He jes traipsed down them stairsteps—right in front of the team. Never even seed it."

"Is he dead?" asked Skinner.

"You betcha," chuckled a burly miner. "Wheel runned right over his chest—flatter'n a pancake. That'll teach him to look where he treads." The man got up from beside the body and, still smiling, left, pushing through the crowd.

"Anybody know this man?" questioned Skinner.

"I thinks he works for Gomper's," answered the matron. "Ya mights ask theres."

"Would you go over to Gomper's store and ask Mr. Gomper to come over here?"

"Wal, I wuz gwan to the greengrocer place, but I'll goes. I enjoys the fuss."

Mr. Gomper soon pushed his way through the crowd. "Oh my God!" he exclaimed softly. "It's Philip Armstead. He's my jeweler. Such a promising young man. Are you sure he's dead?"

"Chest is crushed," grunted Skinner. "Any kin in town?"

"No," replied Gomper, shaken. "He lives alone."

"Would you make the funeral arrangements, Mr. Gomper?"

"I guess I should. He's got a week's pay coming. That should help bury him, won't it?"

"Pretty much should," agreed the sheriff. "If you get Marks to come collect the body, I'll stay and make sure nobody disturbs it."

Gomper looked at the sheriff, tears welling up in his eyes. "A half-hour ago he was a living young man. Talented, artistic, living and breathing and smiling—even joking with me. Now Philip is an 'it.' A thing. No longer human."

"Yes," agreed Skinner.

"Is that all you can say—'yes'?"

"I'm not a good person to ask about death—and probably life, too. I've seen too much death, Gomper. I've seen boys like this fellow lined up dead in fields like wheat when the reaping machine passed through. I've lost my objectivity. I've lost my kids, my friends, my comrades in arms. I'm sorry to say this, Gomper, but my life lately is death. Maybe that's why I'm a good sheriff. I've looked death in the eye and didn't blink. Mr. Death don't blink, either. Now, go get Marks and stop blubbering."

~~~~~~~~~~~~

It was decided to make the drive in two sections due to the narrowness of the Tucson Road. Bert Massey, who lost the D B foreman job to Hugh Foote's fists, was trailmaster. He would coordinate both sections with five drovers in each section. Theoretically the sections would be four or five hours apart so that they could utilize the road's wide spots and turnouts to night herd each section apart from each other.

Having two sections meant two chuck wagons. Opal insisted on driving the second chuck wagon, a hastily-converted ranch wagon. Aunt Polly would ride with Opal and would be the second section's cook. Aunt Polly was unhappy about her selection and spent several hours padding the wagon's hard seat for her considerable derriere.

The first section left at first light, led by Pappy Sloan, a top-hand from the Lazy J. The herd was divided and Hugh Foote, who was to stay behind as temporary general manager of Wilbur ranches, came to see Bert off with the first section.

The first section remuda followed out after the cattle, hazed by the wrangler from the B R. Opal drove the chuck wagon down by the second section to allow Aunt Polly to make coffee for the second section herders.

Opal was excited—and worried. Her ranches were on the line—her slim future in the balance. Hugh Foote came over for coffee and to give her encouragement.

And then came the moment. Sally Lewis, from the Running W, gave the call, "String them beeves out. Let's go to Tucson." Suddenly all Opal's fears vanished in the flush of the effort. For better or worse—her herd was committed. Soon her wagon was swallowed up in the dust of the herd.

~~~~~~~~~~~~~~

Dr. Bezaine, the French born and trained Mine Association surgeon, was used to all types of injuries. He was kept busy treating mine accidents, though most of them were crushing wounds. This patient, strangely, had quite severe burns.

"My friend," he told the man, "you are mos' fortunate not to 'ave zee dommage to zis eye."

"Don't I know it, Doc," said Mike. "Hurt like hell. I wuz hoping you'd have some kinda cream to stop the burning."

"And you zay zee dommage comes from zee pot aches."

"Potash, Doc. Takes the rust off our tools. I got careless and dropped a hammer head in the vat and the alkali splashed over me. I learned my lesson—won't drop no more tools. Just slide 'em in the soup."

"Ah, zee potage. Eet ess zee hour of dinner. I mus' be fors leaving. Please zir—puts zis onguent on zee burns, tous les

jours—ah—every days. Comprendez vous my friend? And ztay far from zee potage."

"I gotcha, Doc," replied Mike, "I'm staying a long way from it."

And that is what he told Olly later that night. "I damn near lost my damn eye on that damn acid. I did lose my clothes. Just dissolved away from me, like if I was wearing clothes made out of newspaper in the pouring rain. Look at my neck 'n' at my wrists 'n' elbows. Geez! It's a wonder I'm still alive."

"Well—it was just an idea," commented Olly. "You're the one who wanted the holes made in silence."

"Wasn't that silent. I was yelling bloody blue murder when that acid hit my skin. Just lucky I had a lot of water with me."

"So—we'll think some more and come up with something else. How about a diversion? You know, mask the drilling noise with another noise," said Olly, smiling at his genius.

"For instance, cannon firing," scorned Mike. "Or a brass band."

"Not a bad thought—the band, I mean. I played tuba in the Scranton Youth Drum and Bugle Corps."

"How come they had a tuba in a drum and bugle corps?" asked Mike, putting more ointment on his neck from a tin container.

I was supposed to play a cornet. But my dad got a good buy on a tuba, instead. And my Uncle Leo was the leader. So I played the tuba. I had good lungs then."

"I played a drum when I was a kid," went on Mike. "My old man stole it when he was in the Army with General Lee in Mexico. Course, he wasn't a general then."

"Your old man?"

"Naw—General Lee. He was a captain or something. When I joined up, after Sumter, I thought I'd be a drummer. But they took my drum and put me in the horse artillery.

That's why I got eardrum trouble. Have to pack it in cotton wool everyday. Never got the drum back. It was a good drum. Had a lot of red tassels on the sides. Had a new head, too. Cost me $1.50. That was a lot of money for a kid. They took the sticks, too." He went silent—looking into the depths of his beer glass, thinking of his lost-forever field drum.

"McKenzie has a cornet," added Olly. "He rooms with me. Only I think he pawned it for those new boots."

"Can he play it?"

"Loudly—and not very well. He can't read notes."

"Me, neither," admitted Mike. "But with a drum, the rhythm is more important. The beat, you know. I used to fake a lot."

"Me, too. Shall I talk to McKenzie? I see him at meals."

"Won't hurt. Find out when he will get the cornet out of hock. We'd have to have a bass drum. A bass drum really makes a lot of noise."

~~~~~~~~~~~~~~

Hugo Dunkelmehl, formerly known as Hugo Schwarzstein, appeared to have turned his life around—for the better. He was an excellent stonemason. His talent and experience soon put him as the leaderman on the dam's face, much to the approval of the other workers, who appreciated his many labor-saving ways of getting the job done right.

He continued to live with the elder, Heinrich Kolb. The elder's home was a house of temperance, Kolb allowing his household a small glass of cherry wine only on certain holy days. Without the drink that had previously dominated Dunkelmehl's life, he blossomed into an intelligent, urbane man. He began taking care of his appearance, shaving his greying beard into a thin version of the popular mutton chops style which accentuated his strong jawline and tanned face.

He began to read, something he had not done since his school days. He read, not only at Kolb's Bible sessions, but for personal profit and pleasure, from Herr Kolb's surprisingly good library. Most of the books were in the elder's native German, which also encouraged the new Hugo.

Another happy circumstance at the elder's house was the elder's second daughter, Eva, a buxom lass of seventeen who had eyes for everything in trousers. The elder's older daughter was a long-faced, austere woman of indeterminate age who, on the basis of prior European study, presided over the colony's experimental garden. Her dinner talk was salted with botanical arguments and an almost daily fealty to some crackpot Austrian named Mendel. Any romantic or maternal instinct in this old maid was wrapped up snugly within the gauze tents of her beloved plants' reproductive parts.

Hugo joined the defense company. Not to do so would have made him conspicuous among the men. Surprisingly, he came to enjoy the soldierly affairs. Eva teased him that it was his Teutonic heritage bursting forth. And he was half-convinced that was correct.

Hugo was serene in his new life. He never thought or even dreamed of his bloody actions at Green Falls. Why should he? The past was gone, as was yesterday, and he was a man for the present. He had his eye on the future—and also on the busty Eva.

～～～～～～～～～～

The young vaquero finally found Jesus Ocampo at the calf shelter, helping old Suarez nurse a bawling calf.

"Mother of God," yelled the good steward, "what have you done to that horse? You could have killed it." He shook his head angrily as he studied the exhausted, foam-splattered mount.

"I had to come swiftly, Señor Jesus," replied the lad, climbing stiffly from his heaving animal. "I have very important information for you."

"Ha!—important information—from my newest vaquero, Uncle Felix!" Ocampo called to old Suarez. "Take this dying horse for a walk. Perhaps we can save it. Now, my boy . . . tell me your great secret, that you were in such a hurry to report."

"It was the wagons, Señor," stammered the youth.

"What wagons?"

"Three big wagons and a smaller wagon, like a cook wagon, Jefe. They came through Agua Mala in the early morning."

"And what did these big wagons carry?" asked Ocampo.

"Large boxes that said 'machinery' and the teams were large—almost double teamed, with big mules."

"And this is important? This what you almost killed a good horse for? Big wagons with machinery?"

"No, Señor Jesus—not just the wagons and teams."

"Then what—for the saints' sake?"

"Jefe, the wagons had no load. They did not press down in the dust of the road. And, Señor, they were heading for our rancho—at a fast pace—very fast."

Ocampo stared at the young vaquero, looking right through him. He stayed silent, thinking, while the youth heard his own racing heartbeat.

Finally Ocampo broke the silence. "No load? The boxes were empty?"

"I think so, Señor. Very light in weight, for sure."

"Heading here? How many men, altogether?"

"Perhaps ten, Señor. Two on each big wagon and out-riders."

"Damn, boy. It's the hide thieves, coming for our herd. They've struck other places. Now it's our turn. What time did you see them come through Agua Mala?"

"Perhaps the second hour of the morning, Jefe."

"And how fast?"

"A good trot, Señor. From big mules."

"Pray God, my son, that we've time to defend ourselves. Can you still ride?"

"For you, Jefe—to my death."

"No, boy. Stay alive to help me. Now quickly, listen to what I need you to do."

~~~~~~~~~~~~~

Señor Jesus Ocampo caught up to his calf branding party at midafternoon. Without the herd vaqueros, who had stayed with their herd, there were three riders plus old Martinez, who drove the wagon and tended camp.

Ocampo had the old man dole out what little food was left to the three riders and then sent him back to the main ranch. Then, bringing the riders to a sandy patch of ground, he drew a rough map of the rancho in the sand. The map finished, he slashed two straight lines through the map, from north to south, dividing the ranch into roughly three long sections.

"Now, my friends, the hide thieves are coming. But we know not where. Here, I have divided the rancho into three pieces; one for each of you. Tomas—you take the east; Jose—the middle; and you, Isaac, the west. You must detect the arrival of the bandits. Seek a high place by day and at night watch by the most logical trail. They must not pass without your observation. They have three large wagons with many draft mules. I think they will choose a wider trail even if it has a harder pull.

"When, by the Virgin Mother's grace, you find them, mark their passage with a pillar of fire at night and a column of smoke by day. No doubt, my friends, two of you will not see their passing, but, I beg you, stay four days at your posts. Perhaps the bandits will return to their lair on a different trail. Again, mark them for us, so that they may be destroyed. Finally—and this I ask with a heavy heart, for I love all of you. Yes—even you, Isaac, you bad-smelling bear. You must fall upon them from ambush to kill their mules, to kill the drivers—anything to delay them. Even at the cost of your life. Do you understand?"

The three vaqueros nodded their comprehension.

"Then," stated Ocampo, rising to his feet, "go with God and do your duty to the hacienda."

~~~~~~~~~~~~~~~

It had been arranged that Opal's trail herd would lay over at Mesa Grande in an open area across from the handful of buildings that was the hamlet. The grass was not abundant there and had to be augmented by two wagonloads of grain, hauled from Tucson.

The water was adequate, though. Mesa Grande boasted a year-round spring which flowed from the granite ridge behind the hamlet. This spring was carried by wooden piping down to the settlement for its use and also the use of the freighters' animals. In fact, the freighters had paid for the piping.

Opal's herd would spend a day in Mesa Grande recuperating from their dry trek from the ranch. The drovers particularly enjoyed the location, being in close proximity to the saloon. Bert Massey's leadership qualities were taxed to the limit policing his thirsty trail drivers at the Swansons' saloon and he was pleased when the herd moved out on its fourth day on the drive.

It always amazed Opal how her cattle, with their huge, dangerous-looking horns, could move down the narrow road without impaling each other. Her drovers, though, did not share her astonishment. They had dodged those long horns too long and had seen too many ripped comrades and gored mounts. They kept well away from the horns, letting their ever-whirling ropes do their talking.

CHAPTER 11

The large, formerly Mexican, haciendas were much more heavily manned than most of the newer, upstart American ranches. They could afford the extra people, for they still operated under the old paternalistic Spanish system. Their riders and workers were paid very little compared to their American counterparts. But the vaqueros had their jobs for life—and the food was good and filling. Whole families were employed on the hacienda, the individual members working at what they generally did best.

The hacienda was a Southwestern and Mexican version of the colonial plantation system. The haciendas did their utmost to be self-supporting, raising different animals for their fabrics and a variety of small crops for their subsistence.

Ocampo had been steward to old Don Benito, the last haciendo, who had been an ill-tempered tyrant. He had been murdered recently, no doubt due to his quarrelsome ways. The only heir, the sons all having died in the constant Apache wars of the previous decades, was an aged sister in Monterrey, Mexico, who preferred that climate and an annuity from the hacienda. This left Jesus Ocampo in full charge of the rancho. A dictator, if you will, but a fair man and nobody's fool.

He had learned ruthlessness and generalship in the dangerous school of Apache and Comanche warfare. The

Mexicans hated the Apaches and the Apaches hated the Mexicans. Their grudge was nurtured in blood to flower in cruelty. This, then, was the fighting background of Señor Jesus Ocampo.

Don Benito had a summer retreat built many years ago, when his ailing wife and active boys were still alive and happy. This retreat was at Lago Verde, a small algae-hued lake fifteen miles south of the main house. With the death of the Señora, the retreat no longer held appeal to Don Benito and it was relegated to a stopover dwelling for passing vaqueros and travelers.

It was to Lago Verde that Ocampo gathered his forces. The first to arrive were the vaqueros from the main ranch; all the riders who still had spring in their spines, good eyes and steady hands for gun work.

Then followed the remuda, almost a hundred strong horses, well broke and reliable. Next came the wagons with camp workers and cooks, food and supplies, grain for the animals, along with the farrier and his forge wagon, the saddle and harness maker, and Tia Rita with her bandages, splints and medicines.

Ocampo had come from posting his observers and he quickly used his headquarters' vaqueros to augment his observers, spreading them ten miles behind the observers. He told off sixteen men into two rider teams—hopefully filling any chinks in the scouting fan.

Now he awaited the riders from the far herds that he had sent the young vaquero to mobilize. Only three riders remained until these vaqueros would arrive. He sent this trio to the highest point on the saucer-shaped hills around the lake to give the alarm. One of the three would detach himself from the group and wait, with saddled horse, half-way to the camp at Lago Verde. When the warning beacon was seen he would gallop the last part of the relay, sparing neither horse nor personal safety.

The plans were laid. Nothing more could be done until the far vaqueros arrived. Ocampo ate and then found a shady spot in which to rest.

~~~~~~~~~

Smokey Watson reined in his horse to allow Judd Payton to catch up to his point position. "Damn, Smokey!" cried Payton, "You're setting a hell of a pace. Never seed the whips used so much."

"Got to," countered the scout. "We got to get in and get out, or we're in trouble."

"Maybe we could ditch those boxes and false sides— might help some," said Payton.

"Not till we start killing beef. They might fool some vaquero—if he spots us."

"How many more miles to go to the red bluffs, Smokey?"

"About ten or twelve. Should be bedded down by dark— hopefully. Moonrise about two or a little later and we'll go to work. That'll give the stock about eight or ten hours rest, before we vamos."

"I'll pass that on to the boys. They're getting hungry," answered Payton, turning his horse to trot back to the approaching wagons.

"Did I say, 'hopefully'?" Smokey asked himself. "Should have said it two or three times."

~~~~~~~~~

The damage to the bombed diversion flume was repaired quickly the following day. The damage to the colony's sense of security took more rehabilitation. To allay fears, a meeting was called the second evening after the blast and the aborted pursuit.

After the obligatory prayers and posturings by the minister and the elder, Major Riemann made a report about the damage and the tracking of the raiders. Then, to let the community talk out its fears, he opened the meeting to questions.

The first was from Frau Fenstermacher, asking if she was safe in her bed. As Frau Fenstermacher was an extremely ugly woman, with abundant facial hair, this brought a titter from the crowd, which was silenced by a determined glare from the elder.

"She means how safe is our village now," rephrased the elder, stepping into the social breach.

"That is a subject that we must discuss tonight," replied Riemann. "That and the dam's protection. We'll get to that later—after the question period."

"You say," began Franz Damm, rising to his feet, "that it appears that these workers of the woman rancher seem to be responsible for the flume damage. I worked to repair that damage. To me—and I'm not an expert on explosions—the damage was small. If they had used a larger device the flume would have fallen and the dam would have been subject to much damage from the water. It seems to me that either the bomb worker was incompetent or this explosion was only to provoke the community. Perhaps to make us take rash action." He looked around, swinging his great shaggy head. "My pardon—perhaps I talk on too much."

"No, Franz," answered the major. "What you say could be very true . . . and we will take your advice in our reaction."

"What has happened to the young women's defense plan?" queried the elder's older daughter, Margot. "We have the castoff weapons. What is the delay in our training?" She knew very well where the delay originated. Her father, the principal procrastinator, stared daggers at his outspoken daughter.

"I'll let the elder answer that question," replied Riemann, with a hint of a grin.

The elder took a deep breath and seemed to implore the heavens for guidance. "Our women are our strength—our inner strength. A quality given them by the good God—to raise and serve their families. Now, it seems that fools and dreamers—that Richard Wagner is one of them—try to portray our women as heroic female warriors, clothed in chain mail, helmeted and armed. Is this how we picture our mothers—feeding their newborn on armorplated breasts? No—a woman's place is the home, tending that helpless infant with the soft concern of loving motherhood."

"Father, I have no helpless infant to nurse," his daughter Margot, reminded him.

"Nor I," said another single woman. She was seconded by several others in the gathering.

"This should be left to God's will, but to satisfy my critics, I will ask Major Riemann if we are so desperate for our safety, so poor in our present soldiery, that we should arm our daughters and mothers."

"Thank you, Herr Kolb," said the major, not looking at all thankful. "If we arm certain women, I do not envision them as being regular soldiers. I think they would be most helpful as an auxiliary force that would augment the men. But there is one place where we could certainly use them and their weapons."

"Where would that be, my good Major?" replied the elder with heavy sarcasm.

"During the workday, when the men are off to work and the village is most vulnerable to attack. A dozen armed persons, firing from the shelter of houses, would slow any attacking body. Hopefully, long enough for help to arrive."

A dozen women in the audience clapped their assent.

"I wash my hands of this business," declared Kolb, disgusted with events. "Do what you want with the ladies. And gentlemen," he smirked, "check under the women's pillows for bayonets before you retire."

The questioning and the rancor over, the meeting turned to its collective response to the bombing.

After discussion, guided by Major Riemann's calm military presence, it was decided to place sentinels at night on the dam and in the church belfry. In addition, a mounted vedette would patrol around the community and, also, the west bank of the dam site, the flank toward the ranchers. Additionally, the men would carry their arms to their work and a mounted patrol would make a sweep of the farmlands before breakfast and scout the road to the dam after their breakfast. These precautions would cost labor and try patience. All agreed, though, the cost was necessary for their peace of mind and the colony's safety.

~~~~~~~~~~~~~

Captain Cabot's request for a residence fit for a gentleman produced a large wall tent from Tucson. Cabot, himself, with Napoleon sawing the boards, built a floor and a partition in this tent, turning it into a bedchamber and a parlor. The tent was also fitted with wooden doors to facilitate entrance and egress. It was to Cabot's tent door that Hugh Foote came on the fifth morning of the trail herd's departure.

Napoleon opened the door, apron tight against his spare waist and a frying pan in his other hand.

"I need to see the captain," greeted the foreman, now the temporary manager.

"I gots coffee, Mr. Foote," said the servant. "You jes sits down an' drinks some an' the cap'n, he'll be rights here." Napoleon set the frying pan down on the camp stove and poured coffee for Hugh. Then he disappeared inside the bed chamber where Hugh heard him waking Cabot.

"Who?" came through the wall, from a graveled voice. "Oh, well—tell him to wait. Bring me some hot water, I need you to shave me."

Napoleon scurried back and forth, finally saying, "The cap'n says to come in—whilst I shave him." Hugh entered Cabot's bedchamber to find Cabot sitting on a wicker armchair. A yellowed towel was wrapped around his shoulders and a lather of shaving soap plastered his face.

"Now, Mr. Foote," grunted Cabot through soap-smeared lips, "what is the import of this most early visit?"

"I'm worried about our boss lady. About what will happen to her when she jumps into that barrel of rattlesnakes in Tucson."

"Pity the poor snake that would strike our poison princess," chuckled Cabot out of the corner of his mouth. "It would find instant death."

"This isn't funny, Cabot," shot back Hugh Foote. "They're a rough bunch with a good piece of their profits to lose. I don't think they'd do her in, more likely mess her up somehow. Break an arm or a leg, maybe—to set her on notice."

"A limb, Mr. Foote. Ladies have limbs."

"Limbs or legs, Cabot, I don't want her hurt."

"Oh my," teased Cabot. "Do I detect more than just concern for Miss Wilbur? A touch of affection towards our shapely employer?"

"Watch your words, Cabot," warned Foote. "I want you to go to Tucson. Use your talent to help her. Back her play."

"I have no orders to follow her to Tucson. Isn't your large friend, Massey, able to play bodyguard?"

"Bert is big and tough. He knows cows. He don't know backroom shenanigans and cutthroat business deals."

"And I do—you think. I state again—I have no orders to leave my post and play nursemaid."

"You got them now. I'm in charge here."

"Temporarily, yes. To be sure. I would need expense money. I do not travel cheaply."

"You'll have a draft. Cash it in Tucson. But if she's hurt—don't return here."

"How negatively you think, Mr. Foote," replied Cabot. "I shall need a hundred dollars. No . . . make it one hundred fifty. We will have our animals to board. Nappy—pack our luggage for a four day excursion. We shall leave after breakfast. Does that suit you, Mr. Temporary Manager?"

"Just make Tucson tonight. I'll get Mrs. Cole to make the draft. Stop by the house and pick it up on your way out. I've got to ride to the B R, we're hurting for horseflesh."

"Oh, Mr. Foote," called the captain. "If our lady asks who authorized my bodyguard escapade, what, pray tell, should I report?"

"Tell her the damn truth, Cabot, my friend." The door slammed noisily behind Foote.

"Isn't love grand, Nappy?" sighed Cabot. "How come I never find love? Don't I deserve it?"

"You gots it, cap'n. Onliest it's your work that you likes."

"Too true, my dark sage. Come, finish up. I smell fun coming up."

~~~~~~~~~~~~~

This was the day the builders came to move the cell bars from the old sheriff's office to the new second floor jail over the brand-new, almost completed, brick jail on main street. Fortunately, only two men, actually a boy and a man, were incarcerated. These two were taken out and chained to the cannon that graced the front of the old militia barracks, which was now the Sweeney Stageline depot and the old sheriff's office.

"There's just enough, counting that section of bars out back," said old man Hansen.

"You're using the folding beds, aren't you?" asked Skinner. "They cost a lot of money."

"Can't move 'em today," stated Hansen. "The bars is an all day job. Maybe more—'cause we have to piece that old section in. That means cutting. Takes forever. No—we'll get the beds tomorrow. And that means drilling holes in the brick to put in the bolts. All takes time."

"Just do a good job. I don't want any escapes due to shoddy work," cautioned Skinner.

"Hey, who you talking to? I was building stuff when you was messing your small clothes."

Just then, Mr. Gomper of Gomper's Department Store came into the office.

"Moving out, I see, Sheriff. Looks like you'll need a new stove—for your new building."

"That is very decent of you, Mr. Gomper," replied the sheriff. "You are a commissioner. How about springing for that?"

"I see what you mean, Skinner. Captain Mosely would never go for it. He's still smarting over the cost of the bricks. But that's not what I came for. I've got a little problem. Could I talk with you outside?"

"Very good," laughed Skinner, "because it seems everybody's big problem was just a little problem when they first come in here. Must be something about this office that just naturally puffs up problems. Maybe its yeast spores in the air?" He led the way outside to the hitchrack.

"This concerns Big Jim Caudelet, Sheriff. You know—the owner of the New Orleans Belle?"

"Indeed I do," said Skinner. "Worked for the brute for awhile, when you fired me and my deputies last year."

"That was pure politics, Sheriff. Our hands were tied by Washington. You don't hold that against me, do you? I had nothing to do with it."

"I was sorta thinking about that hardware job with you— that I didn't get."

"That was my wife, Skinner. She had family to keep at work. Anyway—you said you made more money with Caudelet."

"I did. Had to shoot more people, too. Get back to your little problem for today."

"Remember last week, when my jeweler got killed walking into that wagon?"

"Philip Armstead was the name," stated Skinner.

"Right. Armstead. It turns out that Armstead owed Big Jim money—a gambling debt."

"Not that talented young man you was talking about. How did you put it? Artistic, smiling?"

"Well—I made a wrong judgment, probably. Getting back to my story, Big Jim put the squeeze on Armstead for the debt. Armstead bought some time by giving Caudelet a diamond to hold as collateral. He told Big Jim he would pay back the debt in increments and get the diamond back that way. Caudelet said he went along with it for some modest interest. Believe that or not."

"I'll take not," said Skinner. "Go on."

"So Armstead got killed. Caudelet comes to me. Says he doesn't want the diamond. Wants me to pay for the stone, to pay Armstead's gambling debt. Now—here is where I might have made a mistake. I told Caudelet that gambling debts are not collectible under the law."

"True, true. Continue."

"He says, 'What diamond? I got no diamond.' So now what do I do?"

"Whose diamond is it—the store's?" questioned the sheriff, taking out his pipe.

"Almost wish it was," admitted Gomper. "I dashed back to the store and searched through Armstead's records. It's an almost three carat, marquise-cut diamond. Armstead sent off for a pendant setting from New York, with a ruby frame around it. I went over to the customer to tell her that there would be a slight delay. What with Armstead's death I thought it would give me more time to deal with Caudelet. Boy, was she mad. Sure glad I don't have to lodge with her. She's one . . ."

"Whoa," interrupted Skinner. "Hold on. What's this customer's name?"

"Mrs. Robinson. She runs a boarding house over . . ."

"I know where, Mr. Gomper. And you just made me a very happy sheriff."

"I did?" questioned Gomper. How?"

"How much would you think this diamond's worth?"

"I never saw it, you know. But, retail—we have to ask $250 to $350 a carat, depending on quality. And this was almost three carats, which would be $750 to $1050 plus extra for the large size of the stone. I'd say $1200 to $1500. Somewhere around there. The new setting was $350 wholesale, according to his records. He was going to charge $700. A pretty penny."

"Indeed," mused Skinner. "I will talk to Mr. Caudelet for you. Was this jeweler bonded or insured in any way?"

"Well—I was considering it. But the policy was $90 a year. I passed. A mistake, eh?"

"'Fraid so, Mr. Gomper. I'll talk to Big Jim. Be prepared to pay something, though."

"I should make $350 from the customer. That will help, I guess."

"Don't count on it, Mr. Gomper. Don't count on it."

~~~~~~~~~~~~~~

Smokey Watson spotted the smoke first. It rose black and slender from a butte about three or four miles to the east. Several hundred feet, possibly even five hundred feet above the butte, a thermal breeze caught the thin shaft to carry it almost sideways—where it gradually dissipated.

Smokey jerked his horse around to point out the smoke to Judd Payton. Payton kicked his roan hard and galloped up to his scout.

"Think that's Injuns?" the heavy-set boss asked anxiously.

"I almost hope so," answered the scout.

"It might not be on account of us."

"True, and pigs can fly real pretty," commented the scout.

"What should we do? Got any good ideas?" questioned the boss.

"Only two things to do. Press on—or run like hell. And I vote to run. Course, I ain't running this outfit."

"I don't like the idea of going back the same way we came in," said Payton. "Can you find us another trail home?"

"There's a dry lake on the other side of that ridge. I think I remember a way across at the Salt River. That way we'll be seven or eight miles further west."

"And then there's a dry lake home?"

"Not all the way. Better than half, though," confirmed the scout.

"Pick us a trail, Smokey. I'll turn 'em around—and keep your fingers crossed."

~~~~~~~~~~~~~

The sun was low in the west when the far vaqueros rode into Lago Verde. They came in at the canter, a long dusty company of hard horsemen, a loosely-strewn cavalcade blotting out the red sun with their dirty cloud. Old Papi Sanchez led them in—almost seventy vaqueros. Two of his many sons slid off their horses to help their short, fat patriarch to the ground. Ocampo rushed out to greet the aged retainer. Old Sanchez had always enjoyed a position of respect in Don Benito's fiefdom. If the old don was an earl, then Papi Sanchez was a baron. He had been the rock against which the Apaches and Comanches had dashed. And now that he and his brigade were at Lago Verde, Ocampo's army was ready.

The remuda was called in and Papi Sanchez's riders took fresh horses and then they refreshed themselves in the green water and cut huge slices from the spitted steer at the rear of the house; and, yes, more than a few swigs from the big straw-bound jugs of pulque.

And then a rider came, crazy-mad with excitement, in the second hour of darkness. He galloped his wild-eyed horse, oblivious to the stumble-holes and treacherous terrain, running furiously between the many campfires of Ocampo's army to slide his mount in front of the house where Ocampo and his lieutenants rested.

"A beacon, Jefe!" the rider yelled hoarsely. "From the east. They have come from the east."

"And they do not bring presents of incense and myrrh," laughed Papi Sanchez.

"Then, they are not so wise—are they?" replied Ocampo, pulling on his boots. "Have the riders ready in five minutes," he said to the young vaquero, who had returned to be at his side.

They rode out at a fast trot, a great course of riders, strung out at the van and the trail like a moving cloud of insects in swarm. Ocampo and Papi Sanchez led, with the lieutenants, Segundos and sons riding close-ranked behind. They headed for the break in the surrounding hills and toward their beacon by night.

The moon had come up, throwing its blanched beams on the harsh desert chaparral, making darker smudges of brush and bush. Suddenly, coming fast, galloping recklessly toward Ocampo's force, a rider was seen. The rider fired his rifle toward the stars to gain the column's attention. Ocampo's upthrust arm slowed and stopped the dense throng of riders as the galloper reined in his nervous mount before them. It was the third member of the observers from the hill above Lago Verde.

"Señor!" he panted. "Another fire from the southwest. Now there are two fires showing in the night!"

"This second beacon," snapped Ocampo, ". . . you saw it after the first beacon?"

"Si, Jefe. Felix had left already. A good time after."

"How long after?"

"I am not good with the clocks, Señor. Perhaps like the time it takes me to fill my stomach with food."

"That long, Oscar," laughed Ocampo. "Go back to the house and fill your stomach. You have done well."

"I would wish to ride with you, Jefe," said the older rider. "My horse is still strong."

"Come, then. A brave man is always welcome," said Ocampo. Then turning to Papi Sanchez. "What do you think this second beacon tells us, Don Sanchez?"

"It tells me that either another party comes, which is unlikely, or that the first band has turned from it's path."

Ocampo thought for a moment, then exclaimed, "That is what has happened! They have seen the first signal and have changed their direction—probably to the west."

"They try to get behind the Sawtooth Ridge," spat Gregorio, the headquarters' segundo.

"To make better time on the salt flat," growled old Sanchez. "Let me take half the company to the west, beyond the ridge, while you, my Jefe, take the remainder south. That way we can catch them between us and wipe these Yanqui pests out."

"A good idea, Don Sanchez," answered Ocampo. "But try not to kill them. I have an idea that they may be worth money—and this rancho is desperate for dollars."

CHAPTER 12

It was late afternoon when Opal's trail herd reached Tucson. By the time the last longhorn was hazed into the holding pens down by the river the sun was a burning ball on the purple-hazed horizon.

"Two hundred sixty-three, I tally," called Pappy Sloan, crawling down off the fence rails to hobble over to Bert Massey and Opal.

"Then we're short two," said Massey.

"I know of one," broke in Pappy Sloan. "Stupid critter jes fell off'n the trail and landed in the rocks. It's a coyote's supper now."

"When are you supposed to see the Army agents, Miss Opal?" asked big Bert.

"The man that runs the holding pens said they told him they would be out in the morning. He said they run them through the chute for a look and to tally them."

"I got feed and water coming," Bert went on. "Maybe we can get some of that trail look off by then."

The next morning Bert allowed that they looked somewhat better. Opal was certain they looked fatter and sleeker. Evidently the Army inspectors thought differently.

The older, heavier, grey-haired one named Cobb kept shaking his head as Opal's herd was pushed through the chute into an adjacent pen. The dark-haired inspector, the one named Pratt, just picked his teeth with his tally pencil as he sourly noted the cattle.

Finally the last cow had been pushed through and Opal's men climbed down from the poles with the saddle blankets and feed sacks they had used to swat their charges through the chute.

The two inspectors conferred together in hushed tones for several minutes, counting their tally. After a while they motioned Opal over.

"Not much of a herd, Miss Wilbur," announced the grey-haired one called Cobb. "Not even sure most of them meet minimum standards."

"That's so," seconded Pratt, sucking on a troublesome molar.

"The way I see it, Miss Wilbur," continued Cobb, "you've got only two ways to go."

"Which ways would that be, gentlemen?" smiled Opal, lightning flashes flecking her emerald eyes. Then she held up her hand, slim in a yellow-kid riding glove. "Please, before you answer, let us adjourn to the nearby saloon for refreshment. Shall we?"

"Wouldn't do any good, Miss Wilbur. A few whiskeys aren't going to change our minds."

"Why, Mr. Cobb, Mr. Pratt. Would I think so little of your character as to try to bribe you with alcohol? I am only thinking of a comfortable setting to continue our discussion. Would you deny a lady a seat and a table?"

"Certainly not, ma'am," replied Cobb. "Jack," he told his assistant, "how about going ahead of us and get Doyle to fix up a table—away from the bar? Tell him it's for a lady."

"Why, thank you, Mr. Cobb," purred Opal, putting her arm through the arm of the startled Cobb.

Once in the saloon, whiskey before the inspectors and Bert Massey, she asked the proprietor for tea.

"Only tea I got," said the man, tucking in a stained apron behind his ample belt, "is the green kind that my Chinee cook drinks. I got coffee, though."

"The tea sounds lovely," said Opal. "With sugar, please. Now, gentlemen, you were saying I have but two choices with my herd?"

"I'm afraid so, ma'am," answered Pratt, out of turn. He then looked to his boss, apologetically.

Cobb scowled at his assistant and began, "The first thing is for you to forget about the government contract. Try to sell your herd locally. Any number of ranchers hereabouts would give you a fair price. Course they'd have to fatten up them cows if they tried to sell them—to, ah . . ."

Cobb's sales option petered out to silence as Captain Cabot came into the saloon, looking around sharply at its occupants.

"The government," finished Cobb, eyes on Cabot, who had come up to their table.

Opal twisted in her chair, surprised to see Cabot. "Captain Cabot," she greeted. "I did not expect you in Tucson. Gentlemen, this is Captain Cabot. He is my new regulator."

"We've met," murmured Cobb, tight-lipped.

"I found that I had business in Tucson, Miss Wilbur," stated Cabot, with a tip of his hat. "I don't want to bother your discussion. I will find another table." He went to the next table and sat down facing the inspectors. He laid a brass-action Henry rifle on the green felt of the table.

"Where was I?" asked Cobb, thrown off his stride.

"Advising me to sell my herd to any number of ranchers. They wouldn't be friendly with you? Any number of them—would they, Mr. Cobb?"

Cobb missed her question. He was too busy watching Captain Cabot who had taken a box of shells out of his coat pocket. The Henry rifle used a copper-cased .44 cal. cartridge with a heavy 216 grain slug. Cabot was loading the Henry with these big shells. But before he inserted each shell into the long tubular magazine below the rifle's barrel, he took care to polish each copper shell with a bit of polishing cloth. Then, after examining each shell for dents or defects, he slipped it tenderly and with exaggerated care into the magazine.

"Would they, Mr. Cobb?" Opal prompted again.

"Er, no—certainly not," replied Cobb, his eyes on Cabot's every move.

"And the other option, Mr. Cobb; what was that?" asked Opal.

"Ah—sell them at a penalty to the government."

"A penalty, Mr. Cobb? Why would I be penalized?"

"Underweight beef, Miss Wilbur," put in Pratt. "Isn't that correct, Mr. Cobb?"

"The absolute truth, Mr. Pratt," confirmed Cobb.

"Wait a minute," argued Bert Massey. "There's 263 cows out there. There might be one or two on the skinny side. I'll cut them out and there will be over 250 head of prime beef out there. What do you say? Let me cut any cow you don't like."

"Well, gentlemen?" pushed Opal. "Give the man an answer."

Cobb and Pratt were distracted. Cabot had their full attention, loading the rifle. Finally, Cabot had the tube loaded with its fifteen cartridges. The regulator rose and sauntered over to Opal's table. He stepped in front of the inspectors, looking them up and down, measuring them with his eyes.

He turned to Opal, shaking his head. "It's no problem, Miss Opal. They will certainly fit in normal coffins." He stared at the inspectors again. "See you soon, gentlemen, unless . . ." He left the saloon, walking out into the glare of the morning.

"That man's a mighty dangerous man to carry on your payroll, Miss Wilbur," complained Cobb, wiping perspiration from his face with a stiff forefinger.

"Yes, he is dangerous," replied Opal. "Some one of these days he'll hurt somebody . . . again."

"What were we talking about?" said Cobb.

"I asked you to let me cut out any cow you think too light," replied Bert quickly.

"That seems to be a constructive idea," said Mr. Pratt, his eyes still on the saloon door. "Don't you think so, Mr. Cobb?"

"Capital idea. You're absolutely correct, Mr. Pratt. Tell you what, Miss Wilbur; to show good faith, we'll let you cull them out for us. Just make sure there's 250 head there when you're finished. Now, Miss Wilbur, how about another drink? I think I could use one now."

~~~~~~~~~~~~

As soon as it was light Papi Sanchez saw the dust roiled upward by the wagons of the hide thieves. It hung in the early morning stillness above the deep cleft in the Sawtooth Ridge that was the Salt River. The wagons were leaving the dry river bed, forcing their tiring teams to pull through the sandy banks which bordered the arroyo. Soon—the wagons were on the salt flats, headed for the south and safety.

Judd Payton saw the pursuing riders first and roared to his scout, waving his hat for attention. Smokey wheeled his horse to ride back to his boss.

"God! Look at all those fellows. The fat's in the fire now," the short scout shouted. "We're dead meat, for sure."

"I'm gonna take some of 'em with me!" hollered Payton. "Find some place we can fort up. I'll bring up the wagons." He jerked his horse around to gallop back toward Uncle Walter in the last wagon.

Smokey raced back to the broken ground of the ridge, looking for any place that would provide cover. He spotted a fold in the low cliff and waved to Payton to bring the wagons up. The vaqueros seemed less than half a mile behind Uncle Walter's wagon and were gaining fast.

The big wagons came into the open space before the fissured cliff face, dragging their dust cloud billowing up the face of the stunted palisade. Smokey Watson was in the center of the cloudy confusion, yelling to the drivers to loose the chains of their teams and move the animals into the questionable cover of the cliff. Then the big wagons were frantically manhandled into position and turned on their sides to provide protection.

Uncle Walter's small wagon had lagged behind. His team was exhausted. The pursuing riders, sensing the quick kill of a lamed adversary, swooped across the salt flats, trying to cut off the solitary wagon. Judd Payton fired his rifle at the converging riders, using the heavy Winchester one-handed, like a handgun. He emptied one saddle and dropped another horse—then the rifle was empty.

A fat rider suddenly appeared out of the dust, backed by a dozen vaqueros. Uncle Walter's team went down under their gunfire. Judd saw Uncle Walter's bullet-blasted body swept from the wagon box just before the wagon plowed into the downed team. The wagon jackknifed, spilling Joey, Judd Payton's grandson, flinging him to a heap on the ground.

Payton wheeled his weary roan and grabbed at his pistol in a rescue attempt. It was too late; several vaqueros had flung themselves from their horses to capture the youngster. Foiled in his grandson's recovery, the hide thieves' leader had to retire to the refuge of the wagons.

Papi Sanchez stood in his stirrups to wave his pistol in a slashing motion at the breastwork of the overthrown wagons. Emilio, his eldest son, roared a challenge over the tumult and led thirty charging riders at the barricades. Sanchez saw that the vaqueros still had the advantage of the dust cloud to cover their attack.

Gunfire from the forted wagons twinkled through the dust as more billowing dirt filled the battleground. A horse fell screaming as another raced riderless out of the dirty gloom. Sanchez signalled to his riders to retire and rode out of the dust to form a line out of rifle shot.

The attackers came back, trotting disdainfully through the thinning cloud. Two men were riding double and three more were wounded, one seriously.

"Get men on the cliff behind them!" shouted old Sanchez to Ybanez, a grey-bristled bear of a lieutenant, who made an airy salute and rode off on the southern flank with ten men.

"Find brush and ready five horses with drags," ordered the old general to Emilio. "When the men of Ybanez begin firing, have the drag men start the dust. Make sure you put a nimble man on the first horse and have him ride on the side away from the enemy's fire. Make sure the following riders stay inside the first horse's dust. Do you hear? I don't want any more empty saddles!"

~~~~~~~~~~

"Well, well—look who's here, Thomas," wisecracked Big Jim Caudelet. "It's our old gun-guard come back to see the old folks at home. What's the matter, Skinner—sheriffing don't pay so good? Want your old job back?"

"No, thank you, Caudelet. Saloon business is too rough for me. My legs get cramps every time I think about that gun balcony of yours. I've come to get you out of a predicament. Call it an old favor to a former employer."

"Listen to that bullshit, Thomas," Caudelet told his son. "This sheriff will make a politician yet. Go on Skinner, give me your pitch."

"I'm here to keep you out of jail on a misappropriation charge, Jim."

"Don't call me Jim, Skinner," rasped Caudelet. "Only my friends call me Jim—and I don't have many of them."

"He's got more enemies," grinned son Thomas.

"Misappropriating what?" continued Big Jim belligerently. "It's news to me."

"How about a three-carat diamond that rightly belongs to Gomper's Department Store?" said the sheriff, matter-of-factly.

"Never heard or seen it, Skinner. Now what do you do?"

"Go back and see the County Attorney about an indictment. He might even have to present it to the Grand Jury. Soon as we get an indictment, which we will with our evidence, I'll ask that your gambling license be temporarily revoked on the criminal activities clause."

"You rotten bastard!" cursed Caudelet. "You'd do that, would you?" His huge shoulders strained ominously under his well-cut coat.

"I'd rather talk to you—about a three-carat diamond."

"For Christ's sake, Pop. Talk to him. We'd lose thousands if we had to shut the gambling down," cautioned Thomas.

"All right, Thomas my boy—just for you. What do you want, Skinner? See? I'm talking."

"Gomper needs that diamond," said Skinner. "It belongs to a customer, who was having it reset."

"Oh—for sure, having it reset," agreed Big Jim. "Don't want to have it recognized, like I recognized it."

"What do you mean, Caudelet?"

"I know that diamond and it's not Gomper's or some make believe customer's."

"The customer's real. Believe that—I guarantee it."

"Then you're the bigger fool, Skinner. That diamond was Dickie McFee's. It was in his stickpin. I should know. I tried to buy it a dozen times from him. He wouldn't part with it. I thought he took it to his grave or else sold it to that French doctor."

"How much did you advance Armstead, Caudelet?"

"$525 bucks—hard cash."

"Which you won from him," added Skinner.

"That's not our fault," broke in Thomas. "He was a terrible gambler. He had the same chance to win as anybody.

Our money was in jeopardy—just as always. People always forget that."

"Suppose Gomper gave you two hundred dollars toward the debt," offered the sheriff. "Would you give up the diamond?"

"Everybody acts like I'm a goddam charity," complained Caudelet. "Make it $250 and give me first crack at that diamond—if the real owner is ever found."

"It'll take a while to sift out the rightful owner and you've got to clam up on this deal or you could lose your shot at it. That stone is going to be *Exhibit A* in a murder case."

"McFee's?" questioned Caudelet.

"Just between you and me," agreed Skinner.

"And me," said Thomas. "Should I give it to him now, Pop? It's in the safe upstairs."

"Hell no," scolded his father. "Wait until I get the $250."

~~~~~~~~~~~

Opal had the Army's draft in her clutch purse as she entered the hotel. She stopped at the desk to pick up her room key and saw Napoleon, Cabot's man servant, coming from the bar, with a bottle of whiskey and several glasses on the tray he carried. He went up the wide, carpeted stairs to the upper regions of the hotel. Opal grabbed at her skirt and followed fast behind him.

She caught up with him as he was opening the room door. "Good even's Mis' Opal," he said, making a head-bob into a bow. "Did you wishes to see the cap'n?"

"I do, indeed, Mr. Napoleon," snapped Opal. "Will you announce me, please?"

"Jes' you waits dere, Mis' Opal, whilst I sees if'n he's fit to receives you." He slid through the half-opened door, the bottle miraculously glued to the wavering tray. One minute later, he reappeared smiling broadly, a white jacket suddenly over vest and shirt-sleeves.

"The cap'n will sees you now, Mis' Opal." He opened the door wide and stood to one side. Captain Cabot was seated on a chaise lounge and he hastily rose to greet Opal. He wore a blue silk dressing gown over yellow breeches and two-tone English riding boots.

"Miss Wilbur," he welcomed, unenthusiastically. "How nice to meet here. I'm afraid all I have to offer is bourbon, aside from the pleasure of my company."

"What a lovely room," commented Opal. "Much finer than mine—on the floor under the roof."

"Oh, yes—it is warmer up there, isn't it? This mezzanine floor always seems to catch a breeze."

"I'm surprised you could afford such luxury, Captain. Weren't you just recently describing your dire financial straits?"

"Thankfully, dear lady," confessed Cabot, with a trace of a smile, "I am pleased to be on what is known as a paid expense trip, thanks to Wilbur Ranches."

"And who, pray tell, sanctioned your visit to Tucson?" asked Opal sweetly—baiting her trap with honey.

"Why, your manager, the esteemed Mr. Foote. To tell the absolute truth, I believe he was concerned for your safety—here in the rudeness of Tucson. By the way—I surmise that your business dealings were successful?"

"Very," admitted Opal. "Partly, no doubt, due to your theatrical performance in the saloon."

"Ah . . . I did enjoy that. But I must admit I had to purchase a stage prop, the Henry rifle. I hope you don't mind. My own rifle, the Colt cap and ball, would not have been as effective as the Henry—with its gleaming cartridges."

"How much?" said Opal.

"Of course it was secondhand," went on Cabot, deprecatingly. "Can't find a new one, you know. Thirty-two dollars, including a box of shells. I have entrusted it to Napoleon. He has always been concerned about red Indians. If you need it for the ranch, I'll ask him for its return."

"I'll tell Beatrice to put it down towards him—as a loaned piece of equipage—to be returned if and when you end your employment."

"End our association, dear lady?" stated the captain. "I certainly hope not. Not while Wilbur Ranches needs my services."

"Someday, Captain," answered Opal, "there will come a time when we will no longer need a regulator to protect our borders. You should save your money for that day, sir. Now, I must go. We are leaving after an early breakfast tomorrow. Will you join our party at breakfast, Captain?"

"That sounds terribly prompt, Miss Wilbur. I would rather bring up the rear. But I will see you tomorrow evening at your ranch. Please—let me show you to the door," he said, ushering her out graciously.

Once back on the chaise lounge, Cabot filled a glass with bourbon and smelled its amber surface. Then he sipped the whiskey—savoring its taste.

"Very creditable, Napoleon, you know your bourbon," he announced.

"Tha's six-dollar whiskey, Cap'n," chuckled Napoleon. "Las' months we wuz paying a dollar 'n a quarters. We's in high clover rights now."

"Did you hear our lady employer? 'Save your money for that day, sir.' She would toss us away on the ash heap, Nappy. Talk about ingratitude. I just put the fear of God in those government reptiles, clinching her sale, and she has the gall to tell me my days are numbered."

"She's rights, Cap'n. You knows it, too. Maybes you could finds a nice little ol' saloon somewheres. Wheres you doan have to bes shootin' people always."

"I would lay down and die of boredom, Mr. Napoleon. No . . . How about a small brig on the balmy South Seas? Perhaps the hurricanes would supply adventure. We must save our money, Nappy. No more six-dollar whiskey—unless it is on a travel account, of course."

CHAPTER 13

The requested resupply of Spencer ammunition arrived late that evening, along with several other surprises, in a modest wagon train of freight wagons. The first unheralded event was the arrival, with the cartridges, of seven immigrant families and six unaccompanied males, for a total of forty-two men, women and children.

Escorting this gaggle of Northern Silesians, refugees from Prussian political pressures, was the Senator-Elect from Missouri, Carl Schurz. Schurz, the guiding hand behind the Puzzle River settlement, had taken advantage of the period between his election and his senatorial seating the next March to accompany this latest group of immigrants to Arizona. Actually, he had left St. Louis more than a month after the newcomers, utilizing steam cars and diligence vehicles to catch up with the immigrants.

Mr. Schurz was a tall, gangling man, much the same stature as his good friend Abraham Lincoln; but unlike Lincoln, he always seemed to exhibit a happy, verbose personality. He was confident of his many military, literary and political skills and was considered by many to be a hard driver in his public affairs and duties.

The unexpected influx of new settlers put a sudden strain on sleeping and living space. The elder assigned some of the older children to live temporarily with already settled families, while the church was converted into adjacent men's and ladies' dormitories by a canvas and wood-framed dividing wall which split the none-too-wide aisle.

Fortunately, the Silesians brought with them many skills thus far not represented in the community. A cooper, a wheelwright, several mechanics, six farmers, two miners, a bargeman and a printer were listed. Also listed, to the elder's chagrin, was a brewmaster.

Mr. Schurz could stay only another day before having to depart with the freighters. He would go as far as Tucson with the wagons before transferring to the stage coach for the trip to the railhead.

The next day Major Riemann showed Schurz around the settlement. After that, he took him through the fields, stopping to let him talk to the crew working the big gang plow.

"This soil seems very sandy," commented Schurz, who had farmed in Watertown, Wisconsin, for several years after his own immigration from Europe.

"Yes, it is sandy, Herr Schurz," answered Knapp, the plowman. "But it is adequate and we are constantly adding mulch. All our sawdust and used straw are worked in—and of course, the manure. We even send a big wagon to Green Falls every day to bring back more manure."

"Under most of our land is layer of hardpan," explained the major, "that helps to retain the moisture."

"And your flume will be elevated enough to let the irrigation water flow into the fields?" asked the Senator-Elect.

"Yes sir, the flume's floor will be two feet above the lowest part of the furrow. We start surveying the east flume next week. We have found a good deposit of flagstone about a mile from here for the lining of the flume. There will be a water chest every one-eighth mile, with staunch boards to regulate the irrigation."

"I notice you have a hill halfway down the riverbank. Will that impede the flow?"

"Not after we tunnel through it," said Riemann. "That's why I was so glad to see those two miners you brought; we'll have them digging there as soon as the survey gives us the correct level."

"And here, all along," laughed Schurz, "I thought it would be the brewmaster that you would welcome."

"That, my general, is going to be much more precarious. Heinrich Kolb is going to take a lot of persuasion from a lot of people before he accepts a brewery."

"It seems to me, Major, that a brewery would be a good source of income. Certainly it is one way to dispose of your crops. Perhaps you could influence your good elder by naming the brew after him; maybe call it *Kolbbrau*.

"How about *Heiner's Best*?" chuckled Riemann. "But now we better get to the dam or we will miss our dinner."

That evening the community gave a welcome banquet for the newcomers and an appreciation banquet for their sponsor. A calf and two goats were killed and roasted, along with forty pounds of sausage and sixty loaves of Klaus's Kornbrot. The elder even let Riemann take a small cask of Schnapps out of the medical stores for the celebration saying, "It's against my principles—but we should not let the general think we begrudge him a drink."

As the celebration was drawing to a noisy close, General Schurz beckoned for Riemann to follow. The tall Senator-Elect gathered enough of the boisterous freighters together to unload a last large box from one of the big high-wheeled wagons. They carried it, cursing the weight, into the black-smith's shop. Schurz thanked the freighters and told them to tell the man overseeing the brandy cask that General Schurz wanted each of them to have another drink.

After the freighters left, Schurz lit a lantern hanging from a low rafter and motioned Riemann to pull the soot-blackened canvas that served as the smithy's door across the wide opening.

"I saved this for last," said Schurz, "until I was sure this item was used correctly—for the right purposes. In the wrong hands, it could present problems, both political and moral. I had to be sure. Now if we can find a tool to open it, I'll show you the piece de resistance."

Riemann found several large chisels and hammers and they attacked the stout box. After banging and heaving at the unyielding container, they finally forced its lid loose amid a shriek of nails.

"There," puffed the general, "quick—the lantern—and I'll show you the plum in this pie."

Riemann stretched to slip the lamp's bail from it's nail and shined it into the big box.

"My God—is this what I think it is?" He stared at the pipe-like roll in the box. The grease-coated mechanism looked solid—and heavy. Very heavy.

"A Gatling gun, Major," beamed Schurz. "Complete with tripod and gunner's seat; in .50 caliber."

"My God, a Gatling gun!" Riemann was mesmerized by the lethal shape of the heavy weapon. "I've only heard of them— never saw one."

"I had to talk," laughed the general, "like a Dutch uncle to get the loan of this weapon from the ordnance officials. Your unit's entry into the militia helped greatly. I promised a very complete report from you on the gun's application to desert firing. And one other thing—to the negative, I'm afraid."

"What is that—its weight?"

"No—I was only able to get 2500 cartridges for the testing. So your use of the gun has to be judicious. The ordnance people have had trouble with this hopper type of loading mechanism. They sent plans for a long, single column magazine. I'm sure your blacksmith could make one. Actually, you would, no doubt, need more—perhaps a dozen. You'll have to judge for yourself. And there are other problems, such as extraction and lubrication. That's why I could talk them into a desert test. The lubrication picks up sand particles, you know."

"I noticed, sir, that you seemed to be keeping this gun a secret. Is it still a secret, or should I say a hot potato, politically?"

"That is why, Major, I took my time evaluating our position here. I don't want to do anything that seems like we are seizing land from the cattlemen. The Water Rights Commission idea is slowly moving through the Interior Department. We do not want to jeopardize our position by violence. If you have to defend yourself from hooligans and raiders, that is one thing, but land seizure is out. Do you understand?"

"We always have, General. I told you about the bombing of the diversion flumes and how we backed off—even when we knew that we had caught up with the bombers."

"Good! Take my advice, my friend. It's much easier to be a soldier than a diplomat. One tires your body and the other tries your patience. And, generally, your patience wears out first. Remember that. Cultivate your patience as you would any skill. I learned that as ambassador to Spain when Seward was itching to invade Cuba. It took all my willpower to stay sane and keep smiling."

"Don't worry, General, we won't fire the first shot."

"Nor the second, either, Major."

~~~~~~~~~~

Jesus Ocampo, riding from the northeast with thirty-five men, also saw the great dust plume boiling up from the Salt River arroyo. He immediately signaled a quickening of pace and the vaquero troop plunged into the gloom of the shadowed river canyon.

The almost straight canyon made a two mile cut through the Sawtooth ridge. Ocampo's men made the passage in twenty minutes to find a battle in progress, on the salt flats side. Papi Sanchez was in his element, sweat streaming from beneath his upthrust sombrero, to run down his smiling, jowly cheeks. By now, Ybanez's men had begun to engage the defenders, trading long shots that forced the hide thieves to worry about fire from both their front and their rear.

"You are just in time for the charge, Señor Jesus!" called the old warrior. "I was about to give the signal to make the dust screen."

"Hold the signal!" shouted back Ocampo. "Dead, they are worth nothing."

"Bah!" fumed the older man, fighting his nervous mount. "If we kill them it will teach the Yanquis to leave us alone."

"We can teach their pockets a lesson, also. That it is too expensive to come on our land." Ocampo turned to his segundo, "Gregorio, find me a white flag. I would talk with those men."

"Better the red flag of death, Jefe. But I will find you a white one." The segundo rode off, yelling for one of his men with a white shirt to come forward.

"Now—" cried the steward to Papi Sanchez, "stop the firing—so that I can advance under the white flag!"

The old man shouted to his sons and lieutenants and they rode out to quiet the shooting.

"Ramon would go with you, Jefe," said Gregorio, coming back with a bare-torsoed rider who had a white shirt tied to his rifle. "He does not wish to lose his shirt. I told him he was fortunate not to have on white pantalones today."

The firing died, except for an occasional desultory shot from the wagons. Apparently the defenders were only too glad to save ammunition.

"Come then, Ramon," ordered Ocampo. "Let us see if these robbers respect the white flag." They headed their horses, at a walk, toward the overturned wagons.

"That's far enough, Señor!" came a shout from the barricade when they came within pistol range. "What do you want?"

"I wish to talk—as one merchant to another. Perhaps we can settle this matter more peacefully. Would you come out and parley with me—or are you afraid?"

"I ain't afraid, greaser! Not afraid to die here, too!"

"Come and talk before you say words that can not be taken back!" shouted Ocampo at the wagons.

A pair of horsemen emerged as a wagon tongue was pulled aside from the barricade. They came slowly—nervously checking to their flanks. The riders stopped twenty feet from Ocampo and his flag bearer.

"All right, Señor Ocampo," started Judd Payton, "Why the . . ."

"You know me?" interrupted the steward.

"Not personally. My scout here, Mr. Watson, says he knew you when he worked for the Army."

"Good, then you know that I am a man of my word. My promises, I keep. My threats—also I keep them. How many men do you still have alive?"

"That's for me to know, Ocampo. And for you to find out the hard way."

"The reason I ask, you stinking Yanqui thief, is to set a price for each man. A value on each live man in your robber band."

Payton looked at Smokey Watson and then brought his gaze back to Ocampo. "Are you talking ransom, Ocampo?"

"Together with parole," stated the steward.

"How much?" put in Watson.

"I would have to know how many persons we are talking about. This rancho is very large. Do you know I employ over one hundred twenty men in addition to dozens of women and children? Almost three hundred souls; and this is not a good year to sell cattle."

"You're saying that you need cash?" asked Payton.

"More than revenge—almost more than honor," said Ocampo, looking at Ramon, guiltily.

"How much for our lives?"

"Not only your lives. Also your wagons and animals. You could continue your rotten business—away from this rancho. You could still make money—from other ranches. Perhaps it would lessen my competition—who knows?"

"I repeat—how much?"

"The figure I am thinking about is 15,000 American dollars. In gold. No paper. Perhaps some silver."

"You must be loco. There's no way I could raise that kind of money," shot back Payton. "Those mules and wagons are rented. They're not mine. There is only seven of us left. With luck, I could raise seven thousand. That's a thousand apiece. That's the best I could do. So help me God."

"Then I hope He hears you, Señor Ladron. That is not enough—either for the rancho's needs or my own satisfaction and my men's honor. We leave to return under the red flag. That of no quarter, no surrender."

"Wait a minute, Señor Ocampo," reasoned Watson. "Let me talk to Mr. Payton." They rode out of earshot, where the scout argued with his boss. Finally Payton angrily assented and they returned to Ocampo's position.

"My scout thinks that I can raise money from the men, themselves. He says he's got almost 500 dollars he could throw in the pot. But again, there is no way we could raise fifteen thousand."

Ocampo turned to Ramon. Then he looked at the defender's barricade for long moments. Finally, he pulled his horse around to Payton and his scout.

"I have an fat old man back there. He is like a father to me. He has six sons here and several sons of those sons. If I say attack, he will charge with a smile on his fat face because he is a warrior who loves to fight. And he and the seventy men we have here will smash you. Run over and kill every one of you Yanqui thieves. For it is right. God said you must not steal—and He is at our side. But some of us, perhaps the son or grandson of old Sanchez, will die also.

"What price do I put on my men's lives? I will modify my demand—just this once, Señor. Thirteen thousand. No lower can I go in good conscience." He looked at Payton, his hard eyes showing his determination.

The boss hider turned to glare at his scout, angry at being put in this position. Smokey shrugged—to nod imperceptibly.

"Done—damn you!" spat Payton. "Now what?"

"You will return under escort to Tucson to raise the money. Your men will be confined, hospitably, at my headquarters ranch. You will return in two weeks with the money. If you are not back with the money we will execute one man each day at noon. We will do it the old way, as they did long ago to horse thieves. Your men will be ripped apart by horses.

"Now, Ramon, call in Papi Sanchez and the men."

There was grumbling among the men when they first learned that there would not be a battle, even when Ocampo said each vaquero here would receive twenty-five dollars from the ransom as bonus money. Money was good, they reasoned, but once spent could not be used around the many campfires as would the telling of a fine battle with the gringos. Those stories would last a lifetime.

The wagons were righted and the teams put to them. The Yankees, except for their leader, were bound at the wrists and loaded in the last wagon, the dusty one, for the trip to the rancho headquarters. At the last moment, Payton remembered that he needed authorization to get into the men's bank accounts, and paper had to be found. Pages were ripped from Uncle Walter's supply register and some of the hands had to be loosed for the prisoners to sign away their assets or promise to repay loans.

Then Judd Payton was made ready with a dead vaquero's fresher horse. Ocampo told his headquarters segundo, Gregorio, and the young vaquero, to accompany Payton. The young vaquero was to observe Payton, to see if he was sincerely attempting to raise the ransom. The youth was to report to Gregorio nightly, at a secret location, as to the day's happenings. If any harm came to the young vaquero; if he was made a hostage or otherwise detained, Gregorio was to immediately report the fact to Ocampo and all the prisoners would be killed, by the horses, immediately.

Just as Payton and his two mentors were about to ride south, Papi Sanchez came up, leading a horse which had a body strapped over its saddle. The old man gestured to his sons and the body was lifted from the saddle to be set on unsteady legs. It was Payton's grandson, Joey, dazed but alive from his spill from Uncle Walter's wagon. He was dragged before Payton as Ocampo watched with interest.

"This gringo cub states that he is the grandson of this ladron, my Jefe," growled old Sanchez. "I want this Yanqui thief to return with a piece of memory to help him not to forget his people—that we will most certainly kill if he abandons them. Come here, grandson of a thief!" He grabbed the boy's right ear in a strong, fat hand and in a flash, severed the ear from the youth's head. The grandson screamed in the grasp of the Sanchez sons, blood streaming down the side of his face, the earlobe imperfectly split, sticking out like a red stump.

The old warrior paid no attention to the sobbing boy. He was intent on piercing the upper cartilage of the ear with his big knife. Finally working a hole through it, he walked to his horse to unwrap a rawhide thong from his rifle scabbard. He passed the thong through the ear and knotted the ends with his stubby fingers. Finished, he handed the gory memento to yet another son, who jerked off Payton's hat to snare his neck in the thong's loop.

"Now, thief," chuckled Papi Sanchez, "Wherever you go— you have a piece of your grandson with you. Make sure you remember one thing, you gringo shit—that boy will die last. He will watch all his friends be torn apart, one by one. Sometimes a man does not come apart properly. Perhaps an arm or a leg pulls off—but the body still lives. Then we try again—and again—until it is finished. Remember this, Yanqui."

Ocampo, face flat before this brutality, waved Gregorio off—and the segundo pulled on Payton's reins to get him moving.

"Do you think he comes back, Jefe?" asked one of the Sanchez sons.

"I cannot say. But what I do know is that I want these prisoners and the wagons to return to the big ranch. I have work for those wagons and mules as long as we must feed them."

~~~~~~~~~~~

Opal was hungry. She had just returned from Tucson and was also saddle-sore and tired. But this matter had to be resolved first. It posed a threat to her leadership. She was now red-faced and furious, her green eyes flashing fiery hurt to any interloper.

"Who told you to send Cabot to Tucson?" she demanded.

"I did it on my own responsibility," Foote answered quietly into her tempest.

"You've no right to spend my money—damn you! It's too hard to get."

"I'll spend it—when necessary. Anyway, it worked, didn't it?"

"You've no right—I'm the boss here!" She lunged at him, out of control—hand raised to slap the insolence from his face.

He grabbed her swinging hand, pulling her to him, her bosom heaving against his wiry body. "I've every right to see you safe . . . you silly fool . . . I love you . . . that's why."

"You can't—I won't permit it."

"Too late, boss. All you can do is fire my butt." He swept her into an embrace, locking her hot form in his strong arms. She tried to evade his lips, but he tightened his grip, pinning her to his kiss—for a long moment before releasing her.

"Oh God, Hugh, what have you done?" she groaned.

"I kissed you, that's what—and gave you a squeeze for good measure."

"What have I done?"

"Kissed me back—very pleasant, too."

"I had such good intentions, Mr. Foote. Where did I go wrong? I fended you off—didn't I?" He moved too close again and she pushed him off.

"You still are—regular Miss Ice-Flow."

"I don't want love, Mr. Foote," she said, stepping back. "I want position . . . and security."

"Don't worry—you still have everything. I only kissed you," the foreman reminded her.

"You didn't mean it—what you said?"

"I meant it."

"And so did I—about security and a position of modest wealth."

"So what about us? I can't help how I feel toward you."

"That is why you're leaving, Mr. Foote."

"You are going to fire my butt, then. I said it as a joke."

"Here is my joke—now, Mr. Foote. Pack up. I'm transferring you to the Lazy J. Tell Mr. Thompson that he's the new foreman here—at ten dollars a month more. You—Sir Hugh—will take over his rocky domain."

CHAPTER 14

"Cap'n," called out Napoleon. "Whars you goings?"

"Follow me, Mr. Napoleon," Captain Cabot flung over his shoulder as his horse forced its way through the brushy side bank of the trail. "I am taking a slight detour in the interest of business."

"Monkey business, if you asks dis ole darky," complained the mule-borne lackey, plunging off the trail into the prickly bushes.

Forty-five minutes later found them crossing the underground section of the Puzzle River, a veritable jungle of willow and cottonwood which thrived on the hidden water course's moisture.

Cabot stopped to open his watch, nodding to himself in satisfaction. "Just a little more, Mr. Napoleon, and we'll head for the ranch and supper. I want to get up to those bushes there—on the other side of the farmers' road."

Once at the clump of brush halfway up the rise, Cabot pulled out the Colt rifle and adjusted its peep sight.

"You goings to shoots somebodies elses?" questioned the servant.

"Just one, Nappy. Must keep the Sauerkrauts angry, you know. It's good for business. With luck they will be coming right up to our tent soon, and it will be money in the bank. And talking about the Sauerkrauts, here they come. Our timing was perfect."

After the stinging session with Opal, Hugh Foote went for a long ride to allay his anger and remorse. Like most men faced with a matter of feminine paradoxicalness, he could find no answer, except to blame the woman's complexities or her simplicities. While unsatisfactory, it was at least an answer.

During this grave contemplation of the sorry state of his romance, he had his subconscious guide the rambling course of his horse and he gradually awoke to the fact that he and his horse were well past the Wilbur Ranch's borders. In fact, when he came out from the back of a brush strewn knoll, he saw that he was above the Puzzle River Road that the farmers had improved. He sat his horse, watching one of the farmers' wagons coming along this road, heading for the German colony.

It was a large manure wagon, making slow progress because of its load and flagging team. Two miniature figures rode the distant wagon, the driver listlessly slapping the reins on the plodding team. Suddenly, from an unnoticed clump of bushes lower on the hillside, came the report of a rifle, as the wagon's driver slumped in his seat, saved from a fall only by the actions of the passenger.

Then, from the gunsmoke-marked bushes, two riders broke through, riding fast for the track that wound around the knoll. Soon they were gone, as was the dust of their passage and the white plume of gunsmoke.

Hugh circled his horse to put the hill's crest between him and the stopped wagon. Just his head showed now, as he watched the passenger's frantic response. At last the passenger seemed to give up on the driver and laid the body below the seat. Then, taking the reins and the whip, the man urged the team on towards the German settlement.

"Good God," muttered Hugh Foote, "here I am riding around in a daze while Captain Cabot was shooting Germans.

Makes me sort of glad I'm not foreman here anymore." Shaking his head, he hauled his horse around towards Opal's ranch.

~~~~~~~~~~~~

The prisoners, all in manacles, were sent first in the Sweeneys' spring wagon that Skinner had hired for the occasion. As perversity would have it, the sheriff's jail rolls had recently been increased by unreconstructed Confederate sympathizers who had rioted and tried to ruin the Belle of the Union Saloon upon hearing that General Grant won the presidential election, the Belle of the Union being a Federal hangout. It always amazed Skinner how fervently patriotic were the men who had somehow missed the real battles of the War.

Happy Giles, the dour and dyspeptic jailer, had been prevailed upon to put in extra hours at the new jail, while all hands moved furniture, fittings and firearms from the old office to the brand-new brick building. Deputy Sam took upon himself the task of transferring the eternal flame, better known as the coffee-boiling stove. He successfully managed inadvertently-on-purpose to break six badly stained and chipped cups in the high cause of sanitation and social sensibility.

Finally, nothing was left in the suddenly vast vacancy of the old office except the huge and heavy safe. A salvaged relic of the Drovers' Rest fire—the old Drovers, by the way—not the edifice recently erected to the bacchanalian dreams of thirsty cowmen.

Deputy Sam had coerced the new Drovers owner to let him drag the huge fire-ravaged relic from beneath the charred timbers. It was discovered, after many days spent coaxing the huge rusted door open, that this vault was not really safe in case of fire, as a bushel basket of burnt currency bore witness. Deputy Sam, undeterred, continued his restoration. Now this thousand pound lump of garishly-painted metal sat in solemn solidity, daring all to attempt moving it.

"Let's try to walk it toward the door," suggested Skinner, taking a massive corner. "The trick is to lift it slightly off the floor." Sam looked at Cletus, who made the crazy-man sign, pointing his thick finger at their boss. They all heaved, mostly in unison, to no discernible effect.

"You're absolutely correct, mon sheriff," said Sam. "We're lifting it very slightly. Are you doing your share?"

"I have to watch out for my hernia," stated Skinner, with sudden medical sincerity. "Remember last year and that rock in my privy hole."

"How could we forget? I can still picture Crumbridge carrying you piggyback all over town."

"Wasn't all over town," corrected the sheriff. "I made Crumbridge stick to the back alleys. And I don't have him around anymore."

"How did you get this monster in here in the first place, Sam?" questioned Cletus, suddenly massaging his lower spine.

"Manny Ortiz owed me a favor. I asked him to move it from outside there, where I worked on it, into here."

"I will ask Manny to come over here and give us an estimate," declared Skinner pompously, while probing into his pelvic region, hoping not to find trouble. "This damn thing is just too heavy."

It took Manny a half-hour to arrive, complete with oxen, sledge and a pile of chains. Skinner explained the situation to the little Mexican, who looked at the iron cube with his head to one side, rather as a bird estimating a worm's underground portion.

"So how much, Manny? And don't forget old times' sake."

"Like when I go to jail for drunk, and you make me fix that no-good roof. Twenty dollars. Lots of work. Takes long time."

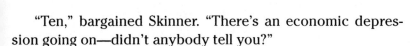

"Ten," bargained Skinner. "There's an economic depression going on—didn't anybody tell you?"

"Frijoles still cost the same. Fifteen—no lower. Take it or leave it."

"Manny, did anyone ever tell you that you caught on to our customs very quickly? I accept—fifteen."

"That's because I'm from Texas. We're smarter."

Manny called to his brother-in-law, who brought a chain into the room to snare the safe. Fifteen seconds later the oxen were dragging the safe out the door and onto the sledge. Ten minutes more and it stood in the new sheriff's office.

"Do I get extra for a fast job?" Manny asked the sheriff, who was fumbling through a desk drawer in search of a pay voucher.

"You made a dollar a minute, ain't that enough? I think you misled us on how hard a job it would be. I almost think it's fraudulent."

"Not in Texas," answered the little Mexican, grabbing the voucher from the sheriff. "In Texas, everything's fair." He rushed out the door, almost knocking over a bespectacled man who peered myopically around the office.

"Sheriff in?" the man asked shyly.

"That's me . . . Sheriff Skinner. Good law makes for a good town. Don't forget me next June at the polls."

"I came because of the shoes. You know—the shoes on that board at the newspaper office."

"Yes?"

"Well, I recognized one pair, the shiny black ones. Is there a reward?"

"Only the satisfaction of a citizen doing his duty for his town."

"No money? I could sure use some. Everybody told me go West and find success. I did, but my condition doesn't allow me to work underground, so I'm a clerk at the Lucky Strike. Don't make as good money as the miners, you know."

"About the shoes . . ." prompted the sheriff.

"Oh yeah. I recognized them from the Mine Association's doctor. His office, I mean. Dr. Dezaine had us breathing problem patients come in on Tuesdays and Fridays. That's how I recognized them."

"Someone there was wearing them?"

"Another patient. Actually he was a private patient. He had throat trouble. Scar tissue. Could only eat mush."

"And the man's name was . . . ?"

"Richard McFee. He said he was a former bartender. I was always fascinated by those shoes. So shiny. Just like ballroom slippers, except I never saw any—ballroom slippers, I mean. He never talked much when we was waiting. Hurt him to talk a lot, I think."

"And you can positively identify those shoes as belonging to Mr. McFee?"

"Oh sure. You see, one of the pearl buttons—they're imitation—I think—must have been replaced. It was sort of pinkish, while the others were all like silver. Grayish, you know."

"And that is how you recognized these shoes?"

"Will I have to repeat this in court?" said the clerk. "I'd hate to lose a day's pay. Can't spare the money, you see."

"I doubt it," soothed Skinner. "But I'm going to take you right over to the county attorney and have him get together with you to make up a statement about these shoes. I really want to thank you. You have been a big help."

"Maybe next time, you can have a reward. People could use it. There's a depression now, you know."

~~~~~~~~~~~~~

Paulie Vogelnester drove the wagon onto the community's square. At this point he cared not for reproach or reprimand from the elder. Groszvater was dead; he was sure of that. Paulie was of the farm and the field; he knew about death, though mostly of animals.

Alerted by his family to the manure wagon's presence, the elder flung back the door, vicious barbs ready to be loosed from the drawn bow of his tongue. The tear-streaked, misshapen head of Paulie stayed the shafts—something was not in order.

"It's Groszvater, Herr Kolb, he's dead," gasped the youth.

"He was an old man, my boy. We must expect things like this in life," placated the elder, coming down his front stairs. Then, he saw the shapeless body crammed under the seat—and the blood.

"Good God, boy, was he injured?" A crowd was collecting about the wagon, drawn as quickly as the green flies were to the manure load.

Paulie climbed down on the wagon wheel to pull Groszvater's body from beneath the seat. He stood in his awkward stance, Groszvater's frail body in his powerful arms. "He was shot, Herr Kolb. An hour from here. By a man on a horse and a man on a mule. What shall I do now?"

"There is no room at the church, with the newcomers now. Take your groszvater to the blacksmithy. Come, my boy, I will go with you."

Major Riemann caught up to the crowd at the smithy.

"What is this about the old man being shot?" he asked Paulie.

Paulie nodded dumbly and lifted his own arm to mutely describe the bullet's path. "A man on a horse and a man on a mule did it, Herr Major."

"Shall I assemble the company, Major?" It was Sgt. Major Klaus, pushing his belly into the conversation.

"No, but double the vedettes and guards tonight—and send a galloper to Green Falls for the sheriff. Tell him we will meet him at dawn, three miles from the settlement. I will have the boy with me—he saw where it happened. I will wait an hour there. If he does not come I will lead a party to catch the assassins. We farmers have ropes, too."

J. Peter Renfrew, the proprietor of Renfrew's House of Rugs, was the band's conductor because he could read notes and had played the piccolo in a Zouave band during the recent unpleasantness. Mike, though, was the undisputed leader of band—even though he played a field drum. Was not he the one that convinced the Mine Association not only to sponsor the miners' band, but also to build a bandstand right next to the Mine Association building?

The Association directors were a little surprised when Mike insisted that the bandstand occupy the sunny side of the building. But their cultural hunger overcame their good sense and they went along with the hotter side. They did bargain, though, that the instruments they were providing would remain the property of the Mine Association.

Today was the ensemble's first rehearsal, taking place on this pleasant Sunday afternoon. As J. Peter Renfrew looked over the dozen eager, but inept, musicians gathered before him, he gave a slight, involuntary shudder and an earnest prayer to any musically inclined saint.

The first piece of music before the band was "The Old Gray Mare," a piece picked for its simplicity and reliance on the rhythm section. This piece went fairly well, if you discounted wrong notes and a dragging pace. Griff, almost hidden behind the bass drum, had trouble seeing the conductor's beat. At least, that was his excuse. But surely he was loud, because nobody heard Harvey at work down below . . . beating a star-drill against the concrete floor of the vault.

"My God, Judah! What has happened? Why are you alone? Joey! Where's . . . ?"

Judd Payton waved a weary hand to silence his wife. "Joey's alive—at least for awhile. Which is more than I can say for your uncle."

"What happened?" she mumbled, suddenly shaking with shock.

"They caught us—that's what. Caught, cut up and hung out to dry."

"How? Why?"

"I been asking myself that—all the long way home. And that's the reason, I guess. The long way, I mean. We tried too much . . . a herd too far. It was my fault. I'm the one that gave the order. I got overconfident. It's all my fault. Like this . . ." He pulled the brown scrap of flesh from his shirt. "It's Joey's ear . . ." And he let out an anguished sigh.

"Are any of the others alive?" . . . Smokey?" The tears were coursing down her crevassed cheeks.

"Uncle Walter and Eddy Cox were killed before we took their damn ransom demand. If we didn't, we'd have been butchered. It was ten to one and they had all the advantages."

"What do mean, 'ransom'? Can we get Joey back?" She grabbed at the idea as a drowning man clutches a drifting plank.

"Not just Joey—everybody." He paused for an unneeded dramatic effect, or maybe in self-pity. "Thirteen thousand in coin . . . in two weeks, or . . ." he stopped, mute with help-lessness.

"Or what, Judah? Tell me, dammit! It's my grandson you're talking about!"

"They'll be ripped apart by horses," he groaned, unable to meet her eyes.

"Ripped apart—God, what savages," she moaned, clutching the porch rail for support.

"It's a savage country. We weren't exactly a traveling Bible show."

"Can you raise that much? That's an awful lot. It will bust us, won't it?"

"Won't do us no good—that's for sure. But I'm gonna try my best. But now I gotta eat and sleep or I won't do anybody any good. And a big glass of whiskey. Maybe it will help me forget how stupid I was."

"It wasn't all your fault, Judah. You said this plan, the empty boxes and all, was Smokey's idea."

"That's what he gets paid for, Mother. He's got a million loco schemes and plans. It was my job to sort out the workable from the crazy. And I screwed up. That's it—plain and simple—and I got to live with it."

"Come, Judah, I'll get you ham and eggs. And I've got fresh corn muffins. You get cleaned up while I get it on the table. Stop feeling sorry for yourself and get going. I want my Joey back, ear or no ear."

~~~~~~~~~~~~

The two vaqueros had made a dry, fireless camp. Earlier they had left Payton, circling to foil detection and doubling back to a hideout that viewed their back trail.

Gregorio, wise in the ways of war, had a small supply of jerked beef and parched corn in his saddlebag. This they ate. Hopefully, the young vaquero could purchase some food on the next day with the few coins that the old segundo gave him. They also set snares braided from their horses' hairs. They were patient—they would wait and see what this Yanqui would do.

~~~~~~~~~~~~

Skinner and Cletus were tardy the next morning because they had gone out of their way to enlist Poke Blaney and his dog pack. Poke was a dried up old-timer who was small in stature and strong in odor—his own, that is. He had deer dogs, rabbit dogs, bear dogs, lion dogs and man dogs. For this expedition he brought a couple of each plus a couple that would fight anything that walked or swam. He called these his alligator dogs and their yellow eyes and scarred hides seemed to guarantee their bravery.

Major Riemann was angry and impatient with the sheriff's lateness. He was accompanied by Sgt. Kiefer and eight mounted infantrymen, their long rifles slung across their backs. Also with the major was Paulie Vogelnester, clinging inexpertly to an unfamiliar horse known more for a good disposition than for speed.

"Show the Sheriff, Paulie," snapped Riemann, "where the wagon was when Groszvater was shot." Paulie struggled his horse around and kicked it down the road twenty yards toward the colony.

"Here," he pointed at a particular spot, marked by a pile of horse apples from yesterday.

"And where did you think the shot came from?" asked Riemann, in German. Paulie pointed up the hillside.

"The smoke came from those bushes and Groszvater was dead."

Skinner caught the "Groszvater" and the "tot" words and waited for Riemann to translate the rest. Then, the whole party rode up the hill. Skinner held them back short of the bushes, telling Poke to sic his dogs on any scent in the clump. Poke got down to cuff his pack into a semblance of sniffing.

"Looks like old Poke is a better smeller than those dogs of his," laughed Cletus. "Now if he can just bark, we could turn the dogs loose and keep him."

Just then the old man *did* almost bark, yelling "Gaa! Gaa!" at the rooting dogs. The dogs took off like a shot, racing and yelping up a narrow animal track that zigzagged up and around the hillock.

"I wish to follow!" shouted Riemann.

"Only under my orders!" yelled back the sheriff, following the dogs.

"I agree—for now!" bellowed the major, signalling his men to follow. Paulie trailed the armed men, holding desperately to the pommel and his horse's mane.

The dogs were more than eager, quickly distancing them-selves from the human pack, who were confined to a narrow trail. For a mile they led their master and the sheriff's party at a mad pace, then suddenly, at a wide spot in a dry wash shaded by stunted trees, the pack stopped—to mill around in confusion.

Poke Blaney rode his horse knee-deep into the circling dogs. "Rosie Honey," he called lovingly, "what's the matter?" A bitch detached herself from the swirl to leap up, whining and barking some secret message to her sweating master.

"Go get it, Rosie-Girl, go on get it, baby," he cajoled. The dog frantically circled Blaney's horse a time or two and then clawed it's way up the hillside to retrieve a bottle half-hidden in the brush.

"Good dog, Rosie, fetch it here, sweetheart," called the old man, sliding off his horse like a teenager. The dog swag-gered back through the pack to lay the treasure at Blaney's feet. Blaney took a sniff and handed the bottle to Skinner, with the comment that there was still dregs of whiskey left in the bottle.

"Not dregs, Mr. Blaney," said Skinner. "Expensive whiskey like this has no dregs—traces perhaps, but never dregs." He handed the flat bottle to Cletus with the admonition to keep it intact, as evidence.

"Looks like our killer's got good taste," commented Cletus. "Sure ain't a down-at-the-heels cowman."

Major Riemann pushed forward to intercept the sheriff. "My sergeant tells me that the men we follow seem to be the same pair that bombed our diversion flume—on the dam we are working on."

"What bombing?" asked Skinner. "I don't know of any bombing."

"It was not reported," the major answered lamely. "We did not want to make an incident of the matter. But we traced two riders, one on a horse and the other on a mule, to the Double Bit Ranch. In fact, we were fired upon."

"Fired upon? —When was this?"

"About two weeks ago, maybe less. The shot was fired in warning, I believe, but it served its purpose. Fortunately, the ranch owner, Miss Wilbur, came out and we talked it out. Not very satisfactorily. We think the two men worked for her, but our proof wasn't very solid—just the hoofprints."

"And that was two weeks or so ago. And now this killing that doesn't make sense."

"It would make sense if you wanted to start a range war—cattlemen against the settlers. That's how I see it, anyway," explained Riemann. "We can't let this continue. That's why these armed men are here. We mean business."

"You were in the War, weren't you? I can tell by the look of your men."

"Yes—under General Schurz. First in Rosencranz's Division and then his Army. That's how I got this," said Riemann, holding out his stiff elbow. "I was a major of infantry. Now, I'm just an engineer trying to build an irrigation system."

"Me, too," answered the sheriff. "Only I was a major in the Army of the Potomac and now I'm a mining town sheriff trying to keep the peace. Well—let's see where trail leads and for God's sake, if we're fired on, don't go starting a damn war. Let me handle it—understand? No shooting."

CHAPTER 15

After breakfast Hugh Foote came up to the headquarters ranch house to make his goodbyes and also to see Opal again.

Opal was the ice queen this morning. Stiff in stance and set in face. The green eyes were lidded now, dampening the flame that lay within. "Rather like a reptile trapped in the sun," thought Foote.

"Please hurry Mr. Thompson along, Mr. Foote," she lectured. "I don't want to be long without a foreman here."

"Bert is capable of running things until Thompson comes," observed the displaced foreman. "I had hoped to get together with old Blackjack and go over any problems. Every ranch is different, you know."

"I can imagine so, Mr. Foote. But you are being employed as an experienced foreman. As such, I should think, you can slip right into Mr. Thompson's role. Of course, if you don't feel up to the assignment, I am sure I can find someone who is."

"Miss Wilbur," grinned Foote, "let me compliment you. Somehow you never disappoint me when it comes to an unfeeling approach to life. Now, I've got to rush off to my exile. But I have one little bit of advice for you."

"If it clears your conscience, Mr. Foote, please give it and go."

"I'll keep it short, boss lady. Keep your eye on your regulator."

"That means?"

"Keep your eye on your regulator. Some enforcers are like cats. You never own them—you just feed them."

"And this cat will scratch me?"

"I'll say no more, Miss Opal. I guess I talked too much yesterday—didn't I?"

"Indeed, Mr. Foote, you did. Godspeed to your craggy canyon. Grow me some fat cattle."

Foote left, swinging up agilely on his horse to trot away from the ranch. Opal watched from the window, seeing his figure get smaller as the distance lengthened. Finally the figure dropped behind a rise and was gone—gone to the Palisade Valley.

"You's a fool, girl," rebuked Aunt Polly. "That was a good man. Good look'n', too."

"You talk too much," scolded Opal. "Didn't I tell you that?"

"Alls the time, chile. I jes doan pays no mind."

~~~~~~~~~~~~

"I hear you wuz looking for me," began the plump, disheveled man as he came into the new sheriff's office. "I had to go to Santa Fe, needed to get some money. I generally don't spend much, except on my inventions. But the automatic door opener cost me a bundle. All the pulleys had to be machined special. And the treadles are cast-iron—had to be done in Tucson. Cost a fortune. So I had to go." He stopped for breath, giving Sam a chance to jump into the conversation.

"Mr. Tittle, I believe?"

"That's me. Handyman, inventor and lately—traveler."

"We've been looking for you, Mr. Tittle."

"It's not about my accelerated axe, is it? That wasn't my fault. The stop had a casting flaw in it. That's why it let the axe head fly off. Besides—that was a very old horse. Swaybacked real bad. Teeth like tusks, you know."

"No," Sam said patiently. "We had a few questions to ask you."

"Can't imagine what you'd ask me."

"It's about a job you did for Mrs. Robinson. Do you remember working for her?"

"Oh yeah, did a lot of jobs for her. Tough to get money from her, though. Always put me off."

"Now, Mr. Tittle," went on Sam, "I want you to remember back awhile, when you were doing odd jobs for her. Do you remember stacking stove wood in her woodshed?"

"She had me over there to beat her rugs. Had to run my lines from the house to the shed. My special tackle, I mean. Snatches up a big heavy rug like it was a dishcloth. It's all in the multiple blocks. For every pound I pull, the energy is increased twelvefold. Just a matter of leverage."

"But she asked you to stack stove wood, too?"

"Yeah. I recall. It was late—close to six—and I was coiling up the tackle and putting it on my cart. That's my special cart with double bushings on the wheels, one inside the other. Reduces friction fifty percent over regular axle arrangements that . . ."

"Come back to that evening, please, Mr. Tittle," interrupted Sam.

"Right. Where . . . oh yeah. I wuz hot and tired—but clients are hard to get, so I did it."

"Did what?"

"Restacked the damn wood. She had it throwed all over, out front of the woodshed. Said she wuz getting rid of a rat's nest in the woodpile. Tore half the pile down. I had to restack it just so."

"What do you mean?"

"That damn box of her late husband's journals she was saving. He was a sea captain and was supposed to have written a lot of journals about the seal trade and the Russians. Saving them for her son; he lives in Boston. Said she wanted to hide the books from thieves."

"And you stacked the wood around the box?"

"Yeah—so you couldn't tell a box wuz under the wood. And do you know the worst part?"

"What was that?" yawned Sam, heading for the coffee pot.

"She hung me up again—for my pay. She had a bill of close to a hundred bucks when finally she paid me off. All that painting and the flagstone walks, about three months worth, off and on. But then I have to go all the way to Sante Fe to trade in those stamps. I made her pay for the trip. Didn't seem right to . . ."

"What!" yelled Sam. "What stamps?"

"Her husband's old stamps. Twenty-five sheets of them. Course there wuz only five or six on each sheet. There wuz one that wuz worth $22.50. Would you believe that?"

"You don't say. Did you sell all of them?"

"Not easily, let me tell you. Would have got more but the dealer said those half stamps weren't worth much since they were cut in two. But I got enough to pay me, plus the expenses. There wuz $37 left over and I wuz going to bring that to her when I found out you wanted to see me. If you're done with me, I'll go and give it to her. Got to keep my clients happy, you know."

"I'd appreciate it, Mr. Tittle, if you'd hold off on that," answered Sam. "And now, I'm going to take you over to the County Attorney's office. I want you to tell him exactly what you just told me."

"Right now?—I wuz getting hungry."

"How about a jelly bun and a cup of good coffee for now?"

"You got no snails kind of sweet rolls? I like them better."

"Afraid not—but these are blackberry jelly buns."

~~~~~~~~~~~~~~

Napoleon was washing clothes in a borrowed wash boiler from the main house. He was sitting on a camp stool, absently pushing a peeled stick into the ballooning fabrics. Now and then he would have to push a piece of firewood under the raised boiler. Napoleon enjoyed—if any portion of a servant's work could be thought pleasant—boiling clothes. It brought back childhood memories of bygone times, when he prattled about while his mother labored as a washerwoman at Stonespring, the Cabot's South Carolina plantation.

When he was six, though, the old Mrs. Cabot, the captain's grandmother, came down one day from the big house and questioned him to determine his aptitude. He must have passed, for he was taken up to the big house to be washed and dressed in fine clothes and given the name of Napoleon. He was to be the boy servant and companion to Master Freddy, Captain Cabot's father. He had learned his letters right alongside young Master Freddy. When Freddy was daydreaming or sassy to the tutor, it was young Napoleon who had his ears boxed. He slept in the big house and ate in the big house; he was a house Negro.

At eighteen, Master Freddy went to England to complete his studies and Napoleon was turned into a footman. He was schooled to serve, to shine silver, to set the great tables and to perform all the hundred duties of a house servant. By the time Master Freddy came back from England six years later, Napoleon was second footman and in training for old Severus' position as butler.

That ambition was killed with the deaths of Master Freddy and his imported Scottish wife in a steamboat blast. Suddenly the infant heir to the Cabot line assumed a primary importance to the dowager grandmother. Napoleon would be valet, counselor and confidant to young Master Claybourne. When war came, an older Clay Cabot presided over the growing list of family shipping lost to the Federals. At last, down to just a pair of fast blockade runners, Claybourne took the sea command of one of them. Six times he made the run from Nassau—sneaking into Charleston the Whitworth guns, the ammunition and all the many essentials that kept the dying Confederacy gasping—to continue the fight.

Then, with the other ship lost, his sole surviving ship was bottled up tightly by the blockade. Cabot volunteered his seamen as infantry. A company come too late to battle— and to wreck. Near dead, Captain Cabot was dragged from the frozen mire by Napoleon, parasites eating at his insides and fever crazing his brain.

Stonespring was a stark pile of blackened timbers, leveled either by Sherman or his disciples when Napoleon took him back, pushing him in a wheeled barrow down neglected, rutted roads. They went past weed-filled fields, ever-conscious of being prey for the roving bands of deserters, hungry freed slaves or plundering Union cavalry that scoured the starving land.

The dowager grandmother lived on, under the generosity of some of her former slaves. She was almost blind, with sticks for limbs and a mind that only meshed in the past. Napoleon had nursed the captain and helped to dig the secreted yams and weave the fish traps that sustained them.

It took a year before Cabot could ride a horse. But there was no horse. The newly-freed citizens had only themselves to pull their plow. Cabot and Napoleon left and walked west; Cabot presuming on his gentleman's status for handouts and meals. Finally came a job as purser on a Natchez steamboat with Napoleon as a steward and waiter. That gave them a stake—a horse, a rifle and a goal—never to go hungry again. Cabot became a hired gun and he was good at the profession; cool, calculating, patient and attentive to his duty.

Suddenly Napoleon's reverie was dashed by the noise of the dogs. If there was anything he remembered from his youth, before the big house, it was the sound of the dogs— after a runaway slave. The yelping packs would send shivers of fear through his little body and he would crawl into the warm fastness of his mother's arms. Now, those very dogs were coming after him. Right now.

He ran from his washing, shouting to the resting Cabot that the dogs had seen set on him. Cabot, at first skeptical, jumped to his feet to hop about, pulling on his boots.

"Get my rifle, Nappy," he said coldly. "And yours, too, with my spare cylinders." Then he strapped on the two heavy .40 caliber French pistols that he very seldom found a need to wear.

"Remember to shoot low at the dogs. High shots are lost, but the low ones will bounce and give you a second chance to hit something."

"They'll be mens coming with thems, Cap'n," groaned Napoleon. "Ain' gonna likes you shootin' theys doags."

"I handle them, Mr. Napoleon," Cabot ordered. "Just you stand behind me and to my left side."

Once they were outside the tent, the pack was louder. Then they saw the scrambling hounds, crazy with the lust of the pack, running straight for the tent.

When the dogs were a hundred yards from them, Cabot gave the order to fire. Cabot's Colt rifle cylinder held five shots, of which three found their mark, tumbling the four-legged victims with the deadly impact. Napoleon got off half a dozen rounds—killing one and wounding another, who continued dragging itself toward the shooters.

Poke Blaney was the first rider following the pack. He screamed at his remaining dogs to come back, though only Rosie and one other older and wiser dog returned from the fray. By now, seeing the destruction of his pack, old Poke was crazy with anger and heartbreak.

"Stay back, Blaney, we'll handle this!" shouted Skinner, furiously motioning to Cletus to take another angle of approach to the shooters. Cletus waved his affirmation, changing course away from Skinner.

"Cease firing!" yelled Skinner, waving his hat towards the pair, who were busily reloading. Then, the white man put his rifle to his shoulder and calmly killed the remaining dogs, those that had continued the attack. Now the black was ready and shot the wounded dog.

"Stop! Stop! I'm the sheriff," Skinner shouted at the men. The white man reloaded, fired at Cletus, hitting the big deputy's dun, dropping it straddle-legged, tossing Cletus over its head into a heap.

Skinner snapped three quick pistol shots at the firers and saw them duck behind the tent. Skinner pulled at his horse and dashed towards Cletus, who had rolled to his knees and was shaking his head groggily. Seeing the sheriff racing up to rescue him, Cletus scrambled over to his downed horse and pulled the Winchester free. The sheriff stuck out an elbow and Cletus grabbed at it and swung up behind him.

"God, Skinner!" panted Cletus into the sheriff's ear. "I'm too damn old for this stuff."

"You're too old?" giggled Skinner. "You almost tore my arm out of the socket." Fortunately, they were not fired upon during their flight.

~~~~~~~~~~~~~

Before the shooting began, Opal's headquarters ranch had been quiet. Before he left, Hugh Foote had declared this day to be a mend and fix day. Several of the hands had gone to Green Falls the night before and were the worse for John Barleycorn. Later on that day they were to sort over the remuda, resetting shoes and doctoring the lame.

There was also a considerable group of riders still at the headquarters ranch, having just come off the cattle drive. They were the extra men from the other ranches who would go home the next day.

When the firing began, this large bunch of hands quickly threw off the effects of the previous evening and went for their weapons, ready to have it out with Indians or rustlers— they didn't much care.

The Wilbur men streamed from bunkhouse, cookhouse and corral, running to defend the main ranch house. Major Riemann's mounted infantry came under their fire as soon as they were seen. By now, Cabot and Napoleon had moved and were firing from the cover of the buggy parked to the rear of Opal's house. Two of Riemann's men were hit, one shot off his horse, before the major could organize a retreat back to Cabot's tent and the cottonwoods' protection.

Skinner dashed over to Riemann's position behind the sparse line of trees. "I gotta stop this mess!" he shouted at the major, pushing Cletus off the shared horse.

"Try this," barked Riemann, handing Skinner an almost white handkerchief.

"Thanks," grunted the sheriff, pulling Gertie from behind the tree to trot toward the main house, frantically waving the handkerchief. He had not gone fifty yards from the trees when a fusillade of shots was fired at him, dropping him from the saddle as his horse turned to gallop back to the tree line.

"Goddam it all, anyway!" yelled Cletus at Riemann. "Tell them men of yours to give me some cover and I'll try to drag him in."

The major shouted something in German and his men, except for the horseholders, poured out a torrent of fire from their long-barreled Spencers, allowing Cletus to run out and drag in the sheriff. Skinner's face was a bloody mask from a wound that had laid open his forehead and scalp.

"We gotta get out of here," snapped Cletus. "And quick. There must be thirty people out there shooting at us. At least the sheriff's breathing."

"They killed my dogs. You should arrest them," sobbed Poke Blaney—tear streams furrowing his dirty face.

"I have a man down out there—Gustav Knapp. I'm afraid we'll have to leave him," said Riemann. "Can you manage the sheriff on his horse?"

"I'll have to. You pass him up to me," answered the deputy, getting on Skinner's horse. Riemann growled to the dog handler to help him and they passed the inert and bleeding sheriff to Cletus, who finally arranged Skinner into a folded position over the saddle while he rode behind him on the sheriff's bedroll.

After a brief conference with his sergeant, the major nodded to Cletus and Blaney to move out along with the wounded settler, whose hurt arm was stuffed into his shirt for support.

Cletus had gone about a quarter-mile down the track when he heard four volleys of fire from the sergeant's rear guard, which was answered randomly by the ranchers. Riemann came up quickly behind Cletus, slowing when he was alongside.

"I'm going on ahead to pick out a place for Sgt. Kiefer to set up a roadblock. The ranchers will be after us like bees on a bear. We've got to sting them a little to slow them down."

Just then Paulie Vogelnester came bumping up the trail, fear showing in his misshapen face. "I heard the guns," he stammered. "I didn't know what to do."

"Help these hurt men, Paulie, to get back to the settlement. Our soldiers will protect you," soothed the major. "Now—go on, kick that old horse of yours to get you off this hill." Paulie could only thump properly with his left foot, but it did the trick. The horse gave a startled look, to tear off down the trail after the wounded men and Blaney with his pair of dogs.

~~~~~~~~~~

The major's comparison to aroused bees was quite apt. After the first shocked surprise at the outbreak of the firing,

Bert Massey rallied one force to drive off the attackers, while mounting another group of riders to either make a flanking charge or a running pursuit. This second force, he commanded personally.

Cabot and Napoleon had retreated to the solidness of the main house, where Opal rushed out to the porch to frantically question them.

"Captain Cabot, sir! Would you have the decency to tell me what the hell is happening? Is it Indians?"

"No, Miss Wilbur, it's the Sauerkrauts. I think it's just a quick raid, though. Only a dozen riders. Probably thought to catch us off guard—after the trail herd business."

"Has anyone been hurt, Captain?" She was trying to look around the house toward the cottonwoods.

"Most certainly, Miss Opal. Mr. Napoleon and I are earning our pay—and the bonuses. Say—you don't give extra for dogs, do you? Killed a whole pack of them."

Opal saw Bert and his troop come trotting up and waved him over. "Where are you taking those men, Mr. Massey?"

"We're gonna make them sod-busters sorry they ever thought about coming here," he threatened, savaging his horse's mouth to control its excitement.

"Don't pursue them past my property, Mr. Massey," cautioned Opal. "I don't want legal trouble."

"This here's Arizona. We got ways of handling these damn nesters—Col. Colt and his six jurors."

"Shut your mouth, you over-fed fool," spat out Opal venomously, "and listen to me. Turn back when you get to my boundary. Disobey me, Mr. Massey, and you're through here. Not exiled like your friend, Mr. Foote, but fired. Do you hear me, Mr. Massey? Or should you stay behind to wash the trail dirt out of those big ears?"

Massey's face turned brick red as he fought to control himself under Opal's tongue-lashing. "I heard," he said angrily, "and so did all these other men. Now they know the bitch they work for."

"Just pray that you still have a job when you return here, Mr. Massey, you impertinent clown."

"You through, or are you gonna chew my butt all damn day? Someone has to have some balls around here, lady—to chase those bastards."

"Go, Mr. Massey. And try to find some brains to go along with your masculine parts," shot back Opal, her green eyes turned fiery with wrath.

Sgt. Kiefer positioned his two men in places with good firing avenues, then found one for himself. He looked to his rear where the horseholder waited, quieting the horses, and planned his escape route. They were to fire on any pursuers, driving them back in confusion with the fire from their repeating rifles, then to continue firing at any exposed frontal attackers.

The next part was the tricky portion, which took guts and experience. At some time the pursuers would try to flank the roadblock. When Sgt. Kiefer felt this threat developing, he was to signal the retirement and they would dash to their mounts to retreat quickly. Then they would gallop down the trail to leap-frog Major Riemann and the other half of the mounted infantry, who were to have another roadblock set up.

Major Riemann warned that they would be able to pull this stunt only once, or hopefully twice, before the pursuers would get wise and split off a force to loop around overland through the rough in hopes of trapping the retiring settlers.

The sound of approaching horses roused the sergeant and his men. Kiefer waved his men down, pointing exaggeratedly at his own rifle to tell his companions to hold their fire—until he fired. Then he waited, rear sight at 50 yards, thinking of Gustav Knapp, his man slain at the ranch yard ambush.

Suddenly the pursuers were in the trail—a big red-faced rider leading the pounding troop. "Ka-pow"—went Kiefer's Spencer and the big rider tumbled sidewards off the trail. Almost immediately the others fired and a horse was down and another rider caved in down onto his horse's mane. Again they fired, frantically working the trigger guards to level more of the big coppercased shells into their rifle breeches. Then, the riders were gone, turned tail and galloping for their lives. Three men were down, crumpled into baggy heaps in the narrow trail. Those three—plus the big leader, were blasted down the slope and several wounded. The hurt horse had threshed about until it, too, slid down the slope into the rocks of the gully.

The pursuers tried another frontal charge after firing a swarm of shots at the defenders. But the charge turned out to be without enthusiasm. One quick volley from Kiefer's men turned the cowmen about quickly and lost them another horse and rider.

A desultory sniping began and Kiefer instructed his men to lay low and not give away their positions. After a while, the sergeant saw half a dozen men rush off the upper trail to plunge into the brush of the gully. He counted to sixty slowly, estimating the flankers' progress.

"Aufsteigen Sie!" yelled Kiefer, motioning to his men, and they raced around the trail's turning to jump on their waiting horses and retire down the trail.

CHAPTER 16

They were an unhappy lot when Sally Lewis, the top hand from the Running W, brought them back to the main house. They had lost five of their number and were angry—at themselves and their enemy.

For once in her life Opal was too shocked for wrath. The five bodies of her men lay out in a row in front of her porch, along with the remains of the German settler killed near the captain's tent. Six dead men, plus several badly wounded, and for what—or why? She had no ready answers. She had no instructions, either, when Sally came to her to ask what they should do next.

He held his hat in his rough, battered hands, uncertain whether to push this she-cat of a woman. Instead, he just chewed—and rotated his hat—waiting for her to make up a seemingly blank mind.

"You's gots to gets dat sheriff man, chile," broke in Aunt Polly. "All dis killin's gots to stops."

"Should I send a rider to Green Falls, ma'am?" asked Sally, unsure of his ground.

"Yes—do that, Mr. Lewis," agreed Opal. "Tell him we have been attacked by riders from the German settlement. The killings should be investigated and people arrested."

"I'll send somebody right away, ma'am . . . and one other thing, ma'am . . ."

"What's that, Mr. Lewis?"

"We oughta move them men someplace. They'll start smelling in that hot sun after a while."

"Then, see to it, Mr. Lewis. You'll be my acting foreman here until Mr. Thompson comes. Do your best for my ranch and you won't regret it."

"Yes'm, I sure will," said the cowman, as he left the office. As he left, Captain Cabot entered, evidently having washed the gunpowder stains from his face and hands and changed to a clean shirt.

"Is he gone to send for more men—from your other ranches?" he asked.

"No, he's sending a rider to get the sheriff," answered Opal flatly.

"Fat lot of good that will do," scoffed Beatrice Cole, swinging into the office on her crutches. "I saw the sheriff go down as your men fired on him. And he was waving a white handkerchief, too."

"How do you know?" said Cabot. "You weren't there."

"Maybe my legs aren't much good, Captain," she sneered, making the title sound like something dirty. "But my eyes are just fine and I saw the whole thing from my window. That deputy—the big mountain man—run out and dragged the sheriff back behind those trees."

"You mean we—I mean our men—shot the sheriff?" asked Opal, appalled.

"Sure did, honey," confirmed the secretary. "If this is a range war, we sure started off wrong. Six dead men and maybe a sheriff, too."

~~~~~~~~~~~~

"Wake up, sir. Please, rouse yourself," said the voice from out there in the haze. "Please, you need to take nourishment. Come now, let me adjust your pillows." A strong arm raised the dense cocoon which was Skinner's head to cram a lump under it. Skinner tried staring hard with his right eye, attempting to pierce the fog.

"One right eye," he giggled to himself, insanely. "Never had more than one right eye. Sure would look funny with two right eyes. Unless, of course I had two left eyes, too. Two left eyes, too. How many eyes is that, Skinner? Motion carried— the eyes have it." The haze closed in tighter and the sheriff fell unconscious once more.

"I thought he was coming to his senses, Onkel Pfaff," said the pretty Miss Kolb, "but he is not ready."

"Sometimes it takes a longer time than others," said the old man, nodding at his wisdom. "We can only wait."

"I will say a prayer for him. He must be a good man; didn't the major say to take special care of him? What happened to his friend, that big man with the leather clothes?"

"I saw him saying goodbye to the major and your father. He is going back to the city they call Green Falls. He seemed to be very upset about this sheriff's injury. I told him it takes time to heal a bad knock on the head, and I saw a lot of them in the regiment. Now, let us see how Fritz is doing with his bad arm. It must be time for the salt soaks."

"Can you do that yourself, Onkel? I want to visit with Hugo. He is on guard until midnight in the church tower."

"Aren't you afraid of taking him from his duty? The lookout guard is very important to our safety. You should not distract him with your silly talk."

"We don't have silly talk, Onkel," she replied, taking off her nurse's apron. "Mr. Dunkelmehl is very intelligent. We talk of worldly things, like what people should do for each other, besides, the major has tripled the guard tonight. There will be two others with Hugo to look for the American raiders."

"Then by all means—go visit with your Hugo, but only for a few minutes or the others will be jealous." The old man watched the girl flying down the hall to see her man friend.

"Ach—love. Be careful, Herr Dunkelmehl. I think you're about to get caught."

~~~~~~~~~~~~~~

Hugh Foote got to the Lazy J just in time for dinner to have been cleared by the cook. But upon learning of Hugh's new assignment the cook was only too happy to fry up some beef and warm up the beans.

No, Blackjack had left for the northern end of the valley right after breakfast. Wouldn't be back until supper—maybe even late supper. Had no idea what Blackjack was doing there. Blackjack didn't tell him about cows and he didn't bother Blackjack about cooking—'cept when he ran out of supplies, which is maybe day after tomorrow.

"Guess I'll groom my horse and wait," said Hugh, pushing the plate back to the cook.

Blackjack was late, tired and ill-tempered, most certainly after he heard that he would have to move to the D B. "God damn it, I've busted my ass on this rocky son of a bitch of a ranch. Now—when I finally get over the hump, figgering I can let up a little bit—I'm yanked off to the damn D B to pull your chestnuts out of the fire. Damm—it's just not fair."

"Get mad at me all you want, Blackjack," chuckled Hugh. "I've been chewed out by an expert—and she's waiting to gnaw on you. Wants you to come, quick. Are you leaving tonight?"

"Hell no, I ain't. Tomorrow I'm telling you about this ranch. It don't look like much, but it's my pride and joy. Only thing in this damn world I got to be proud of. I got no money, no wife or kids, no disgusting vices—except this damn ranch . . . It was my whole life. And now . . . ."

"Let's have a drink and get you some supper," broke in Hugh. "And you can tell me about this rocky empire of yours."

"Not mine—Opal Wilbur's. Tell you the truth, Hugh, if she don't like me taking a day with you, she can just fire my ass.

I'm too damn old to kowtow to some young girl who don't know one end of a cow from another. My niece's husband struck it rich in San Francisco, digging coal. I'll go work for him leading mules, so help me."

"Hold on, Blackjack," said Hugh. "Don't desert the troops so quick. Give her a try. She needs help, you know."

"It's true, then, looks like."

"What's true?"

"That you've been—what do you call it? . . . Smitten—that's the word. You're smitten with her. I heard about it."

"Smitten is a good word for it. She was the smitter and I was the smittee, or was it smotee? Anyhow, she did the whipping—on me. And here I am, Sir Hugh—exiled from the castle to the rocky highlands. Should have brought a kilt and a Claymore sword."

"Well, let me start by telling you about the hands," replied Blackjack. "Now—this cook," he lowered his voice, "he's always trying to tell me how to run this ranch. Always worming information out of me. A hell of a gossip who . . ."

<hr>

"Is the sheriff back yet?" Sam woke with a start. The long hours had overcome the strong coffee to lull him into an impromptu nap. His chair crashed down on all four legs with a thump. Aaron Rose was there, the county attorney.

"Nope," said Sam dumbly, getting up for more coffee. "He's still gone. Just me and Happy to hold down the fort, and I'm stuck with the saloon patrol at night, too."

"I wanted to see him on this Robinson case. I believe we've got enough evidence to go to trial. I can either put up the charges myself or send off to the grand jury in Tucson for the indictment. I had hoped to get the sheriff's opinion."

"I can tell you what he'd say," replied Sam, handing the prosecutor a cup of coffee in a new, immaculate white cup, complete with a handle.

"What's that?" said the attorney, taking a sip. "God, that's awful—too strong and too many eggshells in it."

"Shows what lawyers know about coffee. That's Rebel coffee. Robert E. Lee drank it—just like that."

"No wonder he was always pictured on a horse, or sitting down; his legs had dissolved—from the coffee."

"I refuse to get drawn into a discussion on the art of coffee brewing," intoned Sam piously. "As I was about to say before a certain attorney libeled my talent, Sheriff Skinner would tell you to get the grand jury to hand down an indictment, due to the lady's gender."

"She does indeed, Deputy, have a gender."

"And with it," said Sam, paying no attention, "a big measure of built-in sympathy. A widow-woman, driven by the cruel world to take in boarders to eke out a poor living, and so forth. I can just hear that eloquent brother of yours. Now that I think on it, he must be the smart twin and you the ugly one."

"Now who's libeling who? I'll take your advice on indictments—but not coffee making. I'll have the papers on tomorrow's stage. I should have something back in a week or so. Are you prepared to jail the woman? You can't very well put her upstairs. Murder is no bail, you know. You could, of course . . ."

The noisy arrival of Cletus stopped the attorney in midsentence. Cletus had been in the saddle for the last thirty-two hours; had been thrown violently from his shot dead horse; and now was in no mood to be trifled with by friend or foe.

"The sheriff's been shot," he rasped from a parched throat, pouring a half-cup of coffee from the muddy bottom of the pot. "The shot creased his head pretty bad. He was still out when I left him."

"My word, what happened?" asked Attorney Rose.

"Not really sure," went on Cletus. "Oh Lordy, this coffee is just wonderful. We had Poke Blaney's dogs with us, you know. They picked up the trail and we took off following them dogs. After 'bout an hour, maybe more, we came up to the Wilbur Ranch. This one's the D B, they tell me. There we wuz—dogs all hellbent for leather with the scent, the ranch house coming up when all of sudden we're under fire and the dogs being knocked off right and left.

"We hightails it back to behind some trees and the bullets are flying, let me tell you. The sheriff, he says this has got to stop, so he borrows a white handkerchief and rides out waving it and yelling that he's the sheriff, when he gets hit— knocked right out of the saddle. Well—to make a long story short, we grabbed the sheriff and skedaddled out of there."

"Anybody else hurt?" asked Sam, in his soft voice that seemed to fall in place whenever danger developed.

"One of the Germans killed and one with a bad wing—and my horse killed. I rode the sheriff's back and it's two hops from dead. One thing, though; those Germans set up an ambush for the D B people, covering our retreat. According to them, they emptied three or four saddles there. They got those long Spencers and evidently know how to use them. I tell you, Sam—it's a helluva mess."

"Is it a range war—or what?" questioned Sam.

"I'm damned if I know. We went up there looking into that German's killing and all of a sudden thirty men are shooting at us."

"So—where's the sheriff now?"

"He's in a sort of hospital they got in the German village. There's an old man who claims he was a medical orderly in some German regiment back in the old country. He did a pretty fair job of sewing the sheriff up and bandaging him. Says head blows take a long time to heal. I'd feel better if he were here, with Doc Seevers, but I think the trip would kill him—at least, right now."

"What are you going to do now, Cletus?" asked the attorney.

"I'm going to take care of the sheriff's horse and then myself. I'm black and blue all over from that fall. Then I'm going to sleep for twelve hours straight and have steak and eggs for breakfast. Now—the big question is what are you two defenders of the county going to do?"

"Do?" echoed Sam, "I'm going over and dump this in the lap of our esteemed Chairman of the County Commissioners and watch him squirm like a Mississippi eel."

~~~~~~~~~~~

"One more of those rehearsals, Mike," said Harvey, "and the holes are ready for the nitro."

"Same time, same place next Sunday," replied Mike. "We're gonna start practicing Christmas stuff for our Christmas concert."

"Is there a lot of drumbeating in carols?" Harvey asked, reaching for the salt.

"In some—not all," Mike admitted. "But we're not much good at the soft stuff. Too thin on the melody, if you know what I mean."

"'E means that the clod on that cornet is 'orrible," complained Griff. "Not a bit o' talent at all."

"Stick to the thumping and we're all gonna be rich."

"The new uniforms will be here by Christmas," Mike continued. "Blue with gray cuffs and trousers with red piping. Renfrew wanted Zouave uniforms but the Association wouldn't go for it; cost too much. These should look good. They got silver buttons, 'count of the Silver Association. I'd sure like to see us in them."

"We could wait a bit, Mike," said Griff. "Couldn't we? At least 'til after Christmas, 'n' the concert?"

"Might have to," confessed Mike. "I don't have the transport yet. I was afraid to find someone too early—and have him blab about it to everybody.

~~~~~~~~~~~

To his credit, a page most lightly used, Judd Payton was not a man to let the grass grow under his feet. After a long sleep, two good meals and a change of underwear, he was off to raise the ransom. The first stop was the bank that held the note on his ranch. He renegotiated the mortgage, giving the banker a murderous nine percent, three percent over his previous note. He walked out of the bank with a promise of eight thousand dollars in gold coin.

The remaining five thousand came slower, and took more time, fighting distraught relatives and money interests on behalf of his men. All told he raised $2,150 there. $2,850 to go. On the third day he coerced the mule contractor into advancing $500.00, to be paid back by an increased rental. The wagon company point-blank refused to give a dime and even threatened suit and or mayhem if the wagons were not returned intact.

The tannery representative gave him $1,000 after making him sign an exclusive contract for two years at $1.50 a hide less than market, which with stolen hides was already less than what legitimate hides brought.

With $1,250 remaining to be raised, he was forced to go, hat in hand, to the moneylenders of the underworld. For $1,250 he was forced to pay $2,000 at the end of thirty days, or $4,000 at the end of sixty days. There would be no extension after that; only retribution—to his wife, for starters.

The last day was spent gathering the specie, assisted by two of his ranch hands who prominently displayed shotguns and pistols. This day he was conscious of the young vaquero, always at a distance, watching the efforts involved in loading the mule which carried the ransom.

"You're going now?" objected his wife. "It'll be dark in another few hours. Why not start out early in the morning, after a good night's rest?"

"I'd dearly love to, mother," he explained. "But I'm afraid for the money. I've been dealing with some bad characters lately. I'm afraid they'll try to rob me before I ever get started. Got to go while the going's good."

"What has this world come to? A person isn't even safe in their own house. Is there no law or respect anymore?"

"It's the times, Mother. Too many criminals—looking for any easy buck. Too lazy to work honestly for it, like their folks' generation had to do. Make up some food. There will be three of us for two days. I still got room on the mule for a bag of grub and a couple of canteens."

The sun was low on his left when Judd left his ranch with the mule in tow and accompanied by his two shotgun-toting guards.

"Hey, Judd," called one of his guards, "we're being followed. Did you know that?"

"How many of them, Louie?"

"Only one—I guess. He's not trying to hide or nothing. Just following along behind."

Then Judd saw the smoke, up ahead, to the right. A thin black tendril rising at an angle in the evening wind.

"I think it's time for you boys to be turning back. That smoke up there is my welcoming party—waiting for me. Same as that rider that's trailing us."

"We could ambush that one behind, maybe, if you wanted us to. Benny's got that long rifle of his with him," suggested the man named Louie.

"Forget it. Anything happen to him and they'll kill the boys. Just go on back and hope everything works out all right." After saying their goodbyes and good-lucks, the two guards left. Judd turned in his saddle, making sure they left the young vaquero untouched, which they did, making a wide detour of his position. Then Judd turned his horse and the led mule toward the smoke.

"You mean you tell me that you're not going to avenge the Sauerkraut's raid?" Captain Cabot was angry at the outcome of the morning's battle. He had not anticipated a bloody repulse of the pursuing cowboys and was attempting to bluster his way out of any responsibility in the matter.

"I have not made up my mind as yet, Captain," conceded Opal. "An unthinking reaction could cause us more lives. I certainly learned that today. Can you explain why the sheriff was shot? According to Beatrice, he was waving a white handkerchief and was riding forward at a trot. I can't understand why he was fired upon."

"Obviously you've never been in a battle or gunfight," he said in a superior voice. "In the heat of battle, anything can happen. It's a combination of fear and loose trigger fingers."

"But a man under a flag of truce? Surely . . ."

"Not a real flag of truce, Miss Wilbur. A small handkerchief. Not a four foot white flag—with a bugler playing for a parley."

"So—you did see him waving the handkerchief?" asked Opal.

"Only from hearsay," said Cabot, covering his slip hastily. "I reiterate—an attack is the best defense. Every day will see those Germans more able to defend themselves, or raid us again."

"Just what would you advise, Captain Cabot?"

"Blow up their dam. Do our best to run them off before the authorities get involved and enforce a peaceful resolution.

"You make *peaceful* sound rather odious, Captain."

"It is, or will be if they take that water away from you."

"And how much of a force would this take?" she questioned. "More than we have here now?"

"It would need another thirty men—to hit them at the dam and their settlement at the same time. Also, we would need explosives to destroy the dam. Should send for that right away."

"If I took thirty more men from the ranches, it would strip them to the bone. It would leave only two or three at each ranch. We would be wide open in case of trouble. Suppose those hide thieves would come back, or Indians, even rustlers?"

"In war," he stated, as if lecturing to a child, "the good general has to have the nerve to take the chance—to seize an opportunity."

"Thank you, Captain Cabot, for your counsel. I will think on your suggestions. By the way—who would lead this assault on the German colony?"

"I cannot think of anyone better qualified than myself, Miss Wilbur. Of course, my salary would have to be increased if I took on the added responsibility of sixty or seventy men. It takes a large measure of coordination, you can be sure."

"I'll keep that in mind. Good evening, Captain."

Aunt Polly came back into the office after showing Cabot out. "That mans sho likes to stir up troubles, doan he, chile?"

"Yes, Aunt Polly," Opal said. Then, thinking aloud, she went on, "Why do I feel like a Desdemona asking advice from Iago?"

"I doan knows 'bouts them folks. I onlys wish Mister Foote wuz heres."

"Well, he's not and this is my problem. I am going to solve it my way. Not Captain Cabot's way, or Hugh Foote's way—but my way, by myself."

"What way's thats, chile?"

"That is one of my problems—I don't know, yet."

~~~~~~~~~~~~

"Has his wife been told yet?" asked Mosely, fastening on something solid in this unexpected flood of catastrophe.

"Not yet," admitted Sam. "Figured it was more important to set the wheels in motion. I'll go there next."

"And you feel this is the beginning of a range war?"

"I'm not really sure, Captain," shrugged Sam. "But I think we should treat it like it is. For certain, we don't have enough people to police something this big. Look what happened to the sheriff. They ran right over him and Cletus. If those settlers weren't there, Lord knows what would have happened. Evidently those Germans were pretty good."

"Well, they should be, they've adopted the Green Falls as their hat badges on their uni . . . that's it, Mr. Deputy! That's our way out—without having to hire fifty deputies for a posse."

"What's that, Captain?"

"Technically, that immigrant bunch out there is under the control of the Territorial Militia. They did that in order to get those repeating rifles when we had that Indian scare last year. I had to sign an affidavit to the effect that the troop, or company or whatever they call themselves, was not inimical to the interest of the Federal Republic—and here's the grabber, as the hunter said when he pushed the bear into the trap. They all had to swear an oath to defend the Constitution and the laws of the Territory of Arizona."

"So what do we need to convince them that they are taking orders from us?" said Sam, amazed at the machinations of the political mind.

"An order from the governor . . . better yet, hand delivered by a higher ranking militia officer than that fellow Ramer out there."

"Major Riemann," corrected Sam. "Cletus said he was a major during the hostilities."

"Might have been a major then, but now he's a first lieutenant in the militia. I'll get a galloper off to the telegraph at Tucson. You go see Mrs. Skinner. Tell her if she wants to go to her husband that the county will pay for a hired buggy to take her there. You can make out the voucher yourself."

"Cletus wants to know—what about his dead horse? He wants to buy another as soon as possible."

"I need two estimates from professional horse traders as to the worth of his old horse, plus a report on how it was killed in line of duty. Also remind him that the county pays the rough broke price, not a schooled price, and the estimates should show that. Then I'll bring it up to the full board for a vote."

"What's he supposed to do until then—walk?"

"Sarcasm doesn't suit a public servant, Mr. Deputy. He may rent one until he gets our voucher. Hopefully, he recovered his saddle—or it will be recovered at a later date."

Gen took the news of her husband's wounding with tight-lipped stoicism. "I'll ask Mr. Hansen to drive me out there tomorrow, first thing. He'll need small clothes, I'm sure, and his shaving things. Do you think I should take him a robe and slippers? His robe is not in very good condition, he's always burning holes in it with his smoking. Oh my—I think I should sit for a moment." She groped, ashen-faced, for a chair.

"You just relax, Mrs. Skinner. I'll go see Mr. Ames about a buggy for you for tomorrow. The sheriff is a strong man. I'm sure he'll be just fine, after some rest." As Sam left her she was sitting stock-still on her small cherry wood rocker, staring dumbly into space.

CHAPTER 17

The pain woke Hugo Dunkelmehl—both the hurt from his ankle and the discomfort of a full bladder.

"Onkel Pfaff," he tried to call through the graveled throat. "Help me up. I need to relieve myself."

"So—you're awake, are you?" said the old man, shuffling into the sunlit room.

"Help me get off this bed, old man, before I burst."

"No, I will get a vessel for you, and you must stay in the bed and off the foot for the first week," he commanded, reaching into the bed stand for a pottery chamber pot.

"The foot hurts," complained the new Dunkelmehl. "The bindings are too tight."

"That is the swelling. Soon that will lessen and the ankle will feel better. Are you hungry? I have soup on my stove. And after you eat, I will give you another powder for the pain."

"No," Hugo stated with bad grace. "Just water, and give me the powder now."

Finished with the urinal, he handed it back to Onkel Pfaff, who vanished to somewhere else in the small hospital.

"Oh, God," thought Hugo, "why do you cripple me now—just as everything was going good?" It was all Eva's fault, he told himself as he positioned the hurt foot back on the pillow. After her visit with him last evening he had escorted her down the precipitous stairs from the church tower. At the middle landing, he had turned to kiss her. Certainly not an unnatural thing for a man to do with a girl as attractive as Eva.

And delight of delights, she had reciprocated, kissing him back. After a minute of mutually pleasant kissing, he had become emboldened sufficiently to tenderly grasp her straining bodice. This produced, not the melting of her defenses before his aching ardor, but a startled gasp and a shove from both of her two strong arms.

Off the landing lurched the ardent suitor, reaching for the railing that was suddenly unattainable. Halfway down the staircase he found enough treads to do a little dance before slipping and sliding down the steps to the unyielding door at the bottom.

The corporal of the guard was roused, and Hugo was borne into the little hospital of Onkel Pfaff, who had glared sleepily at the hurt ankle. The blacksmith had to be sent for and an ungainly right-angled brace of wrought iron made to support the rapidly swelling limb. Then the hapless lover was lifted onto a bed, and Onkel Pfaff gave him several powders to help him sleep.

"That is three patients in one day. If I get another, I'll have to give up my own bed," the old man boasted to the corporal. "At least all the noise did not bother the other man in the room."

"You mean that sheriff?" asked the corporal.

"Yes, it's his head, you know. Nothing seems to rouse him."

~~~~~~~~~~~~

Opal awoke from a restless night, promising herself to make a decision about the altercation with the settlers. That was how she was referring to the gunbattle; an altercation. She would have breakfast and coffee—then she would make up her mind, logically.

Breakfast came and was finished. Sally Lewis arrived, looking for orders. "We've gone ahead and dug holes for the bodies, Miss Wilbur. Up under that knoll, it's softer up there. We was figuring on burying them in about an hour. We're just going to paint their names on some rocks for now. Later on you can have real headboards made up."

"I'll come up there in an hour for the burial, Mr. Lewis. Is someone going to say anything over them?"

"The men would like you to, Ma'am, seeing as Hugh Foote isn't here . . . an—anymore."

"I'll find something to read; an hour, then."

"One more thing, Miss Wilbur." Sally was embarrassed, his normally cool gaze now wasted on the edges of the worn carpet.

"Yes?"

"The boys are wondering if they would be going back to their regular ranches—or do you still want them to stay here?"

"I will tell them at the burial. Is that soon enough, Mr. Lewis—for my homesick hands?"

The blue eyes came off the carpet—to pierce hers. "No sense getting riled, ma'am. We take your pay—and give you our best . . . those men up there gave you their lives."

"I need not be reminded, Mr. Lewis. You may leave now." Sally turned and walked out wordlessly.

"You sure handled that in the worst possible way, Opal," observed Beatrice Cole, swiveling her chair around to confront her employer.

"You just put your nose back in those books, Beatrice. This is my problem and I'm going to solve it."

"You better hurry up and solve it cheap, lady. You got a hundred dollars a day worth of ranch hands out there just spitting and whittling, not making you a dime."

"Shut up, Beatrice, I don't need you harping on me."

"You need Hugh Foote, Opal—that's what you need," retorted the bookkeeper, turning her chair away from the angry Opal.

~~~~~~~~~~~~

The leaders of the colony had gathered for a council of war. For once, under the urgency of the moment, there was no bickering or posturing. This was a time to close ranks, which the settlers did with Germanic thoroughness.

All agreed that there were two places to defend; the village, with its houses, shops and barns, and the dam—their hope for the future. Some of their crops, especially the maturing grains, could be destroyed, but farmers were well used to lost crops, they could be replanted.

Work on the dam and the irrigation flumes would suffer with the loss of workers to guard duties. Major Riemann had drawn up a defense plan that called for ten men and the Gatling gun to defend the village. The young ladies' squad, now captained by the elder and his older daughter, would back this force up. Certain houses on the village's outer perimeter would have their shutters loopholed, and other barriers would be erected to prevent attacking horsemen from charging between the buildings of the village.

The Gatling gun was to be manhandled to the church tower where it would be set on a swiveling mount of the blacksmith's design.

Two mounted vedettes would be employed on the far bank of the river, roughly a mile from the village, out towards the ranchers' domains. At night an additional roving mounted patrol would operate there and the vedettes would be pulled back across the river to prevent any accidental encounter.

The dam's defense though, according to the major, would be more complicated, due to unwieldy nature of the dam and its surroundings. A dam, instructed the major, is much like a bridge. The best way to defend a bridge is to establish dual strong-points at one or both ends of the bridge; sufficiently far apart from each other to create a devastating crossfire on any attacker who tried to penetrate the defense zone.

Entrance to the bridge deck or—in this case—the dam's crest, should be blocked with the fire-resistant materials.

Additionally, stated the major, to the groans of the council members, the upstream face of the dam should be protected against drifting torpedoes by a log and chain boom placed about 100 yards from the dam itself. This boom had to be guarded also, day and night.

Riemann let his lecture sink into the members' minds for a moment, then added the bad news. "But here, gentlemen," he continued, "we have a situation where our dam is dominated by the cliffs on each end of the dam. If we built a redoubt at the end of the dam, it would be lower than the cliff and would be useless if an enemy controlled the heights, firing into the strong-point.

"We must, in our case," he pointed out, "secure the cliff with a strong-point that can control not only access to the dam, but the river and the dam itself."

"What type of strong-point, Major, are you talking about?" asked Fenstermacher.

"A wooden, two-story fort with some type of glacis to protect it. Two towers would be better, though, as they could mutually defend each other."

"And how much work would this fort take?" said old Damm, feeling tired already.

"I could only guess," admitted Riemann. "We would only have fifty men or so, when the guards are taken out."

"You're an engineer, Major Riemann," rasped the elder. "You are used to making estimates."

"With thirty men and the mule-drawn scrapers, the glacis could be excavated and the spoils used to raise an earthen flat-topped pyramid eight to ten feet high and ten feet square at the top. We could set three piers on each side as we raise the pyramid. Those piers would support a notched log, ten foot square, one-story redoubt, with a mud roof on split poles."

"So how many days?...Or is it weeks?" It was Fenstermacher again.

"One day for the glacis and earth pyramid. Another day for the erection of the blockhouse. That's if we can set twenty men working on the timbers the first day. We would need those eight pier timbers within the first three hours of the first day. And then on the third day, if we are allowed that much time, we could construct the boom, arm the glacis with sharpened poles and improve the trail to the redoubt."

"Fifty men, three days." Damm nodded his leonine head. "It sounds worth it—to protect a dam we have worked on for a year."

"It is after midnight, now," said the elder, rising to his feet wearily. "What time do you want the workers to be ready, Major?"

"Five . . . no, make it five-thirty. They should assemble with their weapons. I'll have Sgt. Major Klaus ready to issue ammunition, which they will keep with them, at least until the emergency is over."

The council members left, saying they would pass the word on to the rest of the village. Elder Kolb reached out a bony hand to stop Riemann. "Just one moment, please, Major. I have one more small problem to solve."

"Quickly please, Elder—it's late." Riemann had put in a very long day.

"This will only take a minute. It's about Paulie Vogelnester. What with the grandfather killed, it breaks up the team that brought in the fertilizer. Right now, with this trouble, I don't have anyone to replace the old man. And with the shooting, I think it's wise to cancel the manure trips. Too inviting a target, I'm afraid."

"Yes." Riemann was very patient—and very tired.

"So we have Paulie with no work. Is there any way you can use him at the dam?"

"He's good with animals, isn't he?"

"Excellent—almost a kinship—poor lad."

"He can help the miners with that flume tunnel. They can use him to lead that donkey back and forth—dumping the earth. The Schmidt brothers—tell him to go to work with them. Now can I go, Herr Elder? Five o'clock comes very early."

The hands were circled about the open graves; actually in more of an ellipse than a circle—quiet, not joking or skylarking in their usual way. Opal had walked up the half-mile hill from the main house. Cabot was the only man on a horse, which stood quietly, except to twitch at the flies.

Opal walked through the ring of somber men to take her place at the center of the short row of graves. She saw that a blanket-wrapped form lay at the bottom of each hole and silently thanked Sally Lewis for helping her through this ordeal.

"A few months ago," she stated, "I did not know any of you. I didn't know much about Wilbur Ranches, either. But I am learning. You men—and our dead in these graves have helped me to learn. Bert Massey was always there when I needed him. Roy Jones was there when I needed him after the hide thieves struck. The others they were there when the ranch needed them. And they died—doing their job. And I thank them. They gave me and this ranch the greatest gift of loyalty a man has— his life. And they gave it, unafraid and courageous.

"We come here to this lonely place, not to mourn their deaths, for which we are truly sorry, but to celebrate their arisen lives. Not in this shabby burial ground—but in the glorious beauty and bounty of God's heaven. In the palace of Almighty God—where every man is a risen saint. Where every hurt or hate is healed and forgiven. Please, dear Lord, accept these, your children—we pray you, into heaven— washing away their sins in the tears of our prayers and entreaties. We ask this in Our Lord's name and in the name of Jesus. Amen.

"Sally! Please have every man put a handful of Arizona dirt in each grave." She stood, stiff and silent, as the men filed past the graves, throwing their handfuls onto the lumpy remains of their comrades. When the last man finished, she followed—throwing her handful of Wilbur Ranch on the resting place of her dead warriors.

When she was through she returned to her center position. She turned to her men, chin up, beautiful face shining with the inner fire of determination.

"Mr. Lewis and Captain Cabot have asked me what we should do? And I'm sure you are asking what we will do? I'll tell you what we will do. We will fight!" She shouted it out loudly, hoarsely and purposefully.

She had expected a cheer. Had even hoped for a real huzza, like she read that the troops would give to their favorite general. The men took her challenge quietly. A few nodded, a few shook their heads, but for the most part they took her pledge of war gravely; which she had to admit was their right, for they were her soldiers. They had just witnessed the result of fighting, here in this rocky graveyard.

She tried to retrieve the moment. "Go back to the bunkhouse, men. You will have your instructions soon . . . and as of now, you're on fighting wages—double pay." That brought a ragged cheer, at which Opal smiled at her own naivete. Money works better, sometimes, than exhortations of honor.

Cabot and Sally Lewis were at the main house, waiting for her orders.

"Capt. Cabot, go purchase your explosives. Also take a draft from Mrs. Cole to use for enlistment bonuses for new hands. Twenty-five or thirty would be fine. Just so they'll fight. Also bring back more weapons and ammunition. And strong spirits—fighting men need more than coffee. And Beatrice has a list of supplies—food, mostly—to be shipped to us immediately, by fast freighter. If you can find a doctor of some kind, it would be most helpful."

"It sounds like you're finally declaring war, Miss Wilbur." Capt. Cabot was congratulating her, opening the closed ranks of soldiery to her. Opal was leery of being bronzed too early in her military career and chose to ignore his compliment.

"I want you back, Captain, by the evening of the third day. We march on the fourth. See that you are present. You had better leave now. You have much to do."

With Cabot gone she gave instructions to Lewis to have the ranches stripped of men and to increase the remuda. She also wanted scouts sent out to obtain information about the enemy and warn of possible attacks.

Sally suggested a light, hit-and-run raid the next night, aimed at keeping the enemy on edge. She agreed to an eight man force that would not get tied down in any prolonged fight. She wanted a quick slash—and then a faster retreat.

"Who needs Hugh Foote?" she told herself. She was doing just fine.

~~~~~~~~~~

The two vaqueros leading Judd Payton, the old segundo and the younger one from Agua Mala, set a wicked pace across the high desert, parching the animals and punishing the riders. By the time Lago Verde was reached the horses were stumbling and the mule needed constant whipping to achieve any movement.

At Lago Verde the saddles and the specie packs were strapped to four fresh horses. Then, after a quickly downed tortilla and a pint of tepid coffee, the grim-faced old segundo led them north, around the algae-hued lake and through the saucer-shaped hills to the main rancho.

They arrived in the purple shadows of twilight, suddenly riding into the smells of woodsmoke, garlic and cooking chili pepper and the dung of animals and men.

Ocampo came out on the long veranda to meet them, dressed comfortably in the white pantaloons and the sandals of a peasant; only the elegant cut of a dove-gray silk shirt marking him as a lord.

He wasted no time on pleasantries. "You have the ransom? All of it?" he questioned, throwing out his short cigar in an arc of fire into the gloom.

"It's all there." Payton was too exhausted to dismount. "All thirteen thousand. How are my men?"

"Getting fat and lazy on my hospitality. They have been introduced to the mysteries of pulque. They will not be able to travel until tomorrow; by which time I expect the wagons and the animals to have returned."

This brought Payton off his horse, limping up to the long porch. "You mean they're off somewhere?" It was easy to be peevish at the end of a long, hurtful ride.

"Certainly," replied the steward, the dusk not quite masking his smug expression. "You do not think I would feed all those mules for nothing. No—I sent them with some of my men to cut the cedar posts for the new wire we will buy with your money. All the way from your State of Pennsylvania. Those big wagons were a god-send to us."

"I just hope you haven't injured those wagons. They don't belong to me and I'm charged for every little thing that gets broken."

"Please, Señor Ladron, do not try my patience. For thirteen thousand dollars you get your men and equipment back. Not my goodwill. If you ever come again here, I will kill you like I would a bug on the wall. Now—I will count your money and then you can go to your men. Take advantage of my hospitality; it is the last you will get from this rancho."

~~~~~~~~~~~

Genevieve Skinner got to the immigrant colony at noon with Mr. Hansen, the carpenter friend of the family, doing the buggy driving. They had been stopped by a rider guarding the road. A language problem ensued, but was solved by old Hansen using his full command of six German words and a considerable skill in pantomime. They were allowed to continue on their journey after the confusion was cleared.

The colony's village was not a scene of ordered streets and scrubbed front stoops this day. A block and tackle had been erected in the bell tower of the church and a horse was busy pulling up timbers to the shouts of a half-dozen men. Several farm wagons and a large manure wagon were being chained together to make a barrier between two barns, while a group of boys were busy taking down shutters to bore loop-holes in them.

The elder had his younger daughter show Mrs. Skinner to the hospital while Mr. Hansen saw to the needs of the rented horse.

"He's in this room," the buxom girl told Mrs. Skinner in heavily accented English. "My man friend is in the other bed. He hurt his ankle last night while on guard duty. Your man has not roused from his stupor. Perhaps you could be talking to him, making him wake up."

"Sylvester, it's me—Genevieve," said a familiar voice from out there in the haze. "Wake up, and talk to me."

"Thank God, at last somebody that can speak reasonably good English," squeaked the person in Skinner's head. "Tell her to come back later, you want to sleep now. She's always bothering you lately, since Martha has died."

"Martha's dead," muttered the sheriff, his cracked lips barely moving, talking as if in a dream.

"Yes, Sylvester," whispered Gen, clutching his brown hand, which still had traces of dried blood under the nails and in the cracks of the cuticles. "Yes—she's in heaven, Sylvester. But I want you to come back to me. Do you hear me, Sylvester? Tell me that you hear me."

"For God's sake, Skinner," squeaked the voice inside his head. "Tell her you hear her. Then, maybe she'll let us alone. Go ahead, dummy, tell her."

"I hear, woman." The sheriff sounded like a tired boy with a hoarse voice.

"I'll just sit here with you, Sylvester. You sleep some more, and then we'll have some nice broth. It smells very good. Can you smell it, too, Sylvester?"

"Can we smell it? Tell her it's been stinking up the place for the last month."

"A month," repeated Skinner. "Smells."

"No, Sylvester, you can't sleep for a month. Just a little while and it's broth time."

"My God, Skinner, how could you have married such a nag?"

"You're profane," thought Skinner. "Did I ever tell you that?" Then, he drifted off, exhausted—into the blackness.

CHAPTER 18

"There's a lady to see you, Mr. Gomper." It was Mrs. Trent, who was substituting in the jewelry department until the new jeweler would arrive.

"What lady?" grumbled the merchant, holding his finger on a doubtful entry in the sales ledger.

"A Mrs. Robinson. Her file packet, in the safe, had a note pinned to it saying . . ."

"Yes, I know, Mrs. Trent. I want to handle her transaction personally. I'll be right out. Tell her—nicely—to wait."

"I am always polite, Mr. Gomper," replied Mrs. Trent, haughtily making a snicking sound through her too-long teeth. She turned on her heel, the shot in her skirt hem striking the door frame noisily as if to emphasize her politeness.

"Now, what do I do?" Gomper asked himself. "Skinner wants me to stall this woman along. Why am I always getting involved in matters like this? I'm supposed to be running a department store, not some clandestine spy business." He came out of his office smiling, to greet Mrs. Robinson, who definitely was not smiling—scowling was more like it.

"Its been much, much too long, Mr. Gomper. I realize that your jeweler was killed, but this delay is bordering on the absurd. Perhaps I should just take my diamond back and we shall forget about the whole thing—at least with your store."

"Now, now, Mrs. Robinson, we value your trade. You are one of our best customers." Gomper was trying the placating approach.

"Then why should I be kept waiting? It's been a long time since your jeweler was killed. You are treating me very ill—I can assure you."

Gomper switched to the groveling mode. "You are so right, Mrs. Robinson. I extend my deepest apologies. As soon as the stone is in the new setting, I will personally deliver it, myself—in a new velvet-lined box, compliments of the store."

"The new setting is here? How long has it been here, if I may be allowed to ask?"

"Not long," admitted Gomper. "A week, maybe a few days longer."

"A week!" Customers in other departments turned to note the disturbance. Gomper's countenance turned as red as his nose had been for the last ten years. "I want that diamond and the new setting right now. I'll pay you what your charges are at the moment, and send it off to Tucson on tomorrow's stage. Please get the items for me, immediately."

"Mrs. Robinson, I can't." Gomper suddenly looked guilty. He stammered, "It's . . . it's . . . ah, tied up, legally. The Sheriff, you know." Inspiration hit him—suddenly. "It's about Mr. Armstead's accounts. There are grievous discrepancies, you know." He lowered his voice confidentially. "We're trying to hush it up—bad for business, you know." His palms were sweating and felt like Lady MacBeth's hands—sweating blood. "Please—this will all be resolved when the new jeweler comes in a few days and takes a professional inventory for the probate."

"I don't know." She was uncertain of her ground. The legal term had cooled her anger, abruptly. Caution had set in. "You're sure the diamond is all right?"

Gomper had the look of the reprieved. "I give you my word, madam. Your stone is safe in my vault—just waiting to be set."

"Could I see the setting?" she asked—timidly now.

"Most certainly. Mrs. Trent," he called to the sales lady, "please show Mrs. Robinson the fine setting that came in and then make sure to lock up her items in the safe. Can't be too careful—can we, Mrs. Robinson?"

Mrs. Robinson nodded absentmindedly. She was busy trying to figure out what was going on here.

~~~~~~~~~~~~~~

Judd Payton and his roughly-used band of hide thieves were forced to make camp at Lago Verde. They had been escorted by a dozen vaqueros, again under the command of the old segundo, Gregorio. Uncle Walter's wrecked chuck wagon had been cut down to a two-wheeled cart and now carried the band's weapons. This patched-up cart was driven and guarded by Ocampo's men. The weapons would not be turned over until the hide thieves were off the ranchero's land.

The normally big, strong mules were worn-out by overly long days and too little grain. Now they were balking, refusing to proceed beyond their endurance. Only the smell of water had gotten them to Lago Verde. They would, mule-headedly, go no further—voluntarily.

"This is your damn fault!" Judd Payton railed at Gregorio. "You worked these poor animals until they practically got the blind staggers. When's the last time you gave them a ration of grain? Go ahead—ask him," he told Felipe, one of his drivers, who was doing the translating.

"They had no grain," admitted the segundo. "And the grass, what there was in the mountains, was poor. Generally when we work mules, we stop at noon and turn loose the hobbled mules for several hours. The same at night. We stop early to let the mules graze. This last trip, with your mules they did not have the time. The jefe was more concerned with the poles." He offered up an elaborate shrug and a show of empty hands to reinforce this last statement.

"So how do we leave this ranch if the mules aren't fed?" Judd Payton was beside himself with frustration.

Another shrug—this time with a smile for such a simple-minded Yanqui. "We must find food for them, Señor Ladron, what else? Tomorrow we will take the mules to the west side of the lake. There, wild grass grows in the shallows and I will take one thousand pounds of corn from the storehouse here. In two days the mules will be sufficiently revived to get you to Tucson."

"You have that much corn here?" Payton was pleasantly surprised.

"It is hidden in the hills for a time of ill fortune. This is a great rancho, señor. We are prepared. Even for ladrons."

Smokey Watson was sympathetic that night. "A few extra days ain't gonna kill us. Just so's we get back in one piece."

"Every day lost is killing us, Smokey," complained Payton. "I've only got thirty days to pay back those lousy crooks. After that—well, it's too late by then. I'll lose everything. They might even take it out on the wife."

"It's that bad?" Watson had never seen Payton so distressed. "Give us five or six days, back in Tucson, to refit and get fresh mules. Then we can be on the road. How much do you need to pay off the gamblers?"

"Two thousand cash—no excuses—within . . . twenty-seven days now. It's going to be real tight, Smokey."

"Two hundred hides would do it—pay them off. Then you've got more time to pay off the bank loans."

"We won't have time for a decent scout." Payton was playing devil's advocate against the scout's confidence.

"Don't really need one. That Wilbur Ranch we hit last, they'll never expect a return visit so quick."

"Would we take the same route?"

"Why not? It worked like a charm last time, didn't it? Leave Tucson at nightfall, cross the Puzzle at first light. Then you and the wagons can hole up while I find out where the herd is."

"You make it sound easy, Smokey. You're a born optimist. Just so we don't stub our toe again. Joey's running out of ears."

~~~~~~~~~~~~~

As soon as Mrs. Robinson had left the store, Gomper realized that he had made a mistake. "That's their own fault," he tried to rationalize. "I'm not used to all this secret stuff." But the more he tried to shift the blame the more he came to the conclusion that he had made a grievous blunder. Finally, knowing he had to alert the sheriff to his "slip of the tongue," he left his store to confess his mistake. He found Deputy Sam at the sheriff's office.

"You didn't hear?" said Sam, amazed at the usually infallible rumor mill. "He's shot in the head, grazed like. Mrs. Skinner left this morning to go see him."

"Horrible, but I got busy in my office—nobody told me." Gomper was rather glad that Skinner was not available to chastise him. "I came to let the sheriff know that I might have inadvertently said the wrong thing to Mrs. Robinson. A slip of the lip, I'm afraid." He gave a feeble chuckle to coat his shallow confession.

"What was that, Mr. Gomper?" Sam was not laughing.

"I might have exposed . . . that the sheriff was interested in the diamond. You see, she put me on the spot. Wanted her diamond back. Said the jewelry work was taking too long— threatened to take it to Tucson."

"What did you tell her?" Sam was definitely not happy.

"I tried to make it sound like the diamond was involved in probate—with Armstead's death. An irregularity in his accounts, which necessitated a professional inventory by the new jeweler."

"Did she buy your explanation?"

"Well—she stopped her complaining, soon as I said sheriff and probate. She's not the outgoing type, you know. It's hard for me to . . ."

Gomper was interrupted by a dust-covered cowhand coming into the office. "Who's in charge here?" he demanded of the well-dressed Gomper. Gomper hurriedly pointed to Deputy Sam.

"I'm supposed to tell you that the D B Ranch was attacked by some raiders. We shot some of them and they shot some of us. It was them Germans from down by the river. Miss Wilbur just wanted you to know it was them Germans who started the whole thing."

"Quite a walk, isn't it, all the way from the D B?" asked Sam, still not smiling.

"Whatcha mean?" The cowman was tired and this did not help his disposition.

"What I mean is that the information was yesterday's news. What took you so long to get here?"

"Didn't nobody tell me to kill my horse, that's why—smart-ass."

"Go on back to your boss and tell her that the sheriff was shot and it's uncertain whether he'll recover. Tell her we're taking steps to sort the situation out and that she should refrain from any aggressive actions. The Germans have been told the same. Who shot the sheriff—do you know?"

"Wouldn't tell you if I did. Don't like lawmen."

"And I don't like people who shoot lawmen," Sam countered. "Now get out of here or I'll lock you up for conspiracy to kill a peace officer."

"I'll go, deputy," warned the cowboy. "Just you don't go to the D B or you'll get what your sheriff got."

Sam watched the man leave the office, then turned to Gomper. "Another satisfied customer, Mr. Gomper. Just like the department store business, isn't it?"

~~~~~~~~~~~~~~

The vigil of Genevieve bore results. She had gotten almost a half-cup of the broth down her husband's throat. The sheriff's protests were a gauge of his coming to consciousness; the objections increased with the quantity of broth consumed. Soon his eyes were opened to give warning in case of another bout with the broth bowl.

Gen attempted to give advice about her husband's condition to Onkel Pfaff through the pretty Miss Kolb. "He says his head hurts. Can you give him something for the pain? A powder, perhaps?"

"Nein, nein," the old man was emphatic in his response.

"He says," quoted the healthy-looking girl, "that too much morphia obscures the healing. He is more worrying about the kidneys. He must pass water. Can you help him to make water?"

"I can try," replied Gen. "Get me another bowl of that broth."

"I am sorry, but it is gone. But I will have more in an hour, perhaps."

"Just get me an empty bowl," directed Gen. "It will do just as well." When the girl brought the bowl, Gen carried it carefully over to her husband's bedside.

"Sylvester, we have more broth. Would you like it now? . . . Or would you like to try to pass some water?" Soon Onkel Pfaff was smiling at Skinner's specimen, and Gen was feeling more confident about her husband's chances, and her own place in his recovery.

Mr. Hansen had seen to the rented horse, and had found an empty plate at the elder's table. "My usual boarder is in the hospital, with a broken ankle," said Kolb, passing the sausage platter to Hansen. "He's a good stonemason and will be missed on the job."

"Really." Hansen was too busy eating to hold up his end of the table talk.

"Yes, he's only been here a month or so, and already he has been elected foreman of the masons."

"Could I have some more of the potato puree?" Hansen was in his element—eating.

"He had to leave your city," continued Kolb. "He had a fight with an Irisher who was his foreman, bloodied the man's nose. Then the Irisher sent for the police and Hugo had to leave or be arrested."

"Hugo, huh?"

"Yes, Hugo Dunkelmehl. I think he likes my daughter, the younger one. She's a nurse at Onkel Pfaff's little hospital. He would make a good catch for her; and he's religious, too."

"Lucky man. Could I have another piece of that sausage? It's delicious."

"Thank you, it's a special recipe of my family. My wife makes it. You would never guess that below that lovely flavor lies all the undesirable parts of the pig. It's truly a gift from God."

"Oh—God," burped Hansen, suddenly full.

"Yes, my son—the Father in heaven, who guides us all."

"And makes your sausage," said Hansen, looking toward heaven.

"Through our hands, my son. His spirit, our hands."

After thanking his host, Hansen went directly to the hospital to check on Gen and the sheriff. The room was too small for another chair, so he leaned against the wall, listening to Gen babble on about the sheriff's problems. He found himself studying the other patient in the room, the nurse's boyfriend, the stonecutter and mason. The man, feeling Hansen's eyes, nodded amicably. Hansen nodded back. "How's it going?"

"The ankle aches, but Onkel Pfaff says that is the way it should be—hurting." He smiled at his trouble, showing good teeth and a handsome, bearded face.

"Would you be wishing some food, Mrs. Skinner?" asked the nurse. "I have some cooked sausage and bread in our little pharmacy."

Gen accepted, despite Hansen's wigwagging eyeballs. He followed her out of the room. The nurse laid out the sausage and the bread, then, handing Gen a surgical saw to cut the bread, left to check her other patients. Hansen looked down the hall and then ducked into the pharmacy with Gen, closing the door behind him.

"Is the sheriff conscious? I mean does he understand things?"

"Weren't you listening?" scolded Gen. "I told you. He drifts back and forth. But at least he's taking nourishment. Why do you ask?"

"There's a problem, but I don't want to alarm you. I just wish the sheriff was fit and had his pistol handy."

"Are you worried about the cowmen attacking this place? I can hardly believe that would happen."

"Not the cowmen, Mrs. Skinner. It's that other fellow in the room. Do you know who he is?"

"It's the nurse's man friend. She calls him Hugo."

"He's Hugo, alright," stated Hansen. "Hugo Schwarzstein, who killed his wife and kids up in that house on Chinaman's Ridge. I recognized him from the posters. I also did some work in the Grandview Saloon. I think I remember him, a hard drinker with a bad temper. That's what I was doing—fixing tables and chairs. Furniture don't last long in that place."

"He's a murderer?" Gen's eyes grew to goose egg size.

"Now, don't let on," cautioned Hansen. "Soon as the sheriff is up to it, he'll arrest him. Maybe Sam or Cletus will come, and we could tell them."

"Can't we tell the authorities here?"

"I'm not sure they'd believe me. Hugo has sold them a bill of goods. They even think he's religious. Sure is—he kills religiously. No, we can't trust them to do the right thing. Mum's the word. Just wanted to alert you—so you can be on your guard."

"I probably should thank you, Mr. Hansen," she said shakily, "but somehow, I wish you had kept his identity to yourself."

~~~~~~~~~~~~

Captain Josiah Stebbins was a large, heavy man, a fat man, if you will. If the perfect cavalryman was sinewy, slight and lean of form, then perhaps Capt. Stebbins was not the ideal. But, if parade ground displays were discounted, and only hard-fought battles counted, he was a peerless cavalry commander.

At the present time, he was relaxing in a wicker chair, placed on a predetermined flagstone in the breezeway between his quarters and the surgeon's quarters, at Fort Lowell in Tucson.

As it was past the hour of retreat and he was technically off duty, he was attired in linen trousers and a thin cotton shirt. He was smoking his after supper cigar, one of the good ones that he ordered from back East, not an everyday three cent-ers from the sutler. He enjoyed watching the ash grow as he smoked; tight and smooth, getting longer and longer— until it fell, lightly, of its own weight. He turned the cigar, musing on the even burning of the fragrant, green tobacco leaves.

The sound of bootsteps came stamping down the stone walkway, clicking heels in perfect cadence. "Sir," it was that new fresh-faced second lieutenant, what was his name? Cracy, or was it Gracie? "Sir, Major Poole sends his compliments and could you report to headquarters, please?"

"What now, Mr. Cracy?" sighed the good captain.

"It's Jersie, sir—and it's about a telegram that just came in from the Department of the West."

"Duty calls, is that it, Lieutenant?"

"Afraid so, sir."

"Never fear duty, Lieutenant. It's our wife, our mother and our mistress. Duty is comfortable, like an old pair of boots. Speaking of which, do you see my Wellingtons laying around here, somewhere?"

"They are, I believe, sir, under your chair."

"So they are," grunted the heavy captain, capturing the wandering footwear, which he crammed over his bare feet.

"I am ready, Lieutenant," he groaned, pushing his big body to his feet. "Lead us off to the hallowed halls wherein the brains of this regiment reside."

Major Poole, being Major Poole, was upset at any occurrence not exactly described in regulations and manuals. That was the normal nature of adjutants. More especially, adjutants to a widely dispersed cavalry regiment trying to hold down half a dozen scattered forts in an Indian pacification campaign.

Major Poole stared with ill-concealed distaste at Capt. Stebbins' choice of leisure wear. He, personally, was never seen in civilian clothes as he was certain that civilian clothes detracted from the military presence.

"Sorry to bother you, Captain," lied the major, with a smirk that twitched at his fussy little waxed moustache, "but this requires immediate action."

"The cavalry—again to the rescue," murmured Capt. Stebbins.

Major Poole ignored this usual irreverence from the large captain, to continue. "This just came in from General Sheridan's headquarters." He handed the telegraph flimsy to the captain as if it were the Holy Grail—just come over the telegraph wires.

"We are ordered to send an officer-led contingent to the Puzzle River in Green Falls County," read Stebbins, paraphrasing the contents. "To assure peaceful resolution of a dispute between ranchers and immigrant settlers. A local, federally supported, militia company of the settlers under the command of a Lieutenant Riemann is present at the settlers' village, which is unnamed. Said contingent commander, from Fort Lowell, may, upon his rendered judgment, call this militia company to active federal service for an indeterminate period, not to exceed six months.

"The contingent commander may make no permanent dislocations of real property, chattels, inhabitants or natural resources and will confine his operations to preserving the peace, until such time as other governmental entities have relieved him of this responsibility.

"It is the commanding general's express and direct order that military and civilian casualties and damage are kept to a minimum consistent with the constitutional guarantees of the Federal Union. For the Commanding General Western Department, Lt. Colonel Jesse P. Blair, Adjutant. End of message. Want me to make a few choice comments about what little Phil wants?" asked Stebbins, handing back the telegram.

"If those comments do not breach proper discipline," agreed Major Poole, stern-faced.

"This mission could cost the career of its commander. This is work for a politician—not a soldier. I know of this militia company. It's the pet toy soldiers of General Schurz—now senator-elect. He just loves to write articles for the newspapers; and he also has the ear of our new President-Elect, General Grant."

"I'm glad you understand the situation. You are to be the contingent commander, Captain Stebbins." Major Poole was smirking again.

"When do you plan for me to leave, and with what troops?" Captain Stebbins' evening was definitely destroyed now.

"Not until the San Carlos patrol comes in, for sure. We can't cut ourself down to nothing."

"They're overdue now. They were supposed to be back yesterday," the captain pointed out. "They could be in trouble."

"Could be—probably just late. Anyway, it's not your patrol. It's Lieutenant Leigh's responsibility," reminded the major.

"Will I take both troops?" asked Stebbins. "I'll need them for a show of force."

"Only one. Take your pick. Either troop."

"I'll take Sgt. White's, less married men."

"I want you to take Lieutenant Jessey with you. He needs the experience. He's still wet behind the ears."

"It's Jersie. I don't think he's ready yet."

"The War Department says he's posted for duty. Who am I to argue with them? Besides, it's not like you're chasing hostiles."

"If they're shooting at each other, Major, wouldn't you consider that fairly hostile?"

"That's what you get paid for, Captain," stated the adjutant. "Just do your duty."

"Ah, the hair shirt of duty," complained the captain. "How well I know thee."

CHAPTER 19

O pal insisted that Sally Lewis lead the fast raid against the settlers. It was his idea, she argued, and he should know best about its execution. Their scouts were called in for new information about the settlement.

Andrews, the lanky, ginger-bearded cowman, had ridden with Mosby and, as senior, gave the report for both the scouts. "Miss Wilbur, they're digging in on the west cliff, above that dam of theirs, making a trench line and what looks like a raised parapet of some sort. Like what you'd set a field gun on. But I didn't see no cannon."

"How many men they got working on it, Andy?" questioned Lewis.

"'Bout forty or fifty, far as I could make out. And they're hauling timbers in. Guess they're gonna make a breastwork or else line the trench—maybe both."

"Sounds like a tough nut to crack with a light force." Sally Lewis made a sad face. "What about their village?"

"Easier going there—I think. They cut loopholes in some of their shutters and blocked some open spaces off; but there's one big barn just sticking out, asking to be burnt down. Think that's your best bet."

"We could take some lamp-oil." Sally was thinking out loud. "Could get that barn burning, quick. They got animals inside, you think? Like to hurt them for Bert, if we could."

"Imagine so," shrugged the scout, "not really sure. It's always going on dark when they bring the animals back. Too dark to see much from the hills."

"We'll have to cross that river. How deep is it now?"

"By the looks of it—'bout belly deep on a horse," said the scout. "They got people irrigating their crops, hauling water out on horses. They ain't afraid to work, I'll say that for them."

"Well—that's it, Miss Opal," Sally turned to his boss. "We'll go after that barn, then hightail it out of there fast."

"I think you should take Mr. Andrews as a guide," said Opal. "It seems as if he knows the way."

"I was fixing to, Miss Opal," Sally answered. "I want every break we can get."

~~~~~~~~~~~

Harvey had Olly meet him away from the usual night-time haunts of the tunnel gang. He wanted to keep this rendezvous with the nitro man hidden from Mike's suspicious eye.

"It just don't make good sense—this waiting, I mean. The holes are all done—just sitting there."

"Same as all that silver." Olly seemed ready to commit himself, but was waiting for Harvey to voice their common thought. "I think Griff and Mike are more interested in that Christmas concert than they are in getting rich."

"You know that saying, don't you?" Harvey moved his head closer to Olly's. "Opportunity strikes only once."

"But once," Olly corrected superiorly. "We would need help. Tight-lipped help. If Mike found out, we'd be found dead at the bottom of the shaft. He's a bad man to double-cross."

Harvey smiled. Olly had said the word. Now it was out in the open. "It's their fault, Olly, for all this stalling. Serves them right. We got a lot of time and effort invested in this. The question now is—can we get the lift man to switch sides?"

"We're going to have to give him a full share, instead of a half-share, like Mike was giving him. Oh yeah—there's another problem. We'll need a small man to take Griff's place, crawling through the hole."

"That's a problem and there's one more; we're gonna have to get rid of Mike and Griff—permanently—or they'll be on our tail forever," Harvey reminded, grimly. "They got to go, friends or no friends."

"You can buy a lot of friendship with the money we'll have, Harvey. The kind of friends you crawl in bed with. White ones, black ones, yellow ones—you name it—money will buy them all."

"So—when do we do it? We should set a date to shoot at."

"Say three days hence," Olly offered. "What day will that be? We have to work fast."

"Ah . . . the fifth of December," said Harvey, counting the days off on his fingers. "You talk to the lift man. I know a little fellow who works on the pumps. I'll go see him tonight."

~~~~~~~~~~~~~

Mrs. Robinson had spent a sleepless night, trying to remember exactly what Mr. Gomper's words were. The more she tried to reconstruct the scene and the words, the more she felt herself slipping into the mire of self-aggravated doubt.

"It's that nosy sheriff," she told herself. "Sticking his big nose in my business. Who better to get her boarders' belongings than me? The woman who cooked and scrubbed for them. Even took away their pain and suffering . . . But he's after me, I'm certain. That fool of a man, Gomper—I surely wormed the truth out of him. The good Lord is giving me a chance to save myself. Oh thank you, Lord, and I'll not tarry a moment too long. I'll find another town—somewhere. There's always old men with money, looking for a decent place to live—and a little kindness."

~~~~~~~~~~

There were six of them, counting Sally Lewis and Andrews, the guide. The quarter moon shed little light for them to see and they had to trust their mounts' better night sight. Suddenly, they came to the river's bank and the horses hesitated before slipping down the slope and into the river. They pushed on, not allowing the horses to drink—for they could have a furious gallop to safety ahead of them before they were finished this night.

Then they were climbing the other bank, single file, closed up, nose to rump, in anxious anticipation of trouble. Andrews, barely visible, pointed his rifle towards the black loom of the targeted barn. They were moving towards it when the challenge came.

"Still stand Sie!"

Andrews fired immediately at the voice in the dark; three times, as fast as he could work the Winchester. They heard a cry from the direction of the challenger and then the clatter of a retreating rider. The fleeing rider fired four spaced shots, evidently for the alarm.

"The fat's in the fire, Sally!" yelled Andrews. "Set that damn blaze and let's get out of here."

"You other fellows—guard our back!" Sally shouted. "Shorty—bring that jug of lamp-oil up here!" Soon the raiders saw the quick bloom of the yellow fire, reaching up the wall of the barn.

"That's it—we're off—come on!" called Sally and the bunch turned their horses eagerly for the river. Suddenly gunflashes burst out on the far bank of the river. The raiders were back-lighted by the burning barn, silhouetting them to the firers on the other side. They attempted to go around the corner of the burning barn, trying to get the barn between them and the patrol on the far bank.

That move brought the raiders into the Gatling gun's field of fire from the tower. A steady "thug-thug-thug" of Gatling gun slugs caught the group, knocking down horses and riders like wheat under Mr. McCormick's patent reaping machine.

"No more! No more!" screamed Andrews. He never went against machine guns in the Shenandoah and wanted no more from this bullet-spitting terror.

Soon the scene was swarming with villagers, both to contain the fire to the burning barn or to sort out the dead from the disillusioned. Three horses had to be destroyed. Two raiders were killed; Sally Lewis and a young cousin to Señor Aviles, the breeding ranch manager. Shorty Ames had a badly mangled knee, which forced Onkel Pfaff to retrieve the bread knife and take his leg off above the knee. The vidette who gave the alarm had been hit in the back, smashing his right scapular.

Major Riemann put a second mounted patrol into action on the far shore, but not before marking a boundary between the two patrols by setting out two oil lanterns. Two videttes were also added on the village side.

Then a quick council of war was called. "I want to send back the unwounded prisoners on parole," stated the major. "We have no facilities for prisoners here and I think it would be a good idea to let the ranchers know how prepared we are. Perhaps they will stop this insanity."

"But Major, they know we have the Gatling gun up in the tower. They'll take it into account if they attack here again." Sgt. Major Klaus was adamant.

"I hope so, Sgt. Major," smiled Riemann. "As soon as the prisoners have left, I want the Gatling gun moved to the blockhouse by the dam. Then I want a dummy gun installed in the church tower—to fool them into thinking it's still up there to defend us."

"What is left to do on the blockhouse, Major?" asked the elder. "Is it ready?"

"The blockhouse, itself, is ready. Tomorrow we plan to arm the glacis and improve the access route; and also to construct the boom. If we have more time I'd like to build several strongpoints to protect the village. Until then, I would like to increase the village defense force by twenty more riflemen. Actually, those twenty can start some of the preliminary work on the village redoubts tomorrow, leveling the sites and clearing the fields of fire." Everyone was quite satisfied with Riemann's explanation. In fact, the council members were rather elated at the night's results. At the cost of one barn and one milk cow, an enemy force was bloodily repelled.

Major Riemann realized this misplaced euphoria and moved quickly to deflate it. "This is only one small battle in which we have come out fairly successful. Evidently, the raiders only meant to harass us tonight with a small force. If they had hit us with a more substantial attack we could very well have lost the entire village. Tonight we were lucky—tomorrow we might be overwhelmed. Remember that and guide your efforts to see that we come through this safely."

"We pray to God—for His strength," added Kolb. "And now we still have time for a few hours sleep."

~~~~~~~~~~~~

When the firing broke out, Gen was asleep, sleeping the sleep of the exhausted in the bed of the Kolb sisters. The two sisters immediately rose, hurriedly dressed and left for their posts, leaving Gen to grope for her clothing. Once dressed, she crossed the square to the small hospital. At that moment the Gatling gun opened up, adding its racket to the din of the blaze and the shooting from the far river bank.

She ran, terrified, into the safety of the hospital. Onkel Pfaff and the younger Kolb sister were in the little pharmacy adding last minute medical supplies to a haversack that the old orderly hastily grabbed to dash out into the battle.

"He said I should see to the patients—reassure them," said Eva, with little certainty, herself. "Could you help me?" she begged anxiously of Gen. "I have never been in a battle such as this."

"Neither have I, honey," replied Gen, giving the young girl a quick hug for comfort. "But I guess we can learn together. Let's put on a big smile and put your patients at ease."

Gen went into the sheriff's room and turned up the dim lamp. Hugo was fighting his bed clothes in an effort to get to his feet and join the battle. "I must get to my comrades," he explained anxiously, trying to pull his trapped splint from the sheets. "They will need me."

"They'll need you when you've healed. Besides, I think they're doing very well without you. So you just lay back and relax."

Her husband took more convincing. Skinner was awake and wide-eyed at the shooting, trying to put together questions which his brain had trouble framing. Only a few hesitant "whats" and "whos" came out of his scrambled thoughts.

Hansen popped into the room, puffing from the flight of stairs. "You're here, eh, Mrs.? Hell of a way to be woke up. If you're all right, I'm going to help with the fire. How's your husband?"

"Disturbed—along with the rest of us. You go help with the fire. I'll stay here and help Eva. From the sound of it, there will be more patients, although I don't know where they'll put them."

~~~~~~~~~~~~~

Judd Payton and Smokey Watson had problems—almost more trouble than they could handle. It started off with the mule people who were angry about the condition of the returned mules. Quite a few of the animals were lame from the results of the trip, several being actually spavined and made useless. The mule contractor had a dozen or so animals extra to Payton's needs. This dozen usually allowed the contractor to rotate unfit animals to his reserve until they were ready for service.

Now, as the contractor pointed out irately, the reserve was woefully inadequate to furnish the number of animals necessary for Payton's needs.

"That wuz allus our agreement, dammit," scolded the white bearded old patriarch of the mule company, looking to Judd like some Old Testament prophet about to hurl a divine thunderbolt at the miscreant or fornicator; probably the latter because the old man treated his mules with more love than he did his own children.

"I give you the world's best mules—big, strong and healthy. And look at what you bring me back. If I didn't know better, I'd have said you traded the lot off to some Mexican ragpicker."

"That's pretty close to what happened, Ike—except he was hauling cedar posts instead of rags," explained Judd.

"I gave you twenty-eight wonderful mules and you brought me back twenty-four sick puppies, of which I'm gonna hafta put down two, for sure. Maybe three, not sure on Agathocles yet, but Halicarnassus and Xanthippe are done for, thanks to you."

"Not me, Ike. It was that damn Ocampo—who captured us. He said he'd just work the mules for their keep. I never dreamed he'd work them to death."

"Well—it's gonna cost somebody and that somebody is you, Mr. Payton. $175.00 for Halicarnassus, $175.00 for my beautiful Xanthippe—and the jury's still out on Agathocles."

"Put it on my bill, Ike," winced Payton. "You know I'm good for it ... Now, how many mules can I count on—in three days?"

The next stop on Smokey's and Judd's tour of tears was the wagon yard. They knew they would find no mercy there—only angry recriminations again.

"Every Goddamn wheel has to be worked on. Almost every damn tyre has to be cut and shut—plus a bunch of spokes and fellies need replacing. To say nothing about the bedboards busted up. The damage wasn't foreseen in our agreement. I've got a week's work for a wheelwright and a wagonmaker and Lord knows how much for the smith."

"I know, I know." Judd was getting good in the humility department. "Put any unusual charges on my tab. Just try to be fair—or I'll be out of business. This last job has almost killed me. But I need the wagons in three days, plus a smaller wagon. Stout—like an army ambulance, with bows and a good, tight canvas, stained brown."

"Impossible; can't be done that quick. Even if I had to work, myself."

"Bet you a hundred dollars you can do it," countered Judd, looking resignedly at Smokey, who shrugged back.

"I raise you fifty—to one and a half?" bargained the wagonmaster, sure of his hole card—his wagons.

"And people think ill of me and my business," observed Payton. "Done! We'll be here at sundown on the third day."

When Judd got back to his ranch, hoping for a kind word and a good supper or, at the very least, a little peace, he found a cabal aligned against him, led by his adamant wife.

"Joey is not going, do you understand?" She was always good at getting up a fast head of steam. "He's getting a town job with the Haskell boy."

"Not Louis Haskell?" argued Judd. "He's one of my best skinners. I'm counting on him."

"Not any more, you're not. Louis found a job at the slaughterhouse. His lady friend's father has an interest in it. And they found work for Joey there, also. A good job—where he won't have to have his ears cut off. I'll never forgive you, Judd Payton, for letting those Mexicans cut his ear off. You should have stepped in immediately."

"Yes, Mother. I'm sure you're right," recanted Payton—with newly-practiced humility.

Captain Cabot came back early, almost half a day before Opal's deadline. He was accompanied by two dozen armed riders, of which four or five might have been considered as cowmen. The remainder seemed to be made up of the shiftless strata of discharged soldiery that roamed the West—too lazy to work and too scared to steal properly. Most of them still stank of the cheap whiskey that had enticed them to enlist in this range war.

A good sized freight wagon brought up the rear of the Cabot procession. It held the supplies, ammunition and explosives necessary for the campaign.

Captain Cabot was soon apprised of the loss of Sally Lewis and the failure of the fast raid. Blackjack Thompson had arrived the day before; but had so far contributed little in the conduct of the range war. His mind, and energy, it seemed, was still back in Palisade Valley.

The fiasco of the fast raid had hurt Opal's confidence in her martial skills. She blamed herself for Sally's death and had retreated from decision making. This was quite satisfactory to Captain Cabot. Never one to hide his talent under a basket, Cabot stepped into the breach as the war chief. A scout had returned to tell of the making of the boom protection for the dam.

He used this information, to cement his planning position. "Won't do them a bit of good," he told the council of war consisting of Opal, Bennington and Señor Aviles, who had come to avenge his cousin's death.

"The best way to blow a dam is to lower an explosive charge alongside the face of the dam, using the water pressure to direct the force of the explosion against the lower part of the dam's center, where it's the weakest. If we just floated a torpedo of some sort down the river, its explosive force would be along the apex of the dam and would be less destructive."

He paused for a moment, letting this engineering data be absorbed. "Now, what I plan to do is personally lower the charge about halfway down the face of the dam. Anticipating this, I had an attachment made up to convert an empty whiskey barrel into a torpedo with a self-contained fuse that can be lit and then sealed in a pipe that is attached to the bung of the barrel."

"And that will work?" It was Bennington—finally waking from his thoughts.

"I'll stake my life on it," stated Cabot confidently. "You gentlemen just keep the defenders busy and I'll sneak the torpedo down that dam. When they see that dam of theirs blow, those Sauerkrauts will take to their heels—I promise you."

"Sounds good, but . . ." Bennington sounded unconvinced, himself.

"Just you watch and see tomorrow. Now, I want to get Nappy started on the torpedo—while we sort out the new men. I want two troops of men, with each of you gentlemen commanding. Does that suit you, Miss Wilbur?" They all turned to Opal, who had been strangely silent during the discourse.

"If that's the way you want it, it's all right with me. We haven't seemed to have much luck lately."

"We will tomorrow." Cabot ended the meeting on an upbeat note.

Chapter 20

Capt. Stebbins quickly bounced his bulk out of his wicker chair when the San Carlos patrol came in. He went over to join Major Poole on the headquarters' porch.

"Those animals seem to be rather used up," noted the adjutant, primly.

"Not surprised; they're two days late," answered Stebbins. "Probably ran out of supplies three days ago."

"I'm unhappy about this tardiness," went on the major, oblivious to Stebbins' remarks. "What is the sense of making out itineraries if they are not kept? It's disgraceful and quite unmilitary."

"Perhaps you should consult our aboriginal foe? Get him to cooperate on your timetable," proposed Stebbins, with a straight face. "Of course, it would mean teaching him to read."

"Really, Captain, I don't think they have the intelligence to learn their letters."

"Sure didn't take them long to figure out those repeating rifles they stole or bought."

"Sometimes, Stebbins," complained Major Poole, "I'm not really sure whose side you are on—the savage's or ours."

"Oh, ours, for sure, especially on pay day. If it ever comes."

"Those mounts, I'm afraid, will hold you up. No way they'll be fit by tomorrow—in case of trouble." The major was alluding to Fort Lowell's mission to be able to field an immediate emergency force. Rather like the local fire brigade which would react to a conflagration, the ready troop was primed to relieve any one of a half-dozen small forts in the area if they were invested by hostiles.

"I'm only taking one troop. You'll still have one fresh troop for tomorrow and Lieutenant Leigh's bunch will be ready by the next day—at least for an emergency."

"Do you think so? They seem very gaunt," said Poole.

"They're regulars. They'll be ready—if needed."

"I'm inclined to take your advice, Captain."

"That would make General Sheridan happy, I'm sure." Stebbins couldn't stop the smile this time.

"However—I'll talk to Lt. Leigh when he comes in with his report. But in the meantime, I'll put you on alert for moving out tomorrow morning with Sgt. White's troop. What time would you leave?"

"My goodness," Stebbins feigned joy. "I get to set my itinerary. Nine o'clock—more or less. Still want Jersie to go with me?"

"By all means; let him lead the troop. You'll be expedition commander—in overall responsibility."

"Lucky me. How about a scout or two? Feel better with somebody out ahead of the column."

"I'll give you Pecos Bob and that pet Comanche of his. They're giving me nothing but trouble here in garrison. He has been much too familiar with some of the non-coms' wives—according to Mrs. Poole, anyway."

"Me—being led by an amoral—into the quicksands of bovine battle, dependent on a wet-nosed boy lieutenant. What happened to the brave banners of yesteryear? Where's the sparkling sabers of a regiment at the charge? I ask you— what has happened?"

"Are you quite through, Captain? If you are finished with your ravings you may go and tell Lieutenant Jersie to alert Sgt. White's troop. And please, do the Army a favor and at least wear a blouse over that ridiculous outfit of yours when you feel compelled to visit this headquarters."

~~~~~~~~~~~~~~

There was an hour of confusion at the wagon yard. The three big hide wagons were ready, but the smaller wagon was without bows, canvas or a wagon pole. The items had to be hurriedly installed, as the band's meager supplies were transferred from Judd's clumsy ranch wagon and stashed in the newer conveyance. One of Judd's older ranch hands had been talked into taking Uncle Walter's place as cook and driver, over the objections of Mrs. Payton.

Two new men had also been hired on. As they were of unknown quality Judd had to break up a couple of long-standing partnerships to pair them with experienced and steady men.

Then, everything seemed to come together at once. The big wagons were hitched and waiting; the smaller one emerged from a cocoon of workers to rush around the wagon yard—taking its place at the rear of the column.

"That's it, Smokey! Head 'em out!" shouted Payton, his heart beating excitedly with the thrill of the hunt. "And we thank the Lord for what we may receive—hoping for the best."

They stopped at Inspiration Point, ten miles up the mountain, to breathe the teams and to take a quick comfort break, themselves. Smokey Watson led his horse back to the smaller wagon and tied it off on the tailgate.

"I'm gonna get some quick shut-eye, Judd," he said, crawling into the back of the wagon. "Wake me when we're getting close to the Eagle Pass Trail. And remember to keep everything quiet when you go past Mesa Grande."

"You just get your snooze," replied Judd. "You old fellows need a lot of sleep. Us youngsters will do just fine."

Judd Payton rode up to the lead wagon. "That's enough watering the flowers, Gracey. Tell them mules it's time to get going." He gave an owl hoot or two for a signal and led the wagons out.

After another uphill climb, it was the dash down and the climb back up Breakneck Hill, the scorch of new brake-blocks adding their sickly-sweet perfume to the darkness.

Soon they were closing in on Mesa Grande and Judd slowed the teams to a walk. A quiet walk—as all the many articles that would jingle-jangle had been tied or wrapped to silence. Once past the Mesa Grande hamlet, Payton urged the teams to pick up the pace—stretching the big mules into a mile-devouring trot.

It was downhill now where every bit of the drivers' skill counted, trotting fast in the blackness of the night; cork-screwing around curves with always the dangerous canyon waiting to snatch an unwary victim from the narrow road.

Suddenly the lead wagon came rushing around a down-hill bend to confront a small horse-drawn vehicle, lit by a dim sidelight. The horse, seeing the huge, dark shape of the big lead wagon rushing down upon it, did what any sensible horse would do. It moved out of the way—and abruptly went over the road's ill-defined edge, dragging its vehicle and driver onto the rocks below.

The accident took only a few heartbeats. The huge, charging hide wagon, a scream lost in the thunder of hoofs as the small cart careened to its destruction onto the canyon's rocks. Then it was gone, left behind in the gloom of the crazy rush down the dark mountain's winding road. The wagons could not stop, even if they had wished, for speed and the darkness were their only protection. They were the lawless—who preyed and passed in the night.

~~~~~~~~~~~~~

Mrs. Robinson was sure she was being watched. Her every move noted by a large group of sneaking sheriff's deputies. But she would outwit them and flee to keep her freedom. The key to her surreptitious departure, she assured herself, was in keeping her poise.

"If I don't act like a fugitive, nobody will think that I'm escaping the law. If I just act normal, I can deceive that smart-ass sheriff." Armed with this self-advice, she secretly began to prepare for her breakout.

The first and most important item was money. Without money an older woman would be unable to sustain herself properly. Fortunately, Mr. Henderson, although a victim, was also a fine carpenter. She had asked him to make a secret hiding place for valuables in her room and old Charlie had done a fine job of hollowing out a bedpost on her four-poster bed. He bored out the bottom of a leg, reinforcing it with a two inch wrought-iron tube. Entry to this cache was gained by unscrewing the large round foot of the post. The beautiful wooden threads had been waxed and they twisted easily together. Old Charlie knew his business—at least around wood. She lifted the foot of the bed about five inches and set it on a small hinged stand, made by old Henderson, to remove the ball-shaped foot. She then pulled out the cotton bag which held the currency and jewels and put these valu- ables in her clutch bag, replaced the bed foot and lowered the bed to the floor.

In the afternoon she went to the bank, taking care to with- draw only half her savings, as she was afraid closure of her account would send a signal to her watchers. Leaving the bank, she walked a very convoluted course to discourage surveillance, coming, eventually, to the livery stable where she rented a horse and two-wheeled cart.

"I want to leave very early, Mr. Ames. What time do you open in the morning?"

"My man opens up about six, mostly. I don't get up 'til seven—then I go over to Purity's for breakfast," explained the grizzled liveryman, stuffing his mouth with rough-cut tobacco until he looked like a squirrel.

"I was hoping to leave earlier than that," Mrs. Robinson argued.

"Can't—we're closed from ten at night until six in the aunty's meridian—that's Latin-speaking for morning time."

"Could I pick up the horse and cart at ten o'clock? Would that cost extra? It shouldn't, you know. Just because you don't open early enough."

"What'd I quote you—four bucks a day? For a two day trip? Oh, make it an extra dollar. That'll be nine dollars, plus the twenty dollar deposit."

"Good. I'll pick it up at ten. Should I pay your man then?"

"Hell no! He ain't to be trusted with money past six," rebuked Ames. "He starts smelling that booze smell from the saloons and he's the most dishonest man around. Give it to me, right now."

That night, dressed in dark clothing, Mrs. Robinson left her boarding house by the alley gate. Returning with the horse and cart, she opened both sides of her gate and led the horse into the yard. She made her way through the darkened house, alive with the snores and coughs of her venerable boarders, to find the cases with her clothing and personal effects. Putting these in the cart, she led the horse back into the alley and drove the side streets. She kept off Main Street until she passed through Spanishtown, and then it was on across the river to the Tucson Road.

She had not driven a cart or a wagon since she was a girl in Indiana and that gap in her experience, plus the darkness of the night, forced her to drive slowly, letting the none-too-frisky horse establish its own pace—a middling walk.

Gradually, as she ascended the mountain that lay between Green Falls and Tucson, her spirits improved with the knowledge that she was free. By dawn she would be halfway to Tucson. Then it would be the Butterfield Stage and the steam train to a new life in some quiet town—with plenty of old men who needed her kind of care.

She was still full of self-congratulations and hopeful thoughts when the rushing hide thieves' big wagon ran her small cart off the road. She had only time for a quick scream before she and the cart were smashed—bounced and rolled into the rocks of the canyon, thirty feet below the road.

~~~~~~~~~~~~~~

The tunnel gang's plan had worked like a charm. After an hour of frantic work Harvey and Olly were aboard the freight wagon led by a greasy teamster named Sidrach Shannon. This brute wore his beard divided and tied into pigtails bound with strips torn from a red bandanna.

The wagon was pulled by six oxen that required constant verbal criticism along with an occasional whipping and prodding from their master. The scene reminded Olly of a childhood memory of seeing a farmer driving his geese to market, although the farmer had used a long staff rather than Shannon's combination whip and goad.

The silver bars, estimated at eleven hundred pounds troy, were loaded into the bed of the wagon. Manure had been forked over the treasure as concealment, which gave the usually taciturn freighter a laugh, saying it was the most valuable horseshit he had ever hauled. As Olly thought about the successful robbery, he decided the lucky part was finding the foreman, together with Griff and Mike, busy at the working face of a tunnel. A hastily set charge behind a support beam sealed them off and also created the confusion that allowed the breaching of the strongroom floor. It was a simple matter, once the bullion was in the ore trucks and covered with spoils, to spirit the treasure up and out of the mine with the connivance of the bribed liftman. Then, when most of the other miners were busily engaged in saving the trapped trio, Olly and Harvey simply pushed the bullion-laden carts out to between the stored timber piles where the teamster was waiting.

Olly and Harvey had wanted to head directly to Tucson, where they would be met by the liftman, the pumpman and a silver buyer. Shannon talked them out of this idea, explaining that his team could only manage about twenty miles a day and would soon be overhauled on the Tucson Road. He insisted that they take the Eagle Pass Trail from the Puzzle River to where it connected with the Tucson Road. Traveling this route would put them on lonely trails for several days, allowing any pursuit to pass by them.

As the fierce-looking Shannon was the only obviously armed man among them, if you discounted the bits and pieces of dynamite that Olly carried haphazardly in his pockets, his advice was heeded. The oxen were turned toward the Puzzle River and the Eagle Pass Trail.

~~~~~~~~~~~~

Smokey Watson had found a blind canyon in which the hide thieves could conceal themselves while he went to find a vulnerable herd. It was raining as the men unhitched their tired teams. After rubbing them down, they hobbled them and turned the mules out to graze on the scant forage of the canyon.

The cook had made a fire with dried wood brought from the ranch. He had coffee and a big sack of cold corn dodgers ready for the crew. Judd Payton rode down from the crest of the canyon and dismounted wearily by the cook.

"Judd, do I got enough time to put the beans on? I've had 'em soaking in that big jug of mine," asked the cook.

"Go ahead, Felix," grunted Payton, dipping up some coffee for himself. "We'll be here 'til sundown. Figure on feeding us about five—and get yourself some shut-eye. The Lord willing, we'll be skinning hides this night."

The slicker-clad scout came back in the middle of the afternoon with a smile on his dripping face. Judd crawled out from the shelter of the cook wagon to greet his scout.

"I reckon that stupid grin means you've hit pay dirt."

"Found an easy herd, if that's what you mean. Looks like they was making up a small trail herd when they got interrupted," beamed the little scout.

"Small—how small?" Judd sounded concerned.

"Small for a trail herd," laughed Smokey. "Big enough for us, though. Close to three hundred head."

"How far? —Close, I hope."

"'Bout seven miles across the ridge on the D B. If we work fast, we'll be across the river by daylight unless. . . ."

"Unless what?" Judd broke in.

". . . Unless this rain screws everything up. That ridge trail is tough enough when it's dry."

"If we was running late, we could always come back here and hole up until the next night."

"Skinning in the mud—ain't no fun. Takes longer, you know," Smokey put in as he pulled the saddle off his horse.

"We'll manage," said Judd grimly. "Starving ain't no fun either."

"So be it. Wake me up at nightfall," called the scout, climbing into the cook wagon. "And how about finding some corn for my nag? He deserves it if anyone does."

~~~~~~~~~~~~~

The kitchen of the Swansons' saloon and store had an expensive new tin roof. A thing of joy and practicality to Mrs. Swanson who had loathed the former plank roof, as it was a dirt catcher in fair weather and a sieve when it rained.

One nice feature of the new tin roof was its melodiousness—and it was ringing now with the early morning rainfall. Mrs. Swanson was half-awake listening to the music from the roof and half-asleep trying to stretch out her quiet moments before their daughter would awaken, yelling for her pap. Suddenly, she remembered the ritual of her early morning deputy task. The examination of the road in front of their business; the responsibility that rewarded her with the deputy sheriff's authority she enjoyed.

She jumped quickly from her bed, getting a muted cussing from her husband who had gone to bed much later than she, due to his closing the saloon. She stuffed her feet into unlaced brogans, threw a shawl over her head and clumped through the public rooms and across the outside porch into the dripping, gloomy day.

A quick glance is all it took. The newly-rolled wheel ruts were brimming with rain water. At least three wagons, maybe more, had passed in the still hours of night. She tracked back to the saloon and to the bedroom and lifted the baby from her crib. She bounced the child a few times to get her attention and then put it to her breast.

"Mr. Swanson! Rouse yourself! Those wagons the sheriff talked about came through last night. I'll need Jessup's horse. Go see him and borrow it and saddle it up with that smaller saddle of his—not the big one he uses." She took a hand free from her nursing baby to shake his still form.

"You hear?" She punched him again. "I gotta get to the sheriff. Get a move on!"

"Won't do no good," came the sleepy reply. "He's head shot—bad—laid up."

"Who says?" She stripped the quilt from his scrawny, underwear-clad body.

"Them mule skinners last night told me—that's who. Was a big gunfight at the Wilbur Ranch—the headquarters ranch. Ain't no sheriff anymore—lestways, for a time. Lemme go back to sleep."

"No! Get up and get that horse. Somebody will be in the sheriff's office—a deputy or somebody. I promised to bring the word. I'm a deputy myself, you know."

"You done told me that a thousand times already; you told everybody who'd listen," he complained.

"Mr. Swanson—you get your skinny ass out of that bed and get me that horse or I'll introduce my clodhopper to your private parts—now git!"

Fifteen minutes later, with her husband's second best trousers on under her dress and a yellow slicker over it, she kicked Jessup's horse down the muddy road to Green Falls, leaving behind an unhappy husband holding an even more unhappy baby.

~~~~~~~~~~~~~

Opal had trouble sleeping and only the advent of the rain, with its patter on the shingled roof, had finally eased her into sleep. Morning, though, found her problems ominously still present and unresolved. She felt caught up in a current of affairs over which she had no control.

The situation reminded her of a childhood terror. She was in a rowboat with a younger cousin and had lost the oars from their pegs. At once the heavy boat was caught in the river's gentle flow and was steadily borne downstream to the weir.

She and her screaming cousin could see the cleft in the weir at the river's edge, close by the towpath, where the staunch paddles had been removed to let the barges run the staunch. Slowly the rowboat swung with the current and started to slide down the volley of rushing water toward the plunging waterfall.

Then, whether by nature's caprice or with angelic assistance, the boat was caught in a back eddy and pushed away—out of danger—bumping its bulky prow against the slippery mass of the weir. They were rescued soon after by a fisherman who noticed their plight while tending his fish traps.

Opal felt that she was again caught up in something over which she had no control. She toyed at her early breakfast, ignoring Aunt Polly's attempts to humor her.

Beatrice Cole, up early also, stumped in from the outhouse, her crutch tips leaving round globs of mud on Aunt Polly's bleached kitchen floor boards.

"Its abuzz out there, for sure, Opal. Horses and men going every which way." She swung herself into a chair and propped her crutches against the wall. "A few more days of this and you'll be busted."

"I know that, Beatrice. How did I ever get caught up in this mess?"

"It's that Cap'n Cabot," Aunt Polly broke in. "He doan win the wars to frees the slaves—now he's fixin' to have himself another war."

"She's almost right, Opal," said Beatrice. "I'm sorry I ever recommended him. This is all my fault."

"No . . . if it's anybody's fault, it's mine. I'm supposed to be in charge. It looks like I've abdicated my authority ever since Mr. Lewis was killed." Opal paused, trying to see out the window into the rainy dimness.

"It all seemed so simple. Just a small raid, keeping the Germans nervous. Then, all of . . ."

Blackjack Thompson came in suddenly, dripping water from his slicker. "We'll be leaving soon, Miss Wilbur. We're taking the wagon in case we get anyone hurt—if it's all right?"

"Take it. You have somebody to drive it?"

"I got that new kid from my old spread. The skinny blond kid. He's pretty young—don't want to see him get too close to the fighting. Time enough later on when he's grown up."

"How many men will be left here, Mr. Thompson?"

"Not many, I'm afraid, ma'am. Only the cook and the wounded. Oh, yeah—and that darkie of Cabot's, Napoleon. This is a do or die effort I guess; Cabot don't think the old man is up to it."

"Are you going to be all right, Mr. Thompson? You're no spring chicken, either."

"I'm a tough old rooster, Miss Wilbur; and to tell you the truth, since you took the Lazy J away from me, I don't give much of a damn anymore. I'll take on that Gatling gun. Can't hurt me more than you did, if you don't mind me saying."

"I needed a good man here, Mr. Thompson," scolded Opal.

"Pardon me again, ma'am, but Hugh Foote is a hell of a good man. Maybe too good—for you."

"I think that's enough of that. Tell Captain Cabot that I'll be coming with him. Please have my horse brought up here for me. I wish you good luck, Mr. Thompson, and I'm sorry that you feel bad about leaving the Lazy J."

CHAPTER 21

aptain Cabot's force was spread out as they tried to guess the strength of the blockhouse that sat atop the cliff. The square fort stood out starkly in the grey, slanting rain. The bark of the newly-hewn logs had blackened in the rain, making it appear all the more ominous.

Cabot wiped his field glasses again and handed them to Bennington. "I can't tell if that gun's up there or not. What can you make out?"

Bennington took his time, studying the fort, before handing back the glasses. "That firing slit is too damn narrow to see into. If they have a Gatling gun at the settlement, they could very well have a second one in that blockhouse."

"I guess we will find out soon enough," replied Cabot, replacing the glasses in their case. "If there is a Gatling gun up there, it would murder us if we charged right at it in line abreast. I think it would be best if we send a skirmish line up to engage it."

"You mean on foot?" questioned Bennington. "Boys ain't gonna like that. Are they, Blackjack?" he asked, turning to the elderly foreman.

"Afraid not—they ain't much on walking," agreed Blackjack. "Tell you what—let me take twenty men and charge in a loose column down the right. If we can get behind that blockhouse we might find a blind spot and crack it open."

"We could support you with a similar charge down the left," agreed Cabot. "Would you be willing to take the other half of the troop to support him on the left, Bennington?"

"If I do, it would leave only half of that second troop, what with Aviles taking that half-troop of his off to keep the settlement pinned down."

"I'll keep them here in reserve," said Cabot. "They will be adequate to exploit any success that you two may accomplish. Now, gentlemen, gather your riders. I'm afraid that the longer your men stand looking at that blockhouse, the more timid they become."

"Not me," laughed Blackjack. "I've been scared of that damn fort all along."

Blackjack's fears were shown to be well-founded. When his column came to within 150 yards of the fort they started taking both Gatling gun and rifle fire. This firing lessened, somewhat, when Bennington's column attacked on the left and the defenders had to split their fire between the besiegers.

The armed glacis, though, stopped the twin thrusts in their tracks. The combination of the smooth, muddy slopes and the sharpened, out-thrust stakes stalled the attacks, allowing the defenders to decimate the horsemen. The riders hesitated for a long, murderous moment at the glacis, uncertain how to proceed, while the hail of bullets took its toll on their ranks. Then, suddenly, the riders broke under the fire and raced back to safety.

Opal watched the one-sided battle from a rise behind the attackers. She had been placed there for her protection by Bennington and Capt. Cabot. She was filled with disgust and horror at the injuries to her men and loped down the hill to confront her general.

"Stop this insane slaughter, Capt. Cabot!" she cried, riding into Cabot's horse to get his attention. "Is this what you call the art of war? Sending my riders against machine guns! I won't stand for this callousness. This is madness!"

"This is war, Miss Wilbur," stated Cabot calmly. "Your war—for your ranches—remember."

"No, Captain." She stood in her stirrups, furious, the rain mixing with her angry tears. "It's your war. You coaxed and promoted it—why? Is it your love of death and disaster? I want this stopped immediately. Send out a flag of truce or whatever you do to stop the shooting."

Cabot dismounted and grabbed her elbow, pulling her from her horse and down into the mud. Then, with both hands he dragged her to her feet, shaking her.

"Listen up, Missy." He shoved his face close enough for Opal to smell the whiskey and see the wild look in his eyes. "We can't stop, even if I wanted to—and I don't. Now I want you to get the hell out of my way. I've never purposefully killed a woman—not yet. But, I swear to all that's holy or unholy, if you interfere here I'll drop you dead in this mud. Get out of here and let me run this battle. Go down river and cry on Aviles's shoulder."

Opal was frightened. She was intimidated by Cabot and disheartened by the battle. She made her way, wordlessly, to her horse and mounted with difficulty because of the mud and her slicker. Then, still silent, she turned her horse downstream and slowly rode off into the grey rain.

~~~~~~~~~~~~~~

Mrs. Swanson's borrowed horse may not have been up to Pony Express standards—but it was quite sure-footed; a most desirable quality for a ride down a rain-swept mountain road. She almost overlooked the new sheriff's office, not having been in Green Falls for several years.

Sam was busy releasing an under-the-weather prisoner when Mrs. Swanson entered. "Drop everything, Deputy!" she cried, shaking her wet hat too close to Sam's paperwork. "There's trouble afoot!"

"Mrs. Paul Revere, I take it," said Sam, unlocking the smelly prisoner's manacles. "Get yourself some coffee and I'll be right with you."

The freed prisoner started walking over to the coffee until Sam pulled him away. "Not you, Ellis. You buy your coffee somewhere else. Move out now."

"But Sam, it's wet out there," complained the half-drunk miner.

"To tell you the truth, Ellis, a little water would work miracles with your love life," chuckled Sam as he pushed the big miner out the door.

"Now, Mrs. Swanson, what's the problem?"

"Too many eggshells, I'd say. Makes it taste too much of lime. Water's bad enough as it is."

"Not my coffee—the trouble afoot."

"Oh yeah. I'm a deputy sheriff, you know," she said proudly. "Special appointment by Sheriff Skinner."

"I know . . . the trouble?"

"Them wagons, the ones the sheriff was worried about—the hide thieves. Well, they passed my place last night."

"How many? What time last night?"

"Three, maybe four of them," she replied quickly. "Don't know exact about when. Before it started raining—maybe two or three. The mister closes up 'bout one and he didn't hear them. Not sure, really. Emma used to wake me up around two, but don't no more—thank God."

"And you think it's the hide thieves?" asked Sam.

"Hell no, Sam Buller. "I don't know who they was. Could be a traveling circus or Santa Claus—if he was using big wagons. All I know is Sheriff Skinner said to sweep a path across the damn road every night and give it a look-see every morning. Which I done and did and here I am telling you about it. Now, I'm going to get something to eat and get my aching, wet butt back home. I bet Emma's screaming up a storm by now."

She slammed the coffee cup down, slapped on her wet hat and went out to her patient horse.

"Damn and double-damn!" said Deputy Buller. "Everything happens at once and usually ends up in my lap. Well, Cletus, prepare to be woke up."

~~~~~~~~~~~~~~

"I don't like the idea of Opal going off to fight those settlers," announced Beatrice Cole as she stood propped on her crutches, watching the long column of riders trot past the headquarters house. "In fact, I don't like the idea of fighting the settlers."

"Mis' Opal dun spends too much times listening to that Cap'n Cabot. Thas whats I thinks," declared Aunt Polly, with a vehement shake of her bandanna-wrapped head. "I sho wishes Mister Hugh wuz still arounds."

"Well, he's not and I don't know how Opal can get out of this fix." Beatrice left the window to thump over to the stove and its teakettle.

"If'n Mister Hugh wuz here—he'd knows what to do. Maybes I jes go gets him. I kin ride a horse—lest I coulds when I wuz a girl."

"It's close to fifteen miles to the Lazy J. And it's raining," Beatrice pointed out.

"I ain't ascared of a li'l' rain. It's dat lightnin' I doans like. I coulds see dat Mister Napoleon. He'd find me a horse and I could go and tell Mister Hugh to come backs 'n' he'p Mis' Opal."

Aunt Polly found Napoleon in the barn talking to his mule while he gave it a morning brushing. "Whats you doing here, girl? Doan you knows it's raining?"

"Mr. Napoleon, I needs a horse. Ken you gets me one?"

"A horse? What kind of a horse? Where you going in this rain—a good looking young thing like yourself?"

"I's goan afters Mr. Hugh. Mis' Beatrice sez we needs him to stops all dis fighting. An' Mis' Beatrice is the lady in charge nows—what with Mis' Opal done goan."

"When's the last time you rode a horse, girl? It's not easy in the rain, you know."

"Whens I wuz little," replied Polly, patting Napoleon's mule. "Could I borrer dis mule?"

"What? You borrow Simon Bolivar? He wouldn't lets you ride him. He's a one-rider mule and I's the one. You jes gonna hafta tell me what to tell Mr. Hugh and I'll be doing the riding."

"Tell him ever'bodies getting kilt, 'n' he gotta gets here and talk some sense inter Mis' Opal."

"The Cap'n—he gonna be real mad when he hears I went for Mister Hugh."

"You tell him it was Mis' Beatrice tole you. And Mr. Napoleon—I think you is a good man. The kind of a mans a woman should be good to."

"I's an old man, girl. Got the rheumatism in my back—bad."

"When youall comes back, Mr. Napoleon, I's gonna spread some liniments on that back 'n rubs it in 'til you feels like a young boy."

"If'n the back part got feeling too good," grinned Napoleon, "maybe the front part would start feeling frisky."

"We'uns will jes hafta sees about thats, Mr. Napoleon, won'ts we? I gots a lotta loving under all these wet clothes."

"Girl, jes you stay here and I's be back with Mr. Hugh before you knows I's gone." He slapped the saddle blanket on the mule, who turned its head to give him a reproachful look.

"I's sorry, Mr. Bolivar; but tonight I's gonna make it up to you—if'n the Cap'n doan skin me alive."

The repulse at the blockhouse convinced the doubters; a dismounted attack had the only chance of success. The six empty saddles overcame any objections about crawling in the wet.

Captain Cabot set Bennington's half-troop on the left as skirmishers and snipers, firing at the slits and loopholes of the blockhouse. Then, with the blockhouse occupied with Bennington's men, Cabot had Blackjack's men infiltrate the right flank, working down to the river. The fort still dominated the situation, though, and any thought of a coup de main—a quick rush at the blockhouse—was out of the question as long as the Gatling gun still spat out its deadly message.

A rider raced up to Cabot, reporting that Aviles feared a counterattack would be mounted from the village. According to the rider, Aviles was concerned that a part of his men who had crossed the river to establish a firing line along the river bank would be in jeopardy if the defenders mounted a flank attack.

Cabot called up his reserve half-troop—sending them off to Aviles with the warning that they were supposed to be only a blocking force until the dam was destroyed. Then the dam besiegers would move down to the village, to invest and finally ravage it at their leisure.

Blackjack came back, mud-smeared from boots to bandanna, a testimony to the accurate fire from the blockhouse. "We need ammunition—rifle cartridges. Boys started out shooting too fast. I slowed 'em down, but we need more."

Cabot helped him untie the cartridge cases from the pack horse, encouraging him to keep control of his men and continue to besiege the fort.

"Just imagine how those Sauerkrauts in that blockhouse feel—cooped up in there with all that smoke and fumes choking them. Here, you and your men are out breathing good air, cooled by the rain and the breezes."

"If that's true, Cabot," Blackjack answered, "how come I'd be willing to swap with them? Their nice thick fort for my little rock." Still shaking his head at Cabot's logic, he grabbed the cartridge cases and rushed toward his men—taking care to duck behind every bit of cover.

Cabot watched him go back to his half-troop, then turned his attention on the blockhouse. He whistled a little tune through his teeth and had a self-satisfied smile on his face.

～～～～～～～～～～

The stagecoach to Tucson was making good time, considering the rain. Stuart Sweeney, Sr. was driving because of the rain. He thought young Stuart lacked the experience in rainy weather to keep the coach on the slippery, narrow mountain road. Mean Ed Moore was the guard, unhappier than ever in the wet.

"If I'd known it would be raining today," Ed shouted to the elder Sweeney, "I would have spent some of my drinking money on a new slicker. This old one's got more holes in it than Davy Crockett had after the Mexicans got ahold of him."

"I doubt if you would," yelled old Sweeney. "'Specially if it weren't raining. You could have never passed up the saloons to buy it." He had to stop talking to concentrate on the sharp curve coming up.

Suddenly, Ed Moore roused up from his side of the seat, holding on the grab iron to lean over, staring at a spot down over the roadbank.

"Stop this damn coach, Sweeney!" he yelled. "There's some kind of wagon cracked up down there."

The grizzled driver slowly brought the coach to a stop on the slippery surface. "Get down and scotch the wheels, Ed. Horses don't like holding the coach in the slick. And if you're seeing things, I'm gonna cut off some of that whiskey money."

But Ed Moore was correct. There was a smashed cart down on the rocks. The horse was dead, it's neck skewed around unnaturally. There was another body, an older woman's; broken but still alive, gray-faced in the cold of the rain.

They snaked her up on the end of a rope, tying her to a board from the broken cart—the coach's passengers bending on to take the strain while Ed guided the board over the rocks.

Once on the road, they loaded her into the coach, still strapped to the board. The woman was still alive when, an hour later, the coach came to Mesa Grande. There she was deposited with the saloon-keeper, who already had his hands full with a cranky baby.

~~~~~~~~~~~~~~

Gen had fallen into the routine of rising early to help prepare breakfast for the patients at the settlement hospital. The morning meal was always quite simple; bread with butter and tea for those able to masticate or barley broth for those too ill. Skinner had now healed sufficiently to be a chewing diner.

If he could chew, he could not walk with any degree of confidence, tottering from one resting point to the next. He felt dizzy whenever in any position other than prone. Gen, though, was pleased with his progress and kept telling him so—hoping to convince him.

Hugo Dunkelmehl's ankle was better and no longer pained terribly—it just hurt whenever it was not elevated. Onkel Pfaff was thinking of discharging him within the next day or so. He needed Hugo's bed for future patients. The young vedette, who had his shoulder blade smashed in the last raid, was in their hospital room—his bed jammed into the very cramped room.

When breakfast was cleared away, Gen brought in a basin of warm water and prepared to bathe her husband. At that moment the sound of firing was heard from the river side of the settlement. It was soon answered by rifle shots from the village and the firing increased until it was a full-scale battle. The window in the small pharmacy room was shattered with a crash as bullets hit about the building.

Hugo Dunkelmehl threw off his bedclothes and swung both his good foot and his bad foot over the floor, pushing himself, gingerly, to his feet. He stood swaying stiff-legged, looking foolish in his hospital nightshirt.

"Are you trying to seek safety on the floor, Mr. Dunkelmehl?" asked Gen, ever-careful not to get too close to Hugo.

"No—get me a stick to lean on," he ordered. "I go out to join my comrades."

"You'll have to ask Onkel Pfaff; I don't know where the crutches are kept."

"Zen, I go wiz out." He hopped over to the doorway to the hall.

"Hold on, Hugo," grunted Skinner, crawling out of his bed. "We can support each other."

"No! Absolutely not!" cried Gen. "I forbid it. You are both in no condition to help—you can't even walk decently."

"How dare you criticize our apparel, woman," answered the sheriff, shuffling with rubber legs over to Hugo who stood like a one-legged crane, clutching at the doorjamb. "Decent is as decent does; isn't that what your aunt who's-it said?"

"It was Grandmother Eaton, Sylvester—and I am sure she never contemplated a man walking about in his nightshirt. Certainly not a wounded man with long skinny legs that stick out too far below the hem."

"Fie on thee, Mrs. Skinner. This is our kilts—me and my friend Hugo—and we're off to fight the good fight for the honor of bonny Scotland. Right, Hugo?"

"Ja," confirmed Hugo, at a loss for a Scottish accent.

~~~~~~~~~~~

Sam knew it took too long to round up Cletus and the four extra men of the posse, but it could not be helped. The saloons had to be scoured for horsemen who were at loose ends and reasonably sober. The temporary deputy's salary of four dollars a day, plus a buck extra for his horse, was not much of an incentive in a mining town where wages were high and the workers were not required to shoot it out with outlaws.

When they arrived where the trail split at the hidden section of the Puzzle River, both Sam and Cletus reined in, struck by the same thought.

"I know," Sam answered Cletus's unspoken question. "You want to know where we're heading."

"It might prove helpful," replied Cletus, his beaver hat listing soggily under the continuing rain.

"To tell you the truth, I don't know where to start. Got any good ideas?"

"Tracks. Gotta find those wagons' tracks."

"We got tracks, we followed them since leaving Green Falls. Looks like they're from a wagon pulled by oxen."

"Not those tracks. I thought you said Mrs. Swanson thought it was three or four big wagons, with wide wheels."

"She did. Now all we gotta do is find where they were heading to."

"Like I told you before," said Cletus, "We have to find those tracks from those big wagons."

"Can you find them in all this damn water? They'll all be washed out, won't they?"

"Most probably," agreed Cletus. "But what else have we got? Got to play with the cards we was dealt. Let's spread out some and see what we can find."

Sam passed the word to the reluctant posse and trotted his horse over to the other end of the search line. The posse moved slowly down the trail, scanning for wide wheel tracks, but finding only wetness and the ox wagon's muddy ruts.

~~~~~~~~~~

Sam's group was not the only band following Shannon's ox wagon from Green Falls. Three very angry former partners in the tunnel robbery scheme had been quickly dug out from Olly's improvised prison. After a quick medical check by the French doctor at the Mine Association they were sent home to rest and recover their nerve for underground work.

When the crooked liftman quit work that morning, he had thought his working days were over. He had only to catch the stagecoach to Tucson and collect his share of the loot. He hurried back to his room to pack a bag. After that he would walk over to the Congress Hotel and board the stage.

Instead, he found his three former partners, Mike, Eric, and little Griff, waiting to question him. Unfortunately for this newly-retired liftman, the trio was quite anxious to find their wayward loot. The liftman talked, finally, after several of his bones were broken as an inspirational argument. He told of Sidrach Shannon and the wagon of silver. With this information wrung from the unfortunate man, Griff cut his throat, swiftly and almost neatly for such a gory piece of murder.

Their erstwhile partner left awash in his blood, the three next went to the livery stable to rent horses for the pursuit of the ox wagon. Ames, the liveryman, though, was hesitant about renting to miners—to dash about in the mud and rain. He felt they were not competent to handle horses under these conditions and he told them that in his grumpy manner.

Mike had to calm his mates who seemed ready to incapacitate Ames, the liveryman, and steal the horses they required.

"How about a cart or a gig?" asked Mike. "I can drive a two-wheeled cart."

"Nope," said Ames, non-committally, spitting on the floor.

"Whatcha mean—'nope'?" questioned Eric, the foreman, not used to being told no.

"Got the cart rented out, that's why."

"What else you got?" asked Mike, trying to be conciliatory.

"I have a four-wheel trap that I was gonna lay up 'count of loose tyres. But if you take it out in this rain the wheels should be all right, least 'til it gets dry again. It's got single shafts; only one horse."

"How much?" asked Mike.

"Twenty-five for the deposit and six dollars a day."

"We'll take it, for one day," snapped Eric, eager to be gone.

"I figured you would," cackled Ames. "You boys get your money ready while I see if I can find you a noble steed somewhere in my stalls."

Evidently the noble steeds were all hired out, for he finally came back with a mere horse. The anxious trio seemed not to notice though, and even pulled off the tarpaulin that covered the trap to help hasten their departure.

Chapter 22

The hiders had rolled out of their hole at dusk; the big wagons climbing in single file up the slippery ridge trail to cross from Running W country to D B land. A hundred times that black night, Judd Payton blessed the day that he had decided on mule power for his wagons. The mules were more sure-footed than horses. Mules might balk at dangerous situations, but once committed to the task, they would see it through until, at the point of exhaustion, they would again balk—refusing to move another step. This night was not a night to stumble.

All four wagons had dropped their scotch-rollers behind their rear wheels for the climb. These rollers were dragged by chains adjusted so that the rollers traveled a few inches to the rear of the wheel. If the wagon had to stop on the grade, the driver would ease his brake, allowing the heavy wagon to roll back against the scotch-rollers. This took the strain off the team and prevented unnecessary exertion on the animals. Tonight, though, the rollers were being dragged through the mud instead of running smoothly on their iron axles.

Half of the time the rain-drenched blackness prevented the drivers from seeing their leading vehicles, and the reinsmen would have to slack off their reins, allowing their teams' leaders to set the correct pace and interval.

The laborious drive up the spine of the ridge cost the hide thieves over three hours. Suddenly Smokey Watson was stopping them, telling the drivers to wait in place while he and Payton went ahead to silence any nighthawks who might be patrolling the herd.

The drivers and skinners waited, miserable, as the rain found its wet way through and around their slickers, soaking every stitch of their clothing. The mules stood stoically, lifting a foot occasionally, as if testing the trail's surface.

Then a series of storm-muffled shots were heard, causing the mules to prick up their ears and look off into the blackness. The minutes passed anxiously as each pair of men on the soaked wagon seats tried to make small talk, hoping to push away the wet, the cold and their misgivings.

All at once the wagons started moving again, guided by the scout. Another half-mile on the flat and the wagons came up among the impassive cattle. Now, at last, the men knew what to do and they lit dim lanterns, fastening them on upright wagon stakes.

The killing and skinning began. The cook started a low fire—shielded from the rain by a flapping canvas lean-to. Three of his mules were unhitched and led out to pull the heavy hides from the slaughtered cattle. The hiders were hard at work among the herd.

~~~~~~~~~~~~~~~~

The settlers' blockhouse, if not silenced, was fully besieged. The defenders were busy, keeping the attackers beyond the glacis. Periodically the Gatling gun would jam, mostly from powder deposits on the extraction system. Fortunately, Major Riemann had anticipated this, somewhat, and posted a good mechanic to the gun serving crew.

A problem had developed, though, when Cabot's men were able to flank the blockhouse and fire on the rear of the strongpoint. When that happened, the defenders were forced to close the thick shutters that overlooked the river. This trapped the smoke and fumes arising from the blockhouse's firing, making the interior extremely unpleasant.

With the blockhouse engrossed in saving itself, Cabot took advantage of its myopia to sneak his home-built torpedo down to the dam. The weighted barrel with its awkwardly protruding detonating pipe was a heavy and clumsy load, needing the attention of four strong men to get it to the dam's crest.

Once on the dam, the torpedo's porters were exposed to rifle fire from the blockhouse which towered above them. The bullets began striking the partially completed top of the dam, ricocheting wickedly. One of the carrying party was hit almost immediately. He dropped his share of the load and grabbed at his shattered thigh. His life was spewing out between his fingers, and he screamed with the fear and frustration of dying.

"Fire back at those loopholes up there!" yelled Cabot. "Make them keep their heads down." Two of the carrying party had their rifles slung over their backs, and they began shooting at the blockhouse. The other unwounded cowman was futilely trying to save his wounded comrade.

"Forget your friend," ordered Cabot. "He's dead—just doesn't know it yet. Come, I need help with this torpedo. It's lit and we've only thirty minutes or less." With the man's help, Cabot secured a rope around the barrel and lowered it down against the dam's face, letting it settle down slowly beneath the water of the river. Then he yelled at his helper to tie off the rope—suspending the heavy bomb.

"That's it!" yelled Cabot, gesturing frantically. "Get off this dam before the charge goes off! That fuse can do anything when it's cooped up in a tight space!"

The men needed no encouragement bolting off the dam; their haste making them cowards. The wounded man sobbed at them for help and then, weakened mortally, fell silent. The blockhouse, suddenly without moving targets on the dam, turned its rifles on the dying man, the big slugs thumping into his body in a last, merciful salute.

Paulie Vogelnester watched it all, unfolding like some awful dream, before his eyes. Earlier that day, after a quick breakfast, he had been sent to retrieve tools from the quarry. Major Riemann had planned on putting up the second blockhouse, at the village, and needed the additional tools.

The battle, though, had trapped Paulie and his mule-drawn cart on the muddy road out of the quarry. He could not leave without coming under fire from Blackjack's men, who had flanked the blockhouse. In fact, Paulie had tried to leave but had to quickly reverse his direction when bullets began to bang into the boards of his cart.

Then he had seen the attacking cowmen laboriously carrying the torpedo down to the dam. He watched as Capt. Cabot lit the fuse of the bomb, sending blue smoke mixing with the rain in a foggy plume. Then the fuse was capped and the torpedo lowered to its lethal position beneath the water.

Paulie saw it all—the desperate cowmen risking all to place the bomb against the dam—the village's most important structure—the construction that would determine whether the colony would prosper or die in the dryness of the Arizona desert.

As soon as the armed cowmen retreated from the dam, Paulie ran to it. Of course, he was not really running, for Paulie's twisted body would not allow him to run. It was his fastest sideward movement, a crablike wrenching lope that hurt Paulie's body much more than it hurt the sensibilities of the watcher.

But it was movement, even if extremely awkward, and he was soon by the rope that held the bomb, pulling at it with the abnormal strength that perverse nature had wished upon him. Little by little the bomb came up until its tarred body broached the surface. Then, with its huge weight no longer aided by buoyancy, Paulie had to strain to lift it, inch by inch.

Cabot followed his men up the canyon, ducking behind any cover that protected them from the fire of the blockhouse. Finding a well-sited rock, he turned to check on his handiwork and was shocked to see Paulie straining to pull up the torpedo that he had worked so hard to place against the dam.

"Oh, shit! Who's got a rifle? Gimme a rifle!" he cried, watching his work being upset.

"Here—use mine." A Winchester was passed to Cabot. "Throw's a hair left," said the man.

Taking a bead on the monster that was wrecking his plans, Cabot corrected his aim for the downhill shot and fired.

Paulie staggered and turned his misshapen face toward the hill from where his wounding came. Then he continued his work, pulling the heavy barrel from the water with a huge effort, and ripping the weight from its bottom.

Again Cabot fired and one of Paulie's legs collapsed, spilling him to the dam's deck. Now, one-legged, he pushed the barrel over the broken rubble, the detonating pipe wagging insanely in the sleeting rain.

A third shot from Cabot pounded water and blood from Paulie's coat. The poor monster had thrust the barrel up against the side of the diversion flume. With a superhuman effort he lifted the torpedo over his head and shuffled up against the flume.

A shot hit his neck, close under his lump of a jaw, releasing a scarlet spray of blood. Paulie staggered—the torpedo slipping in his grasp. Suddenly, he cried aloud, "Grossvati!" and with his last strength threw the 400 pound torpedo into the flume—where the rushing water carried it off downstream.

Cabot watched his bomb as it traveled through the flume and was spewed out into the river below to bob in the current sometimes above and sometimes below the surface, as if undecided whether to float or sink.

Cabot flung another shot at Paulie, who lay propped against the wooden side of the flume. But it was unnecessary. Paulie Vogelnester was at peace with his problems and the people that had mocked him.

"Damn!" swore Cabot. "There goes our try at the dam. But if we can't get the dam, we can still take the village! Blackjack! Pull out your men. Get them back to the horses. We're pulling out—to go level that village."

"Suits me. I never did take to that blockhouse, anyhow," answered the old foreman. "I'm just sorry, though, we had to lose so many men before we come to the conclusion."

~~~~~~~~~~~~~

The trio of disappointed silver bullion thieves had passed through the deputies' search line, giving them a wet greeting while inquiring if the posse had seen an ox wagon during their searchings.

The big deputy with the sodden beaver hat told them that he had seen ox-wagon traces—but no ox wagon. Must be up ahead though, he said, as the tracks were getting clearer.

Mike thanked the deputies and slapped the dripping horse into a trot. "Wouldn't be long now, boys. Eric, got those pistols ready?"

"They're ready and waiting," answered the foreman, opening the carpetbag to check on the huge pair of Patterson Colt pistols wrapped in oily rags. "Just bring me alongside those sneaking crooks."

Then, through the rain's gloom, they spotted the bulk of the ox wagon and its tall driver striding alongside his plodding animals.

"Easy does it," cautioned Eric, both hands hidden in the carpetbag. "Don't let 'em think we're after 'em."

But it was too late. A cry of alarm came from the ox-wagon. Its driver rushed back to his wagon.

"Whip up that damn horse!" yelled Eric. "Get me closer." Now he had both Colts in his big fists trying to line up his target without falling out of the careening trap. He let off a round, right alongside Mike's ear, causing Mike to jerk out of his line of fire, sawing at the reins.

"Blam! Blam!" Sidrack Shannon's rifle spat red through the rain, lacing a slug through Mike's coat that burned his ribs like a red-hot poker.

"Shoot back, damn you, Eric!" cursed Mike, turning the trap away from Shannon's rifle.

"How can I?" shouted Eric. "You're bumping all over hell—now you're going the wrong way."

"Screw you, Eric. That son-of-a-bitch shot me once and I don't want no more."

"Stop the talk, you two," advised Griff. "'n' just lay back and snipe at them."

Eric did just that, getting out of Shannon's range as quickly as possible. Later, after much discussion, Eric passed a pistol and some ammunition to Griff, who circled around the stalled ox wagon to attack it from the far side which afforded more cover to a shooter armed with a pistol. Shannon had the advantage with his rifle and after a time elected to move the ox wagon away from the attackers. A lucky shot by Eric, though, downed a wheel ox, foiling any early escape. The battle between the former partners in the silver stealing scheme settled down to desultory firing, each side content to wait for the night and darkness.

~~~~~~~~~~~~~~~

Mrs. Swanson left the sheriff's office after alerting Deputy Buller to the tracks thought to have been made by the hide thieves. She had a large breakfast, used Mrs. Purity's facilities and climbed back on her borrowed horse for the long, wet ride back up the mountain to Mesa Grande.

But a smooth setting off was not to be. Mr. Jessup's horse threw a shoe, luckily before she ever got out of town. Wet and angry, she jammed her soaked hat further down on her dripping head and led the horse to the blacksmith and farrier.

This good man was engaged in shoeing an ox. The wild-eyed animal was hoisted above with the ground in a contraption of straps, beams and pulleys that allowed the ox to remain upright while the rain-wet smith worked its hoofs. An ox, unlike a horse or mule, must be somehow supported as it cannot stand on only three legs.

Mrs. Swanson tried to argue her priority, but the smith politely refused her saying, "Wait your damn turn, lady. This ox is docile at present and I'm finishing it before it starts objectin' in any serious manner."

All this delayed Mrs. Swanson, and it was an hour before she could climb back on the borrowed horse and again head down Main Street. A commotion in the sheriff's office aroused her curiosity to make her dismount and seek an explanation. After all, she was a sworn deputy—was she not?

Happy Giles, the fractious night marshal and gaoler, had been rooted out of his bed to preside over the sheriff's office because of Sam's and Cletus's posse activities, chasing after the hide thieves.

Now a bleary-eyed Giles was angrily defending the integrity of the sheriff's office before an equally obdurate mine manager and Mine Association police chief who wanted the sheriff to find what happened to the contents of their bullion room.

"How many damn sheriffs do you think we got around here?" yelled the grizzled gaoler. "The sheriff is shot and laid up—God knows where; Deputy Buller takes Cletus 'n' a posse off after some crooks someplace, waking me out of a sound sleep to do double duty here. What do you want me to do, let them criminals upstairs out—to go looking for your silver?"

"Give me authority to search in the town for the silver. Let us find our silver, ourself," challenged the police chief of the Association.

"Can't. I'm just the damn jailer," admitted Giles. "Go talk to Aaron Rose, the County Prosecutor. Maybe he can think of something. Perhaps he can authorize deputizing those fancy-dressed monkeys of yours."

"See," said the police chief to the mine manager, "You can't count on these two-bit sheriffs when the chips are down. Too few and too damn slow."

"Wait just a minute, you overstuffed, brass-buttoned baboon." It was Mrs. Swanson pushing in from the open doorway. "I'm part of this sheriff's office. I'm the Mesa Grande deputy. See this?" She opened up her slicker to show the badge pinned to her inside coat.

"Don't you dare talk bad about Sheriff Skinner or his deputies. There's all kinds of criminal activities going on that you got no idea of. Now you all listen up. I was headed back to Mesa Grande after tipping off Deputy Buller about them hide thieves."

"Hide thieves?" interrupted the mine manager. "Never heard of that."

"Sure you didn't," Mrs. Swanson snorted. "There's all kinds of criminal stuff happening that the public don't know. Now, I tell you what. I'll swing out of my way to Mesa Grande and hunt up Sam Buller and tell him about this silver business. Then he can decide what to do. Maybe he can split up some of his posse and come back—or something."

"It'll probably be too late," said the police chief ungraciously, "but go ahead and tell him."

"Yeah, tell him. Can't hurt," echoed the mine manager, without much conviction.

"I'll be going then, Mr. Giles." Mrs. Swanson turned her back disdainfully on the mine people to stomp out into the rain.

~~~~~~~~~~~~~

Sheriff Skinner and Hugo Dunkelmehl limped their collective way along the narrow hall and down the tight stairs, emerging into the battleground that was the settlers' village.

"Dis vays," Hugo pivoted the dizzy Skinner toward the shallow trench that attempted to link the riverside buildings now that the big barn had been destroyed.

Skinner shivered as the windy rain quickly drenched the too-short nightshirt. "Where are they?" he asked Hugo, eye and brain still unsure from the concussion. "Damn it—tell me."

"Ober dere—by der river," shouted Hugo. There were four settlers in the trench. One, an older man, was dead, head shot—blood spilling down on a long, greying beard. Hugo grabbed the dead man's rifle, and once sprawled into a firing position that favored his bad ankle, he began firing at the riders before the river.

Skinner took a rifle himself, from a wounded boy who could not control his sobs and cries over being wounded. Onkel Pfaff and Eva Kolb came down the shallow trench from the other end. Eva stopped to say something in a low voice to Hugo. He cut her off with a quick "Ja, Ja" and a jerk of his head for her to keep going, never interrupting his fire.

Onkel Pfaff shook his head about the older, dead settler and motioned to Eva to bring along the wounded boy, now seen to be shot in the hand.

Skinner turned his attention from the trench to where the riders were supposed to be and checked the chamber of the Spencer. He tried to concentrate on the dim figures, willing their outlines to come together normally. He stood erect, his tall white-clothed figure drawing enemy fire. A slug smacked into a charred beam laid before the trench and another buzzed angrily by his head. "Get down, Skinner," he yelled at himself, the voice from his head taking charge. "And start shooting. What did you come out here for, anyway? Trying to be a hero?"

"Shut up," Skinner cried. "Leave me be."

Hugo turned towards him, reloading a tube in the Spencer's stock; as if to ask if Skinner was all right.

"Don't worry about me. Keep up the fire. I'm beginning to see them." And he did see them. The scattered images were coming together to make individuals out of twins and triplets.

Skinner picked a target; the Spencer, as heavy as a six foot miner's drill rod. "Ba-lam" went the rifle, its murderous recoil making his head see twins again. "Shoot between the s.o.b.'s, Skinner," the voice said and he obliged with another blast as a bullet tweaked the nightshirt's wet material above his hip.

"Ha, ha, missed me," cackled Skinner insanely. He fired again, dropping a horse and rider. "Serves you right—you had your turn," he yelled.

Suddenly Hugo was down in the bottom of the muddy trench, his nightshirt running red in the rain. In two seconds he was dead—eyes staring up into the rain, unblinking.

"Goddam you people anyway! You lousy rebels just killed my best sergeant!" screamed Skinner. He grabbed Hugo's wooden cartridge tube holder from Hugo's sodden form and climbed over the debris placed on the trench's parapet.

Now he was stalking his dead sergeant's killers. "Bring up the colors! Fire into them, boys! Keep up your flanks!" He was shouting madly into the rain. He had to stop to load a tube into the Spencer's butt-plate. Then he was off again, firing at his rebels.

The colony's defenders, seeing Skinner's one-man counterattack, hastened to support him, the fat sgt. major leading a dozen riflemen to drive the cowmen back across the river in disorder.

Suddenly, Genevieve was there, clutching her husband's elbow; taking his rifle from him—leading him back to his bed. "How do you do, Miss Genevieve?" said Skinner pleasantly. "What brings you out on such a nasty day?" And then he fainted.

CHAPTER 23

The destruction of the dam was now impossible with Paulie's jettisoning of the explosive torpedo. Capt. Cabot moved all his men to the village. Although his forces still had a precarious toehold on the village side of the river by the entrance road, examination of that flank convinced him that it was too strong to risk a direct mounted assault.

He was still in favor of unmounted assaults, with skirmish lines leapfrogging each other in attack. Not so, his troops. They were cowmen, used to riding and doubly fond of having a horse to ride away from too much trouble—like a Gatling gun, for instance.

Sending Aviles across to command the flank, Cabot had Bennington and Thompson draw up their riders in two long ranks facing the river. He rode down the long line of their front to the halfway point and turned to them and made a hopefully heroic exhortation to press this charge successfully. They were to rid the river of the "damn Sauerkrauts" who would use every drop to water their cabbages, letting the rightful recipients of God's water—the cattle—die, their tongues swollen from thirst.

No loud cheers answered his harangue. But most of the riders seemed to be willing to get this business over with and go back to their normal jobs.

"I'm going up to the other end of the line, Bennington," he ordered. "When you see me move out, bring your men as fast as you can through the river. Start shooting when you hit the far bank and keep up the fire. Don't give them Sauerkrauts a chance to pop up and start shooting.

"B.J.," he yelled to Blackjack Thompson, "count to twenty and bring your line behind us and reinforce our charge." B.J. signaled compliance, walking his horse to the center of his line to lead it from the middle.

Suddenly, it was Cabot screaming, "Now!" And the riders raised a rebel yell as they fought their horses into the river, sliding down the slick bank, their mounts lunging for the footing in the water.

The firing from the other shore opened up when the riders entered the water. The range was long, but here and there a man or horse was hit. The line took no notice, determined to make for the other side.

B.J. Thompson held up his hat. Its lowering would signal his riders to begin the charge. His men eyed the river, each man trying to pick the best course.

Then they saw the barrel in the water, the ridiculous pipe waving drunkenly as the rapid water sloshed the torpedo about. The barrel wavered erratically—then, seemingly determined on its direction, bobbed off for Bennington's charging riders. It exploded in a geyser of water, mud and horse and human parts. The upper third of the line was completely erased. The remainder of the line, shocked, made a quick retreat back to firm ground.

The settlers took this opportunity to mount a countercharge on Aviles's half-troop. His men, disheartened by the blast and the resulting failure to cross the river, withdrew down the road. They then crossed the river at the underground section, joining their friends across the river.

~~~~~~~~~~

Ensign Fenstermacher, newly promoted to command the colony's small mounted troop, halted his men as he saw the cowmen retreating through the thick underbrush above the underground river. He noted their desperate retreat and thought that they no longer required his troop's attention.

He gave the signal to re-form and his men reluctantly gave up the chase to gather boisterously about the young ensign.

Suddenly one of the men heard a shot. The ensign called for quiet and another shot was heard by all. It came from up the rain-darkened road to Green Falls.

"Corporal Damm," ordered the ensign, "take two men and find the meaning of those shots. The troop will remain here at rest, awaiting you."

In fifteen minutes, one of the corporal's men returned with word that an ox wagon was being attacked by three men driving a four-wheeled trap. The ensign quickly formed his small troop to aid in the wagon's defense. The troop pounced on the attackers in two wings, each wing rolling up the surprised gunmen. Some of the mounted infantry dismounted and helped the wagon driver to cut his dead ox loose, allowing the wagon to be brought under guard into the village, along with its attackers. The ensign took note of the extra-deep ruts the ox-drawn wagon's wheels were making in the muddy soil.

~~~~~~~~~~~~

Hugh Foote was more than a mile from the river when he heard the detonation of the torpedo. He had no idea what caused the explosion, but he did know that any escalation of the fighting meant trouble, and the explosion surely seemed to spell disaster to someone.

At the time, though, Hugh's principal problem was his horse. It was played out from too much traveling, too fast. Now it was moving forward by courage alone and Hugh was angry at himself for treating his horse in such a fashion.

"Love a woman—kill a good horse," he told himself. "What if I'm rejected again? Sent off once more in exile.

Ruined my horse—for what?" Just then the horse faltered, missing a step, to jerk back tiredly to its lope, grunting ever harder through its foaming muzzle.

Then, he was atop the last hill and he could see down into the shallow valley. The rain had stopped—but the overcast continued. Hugh was able to slow his winded horse, walking it past the pack animals of the besiegers.

A rider detached itself from the brush to ride toward him and he knew it was her, even from afar. He felt the stir of his heart, but his good sense told him to beware—she had hurt him before. He overrode the warning to luxuriate in the thought of her. Her face, her eyes, her soft, yet firm, body—all worked their magic on him.

They stopped before coming together. She, slim and sure in the saddle; he, weary from riding and wary of her displeasure.

"You came." It was a statement.

"I heard you could use a friend," he said, looking at the green eyes to determine his course.

"Who told you?"

"Napoleon came and got me. Said Aunt Polly and Beatrice sent him. He's worried about what Cabot will do to him when he finds out."

"Cabot's dead. Died in the blast of that torpedo of his—with seven other men. Hoisted with his own petard, the poets would call it. Poetic justice—no doubt. God, Hugh, he went crazy. Dragged me from my horse when I told him to stop. Told me to go away or he'd kill me."

"I'm glad he didn't—kill you, I mean."

"Still in love with me? After all this . . . mess?"

"More than ever. Are you willing to reconsider—maybe?"

"If I were the old Opal, the Opal B.C.—before Cabot—I'd ask for time to think and weigh my options."

"And the new Opal?" he prompted. "What does she say?"

"Don't go away from me, Mr. Foote. Stick really close—forever."

"Suits me, ma'am," Hugh drawled, "if I don't get a better offer. Might find an old lady with five ranches. You only got four, you know."

Their tête-à-tête was unceremoniously interrupted by Bennington, coming up to Opal for orders. "You want us to continue, Miss Opal? I have to tell you the men don't have the stomach for it. They're mostly cowmen, not gunmen. Nothing to be ashamed of, I say. I'm with them."

"As am I, Mr. Bennington," said Opal. "Please take your orders from Mr. Foote now. And you, my dear Mr. Foote, please go down and make a peace with the people down there. I'll agree to anything within reason—about water, land or whatever."

Captain Josiah Stebbins heard the explosion and immediately stood up in his stirrups, holding his gauntleted fist above his head. All along the length of the column he heard the non-coms calling the halt. Sgt. White, who rode next to the heavy captain, looked to him for orders.

"I'm gonna find out what the Sam Hill that was before we traipse into something we might not enjoy," Stebbins said. "Have the men rest . . . and it's a good time to take their ponchos off; it's stopped raining."

He turned to the bugler behind him in the next rank. "Boy—ride up there to where our renowned scout and dilettante is supposed to be and ask him what the hell is happening. When he replies that he doesn't know, tell him Capt. Stebbins would appreciate it greatly if he and his trusty Indian sidekick would go forward and see if it's safe for me and these fine young men in this troop to ride on . . . Got that, boy?"

"Sir," said the bugler uncertainly, "I never knowed what a dilly tent is."

"In the case of Mister Pecos Bob," explained Stebbins patiently, "dilettante means a person who studies whiskey and ladies' backsides."

"Oh—like Sgt. White, you mean," said the bugler, setting spurs to his horse and racing off.

Sgt. White shook his big fist at the departing young rider. Capt. Stebbins chuckled, "You've been found out by your men, Sergeant. They are privy to your private life."

"I'll have that loose-lipped bucko privy to something. Digging a nice deep one, me thinks," Sgt. White smirked.

Second Lieutenant Jersie came forward to inquire about the halt. "Glad you came up, Jersie," said Stebbins. "Saved me sending for you."

"You want my section to lead now—is that it?" the young lieutenant asked eagerly.

"No—dammit—that's not *it*," rasped the heavy captain. "When we leave here we'll move out in two sections. Me and Sgt. White and the first section will move in open column. I want you and Sgt. Flaherty with the second section to come along about a quarter of a mile behind the first section, in as much of a platoon front as the trail will allow."

"Platoon front?" questioned Jersie.

"Dammit, listen to orders before you start asking questions. I want your men ready to fire on foot, in case the first section has to hightail it away from trouble. Go back—tell Sgt. Flaherty and alert your fours and make sure that the horse holders know what to do."

"What about the pack mules?"

"Let old Private Simmons take care of them. Tell him to have hobbles ready. I don't want to lose them—if a few shots are fired. And keep a lane open in your front if we have to retreat through you. Got all that, Lieutenant?"

"Yessir—don't worry, Captain. My section will be like the Rock of Gibraltar—you'll see." The lieutenant sawed at his mount, racing back to his section.

"Enthusiasm, it's called," observed Sgt. White, spitting expertly at a stone in the trail and hitting it dead center. "I used to have it. Think mine leaked out at Shiloh—through the minnie ball hole in my ass."

"A not very heroic location to be shot, I would think," replied Capt. Stebbins.

"I wasn't very heroic at the time—as I remember." He tried for the stone again but missed as his horse pulled at the reins. "Damn," he swore, "I was up to nineteen straight hits and then this stupid nag screws me up."

"Ah—the perils of horsemanship," commented the captain, spotting the bugler galloping back to the troop. "Here comes your privy provider now."

They both watched the young trooper come riding hell-bent-for-leather. Sgt. White used the time to fill up his jaw with rough cut tobacco. Readying himself for war or spitting—or maybe both.

The bugler slid his mount to a stop. "Mr. Pecos Bob Portland's compliments, Cap'n, and he says his interest in alcohol and women's nether parts is purely scientific as he's planning on retiring soon and writing a book."

"And the explosion—any possible word about it from the budding author?" asked Stebbins tolerantly.

"Oh, yes—forgot. Mr. Portland reports there's firing from the valley ahead. You can't hear it 'count of the wind's wrong—but you can see the gunsmoke, he says."

"Thank you son, take your post," ordered Stebbins, turning in his saddle to call out, "Forward! At the trot! Open up the ranks, boys and watch the flanks!"

A few minutes brought the troop up to the scout and his Indian partner, who joined them. "The blast was in the river," Pecos Bob yelled. "Sure scattered whatever's going on down there."

"Good enough, Portland. Bring up the rear with Jersie," shouted Stebbins. Then he called to the bugler. "Blow the canter, boy. Lets get down there."

~~~~~~~~~~~~~

Hugh Foote had called in all the Wilbur riders, gathering them back in the trees on the far bank, with the river between them and the settlers. He was telling the cowmen that the fighting was over and instructing them to return to the headquarters ranch to rest up and catch up on their eating.

Just then, the cavalry was seen coming down into the shallow valley. The settlers were heard to shout loud and long at their rescue.

"I need something white for a flag of truce," said Hugh. "Got anything?" he asked Opal.

"My handkerchief," she replied pulling out a tiny square of lace-trimmed silk.

Hugh looked at the tiny handkerchief and laughed. "They'd have to have a telescope to see that. Don't you have anything more substantial?"

"I don't have a petticoat, Mr. Foote, because of my split skirt. I could give you a pantaloon leg if I could use your jackknife." She dismounted to raise her divided skirt over one leg.

"Don't look," she admonished, slashing at the pantaloon's material by her knee.

"I'm only looking in case you wound yourself. Be careful! That thing's sharp."

"Here—you depraved ogler." She handed the cut-off pantaloon and the knife to Hugh, who slit the tube-like leg open.

"This will do—wish me luck," Hugh called as he spurred his tired horse into the river, waving the ruffled fabric above his head as if his life depended on it.

~~~~~~~~~~~~~

Mrs. Swanson had caught up to Sam, Cletus and the small posse just as the lawmen discovered the blind canyon where the hiders had secreted themselves the previous day. Caught up in the excitement of the chase, Mrs. Swanson refused to return to home, hearth and hungry daughter, insisting on staying on until the kill.

Sam had sent Cletus on ahead up the ridge trail to scout out the way. Suddenly the argument with the lady deputy was stopped when Cletus came slipping and sliding back down the steep trail, much too fast for any expectation of reasonable longevity.

"They're coming back down. Loaded down something dreadful. It's a wonder they don't slide off the damn mountain."

"Can we ambush them someplace?" asked Sam.

"Everything's too open here—and there's close to a dozen of them. And," he added, "we're only six men."

"And a determined deputy sheriff from Mesa Grande," put in Mrs. Swanson.

"Think we'd best get some help," Sam decided. "Cletus, lead off—we don't want to be spotted."

It took two hours of hard riding to get back down to the settlement at Puzzle River and the lawmen were surprised at all the tumult they found there.

The cavalry was patrolling around the settlement's walls, while a truce was being worked out in the church between the settlers and the cowmen.

The news of the hide thieves' return interrupted the truce meeting, as Hugh Foote demanded a recess in the negotiations to allow him and his men to intercept the thieves.

Major Riemann volunteered his troop of mounted infantry, which had returned earlier with the suspicious ox wagon. Hugh Foote gratefully accepted the offer and Captain Stebbins approved the force with the condition that Lt. Jersie and a squad of cavalrymen go along as observers.

Hugh sent Bennington, who was at the truce meeting, to round up twenty cowmen and meet the force on the other side of the river.

Soon a force of close to fifty riders was pounding towards the expected return route of the hiders. Major Riemann had loaned Hugh his horse, as Hugh's mount was exhausted. There was now one other woman to accompany Mrs. Swanson—Opal Wilbur insisted on seeing the remains of her herd.

~~~~~~~~~~~~~~~

With the combined force's departure, Major Riemann and Captain Stebbins had time to investigate the gunfight over the ox wagon. The participants of that fracas had been separately confined since their arrival.

The cause of the argument had soon been discovered—a huge load of silver bullion was found under a covering of very wet manure. Sgt. White had shrewdly taken Griff from his friends, isolating him and threatening him with atrocious dismemberments unless he saved himself with a sincere confession.

Soon, Griff was pouring out his hardened heart, blaming all concerned for his troubles. Dragged before Riemann and Stebbins, he eagerly implicated his former associates. Naturally, he minimized his own responsibilities, swearing that he was coerced into the illegal activities, when all he really wanted was to play in the Mine Association band.

~~~~~~~~~~~~~~~

The descent from the ridge trail was slick and treacherous. They had made wooden drags, lashed together from what poor trees they could find and ballasted with rocks, to aid the downward journey. The drags had a pointed prow that plowed through the mud, slowing the heavily laden wagon to a manageable pace. The problem with the drags was that the leading wagon would leave a set of furrows that the following wagon would have to dodge. The drivers found, though, that if they put their outside wheels in the furrow it would lessen the wagon's always noticeable tendency to try to slide off the wet trail.

At the blind canyon's opening, they stopped to cut loose the drags—the steep part of the trail was passed. Judd Payton dug out a jug of rye whiskey and the men refreshed themselves as they also worked at clearing out the mud from the brake levers and checked their teams and the tackle.

"See that?" questioned Smokey Watson, pointing his head toward the muddy imprints of a half a dozen horses' hoofs.

"Can't hardly miss 'em, can you?" said his boss. "Any chance of going another way?"

"Too damn muddy to go overland. If we take the wagons . . . we got to stick to the trail. But . . ."

"Go ahead—say it," interrupted Payton.

"Well—we could cut the wagons loose and take off over hill and dale."

"And that would be the end of our hide business," replied Payton grimly. "I could never get credit again."

"It would," agreed the scout. "But you'd still be alive. If those tracks was made by the Law—we're all of a sudden talking about getting our necks stretched."

"Maybe they wasn't the Law. Maybe just some cowpokes going someplace. We'd have lost the hides and the wagons for nothing. Maybe we're losing our nerve, too."

"Could be." But the scout sounded skeptical. "And talking about nerve . . . I lost a lot of mine last month. When a hundred vaqueros almost done us in."

"I could put it up to a vote . . . the boys, I mean."

"Why? What made them smarter? You're the boss. That's your job."

Payton looked around, thinking—his lips moving in and out, looking like a lake carp with a beard.

Finally he spat and said, "We go—for home or hell—we go on ahead."

CHAPTER 24

"They're coming—three big wagons 'n' one smaller one," reported Bennington, getting down stiffly from his muddy horse. "They're piled high with our hides—damn them!"

The leaders of the combined force were gathered about a table-sized rock under a cottonwood tree that still dripped water from the recent rain.

"How long before they're here?" asked Hugh Foote.

"Twenty minutes—maybe more. Trail's muddy but they got big teams."

"I don't want any of them to get away." It was Opal, her eyes sparkling.

"They won't," promised Ensign Fenstermacher. "How many are riding horses?"

"Two of them—one ahead; one half-way down the line," answered Bennington, fumbling for his pipe.

"I'll assign three men to each of them. Our long Spencers will reach out for them," the ensign promised.

"They might try circling up—to fight it out," Hugh pointed out. "I don't want any more dead cowmen—if we can possibly help it."

"How about if my men come whooping up out of that gully," said Bennington, "while the ensign's men take a position alongside the road in them rocks? That way, we'd flush them snakes right into the Sauerkrauts' fire."

"My men are not cabbages," said the ensign, angrily. "They are German immigrants."

"You're absolutely right, Ensign," Hugh Foote said quickly. "Apologize, dammit, Bennington."

"Ah—I'm sorry, son." Bennington was red-faced, even with the ruddy, weathered complexion he naturally carried. "We've been so long calling you fellows that—it just popped out. What should I call you fellows?"

"Farmers—is that so bad? We are Arizona farmers. Someday there will be more farmers in Arizona than you cowpeople."

"That's pretty hard to believe, sonny, but let's not fight about that now. Save it for them damn hiders."

"I have a suggestion." It was Lt. Jersie. "I think it would be a good idea if Mr. Bennington's men fired, diagonally, toward the rear of the wagon train. That way, the settlers would not take fire from the cowmen. Also, the ensign's men should hold their fire until the riders have swept by their field of fire." The young lieutenant smiled, proud of his little presentation.

"Good idea, Lieutenant," seconded Hugh. "Hear that, Bob—and you, Ensign?" They both nodded their acceptance.

"I think me and the posse will just stay here," said Deputy Sam Buller. "We can act as sort of a reserve—in case these well-laid plans go astray. Nothing's real certain in this kind of thing."

~~~~~~~~~~~~

Judd Payton kicked his horse into a lope and caught up to Smokey Watson riding twenty yards ahead and to the off-side of the first wagon.

"So far so good," commented the boss man. "Dark in a couple of hours. You still figuring on the Eagle Pass cut-off to the Tucson Road?"

"It'll be slick but nothing like . . ."

His answer was suddenly interrupted by the sight and sounds of two dozen riders, roaring up out of a fold in the ground to the left front. Then the riders were firing at the men on the high drivers' seats of the big wagons.

"Keep them mules going!" screamed Judd, emptying his pistol at the attacking cowmen. "Whip them up! Drive through 'em! Don't stop or we're dead!" he yelled at his drivers.

The driver on the first wagon was hit and his helper was struggling to recover the reins. Smokey Watson saw the problem and galloped up to grab the off leader, bringing the team back on the trail. Then Smokey was hit and crumpling slowly in his saddle, reeling back further and further until he fell sprawling and slipping in the muddy trail. In an instant his body was swallowed up under the hoofs and wheels of the following wagon.

"Smokey!" Judd cried as the third wagon tore his friend to shreds. And then the wagons were through the line of attackers. Judd pulled up to look at his friend Smokey's bloody bundle of a body.

The big 385 grain .52 caliber Spencer slug slammed into Judd Payton, tearing him from his horse and dumping him in the muddy slime of Smokey's burst body, and brains.

Sam saw the ambush falling apart and he growled at his posse to head off the big wagons. They put spurs into their startled mounts and flung themselves at the rushing wagons.

"Drop the leaders!" yelled Sam. "Stop the damn mules!" He fired at the off leader—but the big mule never flinched. It continued its crazed canter, eyes rolling wildly inside its blinders.

Sam rode closer and shot at the beast's head and suddenly it was down, tripping the swing mules behind, sending them in a twisted heap that slid through the mud sickeningly. Then the wagon pole was impaling the muddy trail, levering the big wagon sideways until the wagon's weight and momentum turned it over. The load of wet cowhides spilled and the wagon rolled again and was still—except for the screaming mules that threshed in their broken agonies. The first wagon stopped, Sam turned to the other wagons which had left the trail to drive around the downed lead wagon. Cletus was trying to grab the off leader of the second wagon as Mrs. Swanson was trading shots with the driver's assistant. She fired and the driver doubled up, hit in the stomach and losing the reins. The assistant fired again and Mrs. Swanson had to pull up fast—hit and hurt, slumping in her saddle.

Hugh Foote rode up and killed the man that shot Mrs. Swanson. And then, suddenly, it was over. Cletus had the second wagon's team turned and off the trail in the rough, slowing and stopping it. The other wagons came to a halt in the trail—the drivers quitting the game while still alive.

~~~~~~~~~~~~~~~

Everyone agreed that it was the letdown after all the excitement. Hugh Foote sent a man to find a cow and bring it in for a celebration dinner, which was a generous donation as the cattlemen had little to celebrate. Almost two dozen of their people were dead or hurt in the fighting.

The defenders, the farmers, came out the better—due, probably, to their fortifications. They lost five dead and six wounded. The five dead included Paulie and Hugo. Ensign Fenstermacher was the last person wounded when he attempted to help Mrs. Swanson and had his horse killed, pinning the ensign's leg and breaking a bone.

The celebration dinner was put on the day following the battle. Hugh Foote had sent most of the cowboys back to their ranches after the early morning burial ceremony at the settlers' cemetery.

He took Blackjack and Bennington to visit the site of the latest herd massacre. This day, Opal did not want to see her devastated herd, preferring to stay to help with the wounded of both sides. Onkel Pfaff had Sheriff Skinner moved to

Hugo's old room at Elder Kolb's house, deeming Skinner to be well enough not to require a hospital bed. This was fine with Skinner except that he had trouble lying full length on Kolb's bed, which was much less than six feet long. Instead, he took over a rocker in the parlor.

At a meeting on the evening of the battle, Capt. Stebbins had arbitrarily and quickly brought order to many of the contentious affairs that brought the Federal troops to the Puzzle River settlement.

He first read off a statement that seemed to please no one but himself.

"Upon initial review," he read ponderously, "I find that the recent hostile actions between the cattle owners and the settlers was brought about by a conspiracy planned by one person, a man calling himself Captain Cabot. I find that he misused his position as the rangeland boundary overseer for Wilbur Ranches to promote a range war from which he would profit financially. There is also oral evidence that this Captain Cabot might have been demented during the recent hostilities. Whether Wilbur Ranches has a liability, under Federal law, to the settlers due to this man's commissions, will have to be later determined by the Interior Department and the courts.

"One large bone of contention between the cattle interests and the farming interests is the proper distribution of the Puzzle River water. The dam presently being built by the agricultural interests, seems to me, to alienate the two sides.

"I realize that I am on shaky ground when I, a lowly captain of U.S. Cavalry, ask both parties to come to an agreement that is not sanctified from on high by the omnipotent Washington bureaus and courts. But I feel that peace here depends on mutual understanding between the factions. I intend now, rightly or wrongly—perhaps to my sorrow—to wrest assurances from you that will provide a peaceful solution to the water question.

"Right now—I rule that the Puzzle River's waters be divided equally between the participating factions. One half the flow for the farmers and one half for the ranchers.

"Do I hear any objections? . . . Major Riemann?"

"I agree to the split," said the major. "But I would like to see a water committee formed to regulate flow, reservoir capacity and future operations."

"Who speaks for the ranching interests?" asked Stebbins, looking at Opal Wilbur.

"Mr. Foote speaks for me," she smiled smugly.

"Mr. Foote—how say you—on the record?"

"Your division seems fair to me," replied Hugh, after a moment to think. "I would need time, though, before I could agree on any makeup of the water committee."

"That suit you, Major Riemann?" questioned Stebbins.

"I agree," answered the major.

"Now that the war and the water issues are settled, we come to a wagonload of silver bullion found in possession of various unsavory individuals. I'm told by Deputy Buller that the silver belongs to the Green Falls Mine Association, as it was stolen from the Association. Will you, Deputy, take charge of the silver and the prisoners and return them all to where they should be?"

"Just a damn minute there, Captain Stebbins." Sheriff Skinner, now wearing a smaller cranial bandage, pushed his way out of the rearmost pew, walking slowly and unsteadily up the aisle. His wife, Genevieve, tried to hold his elbow to steady him.

"Let me go, woman." He pushed her helping hand away. "I'm all right now, practically," he said to the onlookers.

"I want you to talk to me. I'm the sheriff here and now I'm back to duty. And Captain Stebbins—to talk bluntly—I'm going to bring the silver and the men who robbed it back to Green Falls. I need to bring them back myself because next June I'm having to run for sheriff and I need the votes this will bring me. And another thing—I want those three hide thieves that are left. I want to take them back to face their crimes and be hanged. I'll leave tomorrow if I can get the loan of a proper team."

"I was about to bring up the hide thieves, Sheriff Skinner, but thank you anyway for your help." Stebbins sounded a little sarcastic at losing a portion of his control of the meeting. "I'll have Lt. Jersie write up the minutes of this meeting by tomorrow morning and I'd like Mr. Foote and Major Riemann to sign as to its accuracy. Then—this meeting is now concluded."

~~~~~~~~~~~~

Skinner's group left the next morning, over his wife's protests. The sheriff and his wife sat in the rear seat of Ames's trap. They were driven by Mr. Hansen, who managed to argue with the sheriff most of the way back to Green Falls.

Next came the former ox wagon now pulled by four heavy-footed horses borrowed from the settlement, as was the driver—who had to work the team from a running board as there was no driver's seat. Seated uncomfortably on the bullion were the prisoners; three former hide thieves and the five retired miners.

Cletus and the four posse members brought up the rear, careful to see that no prisoner slipped his bonds for a run to freedom.

Safely folded in the sheriff's coat pocket was a disposition taken from Major Riemann and Elder Kolb pertaining to the Employment and the Death of Hugo Schwartzstein alias Hugo Dunkelmehl. Also in that pocket was Griff's confession to Sgt. White and Capt. Stebbins.

Deputy Buller was not with the sheriff's party, as he was sent to escort Deputy Mrs. Swanson home to her store in Mesa Grande. Her wound, to the right breast and armpit, was what Onkel Pfaff called a clean wound, and while painful, would heal correctly. She was very adamant about returning to her baby, now that the shooting was over. A travois was expertly built in the settlers' shop and hitched to the horse borrowed from Mr. Jessup for the eight hour trip, that had to be made at a walk.

~~~~~~~~~~~~

"Was it as bad as expected?" Opal was outside to greet Hugh and her two foremen.

"It's something you don't ever get used to," grunted Bennington.

"They murdered young Pedro Aviles," said Hugh gloomily. "He was Aviles's nephew."

"We counted one hundred thirty-seven skinned steers. Hugh wants to take the hides to Tucson and sell 'em. Should bring in some money."

"I figure we got a claim on the wagons and mules, seeing as what they did to us. Blackjack is going to shape it up and leave tomorrow with half a dozen men," Hugh said . . . and then he fell silent.

"Major Riemann took the mules from the last two big wagons and the small one. I think he is going to use them here," said Opal, holding tight to Hugh's arm.

"I'll see him about that. Maybe I'll give them to him after I'm through with them."

"I would like to talk to Mr. Foote, alone, if it's all right with you gentlemen," Opal told the two foremen. They nodded and led their mounts away to care for them.

"What's this all about?" asked Hugh tiredly. "Did I do something wrong—again?"

"I'll know when I hear your answer. Still want to marry me?"

He turned her around to look into her eyes. They were big green pools, inviting him into their depth. "Nobody else asked me today. Why not?—When?"

"How about tonight at the celebration? I talked to . . ."

"Tonight?" interrupted Hugh. "I don't have a clean shirt and . . ."

"Quiet, you—and listen," she broke in. "I talked to the pastor here. He can marry us tonight. Since we're not his parishioners he can dispense with any banns. Now—are you ready, Mr. Foote?"

"Let me see if I can borrow a shirt from the major. Maybe I can trade him a mule for it."

"For a mule," she laughed, "you should get a pair of trousers, too."

~~~~~~~~~~~~~~

Mr. Swanson was very glad to see his wife, even if she was wounded. He had resorted to spooning beer onto a piece of toweling stuck between the baby's gums. Luckily, Mr. Jessup was about and could help with the baby and the lady injured in the accident. Mrs. Swanson's coming, even with only one producing breast, removed a large load from the harried husband's day.

"I'm busier than a rooster on a ship full of hens," he told Sam as they carried his wife upstairs to her bed. "I had to turn the bar over to Jessup's man, Miguel, and I haven't made a dime since. It's nothing but cook, clean out the baby's short clothes and run errands for that damn injured woman. I swear I never seen a person who made so much water. She runs me ragged . . . and the baby . . . thank God the Mrs. is home."

"How'd you end up with the hurt lady?" Sam asked.

"Foolishness—just plain stupidity—that's why," explained Swanson, putting the baby to his sleeping wife's good breast.

"Too damn generous—that's my trouble. My mother allus said it was my biggest fault. Being generous, I mean. When Sweeney brought her in here, I said—sure, set her in the spare bedroom. My guest bedroom—mind you, that I get 75 cents a night for; a dollar if you want clean sheets. Now she's in there for free, I guess. Didn't have a purse or nothing on her. Good ole generous Swanson; stuck again. See? Hear her? She's yelling again. Probably to dump the damn piss pot again. Say, Sam, how about a favor? . . . see what she wants . . . will ya?"

"Why not?" said Sam. "That's my big fault. Can't say no." Sam went to the guest door and opened it to walk inside the candle lit room.

"Well—what do you know," he greeted the lady. "Mrs. Robinson, late of Green Falls. We've missed you."

~~~~~~~~~~~~~~

Hugh Foote dispatched his remaining cowhands back to their respective ranches. The newly-discharged hired gunmen had departed earlier, under the watchful eye of Bob Bennington, to pick up their recompense from Beatrice Cole and to leave Wilbur ranchland for the spotty pleasures of Green Falls and Tucson. Old Blackjack Thompson was delighted to be again posted to the The Lazy J in the Palisade Valley. "Gollies," he gushed, "I feel like I just found my lost child or sumpton. Maybe better. Thanks, Hugh."

"No," assured Foote, "it's me who's thankful, B.J.—to have a top-notch man like you up there. We'll be hiring directly, trying as much as possible to get enough hands to make up for our losses in this damn war. If any good riders come through, feel free to hire them on at the regular rate— cowpokes' wages, that is, not gunfighters'." With a long look around and a shake of his head at the scene of the past bloodshed, B.J. trotted off to his rocky ranch.

Then it was quick time for Hugh to have a good wash and to accept the loan of the elder's second-best shirt (the Major's being unacceptably altered to fit his lame arm). Finally ready, he went into the Kolb house, to catch Opal coming down the stairway. She was also in borrowed attire, a pale yellow linen frock with green piping that almost matched her eyes. "Do I look like a bride?" she asked Hugh from the landing. "The Kolb ladies found this tucked away in a trunk. It still smells a little musty and it's rather faded—but in the lamplight . . ."

"It's just fine," gulped Hugh, struck almost mute by her loveliness.

"Mrs. Kolb is lending us her mother's wedding band—until you buy me my own," she said, leaving the stairs, coming close to put a hand against his chest. "I can feel your heart beating," she breathed, smiling into his face.

"Most probably due to this tight shirt," he grinned back. "Clean, starched and too tight."

"You're not supposed to see me, you know—before the ceremony."

"I want to see you forever—and then some more," he whispered. "Come on; it's near dark. I'll walk you over to the church. Have the Kolbs all left?"

"A few minutes ago. Something about last minute preparations. I guess they'll be needing us soon."

"Are you nervous?" asked Hugh, holding her arm while going down the back steps.

"A little," she answered. "I wish I had brought Aunt Fannie's ivory broach. It would have set this . . ."

"That's far enough!" commanded a figure, detaching himself from the shadows of the outhouse. "Stand right there! How come, Missy, did you forget *my* invitation to this wedding?"

"Why, Capt. Cabot," returned Opal, ". . . we presumed you dead." She suddenly felt an apprehensive rush of blood pump into her body at this unexpected intrusion. That, and Hugh's grip on her arm had turned to steel.

"So it would seem, Missy. But your nuptial gayety is about to be short-lived," sneered Cabot. "Stand away from your paramour, Foote! Because I'm going to kill you. By God, I lost my eye and half my face to that bomb," Cabot rasped on, "but now's the time to settle up our accounts before this mass of pus and ooze does me in. Turn and draw, Mr. Foote!"

"I'm unarmed, Cabot—I'm about to get married in a church—no weapons on me."

"Then I'll just have to lend you one of mine." Using his left hand, Cabot drew the big French revolver on his left hip and tossed it neatly before Opal's feet. "Take up the pistol, Missy—and tuck it into your sweetheart's belt—and then stand aside. As I told you before, I generally limit my killing to men."

"Oh—like this, Captain?" replied Opal, quickly picking up the heavy Le Mat, while simultaneously cocking and firing it in a smooth, almost practiced motion. The massive .44 slug caught Cabot at the juncture of throat and thorax, punching through meat and muscle as if his body were a ripe melon. His wound-ravaged countenance went slack, mouth agape, his one eye round and staring. His blood, black-hued in the evening gloom, bubbled down his already scorched clothing. His right hand fumbled for his pistol, but the fingers had lost their will and he crumpled slowly onto the sandy walkway.

"Ahem," finally said Hugh, breaking the silent spell after the revolver's explosive report. He took the pistol from Opal's still grasp saying, "I understood that *I* was supposed to be the shooter—not you."

"I'm not one to let an opportunity slip by me, Hugh. And besides, *I* wasn't sure of you beating him to the draw."

"Uh huh—and this hurry-up marriage—that's another little opportunity you didn't want to have slip by?"

"My word, Mr. Foote," sighed Opal in her make-believe Southern belle voice—"you *have* found me out. Now, shall we say goodbye to the Captain and go get married?"

"By all means, Miss Wilbur—gotta make the best of our opportunities, you know." He tossed the pistol down and took her hand for the walk to the church.

 Epilogue

The marriage of Opal and Hugh was never ordinary, and never very quiet either. When the two weren't fighting, they were loving. Opal and Hugh, with Aunt Polly's and Uncle Napoleon's help, raised five children and a hundred thousand shorthorn cattle. One child was a U.S. senator and a grandson was to become a WWII corps commander.

The five conspirators in the mine case were convicted, with Mike and Eric being hanged for the killing of the liftman.

The settler's dam was completed in 1870 and named the Paulie Vogelnester Dam at a ceremony presided over by the Senator from Missouri, Carl Schurz. Major Riemann married the older Kolb daughter and went to work for different railways as an engineer. He died of yellow fever while working for a French company on a canal in Panama.

A mural depicting the heroic act of saving the dam was unveiled at the Green Falls County (Arizona) Courthouse in 1923. The mural was financed by public subscription from the school children of that county. The three hide thieves that lived to be convicted were hanged at a very well attended execution in Tucson on July 4th, 1869. A reporter estimated the crowd at over 1,500 men, women and children.

Mrs. Robinson never recovered from the accident. Moved back to Green Falls, she died in the Mine Association hospital there, unrepentant of her crimes.

Sheriff Skinner recovered from his head injury and campaigned vigorously for his election. But certain allegations arose to derail his campaign—but wait; that's another story.

THE

SHERIFF SKINNER SERIES

by Willie Lynch

The Law in Green Falls
ISBN: 0-9715542-0-X

The Sheriff Gets a Job
ISBN: 0-9715542-1-8

Sheriff Skinner and the Puzzle River Water War
ISBN: 0-9715542-2-6

About the Author

Willie Lynch, a long-time afficionado of the Western novel, is a retired army engineer sergeant and transportation worker. A widower, he now resides in a senior community center close to his seven children. He uses the "Skinner" name to honor his uncle who perished in the Great War.